# The Loves of a Lifetime

James B. Styles

ISBN 978-1-63630-568-4 (Paperback)
ISBN 978-1-63630-569-1 (Hardcover)
ISBN 978-1-63630-570-7 (Digital)

Copyright © 2021 James B. Styles
All rights reserved
First Edition

All rights reserved. No part of this publication may be reproduced, distributed, or transmitted in any form or by any means, including photocopying, recording, or other electronic or mechanical methods without the prior written permission of the publisher. For permission requests, solicit the publisher via the address below.

Covenant Books, Inc.
11661 Hwy 707
Murrells Inlet, SC 29576
www.covenantbooks.com

# 1
## CHAPTER

The roar of the fan in the corner of the classroom almost completely drowned out what our teacher, Mrs. Rodman, was trying to impart to us. It really didn't make much difference as this was our last class on Friday afternoon before we were released from school until September. My attention was more directed to the outside as I sat there daydreaming how I was going to spend my summer.

I know one thing for sure, my vacation was going to involve quite a bit of swimming at the lake as well as fishing with my good buddy Roy Earl Duncan. He carried the nickname of Red for obvious reasons. It certainly didn't have anything to do with his appearance, for Roy was a colored boy and for sure my best friend.

Now, I don't pretend to be the smartest, but I've known Roy since we were too young to remember; and to me, in spite of his color and what some people might think, he has always been a fine, loyal friend. Why he has to go to a different school is a mystery to me. Roy has always been a bit on the small side and walks with a slight limp as he fractured his ankle when he was around seven, and it never really healed properly. Now as for me, I'm a good size to be only fifteen, with my sixteenth birthday coming up on June 4, 1928. I'm still growing, and I hope to be as big as my dad someday. I am always around to make sure that no harm comes to Roy, and everybody in Terrell knows it that if they pick on Roy, they have to go through me first.

I've been friends with Roy I guess because his father, Tom, and mine had similarly been associated for years as well. Roy's dad was a foreman at the Cotton Gin and his mom, Dorothy, worked at the

Terrell Western Hotel as a bookkeeper, and they had frequented my dad's grocery store since before I was born and were among Dad's best customers. They even played dominoes on Friday night with some of the other local merchants.

My dad was Big Jack Perkins, and he was called that because he stood at over six feet, four inches and probably tipped the scales at around 250 pounds. He had owned and operated the only grocery store in Terrell from way before I was born. In spite of his size, my dad was as kind and gregarious a man as you would want to know. Yes, everybody loved Big Jack, and he ran his business like that with always a smile on his lips and a funny story he would tell you at the drop of a hat. If you couldn't afford to pay for your supplies, Jack was quick to allow you credit to pay off what you owed.

I was very close to my dad. When he can, he takes me fishing, and in the summer I work in the grocery store with him; and when I grow up, I want to be just like him. My mom is Marion, and she spends her days staying home and taking care of me and my sister, Linda. Linda is off to college in Fort Worth this fall while I will be a junior in high school. Life is sweet.

Terrell is just a small country town located about thirty-five miles east of Dallas. Terrell was founded in 1873 when the Texas and Pacific Railway laid tracks along a road that became Highway 80 going to the west and intersected with Highway 34 that went north to Greenville. Our town had a population of around 8,300 people at least that's what the sign read at the city limits. Downtown consisted of two banks, two hotels, three flour mills, three cotton gins, nine churches, three weekly newspapers as well as my dad's grocery store. We had a small local clinic that old doctor Cartwright would come out from Dallas once a week to tend to anyone that needed help. The closest hospital was in Dallas. This being primarily a farming community, the main business locally was cotton farming.

There were two schools with one for the colored kids and one for the Whites, which I always found curious and didn't really understand. As I left school on Friday afternoon, I walked down to Roy's school to meet up with him and make plans for tomorrow.

"Roy, you ready for summer?"

"You bet I am. What do you want to do on our first Saturday of freedom?"

"Let's go swimming at the lake tomorrow morning then come back for lunch at my house, then maybe my mom can take us into Dallas to see a picture show. There's a new one out called *In Old Arizona* that's a western and is a talkie."

"No kidding. That sounds great to me."

That night after dinner I sat on the front porch with Dad, and he asked me, "Ron, what are your plans for this summer? I do hope you have it in your busy schedule to work in the store with me."

"Sure, I'm always wanting to earn extra money."

"We have Decoration Day coming up on May 30, which is next Wednesday and then your birthday on June 4 the following Monday, so a big celebration week for us, don't you think? By the way, what do you want for your birthday, Ron?"

"Well, my old bicycle is just about worn-out. I could sure use a new one."

"Let me see what I can do."

Decoration Day had been a day of memorials for the fallen soldiers in war that was begun in 1868 by the Grand Army of the Republic, but over the last few years it had been a celebration highlighted by an elaborate picnic put on by our church and a day of games and fireworks, a day that all of Terrell came out for.

On my sixteenth birthday, Mom and Dad did give me a vintage bicycle that my dad had been working on to restore to its former glory. I was so excited at the magnificence of my new ride that I eagerly left to ride the three miles to Roy's house to show it off. As I increased my speed, for some unknown reason, I decided to jerk up on the handlebars to try to do a wheelie, but when I did, the front wheel came loose, and I went tumbling down face-first on to the gravel road, cutting my chin wide open with a two-inch gash. As I lay there in a semiconscious state it took me several minutes to sit up and collect my senses. I checked to see if I still had all my teeth. I took my shirt off and pressed it up against the open wound to try and stem the bleeding then slowly walked back home.

Mom came running out of the house when she saw what a bloody mess I was. "Ron, what on earth happened to you?"

"I don't rightly know, Mom, I just pulled up on my handlebars and the wheel came off, and the next thing I knew I was sitting on the ground bleeding like a stuck pig. I'm not feeling too good right now. I think I need to lie down."

When Dad came in to see what the commotion was, he turned ashen as the color drained from his face. I could see tears starting to well up in his eyes, and he began apologizing profusely, believing he was responsible.

"Dad, don't worry about it. It wasn't your fault. I guess the rough road worked the wheel loose, and I did something stupid by raising up on the handlebars."

"I am so sorry, son. I'll go pick up the bike and fix it for you so you can ride it tomorrow."

I told Dad where I had left the bike, and he brought it back in his pickup truck and worked all night straightening out the bent forks and securing the wheel. But that's the kind of guy my dad was. The next day it was as good as new. Mom patched me up as best she could then contacted Dr. Cartwright to get an appointment with him to sew me up on Wednesday when he made his regularly scheduled stop in Terrell. And now I had a two-inch scar on my chin.

A lot of people said I was the spitting image of my father with brown wavy hair and bright blue eyes and a skin tone that tanned easily. Though I hadn't reached my full size yet, I was still a good-sized boy for my age standing at five feet, ten inches and weighing 120 pounds.

The rest of the summer went by way too quickly, and before you knew it, September had arrived, and it was back to school. Since I had grown some over the summer, I thought I would give football a try. I had never played before, but I felt like I was a decent-enough athlete, so why not. My best friend at school was Joe Carter, and he was our school's quarterback.

"Ron, you need to come out, our team needs you. We barely have enough boys playing as it is, and I feel like you would be a real asset to us. I've already talked to coach Willis, and he's expecting you."

This was true as our school only had an enrollment of around 250 boys and girls, and that included all three high school grades. The football squad numbered only 40 fellows, so barely enough for a starting 22 and substitutes.

Being fifteen now, I was really starting to notice girls, and one in particular I had my eye on was Rebecca Rogers, the head cheerleader. Why not aim high if you're going to aim at all. I figured if I made the football squad and managed to play some, she might just notice me. In my opinion, she was the loveliest girl in school with long black hair cascading down to the middle of her back and the most expressive hazel eyes you have ever seen.

As the fall progressed, my plan worked just like I hoped it would as I became the starting end on offense and linebacker on defense. Yes, Rebecca did notice, and we started dating halfway through the season.

I had enjoyed a growth spurt throughout 1928, and from the beginning of spring, 1929 I was now six feet tall and had gained 10 pounds. Football had helped build up my muscles, but the one who really had grown was Roy. He no longer was an undersized boy, but now stood over six feet, two inches and must have weighed in excess of 225 pounds. His mom and dad had managed to find a brace for his bad ankle, so that now his limp was barely noticeable and no longer held him back. He told me that after he graduates from high school next year, he has been offered a football and basketball scholarship at Grambling State University in Louisiana. With that revelation, I sadly knew instantly that Roy and I would be going in different directions.

*****

The spring semester had ended, and I was enjoying my first Saturday of summer by sleeping in, or so I thought.

"Ron, Ron!"

"I heard you the first time, Mom, but I don't know why you're calling me this early."

"Ron, you have to get up now, it's past 9:00 a.m. and you have work to do at the grocery store with your dad. He's expecting you, so get out of bed and get dressed. I have your breakfast ready."

Growing up in a small town like Terrell has its benefits and its drawbacks. It can be filled with fun things to do like swimming and going to movies and parties with all your friends, but the downside is everybody knows you. There's not much privacy. I'll be seventeen next Tuesday, and I only have one more year of high school. After that I think I want to go away to college like Linda did and leave Terrell behind. I've been dating Rebecca, I like to call her Becky, but she and I seem to have different goals for our future. She's a swell girl that is loads of fun with a great sense of humor. She's very popular in school, being a cheerleader and last year's homecoming queen, so her life is here. I don't think she ever wants to leave and would be happy just getting married and having a passel of kids. Unfortunately, that does not fit into my plans. So I don't see a long-term future for us, so when I decide to leave Terrell after high school, I figure I'll just have to say goodbye to her and hope she understands. No sir, I want out. I hope to go to college then get a job in Dallas or maybe even go into the Army, but I know I want to move on to some kind of a career as soon as I finish high school. As much as I admire my dad, I don't want to work in his store for the rest of my life.

Our home in Terrell is of a Victorian architecture and was built in 1889. It was unique in that it was one of the first homes in Terrell to be wired with electricity and had indoor plumbing. Mom and Dad bought the house shortly after construction was completed. The home had a large covered wraparound front porch where my dad had installed a swing. On the second floor were the three bedrooms, a parlor, and a bathroom. Mom would only let Dad smoke his cigarette or occasional pipe in the parlor or in our library on the first floor. The rest of the first floor had the kitchen, a bathroom, our sitting room, and a dining room. It was indeed a beautiful home made of brick with windows that encompassed floor to ceiling. The wood trim throughout the house was of dark mahogany and featured pocket doors that separated the dining room from our formal living room.

Growing up, one of my fondest experiences was sitting in that swing on the front porch with my dad on a spring afternoon watching the thunderclouds form and move toward us. The wind would increase as the storm approached. There was nothing like the smell of freshness clearing the air and watching as the sky turned dark with the sound of the rain pelting the roof.

Our house was on 1311 Dayton Avenue and was only six blocks from Dad's grocery store on Main Street. That was two blocks south and four blocks west, so it was an easy ten-minute walk unless you counted the time I would detour behind the Terrell Western Hotel to sneak a quick smoke on my way to work. Mom doesn't know I smoke, and I assure you she wouldn't approve, but I figure since my dad smokes, how bad can it be. Besides that, as a young man, I enjoy a good cigarette every now and then. It relaxed me. I get a 50-cent allowance every week plus when I work at Dad's grocery store, he pays me 25 cents an hour, and that can add up quickly. Cigarettes are only 10 cents a pack, and unknown to Dad, I do manage to sneak a package out of the display in his store every once in a while.

I finally arrived at the store and saw my dad behind the counter helping a customer. Dad was well-liked and respected in the Terrell community mainly because of his kindness and generosity. He had such an open and friendly manner with everyone with an almost-constant smile on his face. If a customer of his grocery store couldn't afford to pay their bill, he would in almost every case extend them credit and allow them to pay him back in installments. Only problem with that was Big Jack was a terrible bookkeeper and relied mostly on people's honesty.

Jack saw me out of the corner of his eye and said, "Ron, glad you finally decided to join us. A truck just dropped off a delivery, so why don't you start earning your 25 cents an hour and go unload that shipment. After you've done that, you can bring in the merchandise and start pricing and stocking the shelves."

"Okay, Dad, but is everything alright? You don't look too good."

"I'm okay, Ron, just a little pain in my stomach, probably indigestion, nothing to worry about. Go ahead and get busy."

With that, Big Jack lit up a cigarette and turned to help the next customer.

That night at dinner, Jack still looked like he was in some degree of pain and went straight to bed after he finished eating. That wasn't like him at all as he usually would come outside and sit on the porch swing with us and enjoy a cigarette and some conversation. But tonight it was just Mom and me. She poured some iced tea and brought me a glass, and as she sat down, she said, "Ron, are you ready to turn seventeen next week and become a man? I have something real special for you for your birthday, and I'll give it to you tomorrow after church." We sat there quietly and enjoyed the breeze that cooled off a hot Texas June night. We could hear Jack moaning in pain through the open upstairs bedroom window, so Mom went in to check on him. I followed her in just in case there was something I could do to help.

"Jack, are you okay? Is there anything I can do for you?"

"It's my stomach that hurts, I think. I just took a laxative thinking I was just plugged up a bit, but that only seemed to make things worse. Maybe you should call Doc Cartwright for me. He may be in town. Sometimes he spends the weekend here with some of his family."

As luck would have it, the doctor was still in town, and he came right over. Mom ushered him in to their bedroom, and he closed the door behind him to tend to Jack alone. After a few moments, Doc Cartwright emerged from the bedroom with a concerned look on his face. "Marion, we need to get Jack to the hospital in Dallas. I'm afraid he has appendicitis and maybe some internal bleeding. The absolutely worst thing he could have done was to take a laxative."

While Doc Cartwright called the hospital and made arrangements, I pulled a mattress off and with some blankets and pillows, made a bed in the Model T pickup truck for Dad; and with Mom's help, we laid him down and made him as comfortable as we could. I climbed up in the back with Dad while Mom and Dr. Cartwright rode up front. About halfway through the thirty-five-mile trip to Dallas, Dad passed out, I guess from the pain he was experiencing.

We drove as fast as the old Ford would allow, and after about forty-five minutes we arrived at the hospital. Attendants pulled Dad out of the truck and put him on a gurney. He was taken immediately to the operating room where a staff of doctors and nurses were waiting. Mom and I went and sat down in the waiting room with Dr. Cartwright. The time was now approaching 11:00 p.m. and at this point there was nothing else we could do for Dad. His fate now rested in the hands of the surgical team and God's will. So I went in search of a cup of coffee, hoping to give Mom a little relief.

Mom seemed to be in a state of disbelief as her eyes were glazed over, and she sat there staring off into space, barely speaking seemingly not fully comprehending what had just happened tonight. Dad was always so strong and, in every sense, the rock of our family and was a relatively young man only in his late forties apparently the picture of good health. This just couldn't be happening to him. We sat there the rest of the night waiting to hear from the doctors until I saw the sun starting to appear over the horizon about six thirty in the morning. I decided to get up and stretch my legs and walk outside into the cool morning air to smoke a cigarette, and maybe cry a bit and say a silent prayer for my beloved father.

As I came back into the waiting room, I could see the lead surgeon of the operating team walking down the hall toward us. He sat down next to Mom and said, "Mrs. Perkins, I am so sorry to tell you that we did everything we could possibly do for your husband, but I regret to tell you that he has passed away. I am so sorry for your loss. Is there anything I or any of my staff can do for you?" I sat down next to Mom and took her hand and watched as she started to sob uncontrollably as the realization of what the doctor had just told her began to sink in. "Ron, what will we do without Jack? He was everything to me. I don't know what I am supposed to do now."

We slowly made our way back to Terrell, and Mom just sat there staring out of the window lost in her thoughts while I drove. Doc Cartwright stayed at the hospital to help in making final arrangements for Dad. Once we arrived home from the hospital, Mom's first action was to call Linda at school and let her know what had happened to Dad. Linda was away at college, but with Jack gone, we probably were not going to have the money to keep her in school. Mom then just sat down on the sofa and wept, unable to speak. I knew then that it was going to be up to me to see about the grocery store and to handle arrangements for the funeral with Dr. Cartwright. Our pastor came over that night and sat with and tried to comfort Mom as best as he could.

The next day dawned bright and sunny but cold and empty without Jack. We didn't go to church, and Mom barely would get out of bed and seemed to be in a state of confusion and unclear on what to do next.

On Monday, we had the funeral for Big Jack, and almost everybody that lived in Terrell turned out, for Big Jack was a very popular man. Several people came up to me and said that they knew I was going to be in charge of the grocery store and wanted to pay their debt. But you know what, very few of them lived up to that promise, and in spite of my every effort, the store started to fail. I couldn't collect on the money owed to us, and I no longer could afford to pay for supplies or salaries or overhead. After a couple of months, about the time I was to start back to school for my senior year, I finally had to close the store for good. Not being selfish, but that also threw my plans for college right out of the window.

Mom decided we needed to leave Terrell for good so she could get a job in Dallas to support us. I think she felt like there were too many painful memories in Terrell of her life with Jack. We sold our house, and with what little money we had left after clearing our debts, she was able to buy a modest bungalow in the Samuel Heights area of old East Dallas, and she enrolled me in the new Woodrow Wilson High School. As we pulled out of Terrell in the old Model T for probably the last time, I thought back to my final goodbye with Becky. We sat on that front swing at our old house, and I tried to explain why we would not see each other anymore. It was a tearful goodbye, but I think she understood that my future was no longer in Terrell, whereas hers was.

## THE LOVES OF A LIFETIME

In September, 1929 I enrolled at Woodrow Wilson High School and I have made the decision to tryout for football. I played some in Terrell, but with little distinction and now at a new school with no friends as of yet, I felt like I needed the distraction. Maybe by joining the football team I could make some new friends and be able to eventually fit in at this high school. The head coach liked my aggressive attitude, and at six feet tall and weighing in at 135 pounds, I was a good size for football. So after tryouts, Coach Harris assigned me the position of end on offense and defensive back on defense.

On the first day of practice, I was meeting with the offensive squad and met Robert Hays, who was assigned the position of halfback. It was an instant friendship as Robert and I discovered we had a lot in common. He too was new to Woodrow Wilson High School having transferred in from Fort Worth because his dad had changed jobs. School had just started the fall semester, so neither of us had been able to meet any members of the fairer sex, but that was soon to change. I also became friends with our quarterback, Sammy Mitchell. Sammy was a handsome guy; all the girls wanted a date with Sammy. He stood a little over six feet tall with a thick mop of black hair and a perpetual smile on his face, like he knew something we didn't. So I was starting to make friends a little at a time, being as I am really a little on the shy side.

Robert, Sammy, and I were walking down the hall on the next Monday morning on our way to our first classes of the day when I saw coming toward us, probably the most beautiful girl I had ever seen. She was petite with long blonde hair and striking green eyes. I whispered to Sammy, "You have any idea who that girl right there is?"

"Ron, that's Doreen Winthorp, and we all want a date with her, but so far as I know, she has turned everybody down. Maybe you'll have better luck. Give it a shot."

"Sammy, she is the bees knees, don't you think?"

"The cat's meow, my friend, the cat's meow."

I accepted Sammy's challenge, and as she stopped by her locker, I guess to retrieve something, I walked up to her and said, "Hi, I'm Ron Perkins. I'm kind of new here, and I just wanted to introduce myself." She turned to face me, smiled, and extended her hand to shake mine and said, "Well, Ron, I'm Doreen, and I'm pleased to meet you. Where are you from, if I might ask?" Her hand felt warm and soft in mine, and I suddenly realized that I had forgotten to let her go; I was so mesmerized by her smile and demeanor and those beautiful green eyes.

As soon as I could muster up the courage to speak again, I said, "My mom and I just moved to Dallas from Terrell for my senior year." Then feeling bold, I asked, "Doreen, do you think we could meet at Thomas's Drugstore for a soda after school today and maybe talk with a little more privacy?"

"I think we could arrange that, say thirty minutes after school has let out. A lot of kids go, and I would be happy to meet you there and continue our conversation."

It was at that moment I realized I was still holding her hand, but she had made no effort to pull away as we continued to make eye contact.

"Ron?"

"Yes, Doreen."

"Could I have my hand back now?"

I sheepishly grinned and relaxed my grip to let her go and said, "I'm so sorry, I guess I was so involved in our talk that I completely forgot."

"I'll see you later, Ron." And with that, Doreen turned and walked away, but I was still frozen in place already smitten with this beautiful girl.

Thomas's Drugstore was only a few blocks from the high school and housed a soda fountain and a short-order counter where you could order ice-cream sodas, malts and shakes, french fries, and hamburgers. In one corner, the drugstore boasted a new jukebox that was always playing the popular tunes of the day. There was usually a crowd of kid there in the afternoon, and as I walked in, there was Doreen sitting at a table waiting for me just as she had promised. I walked over and sat next to her and said, "Hi, I am so glad to see you. Can I get you a Coke or an ice-cream soda or anything." She laughed and said, "Sure, Ron, a Coke would just be the berries." I walked over to the counter and ordered us both a Coke, and I noticed that several of the football players were there and were watching me and Doreen with some interest. I figured that it was because they had all been rejected by her and wondered why she was with me, the new guy. So I asked her about that very subject.

"Doreen, can I ask you a personal question?"

"Not too personal, I hope."

"No, it's just that I have been told that you have refused several requests from the fellows for a date, but you agreed to meet me here today. Not that I'm complaining, but why me?"

"Ron, these other guys made it real clear what they wanted or expected from me, and I am just not that kind of girl. I was hoping that you were a little different, being new in school and all. Maybe you would be a bit more intelligent and wanted to get to know me for who I am. Could I be wrong about you?"

"You are definitely not mistaken. I'd really like to find out much more about you. I think you are intriguing and maybe somewhat mysterious, and I was hoping to find that we had many things in common. Like for example, what kind of music do you like?"

"I like popular music in general, and I really like Ruth Etting's songs." After hearing that, I walked over to the jukebox, put in my nickel, and played "Button Up Your Overcoat."

As I walked back to our table, I could see Doreen giving me a very mischievous smile, as if to say, I hoped that I had won her heart. I wasn't real sure of myself at that point or if what I had said and done was what she wanted, but we seemed to have an instant attraction, and Doreen and I became inseparable after that day.

The fact that I was the new guy in school and I was now dating the most beautiful and desirable girl at Woodrow Wilson High School didn't sit too well with some of the other players on the football team that had tried to date Doreen and failed. The next day in school that attitude became apparent as I was walking down the hall and coming toward me were some of my teammates. As they drew close, one of them Tommy Painter, one of our linebackers, took a swing at me with no warning. Luckily, I saw the punch coming and was able to duck. I watched as his hand hit the lockers in the hall with a loud bang. I reacted swiftly with a swing of my own just by instinct, mind you and I was able to connect flush with his jaw. Tommy went down in a heap and looked up at me with a look of confusion. This wasn't supposed to happen to him as Tommy liked to fight and very seldom lost a disagreement, but this time he was lying on the ground with me standing over him.

It seemed to take the fight out of him, and as I turned and walked away, I could hear Tommy holler out at me, "Perkins, this ain't over, not by a long shot. I'll see you again." I found out later that Tommy had been after a date with Doreen without success and didn't take too well to being beat out on anything. I knew I had to watch out for him and be ready for the next time 'cause I felt like a next time was coming and coming soon.

Mom had managed to get a job at Fulton's department store selling ladies' shoes. She didn't make much, but it was enough to keep food on the table and gasoline in the Model T. My intent was to also get a job after school as soon as football season was over, but for now I had football practice most afternoons that took up my time.

I was constantly on the lookout for Tommy as I knew he was still sore at me and wanted revenge. But since he played defense and I played offense, I was able to avoid him as we were preparing for our first football game of the year against the Highland Park Eagles on Friday night. Coach had named me starter at end, and I must say I was very excited about that. Doreen had made the cheerleading squad, and I was hoping to make some spectacular plays to impress her.

As the lights went up on the football field that night, Coach gave us an impassioned pep talk to prepare us to face the mighty Highland Park Eagles, who by the way had won the state championship last year and were favored to repeat and defend their title. They were overwhelming favorites to quickly dispatch the Woodrow Wilson Bearcats. Coach told us in his pep talk that they might have talent, but we had heart and determination. Highland Park was in the wealthy part of Dallas, while we were the poor kids on the east side of town. Add in to that, Highland Park had twice the enrollment that we had.

In spite of all the odds against us, we were eager to take the field. I must say it was quite a rush as we ran out of the locker room, up the tunnel to the field, listening to the screams of encouragement from our home crowd. Well, unfortunately, that was as good as it got as Highland Park was every bit as accomplished and talented as advertised. They whipped us soundly 42-6, but I did catch two passes, one of them right in front of Doreen and the rest of the cheerleaders. So, for me, it was a successful night.

After the game was over and we had showered and dressed, I was surprised and overjoyed to see Doreen standing there waiting for me. "Ron, I hope you are okay. It looked to me that those Highland Park bullies beat you guys up and weren't very nice about it at all."

"I'm alright, I've been hit worse than that, but did you see those two catches I made."

I wanted to make sure that she had noticed the effort I put out and that I was performing just for her. I took her hand in mine as we walked to my old Ford, and as we drove away, I asked, "Do you want to go to the Dairy King for a hamburger and fries before I take you home?"

"Ron, it's getting to be kind of late, and to tell you the truth, I'm not very hungry. Do you think we could drive over to White Rock Lake and just sit and talk for a while?"

Do I need to tell you that I was up for that, and that's exactly what we did. I had a blanket in the truck, and we spread that out on the shore of the lake and sat down to enjoy the warm Texas night under the stars.

"Ron, I want to ask you something, if I may."

"Sure, Doreen, ask me anything. I have no secrets from you."

"Well, this is our senior year in high school, and I am off to college next fall. And I was wondering what your plans for the future were after you graduate."

"I had planned on going to college next year, like you, but my dad passed away suddenly earlier this year, and with that, his grocery business went under. So to be honest with you, I don't have the money to go to college at this time. I don't really know just yet what I'm going to do in the immediate future. I was thinking maybe I could get a good job here in Dallas or I could even go into the Army I suppose." With that I could see the empathy in her eyes, and she put her arms around my neck and leaned in for one of the most delightful kisses I had ever had the pleasure of receiving. It was our first kiss, and it didn't disappoint. It got a little warmer that night on the blanket by White Rock Lake, but it didn't go past some marvelous kissing and holding each other. I had too much respect for Doreen to try anything more aggressive, and besides that, I remembered her words to me when we first met, about boys just wanting one thing from a girl. I was determined to show her that I was different.

It must have been around midnight when Doreen and I loaded up in the Ford for the trip back to her house. She moved over real close to me in the truck, and I put my arm around her shoulders. She would shift gears for me as I steered just so I could hold her close to me. When we arrived at her house, I walked her to her door, and we shared one last good night kiss before I headed home.

I went in and Mom was already asleep, so I didn't have a chance to talk to her. But I was still hungry, so I went into the icebox and found some bologna and made a sandwich with a glass of milk before I turned in for the night with visions of Doreen still flashing through my mind. I always wanted to top off each night with a talk with my mom as we were all each other had in this world since dad died. Linda, my sister, did manage to stay at college on her own and had secured a job with an automobile dealership in Fort Worth and now had her own apartment, so we didn't see or hear much from her. She did tell us that she was in a serious relationship with a fellow named Lonnie, who according to her owned some property in Dallas and was quite wealthy. That sure sounded like Linda alright, always looking for the big bucks.

# 2
## CHAPTER

The next morning, Mom made breakfast for me, and we finally managed to have the talk we missed out on last night.

"Well, Ron, tell me about the game and how you and Doreen are doing. I assume you two had a late date since you didn't get back home until long after I had gone to bed."

"Mom, we were hammered by Highland Park, 42-6, but I did have a couple of catches, so I did alright. And yes, Doreen and I went out afterwards. We just went down by White Rock Lake and talked for a while, then I took her home. Mom, she is a swell girl, and I think I'm really getting serious about her."

"Ron, let me advise you to take it slow and easy. Doreen is a real nice girl, and you shouldn't rush her, if you know what I mean."

I wasn't quite sure what Mom meant by that last statement, but I assume it had to do with sex and me being too aggressive, but she needn't worry about that. Doreen and I had already had that discussion.

Doreen was an only child born on August 20, 1912, to Theodore and Susan Winthorp, so she was a couple of months younger than me, but it appears she was a whole lot smarter. I was going to take her later tonight to a picture show to see *The Light of New York* with Helene Costello and Eugene Pallette. The funny thing about Doreen is I wasn't quite sure about the feelings I was starting to have for her and whether she shared those feelings or not. I'd never been in love before, so I wasn't certain what that felt like. I didn't have those kind of feelings for Becky back in Terrell, so if this was love, it was unchartered territory for me. I hadn't really known Doreen all that long, but I had this strong sense that she was indeed my dream girl and the only one for me.

We went to the picture show and then to the Dairy King for some french fries and Cokes, and the conversation began with my question. "Doreen, tell me about your folks, what does your dad do for a living?"

"My dad is a sales manager for a nationwide pants manufacturer. He's been with his company since before I was born, and my mom is an elementary schoolteacher."

I could tell from that description that they were not wealthy by any means but were doing well and seemed to be a happy family. I decided to hold off on expressing my feelings for Doreen until later, but then she asked a question of me that I did not see coming.

"Ron, where do you think we'll be a year from now? I mean, I know I'm going off to college, probably the university down in Waco, mainly because they have an excellent premed school, and I desperately want to be a doctor someday. But what about you? I know we talked about this some before, but have you given your future any more thought?"

"I can see that this is important to you, but why is my question?"

"Ron, I don't want to scare you off, but it's like you said, we haven't known each other all that long, but I guess my point is I have a plan for my life, and I just want you to be part of it. Just a feeling I have I think."

"We will be in high school until next spring, so please give me some time to figure things out a little better, because believe me, I want the same as you do."

We played a couple of more games in September and into October and finished the season with a mediocre 5-5 record. It had completely slipped my mind to worry about a reprisal from Tommy Painter as it seemed that he had either forgotten about revenge or just didn't see the point anymore. It was pretty much acknowledged around the school and football team that Doreen and I were now a couple, so I think Tommy kind of knew for sure that he no longer had any chance with Doreen.

*****

# THE LOVES OF A LIFETIME

The weather was just starting to turn a bit cooler as we approached the end of October, a refreshing break from the brutal Texas summer heat. One day after football practice, as I was walking toward the locker room with my now best friend Robert when he asked me, "Ron, have you ever played golf?" Now that question came out of the blue, but of course I hadn't. Who could afford the equipment and more importantly the time to devote to a four-hour round of golf. So my answer was of course no. But Robert persisted, "After we shower, meet me out by my car. I'm going to take you to Samuel Park to a driving range there, and I'm going to introduce you to golf." I was not even aware that Robert not only was a fan of the game, but had a complete set of clubs.

After we arrived at Samuel Park, Robert said, "Now, I'm going to give you your first lesson. First thing is to widen your stance and shift your weight from your right foot to your left as you come through the ball. Number 1 rule is keep your head down and watch the ball all the way through your swing. Here take my mashie niblick and some balls, now try your hand at hitting a few. It was totally foreign to me holding that golf club in my hands, and the first few swings I took were comical to say the least. But soon, I was getting the hang of it, and to the surprise to both me and Robert, I was starting to hit the ball fairly well.

"Okay, looks like you've mastered that club, now take my play club and see how you do. With a play club, you can tee the ball up, and you do that by scooping some dirt up into a pile and hitting your ball off of that. But you can only do that in the 'tee box' for your first swing on each par 4 or 5. On a par 3 you use an entirely different club." Well, I listened carefully to Robert's instructions, and soon I was hitting the play club somewhat straight and with decent distance. I could see how one might become addicted to this game.

Robert said to me as we were leaving the driving range, "Let's meet up here a couple more times, and then, according to your progress, we'll actually go out and play a round of 18 holes of golf."

"But I don't have any clubs. What am I supposed to do about that because I don't have the money to buy golf clubs."

"You let me worry about that. I think I can scrounge up some used clubs for you to begin playing with. From what I've seen just tonight, you may very well be a natural at this. Time and practice will tell."

The next day Robert presented me with a set of clubs all of my own that he found for $15.

Robert and I continued to play golf at least twice a week, and my progress has surprised us both. My first goal is to break 100, and I'm getting close. Besides playing golf with Robert, Doreen and I are dating steadily now. I get to see her every day, and every day I look more eagerly to spending time with her. On days when I'm not playing golf, we met at Thomas's Drugstore after school and study together at either her house or mine. On the weekend we may catch a picture show or go roller skating, and there's always bowling or having a picnic at White Rock Lake. As I get more into golf, Doreen had fully supported my involvement and excitement as I seemed to improve with every time I play.

In addition to golf and Doreen, I have been hired at Thomas's Drugstore on a part-time basis as a soda jerk and all-around flunky making 50 cents an hour. So I'm staying very busy these days.

On Wednesday morning, October 30, 1929, I went out to get the newspaper before I was to leave for school and noticed the headline as in large type talking about the stock market crash that happened yesterday. I didn't pay too much attention to it and was not particularly alarmed because we certainly didn't have money for such things as stock market investments, nor did I know anyone that was involved in the stock market. I thought that was for rich people that lived in New York, certainly not us. All I had on my mind was the Halloween party that I was taking Doreen to tomorrow night.

But before long we started feeling the effects of the stock market crash as we saw business start to fail even in Dallas, Texas. Mom was able to keep her job at Fulton's, mainly because she was one of the best salespeople they had, but some of her coworkers were laid off. I was able to keep my part-time job at Thomas's Drugstore as well, but I was concerned about it until Mr. Thomas assured me that at least for now, my job was safe.

Linda, my sister, wrote a letter to Mom telling her that she and Lonnie were okay, that all his investments were in land and property in the South Oak Cliff region of Dallas county. She further informed us that they were planning on getting married in the spring of 1930 and we were invited. I thought that was most generous of her, since in truth she had very little to do with us. I think she looked down her nose at me and Mom as being beneath her, you know we were just poor white trash to her.

Doreen's mom and dad invited Mom and me to their home for Thanksgiving dinner, which I greatly appreciated because it was my favorite holiday. Besides that, since my dad died, Mom has not really had the heart to prepare large elaborate meals beyond what she prepared for just the two of us. To me, it meant spending quality time with Doreen and getting to know her parents better and then we would sit around the radio in their parlor and listen to maybe an episode of *Amos 'N' Andy* or *The Goldbergs'* which was a favorite comedy/drama.

Christmas was up soon, and I had found a charm bracelet for Doreen with several charms, a couple of which were golf related. I had to save my money to get it, but it was worth it when I saw the expression on her face and the tears starting to well up in her eyes. I knew I had done well. Doreen gave me a sweater vest to keep me warm for cold days on the golf course.

The winter of 1929 began mildly enough, but by January of 1930, the weather had turned bitterly cold with a rare early-year snowstorm for Dallas, Texas. But as the months passed by, the cold started to gradually lose its grip, and we were beginning to see the first evidence of spring. By early April, the grass was starting to turn green again, and the flowers were starting to bloom. I hear birds happily singing outside my bedroom window in the early morning hours. I'm in my last semester of high school and that can be both good and bad. It's good because I am finally going to graduate after a very challenging year, but at the same time it means that Doreen will be going off to college in the fall without me. Adding to that, I have made no progress in figuring out what I want to do with my life in the near future.

I haven't as of yet settled on a career path, except I know that college is totally out of the question and joining the military is a remote consideration at best. So that leaves finding some kind of a job that just became infinitely more difficult in today's world with the stock market crash that has thrown the country into a deep depression and put a lot of experienced folks out of work. At this point in time, though I enjoy playing golf, and I am getting better at it, I still don't see how that can produce any kind of career or even a steady income.

Robert and I are playing golf at least two times a week now, and I am steadily improving to the point where I am almost shooting par. Robert, who is an experienced golfer continue to say that I am some kind of prodigy.

"Ron, have you given any thought of entering a golf tournament this spring? I wholeheartedly believe you are ready for competition and just might do fairly well. If nothing else, just think about it. There is going to be a citywide open tournament later this month to be held at the Dallas County Country Club, and I think the entry fee is $10. If you decide to enter, I'll caddie for you. And to sweeten the deal, I found a set of clubs."

Well, I must say that was tempting as I would like to see how I would measure up against a serious challenge. I mean I'm still a punk kid at the age of seventeen, and I would be going up against seasoned professionals and amateurs, some twice my age, but the thought is definitely appealing, so why not give it a whirl. I told Robert to go ahead and sign me up, and he did and paid my $10 entry fee. Robert told me that the winner gets a $1,000 cash prize, second place gets $500, and third place gets $100. Any golfer that finishes in the top ten after third place wins $25. So I figured as well as I had been playing, my chances of getting my money back were pretty good. Besides, I still had a couple of weeks to practice and get my game in shape.

Doreen was firmly behind my new passion for golf and even came out to watch me play a couple of times. She seemed mildly interested but was content to just encourage me. My relationship with her continued to grow stronger as we neared the end of our high school career. I still haven't revealed my true feelings for her, but the time was coming soon as I can barely contain myself, wanting in the worst way to tell her that I love her.

The weather in Dallas, Texas, can really be a mixed bag as it can be sunny and warm one day and pouring down rain the next. Tomorrow is Thursday and is the first day of a four-day tournament, and I feel like I am ready, but my stomach continues to churn with what I am told are "butterflies." I've never been this nervous before, but Doreen has planned to skip school to be there to support me, and my mom has promised she would be there on Saturday to see me play. Robert is my caddie, and I am paired on the first day with a gentleman named John Packard. He is a seasoned veteran of about thirty-two years of age and, from what I've been told, is quite an accomplished golfer and one of the favorites of this tournament. But instead of feeling intimidated, I relish the opportunity to observe up close one of the best golfers in the country. Maybe I can learn something that will help me down the road.

*****

Thursday morning dawned bright and sunny with clear blue skies and temperatures in the sixties with a light wind. Robert picked me and Doreen up at 6:00 a.m. and we were off for the country club to arrive in plenty of time for our 8:00 a.m. tee time. I met my playing partner that morning for the first time, and he seemed to be friendly, maybe polite, would be a better description. He became aloof and was obviously concentrating on his game as we approached our tee time.

The only golf course I had ever played on was, of course, Samuel Park; and even though it was a very adequate course, it didn't compare with the pristine beauty of the Dallas County Country Club. The fairways were a perfect glistening green, manicured so well that you thought you were playing on carpet. Just before the start of the tournament, my sweet Doreen called me aside. "Ron, I have a gift for you before you start playing, and I hope you like it." With that, she handed me a box, and inside the box was a brand-new pair of black-spiked golf shoes. I was almost in tears out of gratitude as I reached for her to give her a hug and a quick kiss. "Doreen, they are magnificent, thank you so much."

"Now, Ron, you go out there and win this tournament, I know you can."

With that, I put on the shoes and made my way to the first tee to join my playing partner.

The first hole was a 397-yard-long par 4 that featured a slight dogleg to the left. If you could stay out of the trees that hugged both sides of a fairly narrow landing area, the approach to the green was easy. John won the coin toss for the honor of teeing off first, and he didn't appear to be even the slightest bit nervous, unlike myself. There was a sizable crowd that had gathered around us, making me even more nervous and apprehensive. I had never played in front of anybody before except for Robert and Doreen. John approached the first tee box, surveyed the fairway and went into his swing motion, and lifted the most beautiful drive I had ever seen, right down the middle of the fairway landing safely some 220 yards later. The crowd cheered his effort, then fell silent as I prepared for my first tee shot of the day. I started to sweat a bit, and my hands were shaking as I went into my swing motion. I came through the ball I thought with a solid impact but was horrified to see my ball careen off to the right and into the woods guarding the fairway. I had really sliced my drive and was now in deep trouble for my second shot.

After a few moments, I found my ball and luckily I saw that I had a slight opening path to the green some 195 yards away. Robert handed me my brassie, and after a few practice swings, I connected solidly with the ball and sent it flying on a direct trajectory toward the green, resting just short but a great recovery effort putting me in good position to pitch up and hopefully one putt for a par. John had hit his second shot cleanly on the green, and it landed about 4 feet from the hole, so he was looking at a birdie attempt and at least a one-shot advantage over me after the first hole. Well, that's exactly how it went. I pitched up and sank my putt as did John. He got his birdie, and I got my par, but after my errant drive, I was most grateful for the way the play turned out.

Hole number 2 was a 445-yard par 5 that was mostly straight and with a generous wide-open landing area for your drive, but the second shot to the green offered a high-risk, high-reward possibility as the green was guarded by a lake that measured around 50 yards across to clear. But if you accomplished that, you were on the green in two, looking at a possible eagle putt. John still held honors, and as he did on the first hole, he blasted a drive that this time carried some 250 yards and landed safely in the middle of the fairway, giving him a clear path to go for the green in two shots.

I approached the tee box and looked back over my right shoulder and saw Doreen standing there in the crowd watching me, and at that moment our eyes met, and she blew me a kiss. Well, that gave me all the encouragement I needed as I went into my swing motion. I too hit a high arcing drive that almost carried as far as John's, but unlike the first hole, this effort carried straight down the middle of the fairway. I was almost 20 yards behind John, so it was my turn to make a decision first. Do I lay up, or do I take a chance and go for the green in two. Being young and impetuous, it was really no decision as Robert handed me my brassie, and I made the decision to go for the green some 215 yards away over the lake. I had always hit the brassie well, but this time I watched anxiously as I knew that as soon as I made contact with the ball, that I didn't get all of it, and my ball dropped into the lake just short of clearing the other side.

According to the rules of the game of golf, I had to take a stroke penalty and drop my ball on the fairway side of the lake where I would now be hitting my fourth shot. I knew that if I hit my jigger well, I could get close enough to the hole to one putt and salvage a par. John, on the other hand, had accomplished a beautiful second shot that dropped down in the middle of the green giving him an opportunity for an eagle or if he two putted, most assuredly a birdie. I was somewhat unnerved after messing up so badly my second shot, so when I hit my Jigger, it came up short, and I two putted for a bogey. John missed the eagle putt but did manage a birdie. Now he had a three-stroke lead on me after just two holes.

So I'm sitting at one over par now, so I looked for Doreen in the crowd to settle my nerves, and sure enough there she was smiling at me and giving me the thumbs-up signal that was most encouraging. As I took in the sight of Doreen looking lovely as always dressed in a light-colored and tailored top and a brown plaid pleated skirt hemmed at the ankles, wearing a Garbo slouch hat that framed her beautiful face and allowed a few blonde curls to peek out. She had been given permission by her mom and dad to call in sick at school under the agreement that she would have to go back to school on Friday. The plan was for Doreen and Mom to be there for me for Saturday and Sunday. Since we were so late in our senior high school semester, rules of attendance were somewhat relaxed as we all had been assured of graduation in May. Robert's girlfriend, Margaret, was set to join us on Friday. Robert and I had also called in sick, which might have raised a few flags if we had not been in our last semester.

The rest of the front nine was mostly routine as I managed to finish with pars on the next seven holes to post a one over score. That put me behind John, who was the leader in the clubhouse at the turn with a two under par score.

The back nine began with a 170-yard par 3, but you had to hit your tee shot over water from tee to green, and there was no place to bail out; it was either on the green or in the water. John of course took honors and teed up first. He fired off a beautiful high shot into the middle of the green, rolling right up to the flag coming to a rest some 6 feet from the hole that was to the back of the green. I selected for my club my spade mashie, and this time I launched a shot with the proper accuracy and distance that was perfectly aimed at the flag, hitting the ground and rolling up to within 2 feet of the hole. This was my first opportunity for a birdie, and I took full advantage and drained the putt. John two putted for a par, so I was able to pick up a quick stroke on him. Now, I was back to even par, and I was very grateful to be only two shots behind John after ten holes.

On holes 11 through 15, I was able to hang in there with three pars, one bogey and one birdie for even-par golf, but next up was the treacherous sixteenth hole. It was a long 425-yard par 4 with an almost ninety-degree turn to the left. One alternative was to hit a lofted drive over the left corner blocked by trees that reached a height of 20 feet or more, ideally landing in the fairway past the turn with only needing a pitching niblick to the green. But you had to be aware of the thick ankle-deep rough that bordered the fairway, so it required a precise shot that was too risky for either John or myself to take.

So the conventional and preferred shot was down the fairway to a landing area that was 225 yards down, but if you hit your drive too far, you were in deep, thick woods; and if you ended up too short you were faced with trying to navigate over that tangle of trees to the left. This hole obviously required a precise tee shot at just the right length and direction. But this is where John ran into a bit of difficulty as he pushed his drive too far, and his ball disappeared into the trees on the right side past the ninety-degree turn. Upon seeing that, I decided to power down some, even though I felt like I couldn't hit my drive as far as John, I didn't want to take any chances. I decided to not use my play club but opted for the brassie instead. I managed to make solid contact, but I didn't push the ball quite far enough to encompass the turn. So I came up a bit short, looking at having to hit a blind shot over the corner with the trees blocking my view. Neither John nor I had an easy second shot coming up.

I was still two strokes behind John, but he had fallen out of the tournament lead to Harry Bonham, who was now at four under par. My options for my second shot on hole 16 were not very appealing. I could try and hit my mashie niblick down the fairway and hook it around the corner into an approach to the green, or I could try and loft a niblick up over the trees and land hopefully in the fairway past the turn. I chose the latter, and I felt like I had hit the shot I wanted as it began to soar over the trees on a perfect trajectory, but it clipped a branch on the way down directing my ball into the thick second cut on the left side of the fairway. Still, it was a marginally successful effort as I was now only 125 yards from the green. I figured if I could accomplish a decent approach shot and one putt, I could preserve my par.

*****

John was having his own set of problems as after exhausting the allowed time to look for a lost ball; he had to take a stroke penalty and drop his ball short of where it disappeared into the thick underbrush. The good news for John was that the drop location left him square in the middle of the fairway, past that severe ninety-degree turn with a clear angle to the green. But he was now hitting three and was still some 200 yards out. That being said, John, being the great and experienced golfer that he was, hit a beautiful shot to the left side of the green coming to a rest some 20 feet from the hole. If he could one putt, he would par the hole, even with a penalty stroke, and that's exactly what he did. I addressed my ball, lying deep in the thick rough, and hit it with my niblick with all the force I could muster, but I came up 10 yards short of the green. I chipped up with my jigger and one putted for a bogey. I finished the day at a one over par 73 and was ecstatic to accomplish that. After the first day, I was five strokes behind the leader, Harry Bonham, at four under par. John finished with a two under score of 70.

The weather on Friday for the second round of the tournament was once again perfect for golf. It was sunny and warm with bright blue cloudless skies, with the temperature a warm for April—seventy-three degrees. There was only an insignificant ten-mile-an-hour breeze out of the south. My tee time on this day was at 11:00 a.m., and I was still paired with John Packard. John continued to be an intense kind of fellow and was more interested in concentrating on his game than conversing with me, which I fully understood. He was statistically still in the running for winning this contest. I knew Doreen wouldn't be in the gallery today, but she and Mom would be there for me on Saturday and Sunday, provided I made the cut. Robert's girlfriend, Margaret, joined us, which always gave him a lift. Margaret was a very pleasant person to be around and fit with Robert perfectly. She was tall and had striking features with bright curly red hair and porcelain skin with bright blue eyes. Robert was a tall, lanky kind of fellow with short cropped brown hair and was obviously very much in love with Margaret and she with him. They were quite the pair.

The day went okay as I was able to salvage another one over par 73. Robert was proving himself to be invaluable to me as my caddie as on several occasions he gave me excellent advice and talked me out of selecting the wrong club for a particular situation. Eighty-four men had signed up for the tournament, and after two days I stood at two over par and in a solid fifteenth place, enough to make the cut for the weekend. I aspired to improve my play on Saturday, especially with Mom and Doreen there, but the weather forecast for the weekend was ominous with cooler temperatures dropping into the fifties with heavy rainfall at times and a gusty wind of up to thirty to forty miles per hour predicted.

The weather forecast was spot-on as Saturday turned out to be an absolutely miserable day with a cold rain pelting us and unpredictable high winds. Luckily, I was no longer paired with John, but with a more exuberant fellow named Fred Baker. Fred was a professional golfer like John but nowhere near as intense. He had a fat cigar stuck between his lips that he struggled with all day to keep it lit through the steady rainfall. He laughed and told jokes, a very personable fellow. Fred stood about five feet nine inches and was overweight, but he had a powerful swing that I envied. Fred started the day at one over par, seven strokes behind the leader, Harry Bonham, who stood at six under after two days. Harry was running away with the tournament, and unless some kind of disaster befell him, he would be the clear-cut winner and walk away with the $1,000 first-place prize money. But inclement weather conditions can be a great equalizer in golf.

Suggested dress for men for the tournament circuit was knickers with argyle socks, a newsboy cap and I had my new black spiked golf shoes that my gal, Doreen, had given to me, and a white shirt and black tie with a plaid sweater vest over the shirt. That was perfect for the beautiful weather we had for Thursday and Friday, but with the constant rain on Saturday, my clothes had become soaked and heavy and uncomfortable. Fortunately, our caddies were allowed to provide us with umbrellas, just not on the green when we were in the process of addressing the ball for a putt. By the third hole I had bogeyed the first and parred the second so now I stood at three over par for the tournament. I was soaked and cold and I saw Doreen, Mom and Margaret standing there in the shrinking gallery cheering me on, hidden under their umbrellas and looking quite miserable in the cold and wet.

I wasn't the only one having a difficult time with the weather as Fred had also dropped a stroke and was no longer laughing or joking around as the conditions continued to worsen. As I was walking along the fifth hole fairway, I stopped and motioned to Mom, Doreen, and Margaret and encouraged them to call it a day, that it was just too hopeless for them to continue. At first, they protested, but I told them how much I appreciated them being there to support me, but to go home before they made themselves sick. The gallery as a whole had dwindled to almost nobody as most had left to seek shelter.

I finished the round with a 74, making me four over for the tournament, but even Harry had dropped a couple of shots, back to four under par, so I was only eight strokes behind the leader. My goal at this point was to finish in the top ten and win that $25 prize. It was a remote goal as I stood in the twenty-first place after three rounds.

The last day of the tournament was cold and overcast, but no rain and the wind had calmed down some, but was still gusting up to around twenty miles per hour. I was scheduled to tee off at 8:30 a.m., once again with Fred and even he seemed to be in better mood. The golf course was soaked after the all-day rain of yesterday, making any extra distance a challenge, but I started out okay as I birdied the first hole; and by the turn at number 9, I had improved to two under for the day and two over par for the tournament. Harry was getting ready to tee off as I made the turn, but it really didn't matter to me, for it was unrealistic to think I had a shot at catching him, but I still felt like I could make it up the leaderboard to that coveted tenth spot.

As I started the back nine, I asked Robert to find out where I was positioned in the standings, and he came back and told me that I was now in a solid fourteenth place. I was greatly encouraged by that, and it gave me the confidence to birdie hole number 11. Now I stood at only one over par for the tournament. I parred holes 12 through 15, then came the treacherous hole number 16. Fred took honors and hit an absolutely beautiful drive as he decided to take the risk and hit to the left up over the trees that guarded the corner and into the fairway past the ninety-degree turn. He was at two over for the tournament, surprisingly one stroke behind me. But I didn't feel like I had the ability to produce a shot with that degree of difficulty, so I hit my brassie down the fairway, but this time slightly past the turn, but still in the fairway with a clear shot at the green.

I was further out than Fred and around 190 yards from the green. The wind was to my back, so Robert handed me the driving iron, and I swung as hard as I could, launching my ball to the leading edge of the green with at least a realistic attempt at a birdie. Fred's second shot also reached the green, but his ball was about 20 feet closer to the hole than mine. I lined up my putt, hoping to get close enough to two putt for a par. I was already at three under for the day, easily my best round of golf ever. The green was still damp, but with the light wind and the sun beginning to emerge from behind the clouds, it was starting to dry out, but still slower than the previous rounds on Thursday and Friday. I stood over my ball, took a couple of practice swings, then struck the ball with a bit more force due to the still wet conditions and watched in anticipation as it rolled across the undulating green on a perfect line to the hole some 35 feet away. Much to my surprise, the ball sat there on the edge of the cup for what seemed like an eternity, then dropped in, giving me a birdie and a four under par score for the day. This brought me back to even par for the tournament with two holes left.

I finished the tournament at even and miraculously had vaulted into the tenth slot, winning a $25 prize. As I walked over to the pay window, the accountant and the PGL official greeted me with, "Great tournament, young man, just how old are you?"

"I'm seventeen, sir, and this was my first ever tournament. I just started playing last year, but I really have learned to love this game."

"That's truly amazing that you have progressed this far in such a short amount of time. Now, before I give you your winnings, I must advise you that if you accept payment, you can no longer be an amateur but will be considered a professional and eligible to join the Professional Golf League. How do you feel about that?"

"Sir, I would consider it an honor and a privilege to be called a professional golfer."

I took my winnings and gave Robert back the $10 he had spotted me to get in the tournament in the first place and an extra $5 for being my caddie. With the other $10 my plan was to take Doreen, Margaret, and Robert out to eat at a favorite Italian restaurant that Doreen favored. I had never in my life shot a 68 in eighteen holes of golf or anywhere near it. Turns out the pressure of a tournament competition or a gallery of people watching and cheering didn't bother me at all, it in reality only served to hone my concentration.

# 3
## CHAPTER

The next tournament on the schedule was to be held in May in Fort Worth, and as a new member of the PGL, I was invited to play. I could see, for the short term at least, that golf may just be my future career as I continued to improve. Now, the question remained, could I earn a living at it? Was I good enough, maybe with a little more seasoning and experience, to actually win a tournament and the rich reward of finishing first? I think I need to triple my time on the driving range to sharpen my skills and eliminate the nagging little mistakes I continuously made at the Dallas contest.

Doreen and I are soon to finish our high school career and then there's summer and after that Doreen leaves for college in the fall. I am not looking forward to not seeing her on a daily basis. I had been looking for a job when Mr. Thomas offered me a full-time position at the drugstore, continuing to be a soda jerk, but also any other jobs he might need me for, such as making deliveries or helping the pharmacist, or working the cash register up front. He has offered me $15 a week for forty hours which is a most generous salary. The job opportunity is wonderful for now, but it doesn't get me any closer to realizing a career that Doreen wants for me. I've always been handy with electrical devices, and if I could eventually make it to college, I would like to pursue a degree in electrical engineering.

I'm thinking that maybe with my job at Thomas's Drugstore and picking up some winnings playing golf, I could eventually afford to enroll in college and join Doreen in Waco at the university. With that in mind, I decided for extra income, I could ask the chairman of the Dallas County Country Club, who I had met at the tournament, and he seemed to like me, about maybe caddying on the weekends. That way I could pick up a few extra bucks and get in some more practice time. Turns out he was agreeable to my proposition, and with that, I started my second job.

All these activities didn't leave me as much time with Doreen as I would like, so I figured it was time for me to tell her how I feel about her and my thoughts on our future together. I have a date with Doreen tonight, and we plan to go to a picture show, then stop by the Dairy King for a burger and fries. The movie she selected was a terrific romance drama called *Morocco* starring Gary Cooper and Marlene Dietrich. As we were leaving the Dairy King, I turned to Doreen and asked, "How do you feel about driving up to our favorite spot on White Rock Lake? I have something I want to talk to you about."

"Ron, you're being so mysterious tonight, but it sounds swell to me. I can't wait to hear what you have on your mind." We reached the lake, and I retrieved the blanket from the truck and spread it out on the shore. As we sat down, Doreen asked, "Okay, Ron, now that we're here, what's up with you."

"For some time now, almost from the moment I met you that day in the hall in school, I've wanted to tell you that I am desperately in love with you. I am really dreading you leaving for the university this fall, I'm afraid I might lose you. I don't want to be apart from you, and I do understand you have plans for your life, but I wanted to ask you something."

As I got down on one knee in front of her, my heart was racing and my hands started to shake as I produced from my pocket an engagement ring I bought with the money I had earned working at Thomas's Drugstore. "Doreen, will you, at some point in the near future, marry me. I know this may be sudden…" I could see tears starting to stream down her beautiful face, and I could tell she was caught completely by surprise. She moved closer to me, threw her arms around my neck, and gave me a hug and a kiss. After a moment, she said, "Ron, I must say I was not expecting this, but I kind of already knew that you loved me, and I feel the same way about you. I can't imagine spending the rest of my life with anyone else. Of course

I'll marry you, but just not right now. We are both still very young, not even eighteen yet, and I am determined to go to college, and you still haven't settled on a career."

"I think I have that part figured out. I now have two jobs, and I'm saving as much money as I can so that maybe in time I will have enough to join you at the university in Waco. I've always had a decent understanding of electricity and how it works, so that I would like to earn a degree in electrical engineering. Also, I still plan to enter golf tournaments in the next year and hopefully walk away with some winnings from that. Does that sound like a good plan to you?"

"Ron, I am so relieved to hear that you have started working on goals toward a future for us together. But you have to understand that I want to go into cardiology, and that requires a bachelor's degree first, that I can do in three years if I work hard at it. Then I have to apply to a medical school, be accepted, and that can take up to four years. After all of that, I have to complete a residency program that can take up to seven years before I can start a practice. I can't earn any kind of a living until I have completed the four years of medical school, so it would be up to you to be our sole support. Are you up to that challenge?"

"I am and I can tell you that I am completely committed to supporting your career. I will wait to marry you for as long as it takes. I will do whatever it takes to achieve my own personal goals over the next few years."

I felt relief wash over me as I knew that Doreen and I had a solid plan for our future together. As we sat there in momentary silence on the shore of the lake, I was thrilled to see Doreen hold her hand up in the moonlight to admire her new and admittedly modest engagement ring. I was the first to speak as there was one more pressing issue on my mind. "Doreen, my love, now that we're engaged and committed to each other, there is one other issue that we haven't talked about…" She stopped me in my tracks and said, "Ron, I know where you're going with this, and yes, I realize we haven't been intimate yet, but I promised my mom and dad that I would abstain until I was married. I hope you understand and can be patient with me, but one of the reasons I chose you over all those other boys was because you, right from the beginning of our relationship, showed me that you were interested in me as a person and what I could offer you other than sex. That is what we're talking about, isn't it?"

"Yes, of course, I mean this is 1930 after all, you know, modern times. But understand I do love you for who you are and what a delight you are to me in every way. You're right, though, I will honor your wishes."

"Ron, I want our wedding to be the most memorable day of our lives, and let me assure you that I feel the same way about our wedding night. But can I ask you a very personal question?"

"Sure, Doreen, you can ask me anything, I have no secrets from you."

"I don't really quite know how to ask this, so I'll just come out with it. Are you experienced, I mean, you know what I mean, don't you?" I could tell she was greatly embarrassed asking that question, but one that she deserved an answer to.

"No, you are the only girl I have ever dated seriously, and I am more than willing to wait for the right time with you, though I must say in all honesty, I have never wanted you more than I do right now."

I could see Doreen awash in the moonlight with her blonde hair in a bit of a disarray and her spectacular green eyes sparkling like never before. I had never seen her look more beautiful. She looked into my eyes and said, "I can't lie, I feel the same way. I must admit there's not much holding me back at this moment, but I have to wait and thank you for being so understanding about this. It's important to me that we wait. I know that when I go off to school this fall that it will cause a hardship on both of us, but you could come to Waco any weekend you wanted to, or I can come back to Dallas. If you come to see me, I'm sure I could get you a room at one of the boys' dorms, and I think a train ticket is only $3. We can write letters every day if you want, so maybe it won't be so bad."

We stayed there at White Rock Lake for a while longer, and we kissed and held each other, now assured that we both wanted the same thing for our future together. But the hour was late, and it was time to take Doreen home.

"Are you going to tell your parents tonight?"

"Yes, if they are still up, but I suspect that I will have to wait until tomorrow morning. But I promise you they will be thrilled for us. They really like you and already feel like you are the son they never had. How about you?"

"No, same here, my mom goes to bed early, so it will have to wait until the morning. But I can tell you that she loves you almost as much as I do. She will be very happy for us."

I told Doreen goodnight and drove home still on cloud nine. The next morning, I got up before Mom, and I made coffee for us, eager to tell her of the plans that we had made.

"Ron, you're up awfully early and you made coffee. What's the occasion? Let me guess, you and Doreen are up to something."

"You are always so perceptive, Mom. Yes, I asked her to marry me, and she said yes under the condition that we wait until she finish medical school. So we are officially engaged."

"Son, I am so proud of you, and I just wish your dad were still here to see this. I know he would be delighted for you as well." Mom started to tear up, overcome with the emotion of the moment, not only in her delight for Doreen and myself, but in suddenly having a memory of Dad and wishing he was still with us.

"Well, Ron, I couldn't be happier for you two, but today is Monday, a school day you know. So shouldn't you be getting ready? And I have to get to the bus stop in the next half hour to go to work myself. So let's get busy."

As I drove to school, I only had one thing on my mind, well, maybe two. I wanted to share my good news with Robert, and I wanted to see Doreen. I didn't have any classes with her, so I knew that it was lunch before I would see her. Robert and I had homeroom together, and I had Doreen's permission to tell him of our engagement.

"Robert, I have some exciting news to tell you."

"Well, by a strange coincidence so do I. But you go first."

"I asked Doreen to marry me last night, and she accepted, so we are now officially engaged. Now what's your news?"

"First of all, I am so happy for you and Doreen, you couldn't be a better match in my opinion. We need to have a party to celebrate the good news. My news is nowhere near as exciting, but what I wanted to tell you is that there is another tournament coming up soon in May in Fort Worth to be held at the Continental Country Club. I think the dates are May 22–25, the week before we graduate. I've been told that the entry fee this time is $25, but the first-place prize is $2,000 with $1,000 for second and $500 for third. Fourth through tenth place earns $50. Should I sign us up? It's considered by the PGL to be the kickoff tournament of the 1930 season, and you really don't want to miss it. If you don't have the $25, I can help."

"No, I can manage the entry fee, so go ahead and sign us up. As you know, I'm still using that hand-me-down set of golf clubs that you found for me, but maybe I can win some decent prize money and buy a new set of Spaldings."

I told Doreen at lunch about the golf tournament in Fort Worth and Robert wanting to throw a party for us, and typical of Doreen, she was enthusiastically in support of both. The party was set for Friday night, and all my old football teammates as well as Doreen's cheerleading team and classmates attended. It was also kind of an end-of-school party as most of us would be going our separate ways after the end of May.

The engagement party was held at Doreen's house thanks to her more than gracious parents and was widely attended by all our high school chums. The celebration lasted well into the night and was one party we would not soon forget. Next big event for us was the golf tournament in Fort Worth followed by graduation and the last summer before Doreen left for the university.

Robert and I called in sick to school for one last time, but I don't think anybody in the school administration really cared one way or the other as we were within a week of graduation anyway. On Wednesday afternoon after school we drove my old Ford truck over to the Continental Country Club. If I thought the Dallas County Country Club was special, it didn't even come close to the magnificence of this place.

"Robert, would you look at this. I don't think I've ever seen a more impressive clubhouse in my life. I can't wait to see the course."

"Yeah, Ron, it's something all right. Kind of intimidating to a couple of poor old country boys like us."

We parked the Ford and walked up the massive stone steps to enter into a cavernous room with walls of what appeared to be white marble with columns supporting a ceiling that must have been at least 30 feet high with a tinted glass skylight with a large crystal chandelier that had to weigh 500 pounds. We walked over to the registration and information desk that was made of dark mahogany wood as were all the wood surfaces in the room. The floor was covered in a rich maroon carpet and to the back of this room were floor-to-ceiling glass windows and a door that led down stone steps to a patio that overlooked the golf course.

Off to the right of the grand entry hall was the dining room that housed what we were told was a four-star restaurant. Off to the left was the pro shop that contained any golf accessory you could think of from a vast array of golf clubs to a complete set of clothing attire. We paid our entry fee and walked through the door at the rear of the building to find the caddie shack for Robert to familiarize himself with the course and chat with the other caddies. I found out that my tee time was 11:00 a.m. and my playing partner for Thursday was one Stephen Jackson.

I walked down the steps past the patio to where the other golfers were gathering. There were ninety-five entries in this tournament, and once again I was the youngest at not yet eighteen years old. We went to a meeting of the golfers and were briefed by a PGL representative on course rules and other procedures. Most of the top golfers were present, and I saw my previous playing partners John Packard and Fred Baker. Harry Bonham was in attendance also. So now we were all set for Thursday morning, but unfortunately neither Robert nor I had a chance to walk the course, so I'm sure there were some surprises in store for us.

Robert and I left early Thursday morning hoping to arrive at the golf course by 8:00 a.m. We thought by doing that we would have time to at least walk the course some before the first players teed off. But we were too late, they had already started, so the course would remain a mystery to us for the first day.

Hole number 1 was a 475-yard par 5 with an elevated tee box dropping off 20 feet to a shimmering, pristine fairway that then rose back up at the approach with a lake guarding the green. The fairway was straight and was lined with beautiful oak trees. The first cut of the rough bordering the fairway was a tangle of ankle-deep Saint Augustine grass. The weather was absolutely perfect for golf with a bright sun and clear blue skies with only a light southerly breeze that was at our back for this first hole. The key on number 1 was a long straight drive keeping it in the fairway and then your second shot would have to be long enough to clear the lake if you wanted to be on the green in two strokes.

Stephen won the coin toss and the right to honors to begin the day. Stephen was a large man that stood six feet, two inches and must have weighed a muscular 225 pounds. I would say he was around thirty years of age and obviously presented a powerful and intimidating figure. He was an experienced member of the PGL tour. Stephen stepped up into the tee box and launched a perfect drive that landed some 230 yards down the fairway, leaving him 245 to the green. My drive was accurate but only around 220 yards, leaving me way short of going for the green in two.

I just needed to hit my second shot at around 175 yards, leaving me less than 100 yards to the green. Robert handed me my mashie niblick, and I nailed the shot as my ball rolled up to the bank of the lake. Stephen was more than likely strong enough to reach the green in two if he caught the ball flush. Stephen hit his brassie for his second shot, cleared the water easily, and landed just short of the green. So we both were looking at a pitch shot to the flag that rested at the back of the green. Since I was further out, I was to go next, and Robert suggested my niblick. I agreed and hit a perfect shot to within 2 feet of the pin. Stephen did well also as he pushed his jigger up close to the pin. We both drained our putts for a welcome birdie on the first hole. I couldn't have asked for a better start.

Hole number 2 was a 170-yard par 3 with a tee box that was elevated above the green by some 50 feet. There was water guarding the green on right side and sand traps surrounding the left and front, so a precision shot was imperative. Stephen went first and launched a high arcing shot that landed in the middle of the green, some 20 feet from the hole, setting himself up for another birdie opportunity. I chose a pitching niblick over Robert's objection that it was not enough club. Turned out he was right as my tee shot fell short of the green and into a deep sand trap. I came out of the sand okay but left myself short of the hole by some 30 feet. Sure enough, I ended up with a two-putt bogey and back to even par golf. Stephen sank his putt and scored his second birdie. On holes 3 through 9, I played even golf for a one over score at the turn.

Hole number 10 was going to prove a wicked test of my golfing skills as it was a 425-yard par 4 with a dogleg to the right over water in front of the tee box and down a fairway that was 30 feet lower than the tee box and the green, making your second shot up over a steep incline a blind shot, provided you successfully negotiated the dogleg turn with your tee shot. The turn was around 200 yards down, so it would require a controlled slice following the fairway. I felt like I had that shot with my play club, against the advice of Robert, who thought a brassie was the safer choice. The penalty of not negotiating the turn to the right successfully with accuracy was a stand of oak trees to the right and trees with thick underbrush to the left and almost certainly a lost ball.

I knew that Robert had been right back on hole number 2, but I felt like I could pull off the shot. I teed up my play club and hit one of the best shots I had ever accomplished as my ball followed the fairway perfectly around the dogleg and nestled into the center of the fairway some 240 yards later. Stephen, being very strong off the tee box went first and chose to fly the corner of the bend and landed his tee shot in the right side of the fairway in the first cut of rough, but still a clear shot to the green. Stephen had finished the front nine at two under par.

Stephen and I both accomplished an excellent tee shot but with different approaches and we were almost side by side in the fairway some 185 yards from the green, but he was in the thick first cut of rough, and I wasn't. Stephen went first and decided to hit his driving iron. He pulled the ball out cleanly and watched as it flew toward the green on a terrific trajectory but came up short, landing in a deep and fluffy sand trap. Now it was my turn, and Robert and I consulted on what club to choose and selected a mashie, taking into consideration the elevation of the green. I hit a superb shot to the middle of the putting surface, some 15 feet from the pin, giving me an opportunity for a birdie to get me back to even par for the tournament.

Stephen came out of the sand trap clean, maybe a little too clean as he flew some 10 feet past the flag, then two putted for a bogey, bringing him back to one under par for the day. I did manage to drop my putt for a birdie. I had picked up two strokes on my playing partner and now only trailed him by one. We were advised that Harry Bonham was in the lead after nine holes with a three under score. So I felt like my chances were still feasible for winning a substantial prize.

I finished the day at even par, and Stephen posted one birdie and two bogeys to also finish at even par. Stephen had been very quiet most of the day, rarely acknowledging me except to occasionally say "Good shot." He was blocking out all distractions to focus on his game. Harry had finished at four under.

Our tee time on Friday was at the same time of 11:00 a.m., and the weather was once again perfect for golf with temperatures approaching the low eighties. Once again I was paired with Stephen, but this time before we began our round, he opened up to me. He did reveal that he had a wife back in his hometown of San Diego, California, and two young daughters. I got the impression that this tournament was important to him. I think he needed to do well to continue his golfing career.

Stephen played better on Friday, posting a round of two under par 70 and found himself only four strokes behind Harry Bonham, who sat at six under after two days. I improved as well as I became more familiar with the intricacies of the course. I posted a respectable one under 71 for the day and the tournament, so I was only five strokes out of the lead with two days left. I easily made the cut for the weekend, and I knew that an added bonus for Saturday was that Doreen and Mom would be there to watch me.

My tee time for Saturday was at 1:00 p.m., and my playing partner would be John Packard, who was also at one under par for the tournament, putting us in seventh place. On this day we all came in Robert's Chevrolet sedan with Mom, Doreen, and Margaret all joining us. The mood on the drive over was festive and upbeat to say the least. I was bursting with optimism today, and my goal was to play myself into one of the top three money slots. I was so grateful at the prospect of having my mom and Doreen in the gallery that day, cheering me on.

We arrived early enough to enjoy lunch in the club restaurant and then Robert and I were off to the first tee while the girls settled into the crowd to follow us. The weather continued to be warm and sunny with only a light breeze. I had played well on hole number 1 on Thursday and Friday, and today was no exception as I secured a birdie to drop me to two under for the tournament. I followed that with a par on hole number 2, and we were off for a hopefully successful day of golf. I played the rest of the front nine at even par and made the turn to hole number 10 at two under par. John seemed to stumble out of the gate with an early bogey on hole number 1 and pars for the rest of the front nine to drop back to even. Harry was just teeing off as we reached the turn and started his day in the lead at six under. I had closed the gap after nine holes and was now only four strokes out of the lead.

We both parred number 10 then moved on to hole 11 which was a 180-yard par 3 with an elevated tee box that was some 75 feet above the green. This particular hole presented a vista of a breathtaking view of the surrounding countryside with downtown Fort Worth visible in the distance. I was first up, and we agreed on a mashie iron. I struck the ball about as well as I could and sent a drive screaming high and on target directly for the pin, landing 6 feet from the hole and rolling up to within 2 feet. I couldn't have asked for a more perfect shot, and I turned to the gallery to see Doreen's reaction. She smiled, enthusiastically clapped her hands, and blew me a kiss. John teed off next and hit a swell shot as well, landing some 20 feet from the hole. We both were able to score a birdie and now I was sitting at three under. Word came back to us that Harry was struggling on the first hole with a bogey, dropping him back to five under. His lead over me had shrunk to two strokes.

Hole number 12 was a par 5 and at 506 yards was the longest hole on the course. It was mostly a straight shot with a stream running down the right side of the fairway all the way past the green. There were tall oak trees and thick underbrush along the left side of the fairway, so a precise tee shot was essential. I teed off and hit a superb drive sending the ball down the middle of the fairway and ending up some 250 yards later. John accomplished a successful drive as well with his ball ending up near mine, but I could tell by his demeanor he was losing patience and was starting to press just a bit.

The fairway narrowed at the 400-yard mark, making the second shot challenging and risky. Going for the green in two was not an option for me, so I felt like I needed to do was hit a shot some 150 yards to set up my approach to the green. Robert and I agreed on a mashie niblick without using a full swing, and the strategy worked perfectly. I had left myself in prime position only 100 yards from the green for my third shot.

John, feeling desperate, chose to hit his brassie and try for an almost-impossible second shot to the green. Predictably he found disastrous results as his ball veered off to the right and into the stream, just about eliminating his chances for a victory in this tournament. He knew instantly that he had made a fatal mistake, and I watched him as his shoulders slumped and he stared into the ground. I hit my niblick into the green and two putted for a par. I finished the day at even par for a three under score for the tournament. Harry had recovered and picked up the stroke he had dropped early on and finished the day at six under par. So with one round of golf left, I was in a tie for fourth place only three strokes out of the lead. John finished the hole with a double bogey and took himself out of contention.

We were jubilant as we left for home on Saturday afternoon, buoyed by the success of the day and with anticipation of achieving the goal of winning third or even second place money on Sunday. Doreen and Mom being there for me were major inspiration and partly responsible for the way the day went. Mom had decided to stay at home on Sunday, saying she wanted instead to attend her church. But I think she was just worn-out with all the excitement and the strain of walking all day. I'm starting to notice that her health is not as robust as it once was, and I worry about her. Life has not been easy for her since Dad died.

# THE LOVES OF A LIFETIME

Our tee time on Sunday was 1:00 p.m., and my playing partner for the last round was a young man named George Wilson. George was not much older than me, and he had done well in the tournament posting a three under score. He was an outgoing sort with a friendly and open demeanor. He was a slight fellow of around five feet and ten inches tall and couldn't have weighed more than 120 pounds. But he did possess a muscular upper body and had been on the pro tour for two years. Word had it that he was a resourceful and smart golfer, that was excellent at scrambling out of trouble.

On the first hole I approached the tee box and surveyed the fairway. Before addressing my ball, I looked to my right to find Doreen, just to give me an added measure of confidence. Next, I swung hard and lofted my drive down the right side of the fairway rolling to a stop at 240 yards with an easy second shot to a position just short of the water hazard, leaving me with less than 100 yards to the green with my third shot. George teed off after me, but unfortunately for him, he hooked his drive off to the left and into the trees, but he was able to find his ball without a great deal of difficulty. However, the only option he had was to punch back out onto the fairway.

George was too far out to make an attempt at the green, so he had to layup with his third shot just short of the water hazard. We both stood on the fairway side of the lake, but I was hitting my third shot while George was on his fourth attempt. I hit my niblick toward the pin that was located on the middle right of the green and watched as the ball rolled up to within 6 feet of the hole. George pulled his approach shot to the left of the green and into a sand trap. He had to chip out and two putted for a triple bogey taking him back to even and for all practical purposes eliminated himself from contention. I was able to one putt for a birdie and now stood at four under par, two strokes off the lead and in a tie for third place.

I played the rest of the front nine at even par and the leader, Harry Bonham, added one more birdie to his score putting him at a tournament leading seven under. I parred hole number 10 and 11 and on number 12, I posted a birdie to move to five under par, keeping pace with Harry and in a tie for third-place money.

I played the rest of the final holes at even par, then waited for the last two groups to finish to see where I stood, praying for at least that coveted third place. I didn't have to wait long as all players completed their round with Harry winning first place at seven under, and I ended up in a tie for third place, splitting the $500 prize money. In the end result I walked away with $250. Tradition was that your caddie was to receive 10 percent of your earnings, but in Robert's case I felt like he deserved so much more. I gave Robert $50 for his invaluable help and support.

Next up for us was our high school graduation next week, but first my dilemma was on how best to spend my remaining winnings. I decided to give $100 to Mom to support our household budget, thus beginning a new tradition of donating some of my winnings to a most deserving Mom. With the remaining money, I decided it was high time that I treat myself to a brand-new set of Spalding golf clubs. That old hand-me-down set of clubs Robert had provided had served me well, but I thought I could drastically improve my game with the latest in golf club technology.

I woke up Saturday morning and met Mom for breakfast. "Ron, are you ready for today?

"Yes, I think I am."

"I just want to tell you how proud I am of you, and I have a small gift for you. I found some of your dad's favorite cuff links, and I know he would want you to have them."

I took the box from Mom, opened it, and saw a set of beautiful silver cuff links that I remembered seeing him wear to church and for special occasions. "Mom, I don't know what to say, except thank you and tell you that I will treasure them always."

Our graduation ceremony was scheduled for Saturday afternoon at 3:00 p.m. on May 31, 1930, after which we were all going out to dinner. Later that night there was to be a dance being held in the gym for all the graduating seniors.

I walked across the stage, received my diploma, and waited in the wings of the stage for Doreen. We spoke briefly as the plan was for us to meet later for dinner with all the parents then we would have our date for the dance.

# 4
## CHAPTER

After dinner, I arrived at Doreen's home to pick her up for our date, knocked on the door, and was rendered speechless at the vision presented to me. There before me stood such a picture of loveliness that it took my breath away. She had pulled her hair back, revealing in full view the classic beauty of her face with her bright green eyes, full soft red lips, and translucent complexion. She was indeed a Grecian goddess. She was wearing a pale green satin evening gown that featured clingy flowing lines and was tightly fitted at her waist and hips, flaring elegantly to the floor. The dress had a high neck and an open plunging back. "Doreen, you are truly lovely tonight. Turn around and let me get a good look at you. I'm quite sure I don't deserve you." Doreen smiled and twirled around gracefully giving me the full picture.

We arrived at the dance around 9:00 p.m., and the band played music of a new swing musician, I think his name was Jimmy Dorsey. His music was swanky with a new tune called the "Tiger Rag." There was also some of Benny Goodman's songs, and we danced until the early morning hours. Afterward, we decided that it was our duty to stay out until the sun came up, I mean this was our last official high school adventure before beginning the summer and the rest of our lives.

We drove over to White Rock Lake to sit on blankets on the shore and watch the dawn break. I held Doreen's warm and sensuous body close to me, relishing her in the night. We enjoyed a long, lingering kiss as the sun started to appear over the horizon. "Doreen, my love, I was kind of hoping this day would never end."

"Me too. It has been marvelous, hasn't it?"

Totally exhausted, we headed back home with thoughts of what the future might bring for us in spite of the Great Depression malaise the country was going through. Surely the government will figure things out in short order and life will go back to normal. But for now we had the summer to enjoy, and in all honesty, the Depression hadn't really touched our lives all that much, at least not yet anyway.

Robert and I had golf tournaments coming up, and Doreen was preparing for college in the fall, but first there was my birthday on June 4 to celebrate as I was now eighteen years of age. Mom and Doreen had gone in together and bought a new pair of black knickers and some argyle socks. If nothing else, I would look sharp for the next tournament coming up in San Antonio in July. Robert did give me some bad news as he had applied for a government job with the postal service, had been accepted, and would be starting his new job in August. That meant he would only be able to caddie for me on the weekend, so I would have to find somebody else to fill in for Thursday and Friday.

I didn't do well in the San Antonio tournament, not even making the cut to play on the weekend. Maybe I was a little too full of myself after the success we had enjoyed in Fort Worth. I have discovered that golf can be a humbling game and plays no favorites. I learned a valuable lesson that not only in golf but in life itself one should not be haughty or arrogant; it won't serve you well. The next tournament that I could enter would be in Scottsdale, Arizona, in August. But it would conflict with Doreen's eighteenth birthday celebration, and I didn't want to miss out on being with her on this important date.

Doreen's birthday signaled both the happiness of her reaching eighteen and the sadness of the fact that within three weeks she would be leaving me for school. It had been a glorious summer seeing Doreen almost every day as our relationship continued to grow stronger, and I eagerly anticipated the day that I would make her my wife. But the day has come, and on a Sunday afternoon, I accompanied Doreen and her parents to the train station to see her off. She was obviously excited to be starting this new chapter in her life while

I was feeling a deep sense of loneliness as we embraced and kissed for what was to be a long time before I would see her again. We stood there on the platform and watched as her train disappeared off in the distance before we turned back to walk to the car for the trip back home. Hardly a word was spoken as I gazed out of the window, wondering what life would be like without seeing Doreen every day. We had been almost inseparable since the day we met in the hallway at school for what seemed like a long time ago. Oh, I knew we would write and maybe I would take the train down to see her on the weekend or she would come back to Dallas on occasion, but it just wouldn't be the same.

Now that the fall season has arrived and I no longer have school to contend with, I'm still working for Mr. Thomas at the drugstore and caddying on the weekends at the Dallas County Country Club for tips. Actually on some weeks I make more with the tips than my salary at the drugstore. So I'm managing to put back a little money every week to move me closer to achieving my goal of eventually joining Doreen at the university. I was hoping to accomplish that within a year or two. Of course, the unknown factor is golf and how much can I earn with that career.

The month of October brings the first real taste of cool weather, and there is the possibility of entering one more tournament before the season ends being held in Tulsa, Oklahoma. The train trip to Tulsa would only cost me $17 round trip. The first-place prize money is $3,000, second place is $2,000, and third place is $1,000. Entrants that finish in fourth through tenth place earn $100. The entry fee is $25. So I'm thinking that in the worst-case scenario, based on past performances, I should be able to win at least the $100 to cover my expenses. Unfortunately, Robert is unavailable to accompany me due to his job responsibility. That means I will have to take whoever is available to caddie for me and hope for the best. I have become comfortable with my new set of Spalding golf clubs and pray that my game will improve to the level of being able to compete for one of the top three prizes.

Mr. Thomas and the country club have allowed me to take the time off to compete in the Tulsa tournament, so I will leave Dallas on Wednesday afternoon, alone with no Robert and no Doreen. After a four-hour train ride, I arrived in Tulsa and checked in at the Oklahoma Hotel, which was located close to the Greater Tulsa Country Club. I was able to walk over to the golf course and get a quick preview. What I discovered was a course that was not too terribly long but promised many hazards with both water and sand traps that would require precise negotiation. This was a course that favored accuracy over distance and power.

*****

Eastern Oklahoma is configured with gently rolling hills and is populated with large elm and cedar trees. The weather forecast is for temperatures in the fifties with a substantial breeze at around ten to fifteen miles per hour, gusting up to 20. I walked into the clubhouse to register and pay my $25 entry fee and to get my tee time for Thursday morning, October 23. Turns out that I am to tee off at 9:00 a.m. with a gentleman by the name of Henry Markham. Henry I am told is one of the older entrants at the age of thirty-nine but has an accumulation of years of experience on the PGL tour and is a native Oklahoman and is very familiar with this particular golf course.

I found out that my caddie was to be an enthusiastic high school senior, curiously carrying the nickname Rocky with the real name of Clifford Hansen. I asked him how he got the nickname of Rocky.

"Well, sir, I guess because I could skip rocks across the Missouri River farther than anybody else. The kids started calling me that, and I guess it kind of stuck."

"That's interesting, but one thing you don't need to do is call me sir. My name is Ron, and I'm only a couple of years older than you."

Rocky smiled and tipped his hat as if to say he understood. I liked this fellow, and it turned out I got lucky in the draw as he was familiar with this course being a native and having played here on numerous occasions.

As I approached the first tee on Thursday morning, I was accorded the honor of teeing off first, and I quickly learned to rely on Rocky and his knowledge of the course. The first hole was a somewhat short 322-yard par 4 with a slight turn to the left, not exactly a dogleg, but the desired shot was to aim for the right side of the fairway to set up your approach to the green, which could easily be reached in two shots. However, if your drive drifted too far to the right, you were essentially in jail as you would find yourself in a thick entanglement of large elm trees blocking your path to the green. This would require you to punch out and layup, costing you a valuable extra shot. The fairway was narrow and was bordered with fescue grass, a thick large blade grass that you did not want to be in. The green was guarded by deep sand traps that surrounded a uniquely small green, so precision was a key.

As predicted, the day began with an overcast sky with a light all-day rain in the forecast with temperatures hovering around fifty-three degrees at my tee time. Fortunately, on the first hole the breeze was at my back. I surveyed the layout of the hole and went into my swing motion. At the suggestion of Rocky, I chose to hit my brassie instead of a play club because of the danger of pushing my drive too far. The desired distance for a drive on this hole was less than 200 yards before the fairway turned to the left.

I came through the ball and hit an excellent drive of some 180 yards staying in the middle of the fairway, leaving me with a direct shot at the green some 142 yards away. Henry was a left-handed golfer, and this was new for me as I had never played with a lefty before. He lifted his drive, using his play club following the left curve of the fairway, using his natural controlled slice perfectly, leaving him less than 100 yards to the green. It was a most impressive display of golfing skills.

We were both set up perfectly for our second shot, but since I was farther out, I was next up. We both hit excellent approach shots and landed safely on the manicured putting surface. We both two putted for pars.

Hole number 2 was a 445-yard par 5 with a dogleg left and a water hazard crossing the fairway at the 300-yard mark. I was up first, but I knew the water posed no difficulty for me as I was positive I could not hit a drive anywhere near 300 yards, and I don't think

Henry could either. So the play club was what Rocky recommended and to put as much power into the stroke as I wanted but to be aware of the elm and cedar tees guarding the right side of the fairway and not drift too far right.

I hit a drive straight down the middle coming to a rest at the 240-yard marker, landing safely way short of the water. For my second shot, clearing the lake was no problem, but I was still 205 yards out from a green that was surrounded by sand traps. Though it was a low-percentage shot, I felt like that with my brassie and the wind still at my back, I had a shot of reaching the green in two. I swung through the ball and intentionally gave it a little more loft to put it up high into the trailing wind to get as much distance as I could. I watched as my strategy worked, and the ball landed softly on the green some 20 feet from the hole, leaving me with a completely makeable putt for an eagle.

Henry had followed my lead and was on the green also lined up for an eagle putt, but a bit further out than mine, so he went first. I watched as his ball came up a foot short, but he tapped in for a birdie and a one under score. As I addressed my ball for my eagle putt, I had watched how Henry came up short, so I put a little extra force into the effort and watched as my ball rolled around the hole and back out on the other side leaving me with a kick-in putt for a birdie. Now I was also at one under after two holes.

As I left the second hole on my way to number 3, I cast a wistful gaze in the direction of the very small group of people that was following us, looking for Doreen and even hoping to see Robert. But, of course, they weren't there, only friends and relatives of Henry, I suppose. Hole 3 was a 164-yard par 3 with a stream cutting across the fairway just short of the green, so you didn't want to be short off the tee. The green was of considerable size and surprisingly there were no sand traps, making it one of the easiest on the golf course. It was just a straight-up shot to the pin located at the back right side of an undulating green.

The wind was blowing across at a twenty-mile-per-hour velocity, making the tee shot somewhat tricky, so I figured a pitching niblick would be enough, but my caddie argued for a mashie niblick, since the hole was on the far side of the green. I have learned in my brief experience of playing competitive golf to rely on the advice of someone far more wiser about the golf course than I, so I took Rocky's suggestion and nailed the shot to within 2 feet of the flag. I drained the putt for a birdie putting me at two under for the round. Henry parred the hole giving me a one shot advantage over him.

We both played even for the rest of the front nine leaving us behind the leader, a fellow named Mac Grey who was currently at three under and one hole in front of us. So I found myself in second place, but the weather was starting to take a turn for the worse as the temperature had dropped in to the forties and the rain was pelting us a little heavier than at the start of the day.

Hole 10 was a straight-shot 340-yard par 4 that featured an elevated green, but caution must be exercised here as the back of the green dropped off into a lake with sand traps guarding the front. The rain was coming down so hard now to the point that it was impossible to keep the grip on my club dry. As I swung through the ball on my tee shot, the club turned in my hand, and the ball sailed wildly to the right and out of bounds. Now I really have to be careful as I am hitting three after the penalty from where the ball left the fairway, still some 220 yards out. So I carefully hit my brassie and saw that the ball came up just short of the green. I was able to chip up and one putt for a bogey, dropping me back to one under for the day. Henry successfully navigated the hole and secure a par to remain at one under.

Hole 11 was a highly challenging 379-yard par 4. The difficulty of this hole, compounded by the rain, was that the fairway started off leading you to the right, only to dogleg back to the left at the 200-yard marker. A thick patch of elm trees blocked your view of the fairway once it turned back to the left. You could choose to attempt to lift your tee shot up over the trees, landing in the fairway past the turn, or you could play the brassie and follow the fairway to where it turned at the 200-yard mark.

The conservative shot was the latter, and because of the deteriorating weather conditions, that's what I chose to do and found the desired success with that decision. Henry chose his play club in an attempt to blast a tee shot over the elm trees but found disastrous results. His shot came up short and disappeared into the thick woods. He was unable to find his ball and had to layup where his ball was last seen which left him in the fairway short of the turn. He ended up with a triple bogey and a two over par score. I managed to reach the green and two putted for a par to stay at one under.

For the rest of the day we fought the weather, but I managed to par holes 12 and 13, birdied 14, and finished at two under. Mac was having a difficult time as well as he had dropped back to two under, leaving us tied for the lead. I was very pleased with my effort and the results after the first day. That was the first time in my golf career that I find myself in first place after one round of golf especially considering the terrible weather conditions. But now I was cold, wet, and hungry and more than a little lonely as I missed Doreen terribly especially and Robert too. I stopped by the clubhouse and sampled the complimentary buffet before checking into my room. I hung my wet clothes up in front of the radiator hoping they would dry before my 11:00 a.m. tee time on Friday. The weather prediction for Friday was more of the same with rain, wind, and cold temperatures; but it was supposed to clear out by Saturday and warm back up in to the sixties with no rain.

The PGL had arranged a free dinner at the Tulsa Cattlemen's restaurant set to begin at 8:00 p.m., so I was eagerly anticipating a steak dinner before I turned in for the night. Once dinner was over, I decided I would jot a quick letter to Doreen and tell her about my experiences so far in Tulsa before calling it a night.

> My dearest Doreen,
>
> I don't have the words to express how much I miss you. It is mighty lonely up here in Tulsa without you. Tulsa is a beautiful city, but the weather so far has been horrible. I played well today in spite of a pouring-down rainstorm and temperatures in the forties, but I shot a two under 70, and I am tied for the lead. I hope your

classes are going well, I have no doubt that they are given how smart you are. Well, I guess I had better go now. I just wanted to get a note to you to let you know that I am thinking of you constantly and wish you were here with me.

Hope to see you soon.

Love, Ron

As I awoke on Friday morning, I checked and my clothes had dried out overnight and were ready for the day. I looked outside to see a light rain falling, maybe not as bad as yesterday, at least so far but still shaping up to be a miserable day again. I dressed and went by the registration desk in the hotel to get them to mail Doreen's letter then I went to the clubhouse for breakfast. After eating I went to the practice area to meet Rocky and warm up for the day. I was still playing with Henry, but Thursday had been a very bad round for him as he had shot a three over par 75 and was five strokes out of the lead. Not an insurmountable task for him but at the best very unlikely. Given that, Henry was in a surly temperament and in no mood for chitchat, so I decided to leave him alone and let him sort out his game on his own.

The field had started with eighty-five golfers, but twenty had already dropped out due to the weather and the course conditions. They might have been a bit premature as the sky was still overcast for the most part, but scattered openings in the clouds were starting to allow rays of sunshine through and the rain had all but ceased. With that the temperature was coming up into a comfortable range.

I started the front nine just trying to maintain pace with Mac, still playing with Henry. As we approached the turn, Henry continued to unravel as he fell further and further behind while though I was not having a spectacular day, it was serviceable. But Mac was starting to pull away and had stretched his lead to two strokes over me. I could see first place starting to slip away, so I asked Rocky's advice about maybe taking a few more chances and pressing a bit more to keep pace.

"Listen, Ron, I'm just a punk kid, but my advice to you would be to play the course and not the competitor. In other words, play your game, not his. Don't worry about what Mac's doing."

Rocky is proving to be far more mature and knowledgeable than his seventeen years of age would indicate. I'm realizing how fortunate I am to have him as my caddie.

I finished the day as I had started it at two under while Mac had increased his lead over me to three strokes as he finished at five under. I still felt secure in my position as the next closest golfer to me stood at one over par. Rocky had invited me to eat dinner with him and his family, and I welcomed the invitation. I went back to the hotel room, took a nice long hot bath, changed clothes, then waited in the lobby for Rocky and his dad, Clark, to pick me up at the appointed time of 7:00 p.m. They showed up right on time, and I could see that father and son were very similar in demeanor. I wanted to be sure and tell Rocky's parents what a wonderful young man he was and what a tremendous help he had been to me.

We arrived at their house, a rather large Victorian home, similar to what I had grown up in back in Terrell that featured a wraparound front porch with a swing and a couple of rocking chairs. I instantly felt at ease as Rocky's mom came out of the front door to greet me. She was a tall woman with striking features of high cheekbones, soft and warm brown eyes, and a rather expressive smile. She was by any measure a beautiful woman.

"Ron, come in. I'm Irene. Welcome to our home. Clifford has told us so much about you. I feel like I already know you."

Rocky's father was also a large man and had a very charismatic personality just like his son. When I met Rocky I was struck by his shocking red hair and the size of this kid as still very young he was around six feet and must have weighed 190 pounds.

I stayed for hours just enjoying Rocky and his family; and after an excellent dinner of ham, sweet potatoes, green beans, and homemade rolls, we adjourned to the front porch to smoke a cigarette and drink a cup of coffee. Rocky's mom soon brought peach cobbler topped with vanilla ice cream for dessert. I needed this companionship, being so far from home and alone, but now I had been adopted by this wonderful Oklahoma family.

Saturday's tee time was at 1:00 p.m., and my playing partner was to be Mac Grey. The next lowest score was at one over par, so that gave me a three stroke lead over third place. As we approached the first tee, I was eager to witness the play of one of the top golfers of the day. I felt like I could learn a great deal from this man. From the beginning, I found Mac to be a friendly and engaging guy, who was supremely confident in his game. He was secure enough to offer help to a young rookie like me. I hoped I would never forget the way he treated me, and I wanted to one day extend that same attitude to some young golfer coming up.

The weather continued to improve as the sky was a bright blue with hardly a cloud in sight and only a light breeze, while the temperature was back up into the mid sixties. You couldn't have asked for a better day to play golf. I finished the day at once again two under par, while Mac had added another birdie to go six under and was starting to separate himself from me and the rest of the field. I couldn't begrudge him his lead as he had been more than kind and helpful to me all day. I was enthusiastic about playing with him again on Sunday. I was still in second place, but now in a tie with the fellow that had been behind me by three strokes at the beginning of the day.

My tee time of 1:00 p.m. on Sunday gave me plenty of time to practice, eat an early lunch, and hopefully settle my nerves. Rocky had this entire tournament proven himself to be a valuable asset as a very confident and knowledgeable young man. I can't explain why I was so nervous on this day. I would guess it's because I had never been in contention on a Sunday before.

Now the time had come to meet Mac on the first tee and finish the last round. Mac had honors as the leader of the tournament. He fired a tee shot that was a thing of beauty as his ball drifted down the right side of the fairway gently curving back to the left and landing safely in the middle some 100 yards from the green. Now it was my turn, and I didn't feel like I possessed the expertise that Mac had demonstrated. So I did what had been successful for me before, and I hit my brassie down the right side of the fairway; but I pushed it too far to the right, and it ended up in the fescue grass of the first cut. I still had a clear shot at the green, but I was some 140 yards out and buried in the thick rough.

Rocky suggested a spade mashie, which, under normal circumstances, would have been way too much club; but I knew I had to dig my ball out of the thick grass. I made solid contact, but the ball flew over the green and into a sand trap. Now I would be hitting out of the sand with my jigger hoping to get close enough to the pin to one putt for a par. Mac, on the other hand, hit a perfect approach shot to within 4 feet of the hole, drained the putt, and walked off with another birdie, putting him at seven under and was now totally out of my reach. I blasted out of the sand trap, two putted for a bogey, and dropped back to one under par for the tournament.

Well, it was just that kind of a day for me as by the turn, I had dropped back to one over par with two bogeys and no birdies. The back nine wasn't any better as I finished out of the money for a fifth-place finish. I guess it was the pressure of trying too hard to keep up with Mac, but I did claim a prize of $100, and I gave Rocky $20 for his help and told him I wish I could do more, but he understood.

I think that more than the disappointment of not winning at least third place was the experience of playing with a great seasoned pro like Mac Grey and having an excellent caddie.

"Rocky, I want to thank you for all your help, and I hope to see you again. I think you have a great career in front of you as a player or at least a professional caddie. Good luck to you."

I learned from Mac how to focus your concentration and close out a tournament with a win. Unfortunately, I did exactly the opposite.

Thus ended the 1930 golf tournament season, with winnings totaling $375, a good start I suppose, but I hope for much better results for 1931.

# 5
## CHAPTER

I spent Sunday night in the hotel and then was off to the train station to catch the Monday morning train at 9:30 a.m. back to Oklahoma City then on into Dallas. Originally, I thought I was going to have to hail a cab, but Rocky's dad graciously agreed to take me. Rocky couldn't be there as he was after all still a senior in high school and had to attend classes. It gave me a chance to talk to Mr. Henson about his son and what a tremendous help he had been to me. He handed me a note from Rocky that contained his address and a request that we write and stay in contact. I truly wanted to keep up with that young man's career, particularly when it came to golf. I felt certain that he had a bright future in whatever career he chose to pursue. So I left my address with Mr. Hansen, boarded the train, and rolled out of Tulsa headed for home.

It was with a somewhat heavy heart as I looked out at the Oklahoma countryside and reflected on what might have been, if I had been able to hold my golf game together on Sunday. I knew that a golden opportunity had slipped through my fingers, and I vowed to work as hard as I could to never let that happen again.

I was due back in Dallas at 2:00 p.m. As I disembarked from the train and walked through the station, I assumed that I was going to have to take a taxi to get home, but there was my old friend Robert waiting on me with a big smile on his face. I knew Mom was at work, and I thought Robert would be too, so I was totally taken by surprise.

"Robert, what are you doing here? I thought you would be at work."

"Normally I would be, but I took today off so I could meet your train and welcome you home from Oklahoma. I wanted you to see my friendly mug as soon as you stepped off the train. So tell me about the tournament, how did you do?"

"Robert, you are not going to believe this, but on Sunday morning I stood at two under par, solidly in second place, with the possibility of winning $2,000. My playing partner was a gentleman by the name of Mac Grey, a kinder man you would be hard-pressed to find who eventually won the tournament. The weather was perfect, but I find it hard to explain what happened other than I lost focus and my game just fell apart and I finished in fifth place. I did win $100 so the day wasn't a complete loss. I was assigned a caddie by the name of Rocky Henson who turned out to be excellent, though not as good as you. I do miss having you on my bag."

On the drive home, Robert surprised me with a revelation of his own. "Ron, I need to tell you something. Margaret and I are engaged and plan to be married in the spring of 1932. I have a good job with the postal service, and Margaret and I are building a solid foundation for our lives together. So the only bad news is that I won't be able to caddie for you again. I'm sorry to let you down like that."

"Don't worry about it, Robert. I will always be grateful to you for introducing me to the game of golf in the first place, and you will always be my best friend for life. Maybe you and Margaret can come watch me play sometime and cheer me on. I would really like that."

Robert dropped me off at home, and I let myself in as Mom was still at work. I went into my bedroom, dropped my luggage off, and proceeded to unpack. I was feeling hungry, so I walked into the kitchen to make a sandwich when I saw a letter from Doreen propped up on the table. She must have mailed it on Thursday before the tournament started and had not had a chance to read the letter I wrote to her from Tulsa. I sat down and eagerly tore open the envelope and started to read.

> My dearest Ron,
>
> I'm on my way to class, but I wanted to get this in the mail to you this morning so hopefully it will get to you by the time you arrive back in

Dallas on Monday. This is just a short note to tell you that I will be coming home next weekend on Friday afternoon on the 3:00 p.m. train, and I pray that you can be there to pick me up. I can't wait to see you and hear all about your adventure in Tulsa and how you did in the tournament there. I love you and eagerly anticipate seeing you this next weekend.

Forever yours,<br>Doreen

    I had mixed emotions after reading Doreen's letter. On the one hand, I was overjoyed at the prospect of seeing her on Friday, but on the other hand, dreading telling her how I blew my chances on Sunday. I knew she would understand and be supportive and kind as she always was, but I was still feeling ashamed at losing out like that. Winning that $2,000 would have accelerated my goal of joining her at the university and realizing my own effort of working toward my degree in electrical engineering. But there's nothing I can do about it now, except just work harder in 1931. One thing I can do is to double my time on the driving range at night to be ready for the upcoming golf season starting in April.

    This would be the first time I have actually seen Doreen in person in over a month, and I nervously puffed on a cigarette as I waited for her train to pull into the station. I was dressed in my best navy blue three-piece double-breasted suit with a white cotton dress shirt and blue tie with two-tone Oxford shoes and my new Fedora.

    As I looked down the tracks, I could see her train approaching, so I lit another cigarette; and as the train pulled into the station, I snuffed it out and looked where the passengers were disembarking. Suddenly, there she was coming toward me with that wonderful warm smile and the twinkle in her green eyes. She looked even more beautiful than the last time I saw her wearing a tan and black form-fitting dress that accentuated her slim figure with her blonde hair peeking out from under her slouch hat. Doreen had the loveliest of smooth tanned skin, and her features were sensual and delicate. She was indeed a first-class beauty, and I was totally smitten with her.

Doreen ran into my arms, and we shared an embrace and the most delicious of kisses I had ever experienced.

"Ron, I am so happy to see you. It seems like it has been such a long time. You must tell me about Tulsa and what all happened and how you did in your tournament."

"I will in time, but all I want to do right now is just look at you and hold you close to me."

I retrieved her luggage, and we walked to my truck. I gave her the bad news of what happened to me in Tulsa, and she squeezed my hand and moved right next to me. Then she smiled that captivating smile of hers and told me everything would be alright. But that was Doreen's nature, always looking at the bright side of life. I hope she knows how precious she is to me.

I drove Doreen home and let her out to freshen up and visit with her family. I was set to come back later for dinner. Our plan was simple for that night. After dinner we would just sit in her parlor and listen to some radio programs and enjoy being together. After a brief time, her parents retreated to their living room leaving Doreen and I alone.

Doreen and I curled up on the couch and held each other while we listened to the swing music of big bands coming from the radio. She had pulled her legs up under her and leaned into me as I put my arm around her shoulders. I think we both were about to drift off to sleep when all of a sudden she sat straight up and asked me a question.

"Ron, do you think I'll still be your girl a year from now? I mean you enter all those golf tournaments, and I do notice those beautiful girls in the crowds following you around. Are you tempted to forget about me and—"

I stopped her right there and told her, "Doreen, there are only two things that really matter to me in life, one is you and the other is golf, though I'm not real sure which is number one."

Doreen had a wry smile on her face as she knew I was kidding. Then she punched me gently in the arm and said, "Well, Mr. Ron

Perkins, I had better be number 1. You could live without golf, but I doubt if you could live without me. And don't you forget it."

"Well, let me turn that question back on you. You're down there with all those handsome virile young college boys, are you ever tempted to forget about old Ron up here in Dallas pining away for you?" At that, Doreen turned serious as the smile disappeared from her face and she said, "Ron, I don't want you to ever think that. In case you don't know, I knew from the moment I met you that there would never be anybody else for me."

Then the subject changed and brightened up a bit. "Ron, do you want children eventually? I mean, I do. I want two girls and a boy. How about you?"

"That sounds fantastic to me. To take it one step further, I see us growing old and gray together. You as a successful doctor and me as a retired golf professional and a wealthy electrical engineer."

As the time was growing late, I left and went home, rethinking our conversation and hoping that my future would play out just like that. I could think of nothing that I would want more. Doreen and I went to the picture show and saw *The Big Trail*, a western with a new young actor that I predicted will have a bright future in Hollywood named John Wayne. After the movie we drove over to White Rock Lake to our favorite spot and enjoyed the cool night air for a time before I took her home.

Sunday morning, I went with Doreen and her parents to church, and then after lunch, it was time to take her to the train station for her return to the university. We shared a last kiss and embrace before she boarded her train, and I watched as it pulled out of the station and disappeared in the distance. Immediately, I felt a wave of melancholy as I could hardly stand not being with her. I knew we would write every week, and I had a planned trip to Waco in two weeks, and then she would be back for the holidays. But still, we would be apart more than I wanted.

Now that cold weather has arrived and the 1931 golf season won't begin until April, I have resigned myself to hitting practice balls every day and playing a couple of rounds at Samuel Park each week, weather permitting. Mom still has her job at Fulton's department store selling ladies' shoes. She was recently given a raise up to $17.50 a week, but she still has to take the bus to and from work. This all adds extra stress to her. She is dedicated to her job and knows that we need that income to survive and put food on the table. I am still working for Mr. Thomas at the drugstore every day until 4:00 p.m. during the week.

I do everything around the store from being a soda jerk to working in the pharmacy. My salary of $15 a week helps out combined with Mom's salary. On the weekend I work at the country club doing odd jobs and caddying some. I mostly help out in the kitchen or keep fresh towels in the locker room. For that extra effort, the club just start paying me .50 an hour plus whatever tips I might earn. So with all that, I am bringing in $20 or more a week, and I try to save some for my college fund. But it is slow going.

The old Ford truck is about on its last leg, but we don't really use it much anymore as Mom takes the bus to work, and I can walk or take the trolley car to wherever I need to go. About the only time I ever need to use the old Ford was when I had a date with Doreen, and now she's gone off to school.

I leave tomorrow, Friday afternoon, for Waco to see Doreen and this will be my first time ever on a college campus. I am almost as excited to see the University as I am to see Doreen. The train leaves Dallas at 2:00 p.m. and arrives in Waco at 4:30. Doreen by that time will have completed her class requirements for the week and we can enjoy the entire weekend together. She tells me she has a cousin that attends school there and lives in the boy's dorm and has graciously provided a place for me to stay.

As I disembark from the train, I see my sweet girl waiting there for me with a taxi standing by to take us to the University. She always looks so beautiful to me that it makes my heart ache already at the thought of leaving on Sunday to go back to Dallas. But first things first, as we arrived on campus, I was awe struck at the sheer grandeur of this place, it was just perfect and I could see why Doreen loved it here. The grass was a brilliant green and closely mowed. The buildings were of red brick with large marble columns and were magnificent.

We walked through the quadrangle with Doreen giving me the grand tour. She pointed out her dorm and then the boy's housing where I would be staying. She showed me the bookstore and the basketball gym and then we ended up by the statue of the founder. We sat there in the shade of a large oak tree on a park bench and just watched as the traffic of kids on their way to and from their class or wherever they were going paraded by us. I was mesmerized by the energy and activity of what a college campus represented. I had a renewed desire to be a part of this life. This exposure gave me even more incentive to do well playing golf this season so I could win enough money to enroll and be here with Doreen.

"Well, Ron, what do you think of my new home?"

"I've never seen anything like it. Do you think it would be all right to walk around campus for a while longer? I really want to see it all."

"We will, then I'll take you in the student union building. I take my meals at the dining hall there, and you can meet some of my friends."

After touring campus for another hour, we had dinner at the student union hall dining room and sat at a large table that accommodated eight people. I was able to meet some of Doreen's classmates, and they all seemed to sincerely enjoy her company. Doreen had such an effervescent personality that both men and women were instantly attracted to her. I am basically a very quiet person especially around people I had just met for the first time, and I enjoyed sitting back watching this scene play out in front of me as the conversation around the table was light and at times hilarious.

Doreen had such a melodious laugh and an easy manner about her that the time flew by, and before I realized it, we had been there for hours. All too soon, it was getting late in the evening and we left to get Doreen back to her dorm before curfew, as the girls had a strict curfew hour, even on weekends. As we arrived, Doreen turned to me and leaned in close for a good night kiss.

"I hope you have enjoyed today and still want to come here someday."

"You know I do. What fun we will have."

I made my way to the boy's dorm, where David, Doreen's cousin, was waiting for me in the lobby. He introduced himself and then escorted me to my room, but before he left, he asked me a rather curious question, "Ron, it may be none of my business, but I would like to know exactly what are your intentions toward my cousin?"

"Well, not to be rude or impertinent, but you're right it is none of your business, but the fact that I've given her an engagement ring and we have made plans to be married as soon as she finishes medical school should answer your question."

"I'm sorry, I didn't know, then the best of luck to both of you. If you need anything, I'll be across the hall. Good night, Ron."

Saturday morning, Doreen had us scheduled for an excursion to Waco park for most of the day. There was a zoo there as well as hiking and bicycling trails. Since Doreen was a freshman, and freshmen were not allowed to have a car on campus, David, who was an upperclassman, graciously agreed to drop us off and return to pick us up later in the day. We packed a picnic lunch of ham sandwiches and potato salad with a couple of Cokes and had just a glorious day. We toured the zoo and explored the hiking trails up to a bluff overlooking downtown and campus off in the distance. That was an absolute perfect spot for our picnic lunch.

We enjoyed the park for another hour as the weather was spectacular with a clear blue sky and temperatures in the high sixties. David picked us up as planned, and back on campus, we retreated to our respective dorm rooms to freshen up and prepare for the evening that Doreen had planned. Around 6:00 p.m., I walked over to Doreen's dorm to pick her up, and as I waited in the lobby, I noticed several other gentlemen callers were there to pick up their date as well. I was further amused by this, thinking what a wonderful time it was to be young and in this magnificent place called the university.

I didn't have to wait long as Doreen came down the stairs, looking as spectacular as always wearing an afternoon dress of navy blue with a white collar that the hem ended just below the knee. She was wearing a beret tilted jauntily over her right eye. Since we had no car, I offered to call a taxi, to that Doreen smiled. "Well, Ron, Waco is not like Dallas. I'm not sure we could even hail a taxi to get here in time. They are scarce here. No, that's okay, it's not a long walk to downtown and the weather is perfectly suited for an evening stroll." With that, she grabbed my hand and off we went.

"There are a couple of museums along the way that you might find interesting, then I have this precious little Italian restaurant I want to take you to. It's very intimate with low lighting, and the food is exquisite."

Once we were seated, the conversation started. "Doreen, I love being here with you. This is indeed a special place, and I can't wait to be here with you. I am fascinated by college life. I am going to work very hard to win some tournament this spring and summer so I can accumulate enough money to finally join you. We shared a dinner of ravioli, five-cheese garlic bread, a salad, and a red wine. After dinner, we walked around downtown for a while then back to campus as it was starting to get late and there was now a chill in the air. I put my coat around Doreen's shoulders and walked her back to her dorm.

"You really know how to show a fellow a good time, my dear. I hope I can come back soon."

"Oh, Ron, so do I. This has just been the cat's pajamas this whole weekend. I love you so much."

We kissed good night then she turned and walked away but not before giving me one more glance and a wink over her shoulder.

Sunday morning we were going to church and then I had to be at the train station by 2:00 p.m. for my trip back to Dallas. I had brought my best suit, a charcoal gray pinstripe number with my Oxfords and a black fedora hat. I walked into Doreen's dorm, and there she was waiting on me wearing a long flowing white dress with a white wide-brim sun hat that accentuated her lovely green eyes and beautiful tan skin perfectly. The sight of her took my breath away.

After church, we had lunch in the dining hall with some of her friends and then it was time for me to go to the train station. David dropped us off and waited in the car while Doreen walked me to my train. As we stood there on the boarding platform, I took her into my arms, and we shared one more passionate kiss. I then turned quickly to board my train as I didn't want her to see the tears starting to run down my cheek. As we pulled out of the station, I watched her for as long as I could until finally she disappeared in the distance.

As I arrived back in Dallas that Sunday afternoon, I was feeling a little down, but then Sunday afternoons tended to make me feel that way as it usually signified goodbye. Robert picked me up at the train station and drove me home. He tried his best to commiserate with me and to understand my feelings.

"Ron, don't be so sad, she'll be here for the holidays, which is not but a few weeks off. So buck up, pardner, it can only get better."

Robert was like that, always finding a way to make me laugh and forget why I was so unhappy. He was right after all; she will be back in Dallas before you know it, and in the meantime we can always write letters.

As I arrived back home, Mom was waiting for me. "Tell me how your weekend went. I am most curious."

"Mom, we had a super time. Doreen showed me around campus, and we went into downtown, and the park, what a terrific place it is. I sure want to be able to go there someday."

"I hope you can too, Ron. You most certainly deserve it, as hard as you're working. How are you and Doreen doing, is everything okay with you two?"

"Really it couldn't be better, Mom. How's your job going, you seem tired."

"I'm doing okay. I think being tired comes with the passing of years as we get older."

So on Monday morning, it was back to my usual routine of work at Thomas's Drugstore until 4:00 p.m. then hit the driving range. That was my Monday-through-Friday routine. Then on Saturday all day and Sunday afternoon, it was doing odd jobs around the country club. The only break I would have from my exhausting routine was taking Mom to church on Sunday morning and then lunch with her. The management of the club would let me play a round of golf for free if the course wasn't busy. Normally the only time the course wasn't busy was if the weather was inhospitable. Fortunately for me, this time of year it was occasionally severe enough for me to get out and play in cold or rainy conditions when nobody else wanted to. I didn't mind. I felt like this opportunity was sharpening my skills and getting me ready for the 1931 golf tournament season.

The days passed quickly, and before I realized it, the Thanksgiving holiday was coming up this week. Doreen would be coming in on the Wednesday afternoon train, and since it was the last working day of the week, Mr. Thomas graciously allowed me the afternoon off to be at the station when she arrived. I watched as Doreen's train pulled in and waited impatiently, nervously smoking a cigarette until I saw her walking toward me with that perpetual smile on her beautiful face.

She ran up to me, threw her arms around my neck, and gave me a long-overdue kiss. "You don't know how glad I am to see you. Let's get your luggage, and I'll take you home." We walked out to the parking lot and she said, "Ron, where's your truck? Did you get a new car?"

"No, my old truck has decided to finally die on me for good, I'm afraid. I had to borrow Robert's Chevrolet. But that is one of my goals for the immediate future, to replace that old truck with something newer and more reliable. Robert has been most generous about loaning me his car, but I'm getting tired of being a bum."

I dropped Doreen off at her house and visited with her mom and dad for a few moments. We had agreed to spend the day on Thursday together and let her have this evening with her folks.

*****

Thanksgiving morning arrived, and Mom and I took the bus to the Winthorp home. Mrs. Winthorp always put on a good spread; and today we were being treated to baked turkey, cornbread dressing, green bean casserole, corn, sweet potatoes, and homemade rolls. The smell of the food was so aromatic that we couldn't wait until it was time to eat this delicious meal. I sat between Mom and Doreen and enjoyed the lively conversation as we enjoyed such a scrumptious meal. Afterward we sat in the parlor talking and listening to the radio until the evening hour. I could tell that Mom was getting tired, and I was prepared to walk her to the bus stop when Mr. Winthorp intervened and volunteered to take Mom home.

As the evening grew late, Doreen's mom and dad retired for the evening finally leaving us alone. We curled up on the couch in front of a roaring fireplace and just enjoyed each other's company until it was time for me to go. Doreen drove me home, and we made plans for the rest of the holidays. She was going to be here until Sunday evening, then back to school to return on Christmas Eve.

The weather was starting to turn bitterly cold, and the forecast was for an unusually cold winter. So we spent most of the Thanksgiving holiday staying close to the fireplace. Sunday came too soon, and I once again borrowed Robert's Chevrolet to take Doreen to the train station.

"I hate to see you go. It's going to be a long cold month here without you. I'll write you every day."

"I know, I want to stay here with you, but I must get back to school. Remember we have a plan for our future, and I must stick to it. Besides that, Christmas will be here before you know it." And with that, she boarded her train and was gone.

*****

Christmas was on a Thursday this year, and Doreen was scheduled to arrive on Wednesday afternoon. The weather had turned for the worst as predicted, and the day she came in, it was drizzling ice with a substantial breeze plunging the temperatures to below freezing. Fortunately for us, Robert's Chevrolet came equipped with a heater and a defroster. The roads were starting to get icy and slick, so I had to exercise extra caution to safely deliver my passenger to her home.

Our plan was for Mom and me to spend Christmas Day with Doreen and her parents, and on this day, it appeared we were going to have a white Christmas as a steady snow began to fall making for a beautiful serene sight as the snow continued. It was so peaceful outside and so warm in Doreen's home as we enjoyed a crackling fire, some eggnog, and sang some favorite Christmas carols. It was time to exchange gifts, and Doreen gave me a snappy Tweed Ivy Cap to wear on cold days on the golf course, and I gave her a set of admittedly fake diamond earrings with the promise that one day I will give her real ones.

We were going to spend New Year's Eve with Robert and Margaret. Robert surprisingly knew of a speakeasy in downtown Dallas that he could get us into. We were all eighteen now and legal, but because of the Volstead Act, we had to drink behind closed doors or in some dimly lit, smoky nightclub. I had never taken a drink in my life, so this would be a new experience for me.

Robert and Margaret picked me up at 9:00 p.m. then onto Doreen's house. It was still a cold night, but I felt like before the evening was over we would warm up substantially. Since I was still limited on my choice of clothes, I chose to wear my charcoal pinstripe suit with my fedora. But as the door opened, Doreen stood there wearing a black silk evening gown that was formfitting with a halter style and a plunging open back, tight at the waist and hips, flaring all the way down to the floor. She wore a mink stole over her dress and looked absolutely elegant.

"My dear, you have done it again, you look marvelous. Are you ready for a night of fun?"

"I can't wait. I've never been to a speakeasy before, have you?"

"No, and I am taken by surprise that Robert of all people knows of one here in downtown Dallas."

We drove down a dark side street. Robert cut the headlights, and we pulled over to the curb and parked as he had been previously told to do. We walked down the street until we came upon a nondescript building. We walked up to a solid-looking door with a slit at eye level. Robert knocked and the slit opened, and once the bouncer recognized Robert, we were ushered in. We were surprised to see how impressive and large this club was. You certainly couldn't tell from the outside, but then I guess that was the point since this whole operation was illegal. But I think that added to the excitement, the danger of getting caught and arrested. We found our table and settled in. Soon the waiter came over and took our drink order. "What'll you fine folks be having tonight?" Robert ordered for himself and Margaret, but I was at a loss, until Doreen spoke up, "Bring us both a rum and Coke, we'll start there." Imagine my surprise as I suddenly realized I was the only one at the table that had never taken a drink.

The band was local and quite good as they accurately played songs by Jimmy Dorsey, Benny Goodman, and Cab Calloway. As the drinks flowed I could feel my head starting to swim. That's when Doreen said, "Okay, big boy, I think you've had enough. Let's dance." When I stood up, my legs all of a sudden felt wobbly, but I managed to regain my composure; and after a few moments dancing with this wonderful woman, I was starting to feel better.

"I've never experienced anything like tonight. Do you think that maybe someday we could do this again?"

Doreen laughed and said, "Ron, I think that's the liquor talking, but sure, we'll do this again soon. But for tonight, maybe it's time I got you home."

I don't remember much after that, but I sure felt it the next morning as my head was pounding. I came out of the bedroom still a bit woozy, and there was Mom sitting at the kitchen table, smiling at me. "Looks like you had a good time last night. Here, have a cup of coffee, it'll make you feel better. The only cure for you, my son, is time. Now go and take you a hot bath and get dressed."

After an hour or so, I felt like I was starting to get back to normal, so I caught the bus and went to Doreen's house. She answered the door and smiled. "You look better than you did last night. How do you feel?"

"Much better. But what exactly happened? Last thing I remember is dancing with you."

"Well, my love, you had too much to drink, and you had to pay the price this morning. But it looks like you have recovered."

We sat and talked, and she filled me in on what happened after I blacked out, telling me that they drove me home and deposited me on my bed and left. So ended 1930.

# 6
## CHAPTER

January 1931 came in cold and blustery, with gray windy days and an icy rain. Even I didn't want to be on the golf course in weather like that. So until things calm down, I'm going to be forced to take a break from golf. I knew the start of the new season was right around the corner, and I hoped that the first tournament, like last year, would be played at the Dallas County Country Club, a course I was intimately familiar with. I felt like that would give me a distinct advantage over golfers with little or no knowledge of the course.

Doreen and I continued to exchange letters at least twice a week, and I always treasured reading them. I decided to keep them all, maybe one day showing them to our children, thinking that they would get a kick out of reading them and seeing that their poor old mom and dad were young once also.

There is a rumor floating around that when the 1931 golf season begins in April, that the Dallas County Country Club will not be the first venue. Instead the first tournament will be held at the Arlington Heights Country Club. I do hope this is not true, for I was counting on my country club being the first to kind of kick off the season on a positive note for me. I am still in search of a caddie now that Robert is no longer available. I've been told that our old high school quarterback Sammy Mitchell would be a possibility. Turns out that Sammy was an experienced golfer and played at the Dallas County Country club quite often when his parents were members. But unfortunately for Sammy and his family, they were caught up in the depression as his dad was heavily invested in the stock market and lost just about everything. It seems that Sammy is quite broke and looking for opportunities.

Sammy still comes into Thomas's Drugstore on occasion, so the next time I see him, I'll approach him about becoming my caddie for this season. Sure enough, a couple of days later, I was presented with the opportunity to have a talk with Sammy. "Hey, Sammy, how are you doing? Mind if I sit down, I'd like to talk to you about a business proposal."

"Ron, I guess you know my current circumstances, and I'm in no position to turn down anything reasonable as long as it's legal, and I'm not real firm on that. What do you have in mind?"

"As you may or may not know, but I'm now playing professional golf. When I started out, Robert Hays caddied for me, but he is no longer available. So I'm in need of a caddie. I feel like I am due for a good year and will pay you 20 percent of what I win, but if I don't win anything, then you don't get paid either. I will pay all your expenses if we go to a tournament out of town. How does that sound?"

"Ron, it sounds good to me, and I would like to do that for you. It seems that I have no other prospects, and my calendar is open. When do we get started?"

I had a long chat with Sammy, and he was totally on board and really grateful for the chance to make some money and have a swell time as well. I always liked Sammy, and I was glad I could help him out. He's a terrific guy. We worked out a practice routine so he could get familiar with my way of doing things and learn what club selection I felt the most proficient with. Sammy was a quick learner, and after about a month, we were optimistic and ready for the season to start.

I've been notified that indeed the 1931 season will begin at the Arlington Heights Country Club in April. It seemed that the Dallas County Country Club will host an event later in the year. So I must adjust and see to it that Sammy and I are ready and take advantage of touring the golf course in Arlington before the tournament. The entry fee was a reasonable $10, and the winnings were substantial. First-place prize was $2,000, second place was $1,000, and third was

$500. Fourth through tenth earn $25. Of course, my goal was to win it all. The field was loaded with savvy veterans that I've competed against before like John Packard and Harry Bonham and my old friend from Tulsa, Mac Grey. I was told that just over one hundred had signed up.

I knew that Doreen was coming home from school for the weekend and would be in the gallery supporting me. Saturday was the only day she could be there as she wouldn't arrive until late Friday afternoon and would have to return to the university on Sunday. Robert told me that he and Margaret would come out on Sunday, and Mom said she would come with Doreen on Saturday. So I will have family and friends there for me most of the weekend.

Sammy borrowed his mom's 1929 Buick for the Wednesday drive to the golf course. It was about the only thing they had that was paid for and still in their possession. This insidious Depression was starting to reach into most households as it increased its pervasive hold on America. But it was heartening to see that golf was continuing to survive as still the most popular participant sport in the United States. Certainly, some marginal golf courses had been forced to close, but most were still operational.

The Arlington Heights Country Club was relatively new, opening for the first time in the spring of 1928. She was a beautiful course, and the clubhouse was magnificent with a Spanish tile roof and stucco walls. The huge archway entrance was bordered in dark, rich wood. Once inside there was a stairway with a wrought-iron railing leading to the second floor pro shop. The large entry room had thick dark carpet, and in the back to the left was the entrance to the restaurant. You could see the golf course through the large arched floor to ceiling windows. The course itself appeared to be in perfect condition for the tournament. We met with the club ownership and PGL representative to find out our tee time and familiarize ourselves with the course rules.

Thursday dawned a bit on the cool side with temperatures beginning the day in the fifties warming to the low sixties with a brisk wind of about ten to fifteen miles per hour, gusting up to twenty. We drew a 9:00 a.m. tee time with a gentleman by the name of Frank

Walters as our playing partner for the day. Frank was probably one of the tallest men I had ever been around. I asked him exactly how tall he was, and he told me he was six feet seven inches. I'm six feet, and he towered over me. But he was slim and athletic and had been on the tour for some four years. He had posted a moderate success record, winning a handful of tournaments over the last few years.

Our time to tee off was up, and Frank had won the coin toss and had the honor of going first. We had been advised this course was somewhat longer than most, I guess as a nod to the future as every year the club and ball technology improved. I still had my set of Spalding clubs, and they had served me well so far, but I was intrigued by the new equipment being introduced.

The fairway of the first hole followed a slight bend to the left. It was a 363-yard par 4 with a suggested drive that moved from right to left to follow the fairway. By all appearances, an easy opening hole. However, that being said, the small green was surrounded by sand traps. A couple of which were over 6 feet deep. If you had the misfortune to end up in one, it would require a precise, lofted shot to escape.

Frank launched a beautiful tee shot that followed the fairway and came to a stop some 250 yards later on the right side of the fairway, leaving him only 113 yards to the green. I followed with an acceptable drive that covered 220 yards but straight and safe for my second shot. I consulted with Sammy, and he suggested an easy mashie niblick with some loft to it, ideally to drop the ball over the sand traps in front and short of the traps in the back. I was able to execute the shot and landed on the green some 20 feet from the pin. Frank hit a remarkable second shot that had his ball rolling up just 2 feet short of the hole. Frank did walk off with a birdie and a one under score while I two putted for a par.

The second hole would prove to be more challenging as it was a par 5, 498 yards in length. The tee box was elevated as the fairway dropped down some 20 feet and had a stream running the width of the fairway at the 220-yard marker. You needed to be certain of your drive as the water hazard was definitely in play. Once you had encompassed the stream the fairway drifted to the right to an elevated green. The fairway was wide enough but was lined with live oak trees that suggested precision was essential.

Frank took honor and blasted a drive easily clearing the water and landing some 280 yards later on the left side of the fairway. I followed suit with an equally powerful drive, ending up in almost the same position as Frank. We were clear of hazards but still had some 220 yards to the green. Frank pulled out his driving iron and followed the right turn of the fairway and landed on the green, in position to putt for an eagle. Sammy suggested a brassie for my attempt, and with the wind to my back I hit what I thought was exactly the right distance, only to see my ball land some 20 yards short of the green. I punched my third shot on to the green but came up some 30 feet short of the pin. I two putted for a par while Frank did likewise and posted his second birdie. I was still at even golf, Frank moved to two under.

It was a routine front nine from that point on as we both parred holes 3 through 8. We were advised that Harry Bonham was in the lead at three under after twelve holes. So I was still in play, not that far out of the lead. But we were approaching hole number 9, another long par 5 at 497 yards. It was straight but had an extremely narrow fairway bordered by live oak trees and thick ankle-deep Saint Augustine grass that comprised the first cut.

There were sand traps that bordered the fairway at random locations all the way up to and including the green, making accuracy with your tee shot essential. Frank must have suffered a momentary loss of concentration and focus as he sliced his drive, and we watched as it careened off to the right and disappeared into the thick grove of trees. After seeing that, I decided to play conservative and selected my brassie. My drive stayed safe and in the fairway at 200 yards distance.

Frank and his caddie disappeared into the woods to find his ball, and after a few moments, they were successful. But it was in a position of being unplayable, so he had to absorb a penalty stroke and hit his third shot from the spot where it went out of bounds.

Frank hit his driving iron, this time with accuracy, but came up some 100 yards short of the green. Sammy suggested my driving iron, and I was able to pull off an accurate shot to some 50 yards short of the green. Frank punched his now fourth shot up on the green and two putted for his first bogey of the day, dropping him back to one under. I lofted my jigger perfectly and rolled the ball up to the hole for a kick-in birdie leaving me at one under for the day also.

Hole 10 was a 383-yard par 4 with a dogleg to the left. The wind was still steady at fifteen miles per hour, but on this hole was to our back. I teed off first and drilled an exceptional drive around the curve of the fairway ending up at 250 yards in distance. Frank followed my lead and drove his ball to within a few feet of mine. We were both left with an approach shot to the green of less than 135 yards in ideal position.

I had not had much of a chance to talk to Frank, but as we walked down the fairway, he started to open up.

"Ron, tell me, what exactly is your professional golf experience? You seem so young but so accomplished at this game beyond your youth. Where did you learn to play with such confidence?"

"Well, I only started playing in the fall of 1929. I was introduced to this wonderful game by my best friend Robert Hays. He's the only instructor I've ever had, and he was my first caddie. I just kind of learned on my own after he got me started. How about you?"

"I grew up in Michigan, and as a boy my interest was in basketball mainly because I had a growth spurt when I was very young, and I was taller than anybody else in my school. It wasn't until we moved to Texas my first year in high school that with your warmer weather and the influence of my basketball coach that I became interested in golf. I discovered like you that I had a natural affinity for the game."

When we had reached our ball, the conversation ended, and we turned our concentration back to the next shot. I went first and chose a pitching niblick, trusting the tailwind to help. The green had a sand trap to the left and right, so a straight shot to the pin located in the back was called for. I lifted my ball on a direct line coming up some 10 feet short, and Frank hit his ball closer to the pin by 4 feet but directly in front of mine. The rules of the day dictated that he didn't have to move or lift his ball for me to hit my putt. He could essentially block my path to the hole. Normally good sportsmanship would indicate that the ball closer to the hole be moved, but Frank apologized and said, "Sorry, Ron, but we're both in this to win, and I'm going to exercise my option and make you go over or around my ball."

Fortunately, Robert had taught me how to use my jigger to jump my ball over one in front of me, and I did just that. Miraculously it came down on the other side of Frank's ball on a correct line to the hole and at the proper speed and it dropped in, giving me a birdie. Frank was so stunned that he missed his putt and settled for a par. Now I have established a one stroke lead over Frank.

That incident put a damper on the rest of the day, as our friendly conversation never resumed. We both played out the rest of the day at even par golf with Frank at one under and me at two under with Harry still in the lead with a four under score.

I was hoping for an early tee time on Friday, but because I was currently in third place, my tee time was set for 1:00 p.m. My reason for wanting an earlier tee time was Doreen was coming in on the afternoon train, and I desperately wanted to be there to pick her up, but it was not to be.

Frank was still my playing partner on Friday, but the relationship had turned frosty, and we hardly spoke throughout the day. Unfortunately for him, Friday was not good as he went from one under to two over due to some uncharacteristic mistakes he made, not to mention his putting, which had been a strong point on Thursday, failed him today. I was able to maintain my two under score as I shot even par for the day.

Sammy and I finished up around 6:30 p.m. and headed for home, satisfied with where we stood after the first two days of the tournament. It turned out that Sammy was a great choice for my caddie as he had proven to be most knowledgeable with exceptional golf instincts. Sammy dropped me off at home with plans to leave for the golf course at 11:00 a.m. Saturday to hit the practice range and have lunch before we started our third round.

I walked in our house and called for Mom.

"Ron, I'm in the kitchen. Are you hungry, I can make you a sandwich."

"No, I'm good, but how are you feeling? Did you have a good day?"

Mom looked very tired and frail, and I knew that the job she worked so hard at was really wearing her down. She was starting to look much older than her actual years. One of my goals for success on the golf course was to include Mom. She certainly deserved it as she had always been so supportive of all that I had attempted in life. We had drawn closer with the passing of Dad.

"Are you going to be able to come out and watch me play tomorrow?"

"We'll see, but I am so bone tired, I may just rest tomorrow and let you tell me all about it when you get home. I hope you're okay with that."

"Sure, Mom, I understand, you just take care of yourself. I'm going to go clean up and go see Doreen. I'll be back later tonight."

I arrived at Doreen's house and rang the doorbell. The door opened, and Doreen flew into my arms, smothering me with kisses. "I am so happy to see you. You must tell me how the tournament is going."

"It's going well, I am currently in third place. And if I can hang on to that, you know what that means. If I can finish there or even higher, I'll win between $500 and $1,000. That gets me one more step closer to my goal. I figure I need at least $3,000 to be able to enroll at the university."

"You are still coming out tomorrow to watch me play, aren't you?"

"You just try and stop me. Of course I'll be there. When do you start playing?"

"We tee off at 1:00 p.m., but Sammy and I will drive over at 11:00 a.m. for a quick lunch and some practice time."

"Margaret wants to come with me tomorrow, since Robert is working, so we'll do some shopping and then be there in plenty of time before you start. I can't wait."

We moved into the parlor and continued our conversation as she breathlessly told me about her studies and life on campus.

I turned the radio on, and as we listened to the music, she leaned into me and promptly fell asleep as did I. It had been a long day for both of us. I didn't stay too much longer as I wanted to catch a late bus home and get a good night's sleep. I was starting to hope that my immediate future would include a car. I was getting weary of riding the bus or bumming rides. The old Ford Model T truck had finally quit altogether.

My playing partner for Saturday was my old friend from Tulsa, Mac Grey. We both held an identical two under score in third place behind Harry Bonham at five under and John Packard at four under. So it appeared it was going to be a tight race the rest of the way.

"Hey, Mac, how have you been? Looks like we're in for a tussle today."

"Ron, glad to see you again. Let's go play some golf and have some fun."

The weather Saturday was picture-perfect for golf with temperatures in the midsixties and cloudless blue skies, with absolutely not a breath of wind. I think with the combination of Doreen in the gallery watching me play and having a fine partner like Mac Grey just added to my confidence, and I felt like I was all but assured of a great day. We both parred the first hole and birdied the second to move to three under for the tournament. We stayed at that score until hole number 6 which was a long 407-yard par 4 that featured a straight fairway bordered for the length of the hole with a stream running up the right side and thick forestation of trees and underbrush on the left. The tee box and green both were elevated with a drop-off of some 30 feet.

I must have come around on the ball with my drive as I hooked it into the trees, but it didn't penetrate too far, and I easily found it. I only had a narrow window to punch my ball back out of trouble, but I was still over 100 yards to the green, hitting now my third shot. Mac had hit a precision drive and second shot, and his ball rested comfortably on the green. I hit my third shot on the green and two putted for a bogey, dropping me back to two under. Mac missed his birdie putt but remained at three under. We finished the front nine with no further change in our score.

As we started the back nine, we were told that Harry was still at five under and John at four under, so we really hadn't lost much ground if any to the two leaders. Mac was one stroke up on me, pushing me to fourth place. I kept my eye out for Doreen, and she doggedly stayed up with us. Occasionally we would make eye contact, and she would give me one of her spectacular smiles. I knew she was riding home with Margaret, and I would see her that night before she left for school the next day.

On hole 14, Mac had added another birdie, pushing me further into fourth place, now two strokes out of third place, and we finished the day that way. John Packard had taken over the lead at six under, and Harry had stayed at five under now in second place. But I knew I had Sunday to make up lost ground. I sensed that Sammy and Doreen were depending on me, even though they didn't say anything and only offered encouragement for Sunday's round. I felt pressure anyway, but that only heightened my resolve to overtake Mac and steal that third-place finish from him. I knew it would be a challenge, but I was up to it.

On Sunday I was to tee off at 2:00 p.m. once again with Mac Grey, standing at two strokes behind him at the beginning of the day. We both parred the first hole, then moved to the par 5 second hole. Mac knew that the stream running across the fairway at the 220-yard marker called for the smart play to power down and layup just short, leaving yourself in position for a second shot to the green.

I assumed that Mac, with a two stroke lead and only one stroke out of second place, would make that smart play, but instead he pulled out his play club and was obviously going for the kill, much to the obvious consternation of his caddie. Mac was a strong golfer, but he hit his drive fat, and the ball dropped into the water hazard. He had to take a penalty stroke and layup by the stream on the fairway side. I took the conservative route and hit my brassie, laying up.

We both were able to land on the green, but I had gained a stroke advantage on him due to his misadventure, and I could tell he still had that errant shot on his mind. If there is one thing I have learned about the game of golf, it is that when you hit a bad shot, as we all do on occasion, you must forget about it and refocus on your next shot. Once on the green, I one putted for a birdie, and Mac two putted for a par. I now had picked up a stroke and trailed him by just one.

We finished the front nine in that position with the two leaders not able to extend their advantage either. It appears we are all playing it safe and protecting our position. It stayed that way until the fourteenth hole. Mac wasn't quite as friendly today, choosing to focus on his game and maybe starting to feel pressure from me coming up on him.

Hole 14 was a short par 4 of some 320 yards with a lake in front of the elevated tee box that in all reality was not in play dropping off to a fairway that turned to the right with a clear approach to the green. There were very few obstacles save for some sand traps to the back of the green. I hit my drive playing a slight fade and following the fairway around to the right ending up 130 yards out in prime placement for a second shot into the green. Mac misplayed his drive and hooked his ball into the left collection of trees and thick rough. He found his ball with a clear path to the green but was still 200 yards out. He selected his driving iron, pulled the ball out, but came up some 30 yards short of the green.

I drove my second shot on to the green and watched as the ball rolled up to within 2 feet of the hole. Mac put his third shot safely on the green and one putted to save his par. I drained my short putt and secured my birdie and now Mac and I were in a deadlock for third place with four holes left.

Hole number 17 was a 185-yard par 3, with water from tee to green. It required a powerful drive and accuracy as the green was completely surrounded with deep sand traps. As I surveyed the hole, my confidence was way up after the events of the last few holes. I had no idea that I was going to be able to pick up two strokes on a seasoned pro like Mac, especially in crunch time on a Sunday, much less the three strokes. It would require to pass him for a third-place finish. This thought was on my mind especially after watching him expertly close me out on that Sunday in the Tulsa tournament.

I was first up, and Sammy and I agreed on a midiron, feeling like that club gave us enough distance and was a more lofted club, giving me the ability to land safely in the middle of the green. The pin was in the back right section, making this shot even more difficult, but I was able to pull it off, ending up some 6 feet from the hole. Mac had chosen a mid mashie but came up some 15 feet short with his ball in position directly behind mine. I remembered the trick Frank had pulled on me on Thursday and chose to do the same to Mac, making him have to jump his ball over mine or go around.

I felt like that at a distance of 10 feet, he was too far away to jump but would have to go around and try to put some spin on his ball. "Sorry, Mac, to do this to you, but I think I need the win more than you do."

"That's all right, Ron, it's in the rules. You have the right. No hard feelings."

With that being said, he shook my hand and addressed his ball. However, his attempt came up short, and he parred the hole while I succeeded in nailing a birdie. Now I was one stroke ahead of him with one hole left.

We both parred hole number 18, and I had my miraculous victory by one stroke to finish third and secure the $500 prize. Mac, being the class gentleman that he was, smiled and embraced me, then offered his congratulations. I really hated to pull that stunt on him on hole 17, but he was gracious about it and took it as just part of the game and was in accordance with the rules of the day.

The ride home was a lot more cheerful than yesterday. I gave Sammy his $100 for being my caddie and for his invaluable support.

"Sammy, you ready to do this again in two weeks in Fort Worth?"

"Ron, I'm in this for the long haul as long as you need me."

I didn't get home until after six, and as I walked into the house, I was struck with the wonderful aroma of roast beef cooking. Mom had prepared a delicious meal for me, to cheer me up if necessary, or to celebrate. She didn't yet know the results of the day but was prepared for either eventuality.

"Mom, I won $500 for third place. I gave Sammy $100 for his contribution, and I want to give you $100 also for our household. The rest goes into savings for my college fund."

"Ron, that's marvelous, I am so happy for you, and thank you for the money."

We had a celebratory dinner and finished out the evening talking about Dad and what the future might bring us.

"I wish your dad could have been here to see what a fine young man you are and revel in your success."

"Me too, Mom, but we still have each other."

# 7
## CHAPTER

Now, it was back to the usual routine of working for Mr. Thomas during the week and the Dallas County Country Club on the weekend. But I was greatly encouraged by the result of the Arlington tournament and eagerly anticipating the next opportunity in Fort Worth. Last year I had finished in a tie for third place. It was by far my best showing of the season, and this year the Fort Worth tournament would be held at the same venue, the beautiful Continental Country Club.

This is the second regional event of 1931 and is being held on April 16–19. I understand that the field is much larger this year with 125 golfers registered, including some of the best in the world. With this much interest, the sponsors of the tournament increased the purse from last year to $3,000 for first place, $2,000 for second and $1,000 for third. Finalists in fourth through tenth receive $150, and the entry fee was increased to $100.

At the golfer's meeting on Wednesday afternoon I was told our tee time would be at 10:00 a.m., and I met my playing partner for Thursday and Friday. His name was Jessie Davis, and he was a young man, maybe even younger than me. I don't know for sure, but I think this just may be his first competition. This presents a new situation for me being the more experienced, but I remembered the help that Mac Grey had given me last year, and I made a decision to return that attitude to this new fellow.

I walked over to introduce myself and stuck out my hand to give his a shake in a friendly manner, and I was shocked by his response. He just looked at me with cold gray eyes and said, "So you're Ron

Perkins. I've heard a lot about you. I understand you're some kind of young prodigy around here. Well, I hope you're ready to accept defeat graciously, for I plan to win this whole thing." He never cracked a smile, just had a look of supreme arrogance and defiance as he then turned and walked off. My immediate thought was that even though I didn't verbalize it was, "You arrogant jerk, you are due for a big surprise if you keep that attitude."

Jessie was a good-sized kid standing over 6 feet tall and weighing in at some 200 pounds, and he had the look of a Greek statue with a highly muscular body with incredibly large biceps that hinted at the fact that he had a powerful swing. He had curly blonde hair and azure blue eyes and looked like he had just walked off a Hollywood movie set. I decided from that initial meeting that it was my mission to teach this young brash fellow some humility. I realize that this upstart was diverting my attention from my goal of winning this event to teaching him a lesson or two, but I felt like I could handle both.

When Sammy joined me after the caddie meeting, I advised him about our partner for tomorrow. "Sammy, you are not going to believe the arrogance and disrespect this guy has for the game of golf."

"Ron, be careful, he may be a real snake, capable of any kind of dirty tricks."

I was so advised and ready for Thursday morning. The weather was a comfortable sixty-five degrees but was overcast with rain in the forecast. The wind at our tee time was at a calm five to ten miles per hour but was predicted to increase as the day wore on.

When I played here last year, I remembered that I had birdied this first hole so as we approached the first tee I attempted once again to try and help my young friend with a little advice about the course since I had the experience and he didn't; it was just the courteous thing to do or so I thought. But once again he rebuffed me. "Perkins, I really don't need your help. I'm perfectly capable of seeing what's in front of me, so why don't you play your game and I'll play mine. Is that okay with you?" Jessie had won the right to go first, and as

Sammy and I thought, he had a very powerful swing and scorched his drive some 260 yards square in the middle of the fairway. This hole was a difficult 475-yard par 5 with a lake guarding the green. The tee box was elevated as the fairway dropped off some 20 feet. This was a spectacular visual hole with a commanding view of the surrounding countryside including downtown Fort Worth. As I was about to hit my drive, I paused to take in this magnificent vista until I heard Jessie say, "Come on, Perkins, we don't have all day."

I turned and smiled at Sammy, both of us thinking, before this day is over, we have to take this guy down a peg or two. He is way too full of himself. I pushed my drive some 220 yards down the right side of the fairway, leaving me 255 yards to clear the lake and land on the green in two. I knew I didn't have that shot, so Sammy selected my baffy, and I laid up just short of the water. This set me up for an easy-approach shot. Jessie looked at me with a sarcastic smirk and said, "Watch this, Perkins, and learn something." He had just 215 yards to clear the lake and land on the green in two. He selected a midiron and landed softly on the green. I was able to land my third shot within 20 feet of the pin, putting for a birdie. Jessie had set himself up for a makeable eagle putt. Sammy and I felt like if he put the eagle put away, then he would be even more insufferable than he already was. His ego certainly didn't need a boost. Unfortunately, he sank the putt and turned and grinned at me. I was able to secure a birdie.

We played the rest of the front nine with each of us scoring one more birdie to make the turn at two under par for me and Jessie at three under. I didn't attempt to engage him in any more conversation as he seemed to be in his own world and didn't welcome any intrusion. I felt like he was going to have to run into some adversity before he came back to Earth with the rest of us, but for now he was in fact leading the tournament after nine holes.

Hole number 10 was a 475-yard par 4 with an elevated tee box and green consisting of a fairway that drops off 30 feet with a dogleg right over water in front of the tee box. The water ordinarily is not in play but just a distraction. The turn came at 200 yards with a blind shot to the green for a second shot.

You could choose a couple of options here, and Jessie chose to blast his drive over the trees on the right, cutting the corner and idealistically landing safely in the fairway well past the dogleg. It didn't work out for Jessie as he had pushed his ball too far to the right, landing short of the fairway and disappearing into the forest. He was a strong golfer alright, that's for sure, but he didn't demonstrate good judgment, just raw power and very little finesse. I chose a controlled fade around the turn with my ball coming to a rest at 230 yards on the left side of the fairway. Jessie was able to find his ball, but his only choice was to punch out to the fairway past the turn, leaving him 200 yards for his third shot approach to the green.

No matter how good you are, or think you are, golf is the great equalizer and can make a fool out of anybody as young Jessie was eventually going to find out. He seemed to prefer his driving irons over his fairway woods, so he selected again, his midiron, thinking that would be enough club. But he forgot to take into consideration that the green was elevated, requiring extra distance. This caused his shot that was perfectly on line to come up some 30 yards short of the green. Now he was hitting four just to get to the putting surface. I chose my driving iron and was able to land safely on the green in two. It was easy to see that Jessie was highly irritated. I erroneously thought that he was blaming himself and all the mistakes he had made on this hole. I two putted for a par, and Jessie two putted for a double bogey. That made me at two under while Jessie dropped back to one under.

As we walked off the green, I could hear Jessie muttering to his caddie. "I hate Texas and this lousy golf course. I should never have left California to try playing here." I'm finding out that this typical of spoiled kid Jessie behavior, blaming everything and not taking his personal responsibility. We both finished the day at even golf but still within shouting distance of John Packard at three under after the first day.

I was holding on to a slim hope that Jessie, after his experience on hole number 10, would have absorbed some humility, but I could tell by the way that he walked up to me after we had finished with an expression of supreme confidence on his face, that he had not learned a thing. "Hey, Perkins, you gonna be ready for another golf lesson tomorrow?"

"Well, Jessie, you never know, and I hate to tell you this, but I am one stroke ahead of you." At that he gave me a sneer and walked off.

Our tee time for Friday is at 1:00 p.m., and it appears that it is going to rain steadily all day long, making the golf course soggy. I think it's going to affect long ball hitters like Jessie more than me mainly because I have never been long off the tee, preferring to play a more measured, conservative, precise game that so far has worked well for me.

Sammy brought his umbrella to help with the now-steady rain, but poor Jessie and his caddie had neglected to prepare and bring any kind of wet weather gear, even though they had been warned that rain was in the forecast. The score didn't change for any of the contenders as we made the turn.

By late afternoon, the rain had turned into a downpour and almost unplayable. But since we were in the next-to-last group on the course, they allowed all golfers to finish the 18 holes for the day. I finished the day still at two under, only one stoke out of the lead and in a secure second place. Jessie followed me in third place at one under. So the pairings for Saturday were self-evident; it appeared that Jessie would continue to be my partner.

A front moved through Fort Worth overnight taking the rain with it. The day dawned bright and sunny with only an occasional fluffy white cloud. Temperatures in the seventies, a perfect California day for golf. Our tee time was 2:00 p.m., and we would be in the next-to-last group to start. We were to be followed by the coleaders John Packard and a gentleman named Jeff Brown that were at three under.

Jessie and I both parred the first two holes bringing us to number 3, a 389-yard par 4. The fairway drifts slightly to the left with a stream running down the left side and deep sand traps placed at strategic points along the right side. The fairway itself was narrow, requiring accuracy off the tee. I was first to tee off, and I launched my shot following the fairway and coming to a rest on the left side at the

220-yard mark. My second shot was at an ideal angle to the green, with a distance left of less than 170 yards. Jessie's drive flew past mine by some 40 yards, and I could see his mood change with that shot. He had been quiet for the most part so far today, but I could see the chatter was coming.

My second shot landed on the green but some 30 feet out, and Jessie's second shot landed directly in front of my ball by 10 feet, and I could sense what was coming next. "Okay, Perkins, let's see just how good you are. You're going to have to go around or over my ball." The greens had dried out in the sunshine and were running quick and smooth, and I could see that I was faced with a double break from where my ball was positioned. I asked my caddie's advice. "Sammy, do you think I can put some spin on my ball and go by his ball on the right side?"

"I think you certainly can pull it off, but you won't know until you try. Go for it."

With Jessie's arrogance and overconfidence, I felt like if I could succeed with this shot, it would unnerve him and throw him off his game. As I stroked the ball, I watched carefully as it started moving around the right side of Jessie's ball correcting on a direct line to the hole and at a good pace and dropping in for a birdie. I looked at Jessie for his reaction, expecting anger or frustration; instead he just shook his head and showed that half smirk I was becoming familiar with and moved toward his ball to execute his putt. He should have learned from the path of my ball, but I guess he was a bit rattled as he missed the putt to secure a par.

We played even par for the rest of the front nine, and as we made the turn, we were told that Packard had increased his lead to five under and Jeff Brown was at four under. That left me at three under and in third place. Jessie was two strokes behind me at one under. Nobody else in the field was under par for the tournament.

The weather continued to be beautiful, and I really had no excuse for not playing the back nine any better than I did, missing several birdie opportunities as we arrived at hole number 18. Jessie had picked up one stroke on me and was now at two under, one behind me.

Hole 18 was a long 509-yard par 5 that offered up its own unique set of challenges. Besides being long, it was bordered by a stream on the right side of the fairway and a thick stand of live oak trees on the left. As the fairway jogged to the right, the stream came around to guard the front of the green accompanied by a 20-foot-deep chasm that was some 30 yards wide loaded with a tangle of rocky underbrush. If you cleared the water you needed to do so with enough distance to also encompass the chasm; otherwise, your ball was most assuredly out of play.

Jessie and I both delivered an accurate drive with his traveling some 260 yards and mine at 240 yards. I felt like I could hit any club I wanted to lay up short of the obstacles in front of the green. Sammy handed me my brassie, and I successfully landed safely in prime position less than 100 yards out for my third shot.

Jessie, even after a powerful drive, was still almost 250 yards out for a sure landing on the green. After I hit, Jessie and his caddie were in an animated conversation that culminated with Jessie demanding his brassie in an obvious attempt to foolishly go for the green in two. An almost-impossible shot even for Jessie. But sure enough he lined up his shot as his caddie stepped back with a look of concern on his face. If he made the shot, he would be in range for an eagle attempt that would put him back in the competition, but if he came up short, then any chance he might have had would be dashed.

I watched as he took some practice swings, then stepped up to the ball to deliver the attempt. Jessie gestured to us all to get behind him out of his line of sight and then stepped up to address the ball. I could see his muscles in his arms tense as he was giving this shot everything he had. He stuck the ball perfectly lifting it up and sending it on a direct line to the pin. The ball kept slowly rising, and for all practical purposes, it appeared as if he had launched the shot of the day.

"Sammy, would you look at that, I think he's pulled it off. We'll never hear the end of this tomorrow."

"I don't know, it looks to me like the ball is starting to lose momentum. Let's wait and see."

About then, the ball did seem to lose altitude and started back down. Just as Sammy said, it came up short and disappeared into the chasm.

But all of a sudden, a miracle happened as the ball came flying back up as if shot out of a cannon on a trajectory directly toward the flag, landing some 5 feet from the hole. Obviously, it had hit a rock at just the right angle and was propelled perfectly back up on the green.

Upon seeing that despair turned into exuberance as Jessie jumped in the arms of his caddie and started to celebrate and rightfully so. It was a gutsy call. You have to give him that. He then turned to me and Sammy. "You guys see that? Look out tomorrow, Perkins, I'm going to leave you in my dust."

"Congratulations, Jessie, it was quite a shot."

It was my turn to hit my approach shot, and I landed safely on the green but still some 20 feet from the pin. I two putted for a par and finished the day at three under for the tournament. Jessie, with his confidence restored, sank his eagle putt and was now tied with me. We were three behind the two coleaders, Packard and Brown, with one more round left. Our tee time for Sunday would be at 1:30 p.m., and I was feeling very optimistic about my chances to finish no worse than third. I remembered what had happened in Tulsa when I collapsed on the last day, and I vowed to not repeat that tomorrow.

Sammy dropped me off at home with plans to leave for the golf course at 10:00 a.m. to give us some extra practice time. I knew we were going to have to endure Jessie's insufferable bragging, but I will just have to ignore him and focus on being the better golfer.

As I walked in, I called for Mom.

"Ron, I'm in the parlor. Come and tell me about your day. How did you do? If you're hungry, I can make you a sandwich."

"No, thanks, Mom, we ate before we left the golf course. To answer your question, I did great today. If I can hold it together tomorrow, I stand a good chance of winning $1,000 for finishing third."

"Ron, that would be marvelous. We can always use the extra money. Maybe I could cut back on my overtime and spend more time with you."

Mom had worked a full shift today and looked exhausted. She was barely able to sit in a chair and read her book. I knew that the only reason she was still up was to greet me and make sure I was okay. I told her to go on to bed that all was well. She has been my hero since Dad died as she has done all that she could to take care of me. Now it was my turn to return the favor. Part of my winnings would go toward my college fund, but part of it would go into our household as well so that eventually she could afford to cut back on her hours.

Sammy and I arrived at the golf course at 10:00 a.m. as we planned and went directly to the practice area to prepare for the day's round, when much to my surprise among the golfer already there was Jessie. He had previously told me, and I quote, "A naturally talented golfer like Jessie doesn't need to spend a lot of time practicing. It's hard to improve on perfection." Yes, he sometimes talks in the third person. He saw me walking up and turned to meet me. "Hey, Perkins, you ready to lose today? Get ready, I'm taking you down."

I looked at Sammy and said, "We need to finish off this palooka today and try to teach him a lesson in humility. Though we probably are wasting our time. I don't think it's in him to behave like a gentleman and show some class." I walked over to him and thought about extending my hand in a gesture of friendliness, but I remembered that hadn't worked before, so I just gave him a warning, "Jessie, you know I have tried on more than one occasion to be considerate to you and offer my help, which you in your arrogance rejected at every turn. Now, I'm done being a gentleman, and I am going to make today my sole mission in life to rub your nose in a humiliating defeat. See you on the first tee at 1:30 p.m., and you better bring your best game."

Jessie had a stunned, quizzical look on his face. It was as if no one had ever stood up to him like that, but soon that usual smirk emerged that seemed to say to me "We'll see about that." But he thought better of responding and just turned and walked away.

# THE LOVES OF A LIFETIME

The weather in Texas can be unpredictable, especially in the spring. Whereas yesterday was a spectacular day for playing golf, today was quite different. The sun had disappeared behind thick gray clouds, and the wind had increased to a steady twenty miles per hour, gusting up to thirty with a substantial chance of rain all day. And, of course, with those conditions the temperature had dropped down in to the low fifties. So this presented a whole new set of challenges; it would be like playing a different course all together.

As our time approached and Jessie and I walked up to the first tee, I could tell he was not comfortable with the sudden change in weather. "Jessie, a little cooler today, not like your Southern California warmth, is it?" I wanted to make sure he had that on his mind, but he turned and looked at me with that annoying smile and said, "Perkins, it ain't gonna bother me, how about you? Besides, just look around at all these beautiful dames that came out to watch Jessie put you down."

With the formalities over, Jessie stepped up to the tee box, ready to launch his first shot of the day. But before he took his first swing, he turned, raised his club to wave to the crowd, then pointed it to me as if to say, "I accept your challenge, and I recognize that you are desperately attempting to throw me off my game, but it will do you no good as I am clearly the superior golfer."

Because of the weather, we both played the front nine at even par as did the two leaders as birdies were difficult to come by. We stayed even until hole number 13, which was a 346-yard par 4. It wasn't a long hole, but that fierce wind was blowing directly in our face. The fairway narrowed at the 220-yard mark, with water on both sides leading to an elevated green surrounded by sand traps. Jessie was still the first to tee off, and he launched a drive of some 200 yards ending up safely in the fairway. I followed suit, and my ball rested within a few yards of Jessie's, both of us with a clear shot of some 146 yards to the green.

Now it was up to the accuracy of our approach shot, and we both smelled birdie opportunity. I chose my mashie niblick over Sammy's recommendation that I go up one club to the spade mashie. As soon as I hit by ball into that gusting wind, I realized that Sammy was right as I came up short and landed in a sand trap in front of the green. Jessie on the other hand had put his ball successfully on the green in perfect position to secure a birdie for the first time today.

So I was almost assured of losing a stroke here, but golf is a funny game and shows no favoritism. I walked up and saw that my lie was decent, so I selected my jigger, approached the ball, and launched a shot on a direct line to the hole. I knew that we had a chance as the ball rolled across the green at the proper speed and fell into the hole for a birdie, my first of the day, taking me to four under for the tournament.

I looked at Jessie, and he had this bemused half smile as if to say, "I've seen you pull off a great shot before, so this time it will not affect my game." But it must have at least distracted him to some degree as he missed his birdie putt and had to settle for a par, putting him one stroke behind me with five holes left to play. Both leaders had suffered a bogey and stood at five under. Now I was only one stroke out of the lead, and my optimism and confidence rose with each hole.

Holes 14–17 didn't change for me and Jessie, but the coleaders had picked up the stroke they had lost with a birdie for each to return to six under. With one hole left I was two strokes back. I was convinced they were both out of my reach, but I did have a one-stroke advantage over Jessie. He was in a foul mood as he could see third place slipping away to me.

Hole 18 had been miraculous for Jessie yesterday, but the weather conditions dictated a different approach. The wind was being unpredictable and was now blowing from right to left, almost assuring a layup second shot, even after the best of drives. Jessie and I followed that formula and ended up at 150 yards from the green, having to traverse the water and that deep chasm to land safely on the green. From my vantage point, I needed to par and hope he didn't birdie, tying me for third place.

I was slightly further out, so I swung through the ball and put my approach shot within 10 feet of the flag with a very real possibility of one putting for a birdie. Jessie put his ball in excellent position at 8 feet from the hole. So it was left to me to putt first, but his ball was not in my path, so I had a clear shot to the hole. I felt like with the wind that the green might be rolling faster than yesterday and the one thing I didn't want to do was to run my ball so far past the hole that it left me a difficult second putt, allowing for the chance of a three putt bogey and totally blowing my lead.

With that in mind, I lined up my putt and had the right speed, just missing on the right side of the hole, leaving me with a kick-in par. That left the door open for Jessie to birdie the hole and tie me for third place. Jessie looked over at me with his usual smug smile and addressed his putt. As the ball travelled across the green, it wobbled just ever so slightly and missed by inches, giving Jessie a par and finishing one stroke behind me. At that, he threw his putter high in the air and watched as it disappeared into the chasm. He cursed me, the weather, Texas in general, the golf course, his caddie, and anything else he could think of. But, of course, none of this was his fault.

I walked over to him to try and congratulate him on playing a competitive game of golf, knowing full well that he was going to reject my overture. He did not disappoint as he said to me with his parting words, "Perkins, you got lucky today, and I hope I never see your ugly mug ever again."

"Well, Jessie, if you play in tour events in California, chances are you'll see me later this year, and I'll beat you again, you arrogant fool."

With that, he had no response and walked off muttering to himself as Sammy and I celebrated winning $1,000, our best ever.

I secured my winnings and gave Sammy his $200. Then we briefly discussed the next tournament coming up to be held in San Antonio in two weeks. I had not done well at that event last year and was thinking about skipping it altogether, but Sammy pointed out to me that we had some momentum built up, especially after beating a punk like Jessie Davis.

So as Sammy dropped me off at home, we agreed to give it a couple of days to think about it and then make a decision. I suppose he was right to suggest we wait, because at this moment I was just too tired to think about golf. All I wanted to do was give Mom the good news and hand her my contribution of $200 to our household budget. That left $600 to go into my college fund that was now up to $900. We had made a decision to hide our cash at home because of the unpredictability of banks. You never knew for sure because of the depression whether your bank was going to stay open or suddenly close its doors, leaving you high and dry.

# 8
## CHAPTER

One thing I wondered about young Jessie was how did he get to be so muscular at such a young age. I posed that question to Sammy on the way home, and he had no clue, so I thought Mom might know. But when we arrived back home after the tournament, Mom was taking a late-afternoon nap, and even though I was eager to tell her of our success and hand her the share of money for our household, I thought better of it. I'll just wait, I knew how hard she worked all week, and Sunday was her only real day that she had to herself. She valued her church on Sunday morning, and when I wasn't in a tournament, I would go with her. Then after church, we would either go out for lunch or eat something she had prepared at home that morning. She would spend the rest of the day reading the newspaper and falling asleep in her chair.

Then as she stirred, I said, "Mom, are you feeling alright?"

"Yes, Ron, I guess I was just tired. How was your tournament?"

"Well, I finished in third place and won $1,000. I have for you $200."

"That's wonderful, Ron. I'm so proud of you, and thank you for the money. Tell me all about your day."

"Well, my playing partner was this young jerk from California, and I edged him out by one stroke to win third place. But I have a question that maybe you can answer. This guy was a year younger than me, but outweighed me by at least 40 pounds, but he wasn't fat. He was very trim and muscular. Sammy and I couldn't figure out how he had managed to get in such magnificent shape. I'd like to do that as well. Do you have any ideas?"

"My only guess would be that maybe he was working with dumbbells. There was a story in the paper about a new trend of young men building up their muscles that way."

"That must be it. We really couldn't ask him, he wasn't a friendly sort. Where would one get their hands on such a thing? Do you think your department store would sell them?"

"I don't know, I could ask my supervisor. But maybe your old high school would have them. I mean football players use weights, don't they?"

"You're right. I hadn't thought of that. I'm still friends with coach. Maybe he would show me how to use dumbbells. See this guy was hitting the ball much farther than me, and as the day wore on I started losing energy and he didn't. Thanks, Mom, I'll run by the school tomorrow."

Monday on my lunch break I was able to go by the high school and talk to coach.

"Ron, yes, we have put our players on a regimen of lifting weights every day, and it has paid off. I would be glad to help you with a program as well if you could come by late afternoon when you wouldn't be in the way. I've been reading in the newspaper about how well you're doing with your golfing career, and we are all very proud of you. If I can help you improve your play in any way, I would be more than happy to. Oh, and one other thing, do you feel like your legs start to get tired late in the day?"

"Yes, tired and sore. Can you recommend something for that as well?"

"If you have a bicycle, start riding it every day for at least five miles, and you will build up your endurance and strength in your legs."

"Thanks, Coach, I'll be back this afternoon so we can get started."

*****

After a long Monday working at Thomas's Drugstore and dropping by the high school to begin my weight training after 4:00 p.m.,

I arrived at home around five thirty about the same time as Mom returned from her shift at work.

"Mom, I took your suggestion and went by the high school on my lunch hour and had a great talk with Coach. You were sure right about the dumbbells. The football players have been using them, and Coach started me on a late-afternoon routine of lifting weights. He advised me to eat a lot of beef, potatoes, and bread. Oh, and drink milk every chance I get. He also suggested I start riding a bicycle on a regular schedule to build up my stamina and leg strength. Do we still have that bicycle that you and Dad gave me back in 1929 for my birthday?"

"Yes, I think it's out there in the garage up against the front wall."

I walked out to the garage, and sure enough, there she was just where Mom said she was all covered in dust with now flat tires, looking really sad. I started tearing up as I flashed back to the day Dad presented the bicycle to me and what happened afterward. I sure miss him. I pulled the bike out and washed it off with the garden hose, greased the chain, then found our old air pump. Once she was ready, I took her for a spin around the block, and she rode as nice as when she was new.

"Was your old bicycle there?"

"Yes, I took her out for a quick ride, and it was as if the old bike was still new. I have one other thing to tell you. Sammy came by Thomas's today, and he has managed to convince me to enter the San Antonio Tournament that runs from April 30–May 3. I'm not particularly excited about it since I did so terrible last year, and I am tired of golf right now anyway. But it's a couple of weeks off, maybe I'll feel better about it by then. For now, Doreen is coming in this weekend, and I can't wait to see her."

Doreen and I continue to write at least twice a week, and of course I think about her every day, so it's work all week and anticipate her coming in on the Friday afternoon train. Robert and Margaret have found a new jazz club in downtown Dallas for us to go to on Saturday night, and I'm excited about that. It'll be like old times as I haven't been able to spend much time with my best friend lately. I get especially lonesome for Doreen, but I miss spending time with Robert also.

I'm waiting in the train station for Doreen, but I had to take a taxi as the old Ford refused to budge, but that doesn't matter. I'm here now and eagerly awaiting the arrival of my girl. Then at that moment I saw her step off the train and onto the platform. I am by no means a fashion expert, but I did take notice of how adorable she looked in a gray knit beret, raked slightly, with her blonde hair peeking out. She was wearing a formfitting, high neckline, and mid-calf-length blue dress. Doreen is a stunningly beautiful woman, very petite but with a God-given voluptuous figure.

Just then she spotted me, ran into my arms, and gave me a long and warm embrace and kiss. "I can't tell you how much I miss seeing you. School can be such a bore without you there to talk to. I pray for the day that you can join me at the university. I know you're just going to love being there with me."

"I haven't been able to tell you, but I placed third in the Fort Worth tournament and won $1,000. Now I have almost a third of what I think I need for my college fund after only two events. I believe that most certainly by the end of the golf season next year, I'll have enough money to enroll for the spring semester of 1933."

"Oh, Ron, that is fabulous news. I am so proud of you and how determined you are to reach your goals."

I dropped Doreen off at her home, and since it was late Friday afternoon and she was clearly exhausted after a long day, I would wait to see her Saturday night. But before I left I wanted to tell her of my plan.

"Tomorrow night, Robert is taking us to a new speakeasy in downtown Dallas. I know nothing about it other than he says it's a real classy joint."

"I'm happy to go anywhere with you, so I'll dress real special for this adventure we'll be going on."

We kissed, and I left for home.

Since this club was a step-up from the one we had gone to on New Year's Eve, I decided to wear my charcoal herringbone tweed three-piece suit with wingtip shoes, red tie, and white silk shirt topped off with my black fedora.

Robert and Margaret picked me up at eight and then on to Doreen's. I walked up and knocked on the door, not really knowing what to expect. Doreen in her words said she would wear something special, and as she answered the door, she did not disappoint. I was at a loss for words as I took in this vision. She was wearing an off-white silk evening gown that hugged her every curve and flowed gracefully all the way to the ground. It featured a sweetheart neckline, and the champagne color perfectly complimented her sensational green eyes and beautifully tanned skin. Doreen is a movie star quality beauty there is no doubt of that. She seems to become more lovely every time I see her. She smiled that captivating smile of hers as if she knew what a spectacular scene she presented and took my hand as we walked out to Robert's car.

"Ron, I must say, you look grand tonight, how do I look?"

"I don't know how you do it, but you manage to take my breath away every time I see you. I've never seen you more beautiful than you are tonight."

Robert drove us into downtown Dallas, and we made our way down some dark side streets until we reached what we had been told was our destination. It didn't look like much, just a large warehouse, but rumor had it that it was the exclusive nightclub in Dallas and only accepted patrons by invitation only. We parked on Elm Street, then walked down an alley to reach a large steel door with a sliding window slot at eye level, reminiscent of the last speakeasy we went to on New Year's Eve. Robert knocked on the door, and the attendant let us in.

Robert had told us we would be dining here as it was not only a speakeasy, but also a supper club. Once inside, I was in awe of the magnificent surroundings as it opened up into this cavernous room with a bandstand and dance floor, surrounded by dimly lit tables just large enough to accommodate four customers.

*****

Each table was covered with a linen cloth with a small unobtrusive low-wattage lamp in the middle. The tables were set up in such a way as to offer unobstructed view of the band and the dance floor.

"Robert, you're right, this is certainly first-class. This room must hold at least five hundred people or more. But one question I have is, isn't this place within a couple of blocks from the Dallas County Courthouse and the police station?"

"Well, Ron, that's the irony of the Volstead Act. Almost everybody drinks, and on any given night, you might spot a judge or two or a prosecutor or maybe even the police chief. They all seem to give this club a wink and a nod."

I sat back and lit a cigarette, and as I looked around, I noticed that there was a bar on every side of the main room with each bartender wearing a tuxedo. The waiters and waitresses were also attired in formal dress. The conversation was light, and laughter filled the room as all there in attendance were having a carefree time, as if the Depression didn't exist in this room for this night. We only had to sit for a few moments before the band came out and started playing soft big band songs of a new artists by the name of Glen Gray. Doreen tapped me on my shoulder and said, "Will you dance with me?" I readily agreed and took her into my arms and felt her warm and soft body next to mine. I thought, I must already be drunk, for this is most intoxicating.

We returned to the table, and the waiter came up to take our dinner order. She ordered a salad and white fish with new potatoes. Remembering what Coach had said, I ordered a thick rib eye with baked potato, then I told Doreen of my new plan.

"The fellow I played with at this last tournament was so much bigger and stronger than me, but he was also a year younger. He could hit the ball much farther and had more energy as the day wore on. So I asked our coach at the high school what he thought, and he suggested weight training, riding a bicycle, and eating a lot of beef and potatoes. I'm trying to put on some weight to help my game. I want to add at least 25 pounds by late summer."

After dinner we ordered another round of drinks and enjoyed ourselves immensely until the early hours of the morning. We left the club around 2:00 a.m., totally exhausted but completely comfortable with each other as Doreen fell asleep leaning on my shoulder on the ride home. I woke her up as we reached her house and told her, "Hey, sleepyhead, it's time to call it a night. I'll come by tomorrow morning at ten thirty to go to church with you and your mom and dad." She yawned, stretched out her arms, and said, "Okay, Ron, sounds great to me." I walked her to her door, and we shared one last good night kiss.

I climbed back into the car with Robert and Margaret and told him, "Buddy, that was one great night. Thank you so much for setting this up. I can't remember when I've had a better time. Hopefully, we can do this again soon."

"Sure, we need to spend more time together. I mean the four of us, you know."

The next morning I met Doreen for church and then we went out to lunch. Once back at her house, I realized it was only a couple of hours before she would have to catch her train to Waco, so we just took up the rest of our time sitting in her parlor and talking.

"You know we have that tournament coming up the end of this month in San Antonio. I wasn't going to sign up for it, but Sammy thought it was a good idea to keep our momentum up. So I figured that if we do go, we could stop in Waco on the way that Wednesday and take you to lunch. You think that would be okay?"

"Sure, I can move my schedule around. That sounds swell to me, any chance I have to spend time with you is fabulous."

Mr. Winthorp let me borrow their car to take Doreen to the train station to see her off. After one final embrace and kiss, I watched as she boarded her train. I stood there until the train disappeared in the distance.

I told Sammy the next day that I would agree to enter the San Antonio tournament, even though I hadn't done well there last year, and I would pick up all his expenses. As usual, Sammy was on board and ready to go. The dates were April 30–May 3 and was being held once again at the San Antonio Heritage Country Club.

We left on Wednesday, April 29, and stopped as planned for an hour layover in Waco. Doreen met us at the train station, and we all went for a pleasant if too brief lunch, and then back on the train for the remainder of the trip to San Antonio. As it turns out, that was the highlight of the trip as once again I didn't even make the cut to play on the weekend. We caught a Friday evening train back to Dallas arriving late that night. It had been an exhausting and disappointing experience. For some reason I just don't do well on that particular golf course. I apologized to Sammy, and as usual, he was forgiving and understanding.

Now I was totally deflated and decided to skip the Dallas County Country Club tournament and just rest and get my mental state back up to the level of enthusiasm I knew I needed to compete adequately. So Sammy and I planned to take the rest of the month of May off but thinking seriously about signing up for the upcoming Western tour. That would start in August and would begin in Scottsdale, Arizona, then on to San Diego, California, and Los Angeles, finishing up in Monterey Bay. The time off would allow me the time to fine-tune my workout regimen, put on some weight, and earn more money to pay for such an expensive trip.

Before I could make that kind of commitment, I needed to talk with Mom and Doreen. It meant that I would be gone a whole month on the road, and I need to see how they felt about it. I'm having to miss out on seeing Doreen as it is with her being gone to school, and I know Mom depends on me to tend to several chores around the house. Not to mention the gamble it would be having to give up my two jobs.

So leaving for a monthlong adventure would present a hardship on us all, and I need to see if Sammy is agreeable to taking off as well. That brings up another consideration in that I would be responsible for all of Sammy's expenses. I could end up blowing my entire college fund that I have worked so hard to build up if I didn't play well. This could be a total loss and a tremendous waste of time. I knew that I had until July 1, 1931, to sign up, so I had plenty of time to decide. Doreen will be home for the summer at the end of May, so I'll just wait until later to approach the subject both with her and Mom.

*****

## THE LOVES OF A LIFETIME

Initially, Sammy didn't like the fact that we were not playing in the month of May, as his caddying for me was his sole source of income. He had been looking for a job, but up until now, none had materialized for him. But eventually he was able to find work in a filling station pumping gas and doing light repair work on customer's cars, you know oil changes, tune-ups, and the like. Sammy had always been mechanically astute, so this was right up his alley. He readily acknowledged that he enjoyed that kind of work. But he assured me that he would be ready to caddie for me again whenever I was ready to go back on tour, even to the possibility of a monthlong California tour.

For the rest of May, I worked my two jobs, continued my weight training, and was beginning to show some results as I had already gained almost 10 pounds, now up to 170. I needed to earn as much money as I could to make up for the disastrous San Antonio trip and prepare for the cost of future events without tapping my college fund. I continued to play golf at my old course Samuel Park, enough to keep my game somewhat sharp, but with no immediate plans to enter a tournament.

Doreen and I would write letters every week, as she kept me informed of her college activities and to tell me that once final exams are over by the end of May, she would be here for the summer. I decided to not mention the possibility of a California trip, preferring to wait until we could talk, once she was home.

Tomorrow, May 29, Doreen is due to come in from Waco on the train. Unfortunately, I will be working at Thomas's Drugstore and can't be there to greet her. Her mom will be taking care of that, so I will see her later that night. I haven't decided whether I will approach the subject of the Western tour right away or wait and give her a chance to get settled in a bit. I may wait until my birthday next week to discuss it with her as this year we both will be nineteen and old enough to make our own decisions. But I do want to talk to Mom first and see how she feels about it.

That night after dinner, I said to Mom, "Can I talk to you about something that's been on my mind. I really need your advice."

"Sure, Ron, what's up?"

"Well, the reason I decided to take the month of May off was for a couple of reasons. One was to rest and build up my money, and the other was to prepare for the possibility of going on the Western tour in August. That would mean being gone the entire month and using up at least half of my college fund hoping to be successful enough to win and cover all the expenses and even add to my savings once the tour is over. But I don't know if I'm willing to take that kind of gamble just yet. Of course as you know, my end goal is to win enough to go to college and marry Doreen. So my question to you is should I go this year or wait until 1932?"

"Ron, you're the only one that knows if you are ready for that kind of what sounds to me like an exhaustive experiment with only the remote chance of being successful. Your competition is probably going to be more than what you face here locally, is it not?"

"Gee, Mom, I hadn't really thought about that, but for sure all the best golfers will be there."

"Let me ask you a question. Are there any more local tournaments you could enter instead to give you more experience and to build up your confidence?"

"Yes, there's one coming up in Houston in late June, and then there's always Tulsa again in October. You've given me a lot to think about. Maybe I should get a little more seasoning and wait until next year to take on the Western tour. Another year will also give me more time to save up some money, build up my strength, and it gives Sammy another year to prepare as well. Thanks, I think that's what I'll do."

As I made my way to Doreen's house, I still hadn't decided on whether to talk to her about my future golf plans. But since Mom had helped me reach a decision, I guess it wouldn't matter a great deal, as I had already concluded that I was going to delay until next year.

I knocked on Doreen's door, and as she ushered me in, she put her finger to her lips to silence me and said, "Well, Mr. Perkins, I am so surprised and glad to see you, won't you come in, please." I was a bit taken aback by this little display of theatre, but I could see the laughter in her eyes, so I played along. "Why, thank you,

Ms. Winthorp, so happy to see you too." She led me into her parlor, closed the door, and at that moment jumped into my arms and started smothering me with kisses. So I had to ask, "Okay, Doreen, what are we doing, why the act?"

"Ron, my very proper and traditional grandmother is here, and I kind of had to put on a drama for her. I hope you understand."

"Now that I know. It was actually fun to have a part in your play."

At that, we had a laugh and sat down on her couch and continued to renew our friendship in our own special way.

"I have to admit something to you. I know you are my girl, but I still worry about all those handsome young men you are around on a daily basis and the temptations you must have to endure. Surely, you go to parties on occasion. I wouldn't think it's all classroom and study time, and I wouldn't expect you to not have some fun."

"Ron, I've told you before that you are my fellow, and nobody comes close to having my heart the way you do. Yes, I go to parties, but I always go home by myself. I will forever be true to you, I promise."

After a while, we left the parlor and went out to sit on the front porch swing as it was getting a little warm inside in more ways than one. It was an unseasonably warm night for May, but there was a pleasant breeze as we sat there rocking back and forth. Doreen nestled under my arm and drew close to me. "Ron, what do you think we should do this summer? I mean do you have any plans for us?" Doreen had always been the kind of a person that wanted to know in detail what the immediate future held in store.

"Well, I don't know. There are picture shows we can see, and we can go swimming at White Rock Lake. I always enjoy seeing you in a bathing suit if you know what I mean. I'm sure we can come up with some other things, like maybe we should take a trip to Galveston or Corpus Christi and take in the beach for a day or two. We could invite Robert and Margaret. Wouldn't that be swell?"

"That all sounds grand, but aren't you playing in any golf tournaments this summer? I was hoping to see you play while I'm home."

"Sammy and I decided to take some time off, but there is a tournament in Houston in late June that I've been thinking of signing up for. Would that be of interest to you?"

"Absolutely, I think that would be great fun. But one thing, I want you to know that I am perfectly capable of paying my own way. I know you can't afford to pay all the expenses for me and Sammy both."

"Aren't you sweet, I don't know how I am so lucky to have you as my girlfriend."

*****

As I left for home, I knew that the first thing I needed to do was to contact Sammy and make sure he was on board with playing the Houston tournament. I'm positive that if I gave him enough time to make his own arrangements, he would be all for it. Sammy has proven to be as valuable to me as Robert was. Then I would have to notify the tournament sponsors of my intent to play and then to verify the event was still being held on June 25–28 at the Bayou Bend Country Club. All easy enough to do. With the added bonus of having Doreen with me, I was now finding myself excited about playing golf again.

The next day I took Doreen to White Rock Lake. There are canoes there you can rent for fifty cents a day, so we took the opportunity to just relax and drift around the lake. We both wanted to spend time alone with no interruptions. We put the canoe into a remote beach on the lake and spread a blanket on the shore to enjoy a picnic lunch of cold fried chicken and lemonade. Once we finished lunch, we both lay there on the blanket, and after a few moments, we both fell asleep with her head resting on my shoulder. An hour or so passed, and as we awakened we loaded up and returned the canoe. That night we went to a new picture show called *Possessed* starring one of my favorites, Clark Gable and costarring Joan Crawford. It was a story about a young girl who leaves her small Pennsylvania home and local suitor for the bright lights of Manhattan and becomes the mistress of a New York lawyer, played by Clark Gable. Kind of a romantic mystery, I guess you would say.

My nineteenth birthday fell on a Thursday this year, which meant that Mom had to work, as did I, so the plan was for a party that night at our house. Mom cooked a big dinner of spaghetti with meat sauce accompanied with fresh, hot garlic bread topped off with a green salad. Doreen of course was there as was Robert and Margaret, and this year Sammy and a new girlfriend he wanted us all to meet came also. Sammy, as handsome a man as he was, never seemed to be able to find a steady girlfriend until now. He met Sarah McKendrick at his place of work. It seems as the story goes, that she is from the small town of Corsicana and would come up to Dallas on occasion to visit her aunt. Well, as it turns out, her aunt was a steady customer of the filling station where Sammy worked, and she brought Sarah with her one day to fill up her car. Sarah and Sammy struck up a friendly conversation at first, but it seems that they had an instant attraction. He asked Sarah out, and they have been dating steadily ever since that first chance meeting. She was indeed a beautiful girl with short auburn hair and big brown eyes. She was tall and slender, and you could tell she was totally smitten with Sammy as he was with her.

I found the chance to talk to Sammy about going to Houston on June 24–28, and he was fired up about going.

"Ron, I'm ready for more golf, believe me. I love my job, don't get me wrong, but golf is now my passion. So yeah, I'll gladly go. But let me ask you something. Do you mind if Sarah goes with us? The train goes right through Corsicana, and we could pick her up there. She'll be no trouble, I promise."

"Sammy, I'm very happy for you and Sarah. I'm so pleased that you have finally found someone that's important to you. Of course, she can go, but I must tell you that Doreen wants to go with us too. But Doreen and I aren't, well you know… I promised her a separate room in Houston."

"Ron, you're not going to believe this, but Sarah made me promise the same thing. We can put the girls in one room, and we can bunk in the other. It'll be so much fun, I can't wait."

I pulled Doreen aside after all had left for the night and informed her of what Sammy and I had discussed, and she was thrilled. It turns out that she had been engaged by Sarah in a conversation and found her to be quite delightful.

So now I had registered with the sponsors of the Houston tournament, and we were all set. Entry fee was $50 and the purse was $4,000 for first place, $3,000 for second, $2,000 for third, and $250 for a fourth through tenth finish. I was told when I signed up that over 125 golfers were playing. So it would be a challenge, but I felt like I had adequately recovered from the San Antonio experience and had my confidence and enthusiasm for the competition back up.

# 9
## CHAPTER

We caught the morning train out of Dallas on June 24 and picked up Sarah in Corsicana as planned and then off to Houston. The mood was light and spirited in anticipation of a fun and successful weekend. As we travelled, Doreen took the opportunity to say, "Ron, can I ask a big favor?"

"Of course, I'll do anything for you, you know that."

"Well, I want you to teach me how to play golf. It so looks like great fun."

My reaction was one of curious delight, but she saw something else entirely. "I can tell by your reaction that you think the idea of me playing golf is patently absurd, that I can't possibly learn, I guess because I'm a girl. Do you think I'm just not able physically or mentally?"

With that, she crossed her arms and sank back in her chair with obvious hurt feelings, until I said, "No, you have it all wrong. I would be thrilled to teach you how to play golf. I just wasn't expecting you to want that. I must say I am flattered and honored and would be overjoyed to be your golf coach."

"It's just that you enjoy the game of golf so much that I want to be a part of anything that you love. Remember, we are in this together for life, you know."

"As soon as we get back to Dallas, I will find my old set of clubs that Robert found for me, and we will go over to Samuel Park and start your golf career. I'll teach you the way Robert did for me. I agree, this will be a lot of fun and one more thing we can do together." That seemed to cheer her up, and we settled back for the remainder of the trip to Houston.

Houston in June is sticky, I guess would be an appropriate word, with temperatures in the nineties and high humidity. I started sweating as soon as we stepped off the train. I had booked two rooms at the Houston Regency Hotel that was close to the golf course. That was our next stop as we caught a taxi to the hotel and checked in. Sammy and I walked over to the golf course for a 2:00 p.m. meeting, and the girls caught a late lunch in the hotel dining room.

At the meeting I found out that I had a 9:30 a.m. tee time, and my playing partner would be a young man by the name of Stan Ford. All that I knew about him was that he was a Houston native and very familiar with this golf course. After the meeting, Stan walked over to greet me with a big smile plastered on his face as he extended his hand to shake mine. "Hi, Ron, I take it we'll be playing together the next two days at least. Listen, I know this course very well, and if I can help you in any way, well, you just let me know." And with that, he gave me a hearty slap on the back and walked off. I'm thinking that this is going to be a pleasant experience, for I instantly liked Stan very much, and I think he liked me as well.

Once back at the hotel we met up with the girls and headed to the bar for happy hour cocktails and decided to call it an early night, in anticipation of a rather busy day on Thursday.

Thursday morning we approached the first tee, and I had won the honor of playing first, but I thought it would be prudent to defer to Stan and follow his lead. The first hole was a 369-yard par 4 with a severe turn to the right. You could attempt to cut the corner, but you would have to go over some tall pine trees. The conservative play was to follow the fairway with a fade shot around the turn that came at the 175-yard mark. If you hit your ball too far to the left or too far straight you would encounter thick rough and trees.

Stan was a burly man with a thick barrel chest and large forearms and biceps that hinted at the power he must possess. Stan stood at my estimation just short of six feet tall and must have weighed close to 200 pounds. He had sandy brown hair, a ruddy complexion, and must have been in his late twenties.

As I expected, Stan pulled out his play club and lofted his drive over the corner above the pine trees, landing safely in the fairway, leaving him less than 100 yards to the green. Realizing that I didn't have that kind of power, at least not yet, I decided on my brassie with a controlled fade following the fairway past the turn. I was able to successfully execute the shot and found myself safely in the fairway but still 170 yards out. The weather was hot, and there was absolutely not a whiff of a breeze with the sun beaming down on us. I looked into the crowd and spotted Doreen, and as our eyes met, she smiled and waved at me, and I tipped my cap back to her. Hard to explain how much that simple gesture meant to me.

Sammy suggested my mashie for my second shot, but I felt like my spade mashie would be enough club, since the pin was in the front of the green and there were no sand traps or other obstacles between me and the green. I was counting on my ability to hit the ball far enough to at least roll up close to the hole. Fortunately, my plan worked to perfection as my ball ended up to within 2 feet of the pin. Stan hit a spectacular shot right at the flag and almost put his ball in the hole on the fly, but his ball rested some six inches for the hole, giving him a tap-in birdie. I drained my putt for my birdie.

As we walked over to the second hole, Stan put his arm around my shoulder and said, "That was fantastic, young man, I think we are going to have an exceptional day. Now this next hole is a par 5, but you gotta watch out and don't hit your drive to the right, because on the other side of those trees is the Humble Highway, and well, if you go there, it's a goner for sure." I saw what Stan was talking about as a drive that drifted right was indeed out of play, but there was an abundance of room to the left, at least for the first 250 yards. This hole was 487 yards in length and mostly flat and straight, but with sand traps running down the length of the fairway from that 250-yard mark on in, both on the right and left side and surrounding the green.

Stan smacked his drive at around 250 yards square in the middle of the fairway, leaving him some 237 yards to the green. I managed some 220 yards directly behind Stan's ball. I hit my driving iron for my second shot and came up some 50 yards short of the green. Stan lit up a fat cigar, put it on the ground, then calmly hit his brassie over the traps in front of the green, with his ball coming to a stop some 20 feet from the hole, in position to putt for an eagle. I chipped up with my jigger, one putted for a birdie, while Stan missed his eagle putt and settled for a birdie as well. We walked off the second green at two under each.

I looked over to see Doreen smiling with pride at me, and my confidence soared. For the rest of the front nine I didn't improve my position any, but Stan moved to three under as we made the turn. Surprisingly, we were in the lead position after nine holes. The only problem with this beautiful course was that the mosquitoes were so aggressive that they were a constant nuisance. Eventually one had to just ignore them and play through the distraction.

The back nine saw no change in the score, and Stan walked off with a one stroke lead over me. I was two strokes clear of the rest of the field. Doreen and Sarah joined us as we walked off the golf course and made our way back to our hotel. Our plan was to find a Houston speakeasy and celebrate the successful day we had just enjoyed. Stan and his lovely wife, Emily, suggested a place they knew of that we could all go for dinner and dancing and agreed to join us. We had a delightful evening and returned to our hotel after midnight. We could sleep in some as we had a 1:00 p.m. tee time for Friday.

I knew all too well not to get too overconfident, for there were some excellent golfers out there lurking such as the likes of Harry Bonham, John Packard, and Mac Grey, all still in contention. I played Friday's round picking up one birdie to go to three under, but Stan had stretched his lead to five under, and John Packard had taken over second place at four under. But after the second round I still had a three stroke lead over fourth place, and I was feeling very good about my game. The disaster that was San Antonio was now safely behind me, and I never gave it another thought.

The four of us went out to dinner Friday night but decided to call it an early evening as there was way too much at stake, and I needed my rest for what promised to be a grueling test on Saturday. I had my sights set on that $2,000 third-place prize and felt like it was there for me and mine to lose.

Saturday was another warm, sunny day, and my tee time was set for 12:30 p.m. Stan was now paired with John Packard since they were the two leaders, and I was in third place now playing with my old friend Mac Grey. Mac started the day at even par, some three strokes behind me, but I had witnessed firsthand what Mac was capable of, and I knew that a three-stroke lead meant nothing with two full rounds of golf left to play. Mac walked up to me and extended his hand for a friendly shake and said, "Well, young man, I see that you have improved your game tremendously since we played together last year in Tulsa. Congratulations on your continued success." That's the way Mac was, always a gentleman and a true pleasure to play golf with no matter the outcome.

Sammy and I both were enjoying the presence of having our ladies there at the tournament with us. I felt like it really boosted my confidence to see Doreen there cheering me on. I think having her watching me impelled me to birdie hole number 1, but then so did Mac. I parred hole number 2 while Mac picked up his second birdie of the day to move to within two strokes of me. I realized at that point that I needed to turn up the intensity, but for most of the rest of the front nine we remained at even golf until we reached hole number 9.

This was a short 355-yard par 4 with the fairway making a right turn around a thick stand of pine trees at the 160-yard marker. If you made the mistake of pushing your tee shot too far to the left there was a lake looming to take your ball out of play. So the preferred shot would be a controlled fade, teeing off with my brassie. I was able to execute the shot as my ball followed the fairway coming to a rest at 150 yards out, for what should be an easy-approach shot.

Mac's drive ended up in the same position as mine, both with a simple shot to the green. Sammy handed me a spade mashie. I trusted his judgment, and the result was a high arcing effort that ended up less than 2 feet from the hole. Mac matched me and wound up less than 6 feet out. We both walked away with a birdie, and I was now at four under, and Mac stood at two under. Stan had pushed his score to seven under, and John was at five under. For the rest of the day there was no change in the standings as all four contenders remained in close competition.

With the prospect within my grasp of winning $2,000 or maybe even more, I was not that far out of second or even first place. Sunday's round would determine who would emerge victorious. I approached Stan before he left the golf course and asked for a recommendation for a restaurant we could all go to for a Saturday night celebration. Stan asked, "What are you and your ladies in the mood for? I can recommend a wonderful barbecue restaurant or a Mexican food café, both of which Houston is famous for. I can take you to either, but you must let Emily and I tag along."

"Of course, Stan, we would be delighted, wouldn't have it any other way."

I asked the girls, and all seemed to be in the mood for a Mexican feast.

We caught a taxi back to the hotel to clean up and dress for the evening before Stan was to pick us up at 7:00 p.m. On the way I told Doreen, "I am so pleased that you are here to enjoy this adventure that we're on. I firmly believe the reason I'm doing so well is because of the inspiration of having you with me."

"Ron, I have had so much fun, and it has been a delight watching you play. I only pray that you do just as well tomorrow, as I'm sure you will."

We walked out of the hotel promptly at 7:00 p.m., and there was Stan and Emily right on time to pick us up. But to my surprise he was driving this beautiful new Cadillac sedan. I had no idea he was so well-heeled, so I asked him, "Stan, it's none of my business, but I was wondering what you do for a living outside of your golf career. Whatever it is, you must be doing it up right. This is a fabulous car you have here."

"Ron, it's no secret really. My family owns a cattle ranch down in the valley, and I have some lucrative commercial real estate holdings here in the city. So the Depression hasn't hurt my family all that much. People have to eat, and businesses need office space, and my family can provide both."

Stan was a most impressive guy, and we thoroughly enjoyed the Mexican restaurant he introduced us to. Afterward, Stan asked, "You feel up to some dancing and drinking? I know of a great speakeasy not far from here I think I can get us into. It'll be fun, I promise."

"Let me guess, you have something to do with the ownership of this speakeasy."

"You guessed right. It is one of my businesses, and I can get us in, no problem."

The evening went by way too fast, and it was time to return to our hotel for a good night sleep and to get ready for what would be a challenge like I had never faced before. This would be the first time since Tulsa that I would be in contention for first place on a Sunday. We thanked Stan and Emily for a thoroughly entertaining night. We entered the hotel, and I walked Doreen to her room and said to her, "Have I told you how lovely you looked tonight and just how much I love you? You are always so beautiful." We arrived at her door and shared one last embrace and kiss for the night.

Doreen closed the door behind her, leaned up against it, and said to Sarah, "I don't know how much longer I can hold out. I've never been with a man, but I want Ron so badly, I can taste it. He has been so patient with me, but I'm starting to lose my resolve. Sarah, what should I do?"

"Honey, let me give you a piece of advice. You are finding yourself in a no-lose proposition. That man loves you with all of his heart, that much is very evident. So if you do give in, it will be wonderful, I promise, and if you choose not to, well, he's not going anywhere. So just follow your conscience."

I walked back to my room and went in and said to Sammy, "Brother, I don't know how much more I can stand. I love and want that girl so bad, I am just about at my wit's end. I want to respect her wishes, but not having her is literally driving me crazy. What do you think I should do?"

"Ron, you and Doreen have been together since high school, and things between you two are going swell, aren't they?"

"Well, sure, Sammy, we have a wonderful relationship, none better than what we have."

"So why are you in such a rush to monkey things up? You have the rest of your lives to be intimate. Just relax and talk to her about the way you feel, but I certainly wouldn't push the issue."

"Thanks, I guess I just needed another guy to talk to."

The next morning we made our way to the golf course for an appetizing Sunday morning brunch at the club and then Sammy and I went to the practice area to hit a few balls before our 1:30 p.m. tee time. We were informed that the four leaders had separated from the rest of the field by more than four strokes. Mac was at two under and the next closest was at two over par. So if I could just maintain my position, I most certainly would win that third-place prize. And who knows, maybe one of the two leaders would stumble somewhere along the way. First or second place was not out of the question.

It appeared that we all started the day trying to play conservative and protecting our position, so for the first few holes everything remained unchanged from Saturday. We were in the next-to-last group with Stan and John teeing off after us. At least that was accurate for the first seven holes.

Hole number 8 was one of the most challenging on the course. It was a 445-yard par 5 with a double break of a fairway that started out leading to the left for the first 200 yards, then broke back to the right for the next 150 yards, then once again back to the left on into the green. The fairway was somewhat narrow with tall pine trees bordering both sides of the fairway and sand traps placed strategically all the way up to the green. It was a tricky hole that prevented you from being greedy. The suggested play was a brassie off the tee, followed by a long iron, then a short iron on in. I could tell that Mac was getting impatient as he was still two strokes behind me and desperately wanted to move up the leaderboard. He knew he was starting to run out of holes to play.

I decided to follow the recommended procedure, and Sammy agreed. I looked into the crowd, and I could see Doreen with something of a worried look on her face as she raised her hands up, showing me crossed fingers, wishing me good luck. That gesture gave me the confidence to execute my shot perfectly, driving my ball to just past the first turn, in prime position. Mac, on the other hand, pulled out his play club and hammered his shot past the first turn and into the fairway some 50 yards past mine. At that point, I knew he was going for it all in two shots, trying to make up some ground right here.

I stuck with our plan, and Sammy handed me a mashie niblick to negotiate the right turn. As I swung the club, I knew instantly that I had made solid contact, pushing my ball to within 100 yards and on the right center of the fairway. As I had predicted, I watched as Mac drilled his second shot with enviable precise execution, landing on the green, some 25 feet from the hole, with an opportunity for an eagle putt. I hit my pitching niblick into the green some 20 feet from the pin, a bit closer than Mac. As luck would have it, he made his eagle putt, but I was able to one putt for a birdie, moving my score to five under. But Mac was now only one shot behind me at four under. I knew at the beginning of the day that a three-stroke lead over an accomplished golfer like Mac Grey would probably not be enough.

I was told by an official that I was now tied with John for second place at five under, two strokes behind Stan at seven under. But that changed very quickly as John birdied the next hole to regain his one-stroke advantage. There were no further changes in the standings as we neared the eighteenth hole and the finish for the tournament. Mac was one behind me, and I was one behind John. This last hole was a short 310-yard par 4 with a fairway that turned to the right. I knew that Mac was going to take his last shot at tying me or passing me for third place. Mac is a swell fellow, but he is still an intense competitor. Even on this short hole, Mac chose to hit his play club, fading his shot around the bend, setting him up for a short chip to the green and a chance for a birdie.

As the fairway turned to the right, there was a water hazard just past the turn, so if you hit your drive too far to the left or too long, you were most certainly in trouble, probably looking at a lost ball and a penalty stroke. Unfortunately for Mac, he got all his ball alright, but it didn't fade like he wanted, but went straight and landed in the water. He knew what that meant, that he would have to drop a ball where it left the fairway and was now hitting three into the green, with his attempt at a birdie now all but gone. Mac, being the gentleman that he was, rested his arms on his club, turned to me, smiled, and tipped his hat as if to say, congratulations, you just won $2,000.

Sure enough, I parred the hole, and Mac bogeyed, giving me a solid third-place finish. As we walked off the eighteenth hole, Doreen ran up into my arms and kissed me right in front of all those people. But I didn't care, I was too excited and relieved to worry about what other people thought, only that they now knew I was a lucky guy to have such a beautiful girl kissing me.

I picked up my winnings and happily handed Sammy his $400, then we took a taxi back to the hotel to check out. Stan, who had won the tournament, stopped by to congratulate me and to give us a ride to the train station for our triumphant journey back to Dallas.

"Ron, I'm so happy for you guys. It was a well-deserved victory. If you're ever back this way, be sure and look me up. We don't need golf to get together and have a good time."

"Congratulations to you too for a most impressive win, and the same applies if you are ever in Dallas. Let's do get together again. I owe you for your hospitality. I'll never forget how kind you have been to all of us."

We were all exhausted and slept most of the way back until our stop in Corsicana to let Sarah off. I watched as Sammy walked her off the train, and when he came back on, he blessed us with a revelation. "Ron, Doreen, I think I'm in love. I want to marry her. Isn't she just the bee's knees?" Doreen and I had to laugh at Sammy's exuberance and really couldn't blame him as we all really liked Sarah. She is such a swell girl and absolutely perfect for Sammy.

Sammy had his Buick at the Dallas train station, and we dropped Doreen off first; and as I was getting ready to leave, she said, "Ron, this was such a fantastic experience. I'm so glad you brought me along. I hope I see you tomorrow. I love you, good night." She kissed me good night then Sammy drove me home. I couldn't wait to tell Mom of my win.

It was late Sunday night by the time I arrived home, and I fully expected for Mom to be in bed. I carefully unlocked the front door and walked in trying to be as quiet as I could. But then I saw her sitting in her chair in the living room, sound asleep with a book on her lap. She had tried desperately to stay awake until I returned home, but fell a bit short of that goal. I walked over and gently touched her on her shoulder. She slowly opened her eyes and with sleep in her voice, said, "How did you do in Houston, and what time is it? I tried to stay awake for you, but I guess I didn't make it."

"Mom, we did great. I finished in third place and won $2,000."

I handed her $400, leaving me $1200 for my college fund. Now I had saved well over $2,000, well on my way to my target amount of $3,000.

"Oh, Ron, that's marvelous. I'm so proud of you. How is Doreen, and did she enjoy the weekend in Houston?"

"I think she had a swell time, at least I was so grateful for her being there to cheer me on. She told me on the train on the way down there that she wanted me to teach her how to play golf. She's a real peach. Now, you need to go to bed. I know you have an early morning."

Monday it was back to work as usual for both Mom and me. But I was ready to get back to a normal routine after such an exciting and profitable weekend. Now my schedule contained a couple more responsibilities in addition to working at the drugstore and the country club on the weekend. I was continuing my weight lifting program every afternoon at the high school as well as taking Doreen to Samuel Park for her golf lesson.

I was starting to see some results from lifting weights, riding my bicycle, and beefing up my diet as my weight was now up to 185. In addition to that, when I started Doreen's golf lesson, I had the opportunity to drive some balls on my own, and it sure felt like I was getting considerable more distance. I felt stronger, and I seemed to have more energy.

Sammy came by work one afternoon and brought me some good news. "Ron, listen, I know you are really in bad need of a car, since your old Ford up and died on you. One of my good customers came in today and told me that he wanted to sell his old car, that he had already bought a new one and just wanted to get rid of it. It's a very clean 1930 Dodge two-door sedan, and he only wants $200 for it. It's a great car and a very good price. I should know, for I'm the one that's been performing maintenance on it the last year. If you want it, I can set that up for you."

"Wow, Sammy, that's great news. Of course, I want it. I'm tired of riding the trolley or bumming rides off you and Robert. Sure, let me get my money out of my secret savings account, and let's go pick it up."

My secret savings account was a coffee can under my mattress. Sammy drove me over to his customer's house, and there it was, this beautiful dark green Dodge sedan just sitting there waiting for me. I paid the gentleman for the car, picked up the title, and drove her home. She hummed like a brand-new car as I was certain that if she had been in Sammy's hands then she was first-class all the way. I arrived home before Mom finished her shift, and I couldn't wait to show her our new car. I knew she'd be excited.

## CHAPTER 10

I was sitting in the living room reading the newspaper when I heard the front door open. Mom came in and said, "Ron, whose beautiful car is that sitting in our driveway?"

"That's now our Dodge sedan that Sammy found for us. I paid for it out of my college fund."

"It looks expensive, are you sure we can afford it?"

"It was only $200, a real steal, but yes, it's paid for and belongs to us now. We can finally have that old Ford towed off."

With that, Mom sat down in her chair and began to cry very quietly. "Mom, what's wrong? I thought you would be pleased."

"I am, believe me, but that old Ford truck is the last thing that we have that belonged to your dad. I'm just going to be sad to see it hauled off. Do you think we could keep it a little longer? I know it doesn't run and probably never will again, but I just can't bear to see it gone."

I sat down next to Mom and said, "Of course we can hang on to it. I just didn't realize how much it meant to you. There is no hurry, we'll keep the truck as long as you want to. Maybe one day I'll get Sammy to take a look at her and see if we can get the old Ford running again. If it's okay with you, I want to drive over to Doreen to show her."

"You go ahead, I'll be alright."

When she answered the door, I said, "Doreen, I have something I want to show you. Can you come outside for a moment?"

She walked with me out to her driveway where my shiny, almost-new Dodge sat. "What do you think, ain't she grand?"

"You finally have yourself a new car, I'm excited for you. I know how badly you and your mom needed a replacement for that old Ford that doesn't even run anymore. So congratulations, when can I go for a ride?"

"No time like the present. Tell your mom we're leaving and we'll run down to the Hamburger King for a Coke."

We took a nice drive around White Rock Lake then back to her house. We sat on the porch swing, drank some lemonade, and just had a conversation.

"Are you ready for your first golf lesson?"

"You know I am, when can we start? Mom and I went out and bought for me a new golfing outfit, just for the occasion. I do want to be stylish you know."

"How does Saturday morning sound to you for starters? I don't have to work at Thomas's and I already asked the country club if I could have just this Saturday morning off, and they agreed. I can pick you up around 10:00 a.m., and we'll start out with getting you familiar with all the different clubs and what purpose each club serves. I'm going to train you at Samuel Park. That's where Robert started me off. We can hit some practice balls and then maybe even play a few holes. Samuel Park is a relatively easy and short course without a lot of obstacles. I think you'll love it."

"Sounds great to me, I'll be ready."

I stayed with her a little longer then left for home. Doreen and I would see each other almost every day during the rest of the summer, if nothing more than taking a walk or sitting on her porch swing. Besides golf, sometimes we would take in a picture show or drive over to the lake for a swim. I so enjoyed just being with her as I knew that all too soon she would be going back to school in the fall.

*****

I drove over Saturday morning to take Doreen to Samuel Park for her first golf lesson. When she opened the door, I was stunned to see how beautiful she looked in her new golf attire. Doreen was always a very fashionable girl, and her choice for a golf outfit was no exception. She was wearing a wide-brim straw sun hat and a blue two-piece dress with white trim and a pleated skirt. She had selected the proper rubber sole shoes for her golfing experience. After taking this picture in, all I could think to say was, "Well, aren't you the cat's pajamas. You look absolutely fantastic. Let's go have some fun."

We arrived at Samuel Park and made our way to the practice range. I brought my original set of clubs that Robert had found for me. These would now be Doreen's, but I wanted to see how she did with them just the way they were. I felt like I might have to cut the shaft down to accommodate her height. "Now, Doreen, the first thing I need to teach you is how to grip the club." I handed her my jigger, being the shortest club in the bag and the easiest to learn. "Grab this club and interlock your fingers on the shaft. Now that you've done that, I want you to take several gentle swings with the club in a sweeping motion. Now that you have a feel for that, I'm going to put a ball down, and I want you to just make contact and keep your head down and your eyes on the ball."

Doreen carefully followed my instructions to the letter, and before long she was hitting the ball straight for the most part and at a distance of some 50 yards. We went through that for a half an hour, then I decided she was doing so well, it was time to take the next step. "Now, let me give you a mashie niblick, and I want you to tuck your right arm up against your body as you go through your swing, keeping your left arm as straight as you can. Once again, keep your head down, eyes on the ball, and easily swing through. Don't try to kill it." Her first attempts, like mine once were, was a bit of a failure, but she kept at it; and after several attempts, she was starting to show some progress. She doggedly stayed with it until I could tell she was really starting to tire, so I called a halt to today's lesson.

"I think that's enough for today. You've done remarkably well for a first lesson. I'm very proud of you. It takes a lot of practice before it becomes comfortable, but I can already see that you have what it takes to be a good golf player. I'm going to take these clubs home with me and cut the shaft down and regrip to better accommodate your height. This will make this process easier for you."

"Thank you so much for your patience with me. I so want to be good at this. I know I'll never be as accomplished as you are, but at least we can eventually play together some, and you won't be embarrassed by me."

"I would never be embarrassed with you, don't ever think that."

"If it's okay with you, I don't want to wait until next Saturday to try again. So whenever you have done what you need to do to alter my clubs, then let's get back out there."

"I should have them ready in a day or two, and I was thinking anyway that we should play during the week in the evening. It'll be cooler, and we should be able to get in an hour or so before it gets dark. The country club let me have today off, but I usually have to work there on Saturday."

Our next opportunity to play came in the next Wednesday evening. I could get off work at 4:00 p.m., do my weight training for an hour, pick Doreen up, and be at the golf course by five thirty with plenty of daylight left. I had her clubs modified and ready for her to try out.

*****

"Ron, I've been practicing at home what you taught me last time, and I'm eager to take the next step."

"What have you been practicing with, I have your clubs."

"Well, I have become so adept at this with a broom handle that I'm considering adding it to my bag."

Doreen shared that with me as a joke, but I admired her tenacity and her desire to learn the game of golf. But that was her personality; she always went after her interests with just that kind of vigor.

"Okay, you remember what we went over last time? I assume you do, since you've been practicing with your special broomstick. I want to encourage you to do as much of that as you feel able to. It will only make you a better golfer."

"I'm ready for the next step."

"Okay, we're going to start with a midiron, but first of all tell me how the club feels since I cut down the shaft."

"It's perfect for my height and a little lighter, I think."

"Good. Now, using the grip that I taught you, go into your swing motion. I want you to have your feet set at shoulder width. That wider stance will give you a good, strong base. When you swing the club, turn your body at the waist only. Don't go rocking back and forth, that will just throw your balance off. Start with your weight on your left foot and move back with it on your right and then follow through moving back over your left foot and see how that feels to you."

"Okay, let me try that a few times and then I want to hit some balls."

She had a bit of a problem adjusting to a motion that was obviously foreign to her, but it wasn't long before she was hitting the ball with some accuracy and distance. It was a miracle that her form did not lend itself to a slice or a hook but went straight for the most part. I could see the excitement in her eyes as she could feel the progress she was making. She put her club down and took a rest and said, "This is so much fun, I can already see why you love it. It can be very addictive. How long do you think it will be before I can actually play a round of golf?"

"I don't want you to get ahead of yourself. It may be discouraging to you if you try to play before you're ready. Let's put in some more practice time, and I'll let you know when I think you're ready. Robert had me practice just like we're doing now for several days before he let me actually play the game."

From that first practice round through the next several, Doreen made it quite clear that she was, in her mind, ready to meet the challenge of playing eighteen holes of golf. I knew from my observations that she was showing remarkable signs of progress and, in all honesty, was becoming quite accomplished long before I agreed to actually playing a game with her. I wanted to protect her from becoming discouraged and suffer a setback and dampen her enthusiasm. She had such a passion already for the game. But I shouldn't have worried about that for Doreen was an eternally optimistic and enthusiastic person about golf and life in general.

"So the day has come for your first actual round of golf. Are you excited?" I knew that was a foolish question before I asked it. Samuel Park golf course is heavily wooded but with no water hazards and very few sand traps and was comparatively speaking a short golf course. The first hole was a 150-yard par 3 for men, with the ladies' tee at 100 yards.

I teed off first and hit my spade mashie onto the green. I recommended a driving iron for Doreen as I had no idea how far she could accurately hit the ball. I could see her trembling in eager anticipation, and as luck would have it, she came around on the ball and pushed it into the trees on the left. "That's okay, that is to be expected on your first attempt. Let me put another ball down for you, and you try again." This time she hit a perfectly executed shot covering the 100 yards to the green. She threw down her club and jumped into my arms, squealing with delight. I knew this was going to be a fun day.

I had worked with Doreen on her putting technique, and she seemed to take to that quicker than any other aspect of the game. She had excelled in measuring the exact amount of force you put on the ball to make it cover the distance to the hole as well as reading how the green was breaking to the right or left, or not at all. Now we were on the first green, and she was going to have her first attempt in a real situation. Her ball rested some 25 feet from the pin with an obvious line breaking to the right of the hole, that should curl back to the left.

I watched with great pride as she kneeled down and carefully sized up what this putt would require. She tapped the ball with her putter and ran it up to the hole on a perfect line only to have it come up inches short. She finished with a par.

"Congratulations, you just parred your first hole. I think you may do very well at this game of golf."

"Thank you, it's only because I have an excellent teacher. What's next?"

"The next hole is a 400-yard par 5 that has an elevated tee box with a fairway that drops down some 20 feet, then back up to the green. It will take you around a bend to a straight shot to the green that has a sand trap to the left and right. Now, for the first time you will get to use your play club, which may be the most difficult club to master that you have in your bag. I've avoided teaching you how to use it for just that very reason."

"Why is it so hard to learn? It doesn't look that different from some of the other clubs."

"It's because what I have trained you on so far is called irons, and this is a wood. It has a different hitting surface and will push the ball farther, plus the fact we can tee it up."

Doreen had this confused look on her face, so I explained, "Look, I'll demonstrate. We can scoop up some dirt under the ball to pull it up off the ground, making it easier to hit the ball." Once I had her set up, she addressed the ball with her play club, and not being used to the concept, she solidly hit into the dirt under the ball.

"Whoops, I guess that's not what you wanted me to do." She covered her mouth with her hand and started laughing at herself, and of course I had to join in, not laughing at her attempt but at the precious way she reacted.

I reteed her ball, and now that she understood what we were trying to do, she hit a very acceptable solid shot straight down the fairway at about 140 yards in distance. She turned to me and said, "Whatever are you talking about, I love the play club. When can I hit it again?" I just had to shake my head in bemusement at the way she approached the game of golf and how it was no different from the enthusiasm she showed for life in general.

We had a ball playing nine holes before darkness set in, and her only question was, "When can we play again?" Doreen has such a zest for life that I had never seen in anyone else with such desire to excel at everything she tried, whether it was golf, her studies and career, or her relationship with me. What a wonderful life we were going to have together.

I chose not to do any more tournaments in the summer of 1931, choosing to spend my golf time with Doreen instead. She would be back off to the university soon, and I would once again be without her. So my thought was to enjoy the rest of the time we had before the fall and rejoin the tour in the spring of 1932.

For Doreen's birthday in August, I planned a party for her at my house with Robert, Margaret, and Sammy. Sarah even came up from

Corsicana to join us. The next day on Friday, I booked a tee time for us at the Dallas County Country Club, making a foursome with Robert and Margaret. Sammy and Sarah declined to join us, saying they had other plans. The manager of the country club allowed us to play even though we weren't members because I worked there on most weekends, and we had a great working relationship. He knew how important this was to me. He had always been very kind and generous gentleman.

I wasn't aware that Margaret was such an accomplished golfer in her own right, but she proved to be most impressive and an inspiration to Doreen. It turned out that Robert had continued to play whenever he had a chance and had been teaching Margaret just like he did with me. Margaret and Doreen had been friends since high school, so the day was filled with laughter and friendly teasing whenever anyone hit a bad shot, and needless to say, there were more than a few of those.

After finishing our round of golf, it was now late afternoon. Plans for the night were to revisit the speakeasy in downtown Dallas for dinner and dancing. This time, we are taking my Dodge sedan, and I picked up Doreen first at 8:00 p.m. She looked radiant as always wearing a black flowing gown with a sweetheart neckline. We picked up Robert and Margaret and arrived at the club at eight thirty. We danced until after midnight, but after a day of playing eighteen holes of golf and then going out for dinner and dancing, we were all exhausted as I drove us home.

*****

Doreen and I played golf a few more times, and then all too soon, it was time for her to return to school. It always made me exceedingly sad to see her train pull out of the depot, knowing it would be at least a month before I would see her again. As for me, it was back to my usual routine of working my two jobs and continuing with my weight training to get ready for the 1932 golf season.

She was to start her classes on Tuesday, September 8, with plans for me to join her for homecoming weekend on October 22–25.

In the meantime we were to exchange letters at least twice a week. At first her letters were light and filled with information about her classes and studies, but around the first of October, I had the sense that her letters changed in tone. It was as if she had something on her mind but didn't know how to express it to me in a letter. Of course, my imagination started to run wild, thinking that she had met someone else and didn't know how to tell me she was breaking up with me. So I thought my best course of action was to telephone her at her dorm and just ask her straight up what was going on.

For some reason, I was exceedingly nervous about calling her, and it took me several days to work up the courage. I suppose it was because I didn't want to hear bad news. By this time I was convinced that she was going to tell me that we were through. I had finally decided to write her a letter telling her I was going to call her on the dorm telephone on a day that I knew she didn't have an early morning class. As the phone started ringing, my hands began to sweat with dread at what I imagined she was going to say to me.

Finally the phone was picked up, and an unfamiliar voice said, "Hello, who's calling?"

"Hi, my name is Ron Perkins, and I'm trying to reach Doreen Winthorp. Could you possibly call her to the telephone?"

The phone went dead for a few moments, but soon I heard, "Ron, how are you? Is everything okay?"

"I don't know. That's why I'm calling instead of writing. Your recent letters have been, I don't know, different I guess. I just feel like there is something going on with you that I need to know about. Am I wrong?"

Doreen didn't say anything for a moment or so, then I could hear her crying, and I assumed the worst was about to happen. "Oh, Ron, I'm so ashamed. I do need to tell you something, but I didn't know how to express it in a letter. I'm afraid I haven't been true to you. There is a young man in one of my classes that one day asked me to go to coffee with him. He said he wanted to discuss some of our study issues. So I innocently went, but soon realized he had more on his mind than just studies. I told him as politely as I could that I was engaged and was not interested in dating him, but it didn't deter him at all. He promised that if I went to a party with him just one time that he would leave me alone. Foolishly I fell for it and went with him. At this party, he started getting fresh with me, so I ran home to get away from him. Now he won't leave me alone. He stops by my dorm unannounced and waits for me in the lobby. He follows me after our class together trying to talk to me, and get this, he sends me love letters. I'm so sorry I let this happen."

"It sounds to me like you have nothing to be sorry about. You've tried to discourage this fellow, but he won't listen. Doreen, I don't think you've done anything wrong. Tell me his name, and when I come down there next week for homecoming I'll have a talk with this gentleman."

"His name is Scott Franklin, but I hope all you're planning to do is talk. He is a big fellow, plays football I think."

"Tell me what he looks like, so I'll know when I see him."

"He is a little taller than you and has short blonde hair, but I promise you'll know him instantly when you see him."

My weight training for the last several months had paid off as I had now reached my target weight of 185 pounds, so I am feeling strong and confident. If I do find this fellow unreasonable, I am certainly not afraid of a confrontation. I've always been able to handle myself in a scrape.

My train arrived in Waco late Friday afternoon, and as I stepped off the train, there was Doreen waiting for me. She ran up to me with tears in her eyes and threw her arms around my neck. "I am so glad you're here. You just don't know how much I've missed you."

"I assure you I feel the same way. But I promise you we'll have a wonderful weekend as soon as we get this Scott Franklin situation resolved."

We dropped my luggage off at the boys' dorm and went out for dinner. Once again, Doreen's cousin David had secured a room for me.

"What's up for tomorrow?"

"Well, I'm taking you to lunch at a cozy little café by the campus, then the game starts at 2:00 p.m. After that, there's a dance being held in the gymnasium building. That's probably where we'll run into Scott. See he also asked me out to the dance, and of course, once again, I turned him down. Like I said, he plays halfback for the football team, and his number is 31. I'll point him out to you. But, Ron, be careful, he has a reputation of being a brawler. Just talk to him and leave it at that. I don't want to see you get hurt."

The day couldn't have gone any better. Through lunch and the football game, I felt drawn closer to Doreen than ever before, and I could sense that she felt the same way. The trouble with this Scott Franklin fellow has united us against a common foe. As I waited in the lobby of Doreen's dorm for her to come down, I could only think of having a swell evening with my lady. I wasn't worried about what might happen with this fellow. I was fully confident that I could handle him.

Doreen came down the stairs looking delightful as usual, and we walked over to the gym for the dance. We found a table close to the dance floor and listened to the band playing. So far there was no sign of this guy, so maybe he decided to not show up. "Ron, dance with me." We walked out on the floor and began to dance when Doreen squeezed my hand, and her body shuddered. At the same time I felt a tap on my shoulder. "I'm cutting in, buster." I knew this had to be Scott as I turned to face him.

"No, you're not my friend."

Doreen was right; he was a rather large fellow that stood at least six feet, two inches and probably outweighed me by 20 pounds. I could tell from his demeanor and the tone of his voice that he was a bully and was used to pushing people around.

"As a matter of fact, I'm telling you just this one time that you are to totally leave Doreen alone. No more contact of any kind, do I make myself clear?"

"Big talk, and what are you going to do about it if I don't."

"Well, Mr. Franklin, we can settle this right now if you would like to step outside."

By this time, the crowd around us had stopped dancing to watch this drama unfolding in front of them.

Scott was known on campus to be a brute that nobody messed with, not even other football players. Rumor had it that a fellow challenged him in a dispute over a girl, and Scott put him in the hospital. We walked outside and squared off.

"Ron, don't do this, he's going to hurt you, and I can't bear to see that."

"Don't worry, I got this." I looked in Scott's eyes, and I may be wrong, but I thought I saw some fear and concern. I don't think very many men had ever stood up to him before now.

As we stood there face-to-face with a ring of onlookers surrounding us, I said to him, "I want you to remember that when this is over, you asked for it. I tried to give you an easy out, but you were too stupid to take it. That seemed to enrage him as he bowed up and launched a right cross at me, but I saw it coming and ducked under and came back with a left uppercut to his jaw, knocking him off his feet. He lay there for a moment as his eyes glassed overlooking up at me with a confused expression and blood dripping from his mouth. He jumped back up and bull-rushed me, but I brushed him aside and hit the back of his head with my right fist, and once again he went down in a heap. The crowd gasped as he came up on one knee, obviously stunned.

I patiently waited as he came to his feet, and at that moment, I decided it was time to finish him off. I threw a right cross at the side of his face as hard as I could hit him, and once again he went down, but this time he didn't get up. I had knocked him unconscious. Two of his teammates pulled him back up to a sitting position, but now the fight was over as he didn't want any more of me. I kneeled down in front of him and grabbed his jaw in my hand and said to him, "Now, Scott, I want to make sure you hear me. If you don't leave Doreen alone, I'll come back and finish you. Do I make myself crystal clear?" Groggily, he responded with, "I got it." And that was the end of Scott.

"Are you okay?"

"Yes, I'm fine. That palooka never laid a glove on me. I guess all that training I've been doing for golf paid off tonight. If he so much as looks at you the wrong way, I want you to call me, and I'll come back and fulfill my promise to him."

I put my arm around Doreen's waist, and we walked back to her dorm and sat in the lobby until it was time for her curfew. The rest of the weekend went off without any more incidents. As a matter of fact, we never saw Scott again. Doreen dropped me off at the train station on Sunday, and I knew that the next time I would see her would be the Thanksgiving holiday.

The weather in late November had turned a mite chilly as I stood there smoking a cigarette waiting for Doreen's train to roll into the station. I only had to wait maybe a half hour when her train finally arrived. We retrieved her luggage, and as we walked to the car, the first thing I wanted to know about was Scott. "Well, tell me, have you had any more trouble from our aggressive friend?" Doreen smiled and said, "Before you came down, he would sit next to me in the class we shared. But now, he sits as far on the other side of the room as he can get. Plus, when class is over, he sits there and waits until I am out of sight. I truly believe he thinks you're coming back to kill him if I tell you that he has been fresh with me again." We both had a good laugh at that, and I was reassured that we would have no further trouble out of Scott.

The Thanksgiving holiday passed all too quickly, and it seemed like we had no time together before I was putting her on a train back to Waco. But we had Christmas coming up in a month and then New Year's. Time seemed to be passing in a blur as we went through the Christmas holiday and Doreen was back in school. But we felt like we had a lot to look forward to in 1932.

I was starting to worry about Mom's health. She had never been a physically strong woman, and her workload at the department store appeared to be wearing her down. I was hoping that the money I was winning playing golf would help to ease the number of hours she had to work. She seemed to be always so exhausted to the point that when she finished her day at work and took that long bus ride home, then cook dinner for me, she had no energy left. All she could do was sit in her chair and read, then off to bed early. Part of my goal in life was to earn enough money so she could quit her job entirely and enjoy life a little more. Losing Dad in 1929 had been especially hard on her, and I could see she was still grieving.

It's always cold in Dallas in January, and this year brings in a rare snowstorm, paralyzing the city. So neither Mom nor I can get out to go to work, so we'll just stay in the house and try to keep warm until the weather improves. In Texas it always does eventually, and after a few days, the temperature was back up in to the fifties, and the sun was out, melting the snow.

I was eager to resume my career in golf, so to keep my game sharp, I tried to at least twice a week go over to Samuel Park and practice. On several occasions, Robert and Sammy would join in, and we would play some competitive games while we practiced, like who could hit the ball the farthest and who was the most accurate. Sammy had always been the long ball hitter before, but now after the regimen I had put myself through, I was flying my ball past his by some 40–50 yards. He was most impressed and was ready for the new golf season to start, more optimistic than even I was.

Doreen came home from school in March, and we spent a terrific weekend together. We played some golf as she was now very enthusiastic about the game, and we took in a comedy picture show called *This Is the Night* starring Lili Damita, Charles Ruggles, Roland Young, Thelma Todd, and new fellow named Cary Grant that everybody says is brilliant and may have a long successful career ahead of him.

I was the first to approach a subject that was weighing on my mind. "Okay, what's going on with Scott? Has he bothered you any more since our last meeting?"

"No, not at all. As a matter of fact, I haven't seen him anywhere on campus this whole semester, and we no longer have any classes together. Rumor has it that you humiliated him so badly that he became the laughingstock of the football team and transferred to another school at the end of the fall semester."

"Well, good riddance if you ask me."

As the weekend came to a close and Doreen left to return to the university, we were resigned to writing letters until the end of the semester in May. Her goal remained to try and finish undergraduate school in three years, and with her grades, she was well on her way. I would have been surprised at any other results as Doreen excelled at everything she attempted.

The first regional tournament of the year was being held at the Riverside Country Club in Dallas on April 7–10. I was not familiar with that particular course, but understood that it was tough but well designed and featured great risk but great reward at the same time if you had the nerve to take chances. Word had gone out that it would be a $100 registration fee, and the purse would be $4,000 for first place, $3,000 for second, $2,500 for third and $150 for a fourth through tenth-place finish. This would be my first tournament of the 1932 season.

I signed up for the tournament at Riverside. Sammy was more excited than I was as he was ready to get back into action. I felt like 1932 was going to be a very good year for golf, and my plan was to try and earn some winnings at a couple of local events and then take the Western tour that I had declined to do in 1931. This season was going to be my push to finally earn enough money to enroll at the university in the spring of 1933. I felt like scaling down on the number of local events to get myself ready for what would promise to be the grueling challenge of the Western tour was a sound plan. I knew it would be expensive and a gamble, but I was confident that I could win and win big in California. Maybe, I'll get to play with my old friend Jessie again.

The field turned out to be 120 golfers, including some of the most talented in the game like John Packard, Harry Bonham, and Mac Grey, as well as my old friend from Houston, Stan Ford. I sought Stan out at the golfer's meeting on Wednesday and told him, "Hey, old friend, glad to see you here. Maybe I'll have the opportunity to show you the same hospitality you did for us down in Houston. Did you bring Emily with you?"

"I did, and she wants to see you and Doreen again. She talks about you two quite a bit and how much fun we all had. Is Doreen here with you?"

"No, she's at school, and Sarah still lives in Corsicana, so I'm afraid it's just me and Sammy to show you around. We'll talk later, maybe we'll be paired up again."

The first hole was a long 175-yard par 3. My playing partner for the day was a gentleman from Oklahoma named Ollie Sims. After my introduction to Ollie, I was shocked to see that his caddie was my old friend Rocky from Tulsa who had caddied for me there back in the fall of 1930. I reached out to shake his hand. "Rocky, you remember me? You caddied for me back a couple of years ago. How are you doing?"

"Yes, Mr. Perkins, of course I remember you. I am so glad to see you again."

After the introductions we set about the business of golf, and I was able to birdie the first hole and moved on to the par 4 second. I had not played a competitive round of golf since I had started my training regimen, and I was curious to see if I could actually add more distance to my tee shot and not lose the accuracy that my game depended on. This hole was 313 yards in length, and the fairway was relatively straight with very few obstructions. I teed off first and surprised myself as I launched a tee shot coming to a rest on the left side of the fairway at the 260-yard mark, leaving me a chip shot with my jigger to the green. After two holes I was now two under.

I finished the front nine at two under and added one more birdie on the back nine to finish the first day at three under par. The weather had been picture-perfect for golf and remained that way on Friday as I shot a round of even par, staying at three under for the tournament. The weather forecast for Saturday brought about a change as the temperature dropped into the fifties, cold for April, with a steady rain and winds gusting up to thirty miles per hour.

On Saturday because of the inclement weather, I played the round at one over, leaving me at two under for the tournament and tied for third place. Sunday wasn't much better as I finished in a tie for third place and split the $2,500 prize money, taking home $1,250. I gave Sammy his cut of $250.

As Sammy and I left the golf course and started our drive home, I said to him, "I wanted to let you know that I am seriously considering signing up for the Western tour this summer in August, and I hope you are on board with that. You know I can't go without you, and of course I will pick up all your expenses plus your usual 20 percent cut of the winnings, if there are any. I'm thinking we do the Fort Worth tournament in May and then take June and July off. Is that okay with you?"

"Ron, I'm there, sounds like great fun and a real opportunity for us to make some greenbacks. I think you told me last year that we would be gone for the entire month of August, is that still right?"

"Yes, I'm afraid so. For me, I'll have to make arrangements with Mr. Thomas and the country club and of course Mom and Doreen. But I think I can make arrangements to the satisfaction of all involved. How about you?"

"I think the filling station will allow me to go, but I do have something I need to talk to you about. Sarah and I have become quite serious, and last week I asked her to marry me, and she accepted. We plan on being married in June, and with this new possibility of spending August on the road in California, I hope you'll allow me to take her with us. But don't worry I'll pay her way, you won't have to. I promise you she will not cause any problems or be a distraction in any way. Is that okay with you?"

"Sammy, I'm shocked and very happy for you and Sarah, and of course she can come with us. I think that's swell."

"Maybe you could ask Doreen if she would like to go as well. I know you two aren't married yet, but we could make some kind of arrangements to accommodate her."

"I hadn't really thought of how I was going to explain to her that I would be gone a whole month without her, but that's an excellent idea. I can only hope that she will go for it, but I don't see why not. It would be a grand adventure for the four of us. I'll talk to her when she comes home. Oh, and by the way, Robert and Margaret are getting married in June as well."

I now have another $750 to put in my college fund bringing my total up to $2,650 and very close to my goal of $3,000. I realize that if Doreen goes with us to California, that paying for her, Sammy, and my expenses will cost me around an additional $1,000 at least. But I truly believe I can win at least double that amount in California.

I decided it was time to clear my future golf plans with Mom, so as I arrived home, I called for her to give her the good news of the day.

"Well, we did okay. I finished in third place and had to share the winnings with another fellow that tied me, but I still walked away with another $1,000 after I paid Sammy, and I have $250 for you. I'm getting very close to my goal, and the likelihood of going to college is getting closer to being a reality. But I do want to talk to you about something. Do you remember last year when we discussed the Western tour and we decided that I wasn't ready?"

"Yes, I do remember, and I know that you have been thinking about this for a year now, and you feel like you're ready to go now, that it's your time. Am I right?"

"Yes, I've worked it out with Sammy, and he is on board. One other thing I need your advice on is he wants to take Sarah with us, and I want to ask Doreen to go also. What do you think about that?"

"Ron, that's an awful big step in a lot of ways. First of all, have you talked to Doreen yet? And second, if she does agree to go, how can you pay her expenses as well as Sammy's and your own? Then there's the fact that you have decided to honor her request of no intimacy until after you're married. How are you going to address that? It's quite a bit to think about, plus the fact that I will miss you terribly, you being gone a whole month. Do you realize that in your whole life, you and I have never been separated that long?"

"Mom, I can appreciate your concerns, and I have taken into consideration all that you are worried about, and I think I have it all worked out. I can afford all the expenses only if I win in California and win more than once. I know this will be a risky gamble, but I think I have it in me to be successful. As far as Doreen and my promise to her, I will arrange for her to have her own room the whole trip. I plan on talking to her as soon as she comes home from school."

"One other thing, son, don't you think that the girls will be a distraction, interfering with your focus on your game?"

"Not at all. Quite the opposite in fact. Every time she has been there at a tournament, I have performed better."

"Sounds like you are ready to take this next step both in your golf career and in your relationship with Doreen. I will miss having you here, but don't worry I'll manage. You have my blessing."

Sammy and I worked the Fort Worth tournament but finished out of the money. I can only assume that my concentration was already on the Western tour and talking to Doreen about joining us on our journey.

# 11
## CHAPTER

Today is the day that Doreen arrives home from college, and as I wait for her train to pull into the station, I'm trying to decide how I'm going to approach her about the possibility of joining me, Sammy, and Sarah for the California tour. Soon her train comes to a stop, and I see her disembark. I am always surprised by how each time the thrill of seeing her almost leaves me speechless. As she runs into my arms, I push her back a bit to take a good, long look. "Doreen, what are you wearing?"

"Hey, you never seen a girl in trousers before? I'm a modern 1930s woman. What do you think?" She stepped back and twirled around so I could take in the full picture of how stunning she looked wearing black trousers with a white blouse and a gray ladies' felt fedora hat jauntily raked to one side.

"Doll, you always look good to me."

She put her arms around my neck and gave me a hello kiss that lasted long enough to elicit some laughter and friendly catcalls from passing strangers. We retrieved her luggage and walked hand in hand to my car.

"How are your studies going?"

"I am doing so well that it looks like I'll be able to graduate after the spring 1933 semester, and then on to medical school in the fall. That is, if I'm accepted, and I see no reason why I shouldn't. I am after all a straight A student. I may can even enroll for the summer session. Of course, by then, I will be Mrs. Ron Perkins, married to a freshman student at the university studying electrical engineering."

With that, we laughed and realized that we still held the same dream, a dream that was getting even closer to fulfillment.

I decided to wait until later to talk to her about going to California, just so she could rest and visit with her family before I asked for a decision of that magnitude.

"Ron, I wanted you to know that I took my golf clubs with me to the university, and I have been practicing almost every day. When can we go back to Samuel Park and play again?"

"Tomorrow is Saturday, and I can probably get us a tee time in the late afternoon. But don't you want to rest for a day or so before playing eighteen holes of golf?"

"No, I think if I get a good night's sleep, I'll be good to go. So if you don't mind, go ahead and get us set up."

I picked Doreen up at 2:00 p.m. We arrived in plenty of time to hit some practice balls. As I watched her hit a few, I was immediately impressed with her poise and concentration. When it became time for us to tee off, I noticed a sly smile come across her face as I addressed the ball. It soon became obvious to me why she had this confident air about her. She stepped up to hit her first shot on this par 3 and launched a high soaring effort aimed right at the flag. It appeared she had dialed in the right distance as well. I could tell she had indeed been putting a lot of energy into improving her game. From what I observed, she was doing every step I had taught her and was doing it flawlessly.

"My goodness, I can tell you have been working hard. I am truly in awe of how quickly you have grasped the fundamentals of golf." She continued to perform with very few mistakes and almost broke 100. I knew it wouldn't be long before her ability would take her to a score far exceeding that. Doreen was a natural talent.

As we drove home from the golf course, I could tell she was exhausted, far more than she was willing to admit.

"Why don't I drop you off, go home, clean up, and come back in an hour or so. Then we can go out to dinner anywhere you would like. How does that sound to you?"

"Sounds dreamy, I certainly welcome an easy night for us. I'll see you in an hour."

After dinner we drove back to her house, and as we sat on her couch in the parlor, I decided it was time to explore how she would feel about taking the California trip with us. "I have some news for you that I don't think you are aware of. You know that Robert and Margaret are getting married on June 11, but what you don't know is that Sammy told me that he has asked Sarah to marry him, and she accepted. They are getting married on June 25."

"Are you kidding me? I am so happy for them. I think Sarah is such a darling girl and just perfect for Sammy."

"It does make me wonder, if we shouldn't go ahead and join them instead of waiting until next spring. How do you feel about that?"

"Ron, I would really love to. You know how I feel about you. But I really want to finish my undergraduate studies first. So as much as I may want to, I think we should stick to our original plan and wait."

"I suppose I would have to agree that maybe the timing isn't quite right for us to get married now. But let me ask you about something else. Sammy and I have committed to go on the Western tour in August for the whole month, and he is taking Sarah with us. I wanted to ask if you would go too. I don't think I can spend a whole month away from you this summer. I'll pay all of your expenses and arrange separate accommodations for you for the entire trip. What do you think?"

"I'm surprised, I wasn't expecting this. I'm not saying no. I just want to think about it for a couple of days before I give you my answer. It does sound like fun, and I've never seen California, but I also need to check with Mom and Dad first."

We talked a while longer, and I could tell she was leaning in my direction but with some reservations.

"Would it help if I talked to your dad and assured him that you will be safe and secure?"

"No, I will soon be 20 years old, so I can make decisions on my own. I just want to have the time to think about it, and if I do decide to accept your invitation, I want to clear it with them. I want to make sure that they don't have something planned for my birthday.

I left for the night with plans to take Mom with me and meet Doreen and her parents for church the next morning.

After church, we all went out to lunch, and Doreen took me aside and said, "I talked this over with Mom and Dad last night about the trip to California, and they agreed it would be great fun and an opportunity for us both to have a wonderful adventure. They trust you, and know that you have always had my best interests at heart. So, yes, I'm going to spend the month of August in California with my best friend and the love of my life. Dad told me that he had something special for me for my twentieth birthday, but it could wait until we got back."

Now we were all set to leave for the West Coast on Monday, August 1, on the train to our first golf tournament in Scottsdale, Arizona. We would arrive there on August 3. There was one more thing I had planned for Monday for Mom. I decided that it was time we stepped up in to the 1930s and had a telephone installed. I wanted to be able to call Mom from the road just to check in on her from time to time. We had not had one since we moved to Dallas. Anytime I needed to use the telephone, I had to call from work or use Robert's or Sammy's. I was tired of doing that.

The next event to be celebrated is my twentieth birthday on June 4. This is a bittersweet time for Mom. This will mark the third anniversary of the passing of Dad the day before my birthday in 1929. So part of the occasion will entail a visit back to Terrell on Friday to visit Big Jack's grave. It seems to give Mom some comfort.

My birthday happens to fall on a Saturday this year, so Mom, Doreen, and I invited Robert and Margaret, Sammy and Sarah to White Rock Lake for a picnic. Part of the charm of White Rock Lake is the various activities it offers. There is of course swimming, but also canoe rentals, and an area along the shore that is specifically for picnic lunches with tables and small grilles, surrounded by large oak trees that provide welcome shade from the sun.

Mom and I packed cold cuts of ham, salami, and bologna, bread, potato chips, condiments, and lemonade, enough for all to enjoy. We rented canoes, swam a bit, and had a leisurely lunch, making this one of my most memorable birthdays ever.

No sooner had we wrapped up my birthday than it was Robert and Margaret's wedding on June 11, the very next weekend. Margaret is a wonderful girl and is perfect for Robert. She stands about five feet, four inches with red curly ringlets framing her porcelain white face featuring beautiful blue eyes. She is an Irish lass, and I don't think she has ever had a bad day as every time I am around her, she has a smile on her face and seems to enjoy life to the fullest. I have been asked by Robert to be his best man, and Doreen has been asked to be the maid of honor.

Robert and Margaret's wedding went off without a hitch. We saw them off for their honeymoon to the Texas Gulf Coast. I've never seen Robert more at peace. They are indeed made for each other with lots of happy years ahead of them. Robert has achieved the great American dream with a loving wife, a steady government job in these uncertain times, a comfortable home, and an almost-new Chevrolet. It just couldn't get any better for them. I hope that one day, Doreen and I will enjoy the same fulfillment.

The last major event of the summer before we begin the Western tour in August is Sammy and Sarah's wedding on June 25. I was not asked to be best man, that honor went to our old linebacker from high school, Tommy Painter, while I served as a groomsman.

We all agreed to pass on entering any events in July, preferring to prepare for the Western tour in August. Instead, while Sammy and Sarah were gone on their honeymoon, Doreen and I continued to play at least twice a week at Samuel Park. She was showing remarkable progress in her game as she was now scoring in the low nineties. Excitement and anticipation are mounting as we move ever closer to our departure date of August 1.

Sammy and Sarah have returned from their honeymoon, and all seemed to be eager for our adventure as we met at the train station in the early morning hours of August 1 for a 6:00 a.m. departure for Scottsdale, Arizona.

I have booked two sleeper cars on the Sunset Limited and have made all the necessary arrangements. This is something that Sammy ordinarily does, but he has been understandably otherwise occupied.

We are signed up for contests in Scottsdale, Arizona, San Diego, Los Angeles, and the Monterey Peninsula. Now we just have to get there.

"Doreen, I want to explain to you that even though we will be sharing a sleeper car, we have an upper and lower birth. So I am technically honoring my commitment to you and your dad. I just couldn't afford three sleeper cars, and I didn't feel like I could separate the newlyweds. I hope you are okay with the arrangements."

"I'm not worried about it in the least. You have proven yourself to be a gentleman and a man of your word. But I must warn you that you will see me in the morning before I have a chance to put on my makeup."

"I have seen you without makeup before, and I find you every bit as enchanting either way."

We left on the train out of Dallas on a connecting route to San Antonio where we would catch the Sunset Limited on into Arizona. The trip would take two days arriving in Scottsdale early Wednesday morning in time for the golfer's pretournament orientation. As we settled into our sleeper berth, Doreen asked, "Ron, I brought my golf clubs at your suggestion, but do you think there will really be time for me to play with you?"

"Yes, there should be several opportunities where we can squeeze in a round or two for just us. I don't see why not."

"I have another question about where we are staying along the way. I mean do I have a room all to myself, or will I be sharing a room with Sarah at any point?"

"The PGL has provided all the golfers and their families with adequate hotel accommodations all the way up to the Monterey Peninsula. To answer your question, you will have a hotel room to yourself at every stop. Sammy and Sarah have their own room of course, and I have mine. It's more expensive that way, but it is worth every penny to have you with me on this adventure."

I could see by the expression on her face that she was absorbing all the information and seemed to be satisfied with all that I had covered. We left our berth and met Sammy and Sarah in the dining car for breakfast.

"Are you guys settled in and is everything comfortable for you?"

"You bet, we are ready for Arizona. This is going to be such a venture, and I believe a highly successful one at that. I truly believe, Ron, that you are going to enjoy at least one tour victory."

We settled in to enjoy a selection of a delicious breakfast of eggs, bacon, sausage, potatoes, pancakes, virtually anything you could possibly desire. Juice and coffee were provided in abundant amounts.

After two days on the train, we finally rolled into Scottsdale in the early morning hour and took a taxi to the Desert Heights Country Club and resort center. The clubhouse was a one-story structure built like an old Indian pueblo with thick adobe walls and a flat roof. The door to the main entrance was a large arched entryway that opened up into this magnificent and bright interior. At the back of the room were floor-to-ceiling windows that revealed a view of a terrace leading down to a swimming pool. Just past that was the golf course. I had been told this was a traditional desert course with manicured fairways and greens, but the rough was pure desert with sand and cactus as well as mesquite and thorn acacia bushes interspersed with occasional rattlesnakes. So caution was emphasized if you wandered off the fairway.

We made our way to the resort restaurant for a light lunch before the player and caddie meetings that were to start at 2:00 p.m. The girls were free to explore the amenities offered by the resort while Sammy and I were at the meeting. I learned that my tee time for Thursday would be at 9:00 a.m., and my playing partner would be a gentleman by the name of Ernie Hudson. I tried to find him at the conclusion of our orientation session, but he was nowhere to be found. So introductions would have to wait until our Thursday tee time. The purse for this tournament was $3,000 for first place, $2,000 for second, and $1,000 for third with fourth through tenth earning $150. The entry fee was $100.

The large prize money was reported to be in the California events. I was told that the Monterey Peninsula tournament offered a $10,000 first-place prize. If that was true, then winning there would certainly be a dream come true. But the reputation of that course is that it was extremely challenging, boasting of high reward for high-risk shots, if you were willing to gamble on your golf ability and could control your nerves.

After the meeting had concluded, we met the girls and made our way to the Desert Heights Resort Hotel to check in to our rooms. As I promised Doreen, she had a room all to herself. Since the temperature was hovering around one hundred degrees, typical for an afternoon in Southern Arizona, we decided to visit the swimming pool. After an afternoon of swimming and enjoying the sun, we retired to our rooms to change clothes and prepare for a dinner in the hotel restaurant. After dinner, we discovered the hotel had a small piano bar, so we decided to have a few drinks before calling it a night.

The next morning we were up and sampling the hotel complimentary breakfast buffet in plenty of time before our 9:00 a.m. tee time. Sammy and I left the girls there and made our way to the practice range to hit a few before our tee time. The girls joined the group at the first tee that would be following us for the day. As always, I looked to find Doreen in the crowd. Seeing her there was calming for me and gave me the incentive to play well.

The day, even at the early morning hour was already warming up, but because we were essentially in the desert, the humidity was extremely low, so it wasn't that uncomfortable, at least not yet. I had eighty-sixed my sweater and was playing in a white shirt, black tie, and summer knickers that Mom had given me for my birthday. My playing partner finally showed up just in time to tee off.

"Hi, young man, my name is Ernie Hudson, and you must be Ron. I am so pleased to meet you."

Ernie was a slight fellow, only about five feet nine inches, but with a compact powerful build.

The first hole was a straight 349-yard par 4 featuring a narrow landing area at the 250-yard marker. But with a straight tee shot you should have a clean shot to the green that only had a sand trap in the back side. This hole was custom built for birdies. This was going to be first real test to see if all the weight training I had been doing for the past several months would now pay off. I teed off with my play club hoping to drive the ball with accuracy and distance, setting me up for an easy chip shot to the green. As I came through my swing motion and made contact with the ball, I instantly knew I had hit a solid shot. But as I rested my club and watched the flight of the ball, I was amazed that it seemed to fly forever, coming to a rest in the fairway, some 280 yards later. Now I was blessed with only a 69-yard chip shot into the green.

After a few moments, Ernie said, "That was a great shot, my young friend. Tell me, are you going to be doing that all day?" We both laughed, and I said, "Ernie, I can only hope so." Ernie lined up his tee shot and hit a beauty, splitting the fairway and coming to a rest after 240 yards. Ernie was up next and hit his second shot safely on the green, but some 20 feet from the flag. I was able to produce a splendid shot, coming to a rest within twelve inches of the hole, for a kick-in birdie, and I was off and running. Ernie two putted for a par.

Hole number 2 was similar to the first, but this time we both scored a par. Hole number 3 was a long 175-yard par 3, with the distance from tee to green being all desert with an abundance of mesquite and thorn acacia bushes. Your only option was to land on the green. We both accomplished the required shot and walked away with pars. Now after three holes I was one under, and Ernie was at even for the day. I was told I was two strokes out of the lead. The usual contingency of players were in attendance. There was Harry Bonham and John Packard as well as Mac Grey and my friend from Houston Stan Ford. But oddly enough, the one I expected to be there, wasn't. Of course, I'm referring to Jessie Davis, the California kid.

The front nine saw Ernie pick up a birdie to tie me at one under, now four strokes out of the lead. I looked for the girls in the crowd following us and spotted Doreen and Sarah still there with us. Doreen had chosen to wear a long white cotton dress with a wide-brim straw sun hat. She appeared to be unperturbed by the heat and beautiful as always. When I managed to look in her direction, our eyes met, and she gave me an encouraging smile and put her hand to her lips to blow me a kiss.

As the day wore on, the heat was beginning to intensify, and I was starting to feel my training regimen of riding my bicycle daily to strengthen my legs and to increase my endurance starting to serve me well. I noticed that Ernie was starting to wilt. He was constantly taking his hat off and wiping his brow with his forearm as the sun beat down on us and the temperature rose to what must have been close to one hundred degrees by now.

We walked over to hole 14 where an aid station had been set up for the golfers with water and damp towels available. Ernie and I both took the opportunity to take deep drinks of water and wash our face with the cool towels. I knew that Doreen and Sarah had planned ahead, wearing light clothing and bringing with them from the hotel, thermoses of cool water, and they looked none the worse for the conditions of the day.

Fourteen was a long 495-yard par 5, with a swath of the desert cutting across the fairway at the 230-yard marker that was some 50 yards wide. It would take a tremendous drive to clear the hazard, but after being refreshed by the drink of cool water and feeling reenergized, I consulted with Sammy about the prospects of going for the distance with my play club. "What do you think, can I make it?"

"Well, there is no wind and the air is dry, I mean, what do you have to lose. I'd take a shot at it if it were me."

I took a long look down the fairway trying to build up my confidence and hoping that my work all these months would not betray me, as I lined up for the longest drive I've ever attempted.

As I started my swing, I could feel the muscles in my arms flex. I came down through the ball making solid contact and stood back and watched as the ball continued to rise on a straight trajectory following the fairway, clearing the desert easily, landing safely with only 210 yards left to negotiate.

"Well, I thought your drive on the first hole was good, but, son, that was awe inspiring."

Ernie decided to not try to duplicate my effort, choosing to lay up short. Ernie was still 275 yard out and selected his driving iron for his second shot to put himself in position for an easy approach.

My decision was to go for the green in two, putting me in line for an eagle attempt. Sammy suggested that I also use my driving iron, but I felt like I had more control with a brassie, so I overruled him and struck what appeared to be a perfect shot as the ball landed gently on the green, but still some 20 feet from the hole. I missed my eagle putt and settled for a birdie. Ernie made his putt, and we both had dropped our score to now two under par, only three strokes out of the lead.

That's the way the day ended, and as we left the eighteenth hole, I shook hands with Ernie and told him I would see him tomorrow. We were told we had a noon tee time for Friday. Sammy and I met the girls, and we walked over to the resort hotel for a late lunch. A visit to our rooms to change into swim attire, then a cold iced tea and a table by the swimming pool sounded like the best way to spend the rest of our day.

Friday didn't bring any change in our score as we both remained at two under par, but the leader was at four under, so we were still in the game. We both easily made the cut and said goodbye to some thirty golfers. I felt lucky to be tied for third place at this point in the tournament. I didn't think I had played my best golf, but I still had the confidence that I could improve my position over the weekend.

As we left the golf course, I wanted to go to my room, change clothes, and take a hot bath before meeting the girls for dinner. Doreen walked with me to my room, and I could tell there was something on her mind. "Ron, can I talk to you, it'll just take a moment."

"Sure, is there something wrong?"

"No, there's not a problem, except I'm feeling guilty about costing you the extra expense for a room just for me, and I'm starting to feel a little lonely staying by myself. Do you think it would be possible if you and I shared a room? I see that all the rooms have twin beds, and if you will promise that at no time will we, let's say, you know, go all the way, then I would really like to do that. We are after all sharing a berth on the train, so why not a hotel room?"

"I would love to do that, but I'll tell you up front that it will be difficult for me to keep my hands off you. I will agree that it will be a better arrangement, both from an expense standpoint, but also it will give me more time to be with you."

"I'm just as concerned that I won't be able to keep my hands to myself, as well, but we are mature adults, and we should be able to respect each other's wishes. Don't you think?"

So with that, Doreen and I were going to be roommates for the remainder of the trip. Later that evening, as we were on our way to dinner, I stopped by the registration desk and cancelled her room for the rest of our stay there.

I hadn't told Sammy and Sarah about our new arrangement. I felt like it was better to keep that between Doreen and myself for now. So as we finished dinner and were on our way back to our rooms, we cautiously waited until Sammy and Sarah had retreated for the night, before we went into what was now our room. Not that we were lying to them, it just didn't seem like the right time to include them in our private affairs.

Once I was in bed for the night, I watched as Doreen emerged from the bathroom. In the dim light, I was surprised as she came over and sat next to me on the edge of my bed and leaned in to give me a good night kiss. I reached up and pulled her in close to me, and in an instant, we were in bed together for the first time. "You know how much I want you. I think this is going to be far more difficult than we thought." Doreen smiled and said, "Well, Ron, just consider it a dress rehearsal for what it will be like when we are finally married, just without sex at least for now."

And with that, she pulled away from me and snuggled in her own bed for the night. But I could sense her looking back at me as I was to her in the dark, both of us dreaming of what was to be our future. With that thought in mind, I was finally able to go to sleep.

The next morning I awoke before her and quietly went down to the restaurant for coffee. As I reentered the room, she was sitting up in bed smiling at me. "I'm sorry, I didn't mean to wake you, but I just wanted you to have some coffee to start your day. There's no rush, we don't tee off until 1:00 p.m., so we have plenty of time to relax before we go down for a late breakfast."

"Thank you so much. That's very considerate of you. You know, I truly believe this arrangement we find ourselves in is going to work just fine. I mean we are no longer silly teenagers, but young, mature adults in full control of our emotions and urges, don't you think?"

"Well, I'm not so sure on my part, but I will certainly give it my best effort. I am just so grateful that you were able to come with me on this great adventure. As far as sharing a room, no matter what happens, it just makes it sweeter."

Once we were dressed, we went down to the restaurant to meet Sammy and Sarah for a Saturday morning brunch, before putting in some practice time before teeing off. As I approached the first tee, Ernie was already there waiting on me, eager to go, I suppose.

The day began without any change in our score as we both parred the first four holes, but number 5 coming up was the third most difficult on the course. It was a 367-yard par 4 with a fairway that turned almost ninety degrees to the right at the 175-yard marker. There was desert and out of bounds to the left and a lake on the right. If you had the nerve, you could attempt a drive of 230 yards and fly over the lake to the fairway on the other side, leaving you a short approach of 140 yards to a green that was surrounded by sand traps. This is why hole number 5 is considered so difficult as it presents a number of challenges.

The skies were bright blue with hardly even a cloud in sight. The temperature was approaching a steamy one hundred degrees, and there was virtually no movement in the air. So the weather conditions would not be a factor; it was just a matter of if I wanted to take the risk. I felt like the 230-yard drive was no concern, but my accuracy was.

I talked with Sammy about the prospects of flying the lake with my play club, but at his suggestion, I decided to power down to a driving iron to make the turn at 180 yards, leaving me a substantial distance to the green of 187 yards. I knew choosing that option made the likelihood of making the green in two, difficult at best. But I was able to drive the ball around the curve to the 190 marker, leaving me 177 to the green and in perfect position sitting at the right center of the fairway with a great angle for my approach shot. Ernie for some reason chose to try and fly the lake with his play club. He should have known better. He was no power hitter, and his ball came up short landing in the lake.

I could tell by the look on his face that he knew he had made a tragic mistake. He was now hitting three from a position where his ball entered the lake, leaving him over 200 yards to the green, still having to encompass the lake. He lined up his shot, and using his brassie, he hit it well but still came up short of the green. He ended up with a double bogey, dropping him back to even par for the tournament. I was able to reach the green and two putted to preserve my par and stayed at two under.

We finished the front nine with no further change in our respective scores. As I began the back nine, I was informed that I was in a tie for second place, three strokes behind the leader. I was hoping to maintain that position and have a strong Sunday finish. I watched as Ernie continued to unravel and slowly drift further back in the standings. He continued to struggle on the back nine with three bogeys in a row. He finished with a birdie on hole number 18 to end up at two over par for the tournament.

After walking off the course with only Sunday's round standing between me and second-place money, I felt encouraged and confident. Knowing that I now would be sharing a room with Doreen even added to my feeling of comfort as we further explored our relationship. Before this trip, we had never spent the entire night together. Even with the agreement we have, it was still a new level of intimacy between us, and I was relishing the experience.

Sarah turned out to be a very sensitive girl as she picked up on the new interaction between Doreen and me.

"Is there something going on with you two? It just feels different, but I can't quite put my finger on it. Just the way you look at each other is not the same as yesterday. Come on what's up? You can tell Sarah." Sammy was looking on with amusement as he too ascertained that there was a new feeling in the air.

I looked at Doreen, and she smiled at me as if to say you have my permission. "Now, don't read too much into this, but yes, we have abandoned the plan for Doreen to have her own room. She is now sharing one with me for the rest of this journey, but we are doing nothing more than sharing a room for purely economic reasons. I promise nothing else is going on. We have an agreement."

"Okay, Ron, if that's what you want us to believe, it's alright with us. You both are adults, and we approve whatever is going on."

"Good, now that's out of the way, let's go eat and get ready for tomorrow. I plan on taking that second place money."

I could tell that Sammy and Sarah didn't exactly buy our story but were happy for us anyway.

Doreen and I retired to our room, and I took bathroom time first. I came out in my pajamas and crawled into bed. I decided to read a magazine article before I called it a night while Doreen was making her final preparations. Soon she appeared, but instead of settling into her bed, she came over and nestled up close to me. "What are you reading?"

"Just a story all about the future of golf. It's very interesting. It talks about how popular this sport is becoming. Virtually anybody can play, no matter your age or gender."

"Read me some of it, maybe it will put me to sleep. I'm too excited to call it a night just yet."

I started reading to her, and before long I noticed her breathing had become very easy and quiet, and I knew without looking that she had fallen asleep with her head resting on my shoulder. I gazed at her angelic face, stroked her hair, and thanked God she was mine. Before long, I too fell asleep and woke up the next morning with her still by my side. I, once again, without waking her, slipped out of bed, dressed, and went down to the restaurant to bring coffee back. When I entered the room, Doreen was awake and greeted me, "Good morning, Ron. I see I'm not in my bed. Can you tell me what happened last night, I can't seem to remember."

"Well, I started reading to you, and in a matter of moments you fell fast asleep in my bed with your arms around me and your head on my shoulder. I thought about waking you, but you were sleeping so peacefully, I didn't want to disturb you. Eventually I fell asleep also. Don't worry, I didn't break my promise to you."

Under her breath, I swear I heard her say, "Maybe, it's time you did." But I can't be sure.

Our tee time for the last round on Sunday was at 1:00 p.m. I started the day at two under par, tied with Howard Ralston, who was now my playing partner. We were three strokes behind the leader, my old friend Harry Bonham. Howard was a new acquaintance. He was an Arizona native and very familiar with this course. He was somewhat friendly in a polite way but was all business about his golf game. The surprise about Howard was that he played left-handed. I had not competed against a southpaw since Henry Markham back a couple of years ago in Tulsa. We worked our way through the front nine and both stayed at two under as we made the turn to the back nine. We had separated from the rest of the field that stood three strokes behind us.

Hole number 10 was considered to be the second hardest on the course and for good reason. First of all, it was a 378-yard par 4, requiring one to tee off over 150 yards of desert wasteland, before the narrow fairway picked up. That left 228 yards of fairway, with a lake bordering the left and deep sand traps surrounding the green. The ideal drive would be 230 yards to the right side of the fairway, leaving you 148 to the green, but accuracy was necessary. You wanted to be able to drop your second shot over the sand traps in the front, but stopping short of those in the back of the green. The green itself was comparatively small. This made pinpoint accuracy a must.

The weather was stifling with cloudless blue skies and the temperature now in all likelihood well over one hundred degrees. Howard was first up and launched a beautiful tee shot of 240 yards square in the center of the fairway. I was able to follow his lead, but my drive came to a rest some ten yards short of his, but I was in a more desirable right center position. This gave me a better angle to the pin. I still had to cover 158 yards, so Sammy handed me a spade mashie. I seldom disagree with Sammy, but I felt like with the heat, plus starting to tire some, I wanted more club, so I lobbied for a mashie. Sammy reluctantly handed me the club, expressing his opinion that it was too much club. I struck the ball cleanly but did take some velocity off my swing and planted the ball in the center of the green, some 20 feet from the flag.

Howard observed the result of my shot, and even though he was ten yards closer, he chose a mashie as well. But I don't think he took into consideration how much closer he was than me, and he didn't power down on his swing like I had. So when he hit the ball, it flew over the green and landed in one of the sand traps on the back side. He chomped down on his cigar, turned red in the face, muttered a curse, and angrily walked off, in deep conversation with his caddie.

This was no ordinary sand trap, as Howard found his ball at the bottom of a six-foot wall, with the flag within 10 feet of the trap. It would require a skilled shot straight up in the air to clear the wall, then travel no farther than 20 feet, an almost-impossible task. But Howard did the best he could muster, coming out of the trap successfully, but too strong as his ball landed 30 feet from the hole, leaving a difficult putt for a par. He missed the putt and had his first bogey of the day, dropping him back to one under. I was looking at an undulating green with what appeared to be a hard breaking left to right putt. I aimed my putt with that in mind but came up just a few inches short, leaving me with a kick-in par. I now had second place to myself.

We played the rest of the back nine without our score changing, and I was able to secure second place and the $2,000 prize that went with it. This was a cause for celebration. I picked up my winnings and gave Sammy his $400. We returned to the hotel for our last night in Scottsdale, for tomorrow we are on the train bound for San Diego, California, and the next stop on the tour.

We enjoyed a celebratory dinner and then retired to our rooms. I told Doreen I want to call Mom and tell her the good news. I'm sure she's waiting to hear from us and eager to try out her new telephone.

"Mom, I wanted to call and check up on you and let you know we won second place and $2,000. Tomorrow we are on our way to San Diego. How are you doing?"

"I'm getting along just fine. I'm so glad to hear from you. Congratulations on your win. How are you and Doreen getting along?"

"Well, she's sitting right here with me, and we are having a swell time. I'll let you go now, and I'll call you from California tomorrow."

# 12
## CHAPTER

We left Scottsdale at midmorning and boarded our train for San Diego due to arrive by late afternoon. The tournament was being held at the Whispering Pines Country Club. We had reservations at the hotel in the resort center next to the golf course. I had promised Doreen that we would have the opportunity at some point during our trip to play a round of golf. The sponsors had closed the golf course the entire week to accommodate only golfers that were registered. This gave us the opportunity to play practice rounds and familiarize ourselves with what for sure was a challenging golf course.

The clubhouse and resort hotel architecture was in a Spanish motif with thick stucco walls, red tile roof, and heavy dark wood accents around the doors and windows. It was a magnificent display with a setting on the Pacific Ocean that offered unforgettable views.

We checked into our room on Monday and now had ample time to explore San Diego, including downtown and the beaches. After settling in, we took Tuesday morning to explore the city. I think we all were impressed at how beautiful and picturesque this place was and what a delight it must be to actually live here. That afternoon we made our way to the pristine white sand beaches and marveled at the magnificence of the blue Pacific Ocean.

Wednesday morning, we were set with an 8:00 a.m. tee time for the four of us. I was not aware that Sarah played, but it turned out she was an accomplished golfer in her own right and played very well. She was no match for Doreen, however. Doreen's game had improved beyond my comprehension. I had no idea she was such a naturally talented athlete. We finished our round at noon and adjourned to the hotel for lunch. Sammy and I had a 2:00 p.m. player's meeting, and the girls returned to the rooms to freshen up and go on a shopping expedition.

At the meeting we discovered our tee time would be at 9:00 a.m. on Thursday, and my partner would be a San Diego native by the name of Joe Thompson. The purse would be $4,000 for first place, $3,000 for second, and $2,000 for third. Players that finished fourth through tenth would win $200, and the entry fee was $200.

After the stifling desert heat of Scottsdale, Arizona, it was a relief to be in the Mediterranean climate of San Diego with temperatures mostly in the eighties with slight humidity blowing in off the Pacific Ocean, ideal conditions for golf.

Our room at the resort hotel was one of luxury I was not familiar with. It was a spacious suite with comfortable twin beds and a large bathroom with both a tub and shower. We had a sitting room adjacent to our bedroom with a couch and chairs, and we had a spectacular view of the ocean from our third floor picture window.

"Are you regretting giving up your own personal room to move in with a chump like me?"

"Oh no, quite the opposite. I am enjoying myself and your company immensely. It certainly seems like we are entirely comfortable around each other in every way."

I met Joe on the first tee Thursday morning, and he had the honor of going first. I was grateful for that since he had experienced playing this course many times. Joe was a quiet man in demeanor, a man of few words, but hopefully as the day unfolded, I could learn from him and his knowledge of this course. However, he didn't show any indication of being forthcoming with advice, so my only option was to observe and try to follow his lead.

The first hole was a 364-yard par 4 that was relatively straight but with a drop-off of a fairway leading back up to a green that was encompassed by deep sand traps. I was told that the fairway grass was called Kikuyu and the greens were bent grass. The rough bordering the fairway was ankle-deep California fescue that was very thick and tangled. The rough was something you wanted to avoid at all costs as this grass would literally grab your ball and hold it, requiring a swing of some velocity to free your ball with any kind of distance. The fairway was lined with large eucalyptus trees, requiring accuracy off the tee box.

Joe nailed his drive some 240 yards, landing safely in the center of the fairway, leaving him a second shot of 124 yards. Because I find myself able to push the ball with greater distance, I chose to play conservative and tee off with my brassie and ended up safely at the 220-yard mark. Sammy handed me the mashie niblick for my second shot. I was able to drive the ball to the right side of the green, some 20 feet from the hole. Joe was considerably more accurate as his ball came to a rest within 5 feet of the pin. Joe secured his birdie while I two putted for a par.

The score remained that way as we walked up on what was considered to be the highest handicap hole, number 7. It was a 387-yard par 4 with the Pacific Ocean on the right that provided a steady yet unpredictable breeze coming in at a right to left angle. It was a beautiful setting, but if you pushed your drive too far to the right, your ball would sail over a 30-foot-high cliff and into the Pacific. The left didn't offer much solace as it was lined with a thick assortment of pine and eucalyptus trees with an abundance of pine straw and the aforementioned thick California fescue.

I could now see why this was the number one handicap as it presented multiple challenges. I looked toward the crowd to find Doreen. Once our eyes met, she blew me a kiss and smiled at me as if to say, "You can do this, don't worry." Joe teed off and flirted with the ocean as he intentionally hit a swooping draw above the cliff and the ocean below, curving back to a perfect position in the fairway. I don't think I had ever seen anybody accomplish a shot quite like that; it was most impressive.

I chose the more conservative route, selecting my play club and fade my shot more to the left side of the fairway. But I overcompensated and went too far left with my ball ending up in the dreaded California fescue.

I knew my miss hit had cost me as I still had 180 yards left to negotiate, so Sammy handed me my driving iron. I took as vicious a cut at the ball as I was capable of, and here my weight training came into play. I watched as the ball sprang free of the fescue on a direct course to the green, coming up ten yards short. Joe had dropped his ball on his second shot within 15 feet of the flag, putting him in position for another birdie.

I dropped my jigger shot within six inches of the hole, preserving my par, while Joe completed his birdie effort to go to two under as we approached the turn. I was unable to pick up any ground on the back nine, playing even par golf for the day, while Joe picked up another birdie to go three under.

Friday's round didn't yield any change in my score as I was finding this golf course most challenging. But Joe didn't improve either as he finished the day still at three under. Hopefully, Saturday will be a turning point for me as in the current standings I am in twelfth place, way out of the money.

For Saturday, I made the cut, but barely, and I was now paired with Ernie Hudson, my playing partner from Scottsdale. We both were at even par, eight strokes out of the lead. Our score remained that way until hole number 12, which was a very short 105-yard par 3, but it was considered to be the second hardest hole. The reason for that was it featured an elevated tee box of some 50 feet above the green that looked like a postage stamp down below us. It was surrounded by sand traps with the Pacific Ocean on the right that produced unpredictable wind gusts.

One would think that the proper club for that distance would be the jigger, but not necessarily as many golfers misjudged the distance. Using that club tended to produce a shot that came up short, ending up with the ball in a sand trap that guarded the front of the green. With that in mind, I decided to take a cut swing with my niblick, trying to hit a high, arcing shot just to land somewhere safely on the green. As I launched the shot, I felt like I had hit it way too hard, but a gust of wind caught it and dropped my ball gently on the green. My ball rolled up to some 10 feet from the flag, giving me a reasonable chance at my first birdie for the entire tournament.

Ernie was not as successful as he overshot the green and landed in a sand trap on the back side. He was able to recover, punched out, and one putted for a par. I sank my putt for a birdie giving me a one under score. With that birdie I was able to move up to eighth place as the leader remained at eight under.

Hole 18 saw me finish with a birdie, and Ernie posted an eagle, moving us both to a two under score with only Sunday's round remaining. As we walked off the golf course, I asked some of the local fellows where would be a suitable place for Sammy and I to take the girls out on the town. It was suggested to me that the Pacifica Palisades Hotel had a wonderful indoor and outdoor combination dinner and dancing club that was first-class all the way. The outdoor part of the club was on a pier that jutted out over the Pacific Ocean, with the indoor featuring dining facilities and a large dance floor with usually a famous band performing.

When we got back to the room, I asked Doreen, "It's time we went out and had some fun, don't you think? Let's get way from golf for an evening and enjoy what San Diego has to offer. Some of the local golfers told me about this really swell place right on the Pacific Ocean, perfect for dining and dancing."

"That sounds delightful. When Sarah and I went out shopping, I found this divine new evening gown suited just for this occasion, and I think you are going to absolutely love it."

I dressed first in a three-piece navy blue pinstripe suit and waited for Doreen to emerge from the bathroom in this mysterious new dress. Doreen never disappoints, and this was no exception as she entered the room wearing an elegant emerald green evening gown that appeared to be made of silk and virtually hugged her every curve. I must have had my mouth wide open as she laughed and said, "You must like. You can close your mouth now and be a dear and come zip me up." I walked over, zipped up her gown, and gave her a gentle kiss on her bare neck. With that, she pushed back up against me. "We're going to have a marvelous time tonight, I can just tell."

We were waiting to meet Sammy and Sarah in the lobby. When they appeared, Sarah looked stunning in a white evening gown that perfectly set off her deep tan, auburn hair, and soft brown eyes. She and Sammy both had that dark, exotic look about them and were in every sense a perfect match.

We arrived by taxi at the Pacifica Palisades Hotel, and it was everything I had been told it was. The hotel was in the popular Southern California Spanish Mission decor with thick white adobe walls and red tile roof. Entry into the hotel was through a large arched doorway into the main foyer. As we walked through the lobby, we found our way to the hotel supper club. It was a large room decorated with murals of California scenery on each wall and intimate tables for a party of four seating with soft velvet chairs. As the maître d' guided us to our table, you could see heads turn to look at Sarah and Doreen as we walked by. They both had to be the most glamorous ladies in the hotel. There was a large dance floor in front of a massive bandstand. The band tonight was orchestrated by the famous Benny Goodman. The song they were playing fit right in with the night, I think it was called "Let's Dance."

We ordered dinner, and Doreen chose a sweet and spicy chicken with roasted sweet potatoes and asparagus, with a dollop of chili-garlic sauce to add some spice to her meal. I, in keeping with my training, ordered a thick porterhouse steak with a loaded baked potato. Sarah ordered asparagus-stuffed chicken filled with provolone and parmesan, while Sammy joined me with a T-bone steak and french fries. We had water and iced tea for drinks since this was still prohibition, and this place was no speakeasy.

We danced and enjoyed the evening until midnight, then decided to call it an early night. I had an important round of golf to play tomorrow. But before we left, we walked out on the pier overlooking the ocean to feel the cool breeze and listen to the waves crashing against the shore. Doreen began to shiver, so I took off my jacket and wrapped it around her shoulders. She leaned into me, and we stood there for several moments taking in the beauty of the Pacific Ocean and the moonlit night. As we were leaving, Doreen said, "Well, wasn't that just a gas? I can't remember when I've had a better time."

Back at the hotel, we dressed for bed, discreetly of course. As I was preparing to douse the lights for the night, Doreen came over and sat on the edge of my bed. "Ron, it was an absolutely marvelous night, one that I'll never forget. I truly believe that we have many more in our future just like tonight, don't you think?"

"I couldn't agree more. I am convinced that we are just at the beginning of our life experience for many, many years to come."

She gave me an exquisite good night kiss and then retreated to her own bed for the night. I looked in her direction in the darkened room and listened as her breathing indicated she had drifted off before I finally fell asleep myself.

As I awoke Sunday morning, I was surprised to see Doreen sitting at the side of my bed smiling at me. "Good morning, you're up awfully early. Is that coffee I smell?"

"Yes, I felt like it was my turn to fetch, so I dressed and quietly made my way down to the restaurant. I've been sitting here for the last few moments just watching you sleep. Were you dreaming?"

"I'm always dreaming of you, my love."

"Today, I find myself six strokes out of first place and not even in the running for third place. But I feel inspired, especially after last night to go out and post my best round of golf ever. My goal is to shoot no worse than four under and finish in the money."

"I have confidence that you will do just that, and I will be right there with you all day."

My tee time was at 11:00 a.m. with Ernie still my partner for this last round. We shook hands and wished each other good luck for the day. Ernie and I both stood at two under with the leader at eight under. Second place score was seven under par and third place was at five under. So clearly we had our work cut out for us to try and move up to at least third place.

Maybe I was too excited or overconfident, but I started the day on hole number 1 with a bogey, dropping me back to one under par. I could not imagine a worse start for the day. Now I really had ground to make up. My goal of posting a four under score was already starting to slip away from me. I stayed at one under until we reached hole number 9, which was a 452-yard par 5, featuring a fairway that turned to the right at the 200-yard mark. It was bordered by thick California fescue and a mixture of pine and eucalyptus trees. The desired tee shot was one of a gentle fade around the turn, following the fairway for an easy approach. There were deep sand traps in front and to the right of the green.

Ernie teed off first but was unable to drive his ball around the turn as it went straight and into a grove of pine trees and pine straw. The only shot he had was to execute a hook shot around the trees, but he pushed it too far ending up in the thick rough. I was able to execute a perfect drive as my ball followed the fairway coming to a rest at the 260-yard marker, leaving me a clear shot to the green at a distance of 190 yards. Ernie was now laying three and still over 200 yards from the green. He pulled his brassie, but as he made contact with the ball, it immediately drifted too far right. He ended up with a double bogey and for all practical purposes eliminated himself from contention.

I chose a driving iron for my second shot to easily cover the remaining 190 yards. The San Diego weather was ideal with a bright sunny blue sky and virtually no breeze. I swung down hard on the ball and watched as it lifted up on an exact line to the flag, coming to a rest at only 6 feet from the hole. I finished with an easy putt for an eagle, making up for the bogey on the first hole and now I was at three under, only five strokes behind the leader.

I followed up on hole 10 with another birdie and moved up to now four under and followed with a par on 11 and a birdie on 12, now at five under, only one stroke out of third place. I was having quite a day. I parred hole 13 through 16. The golfer one stroke in front of me at six under had picked up a bogey, and now I was in a tie for third place. My goal was to finish the last two holes with at least one birdie and hope he didn't duplicate my effort, giving me third place outright.

The Pacific Ocean bordered hole 17 on the left with the fairway curving at a right-to-left direction. This was a 347-yard par 4, and the ideal drive was with a slight draw, of course keeping it from being too much of a draw and in the fairway. If you drove the ball too far, then the Pacific Ocean came into play. I felt like my driving iron was my best option to tee off with as there was a brisk left to right breeze coming in off the Pacific, making any drive treacherous. My reasoning was that I could hit my ball almost as far with a driving iron as my play club but could maintain a low trajectory, keeping the wind from being a factor. I went into my swing and hit the desired drive as my ball came to a rest 150 yards out.

With the wind influencing my decision, I knew that my next shot would be into the wind, so I went up one club to a mashie and was able to drive my ball to within 3 feet of the pin and sank the putt for birdie, taking me to now six under, alone in third place and only one stroke out of second place. I had reached five under par for the day, surpassing my goal of four under with one hole left.

I was having the kind of day that all golfers dream of. I could do no wrong as I approached the last hole. I parred 18, but the good news was that the gentleman in second place ahead of me had faltered, and I was now in a tie for second place. As luck would have it, he bogeyed 18, handing me second place outright and the $3,000 prize money.

We walked off the eighteenth green in an ecstatic mood as I realized I now had enough money to finally register for college for the spring 1933 semester. After paying Sammy $600 and wiring the same to Mom, I still had $4,600 saved with two more tournaments to go. Next up was Los Angeles.

We stayed one last night in beautiful San Diego, a city we all liked and regretted to leave. Maybe one day, Doreen and I could come back for a visit. But for now, it was onto the next contest, the Los Angeles Open, being held at the Southern California Country Club. We had booked rooms close to the golf course at the Roosevelt Hotel.

Monday morning we had one last breakfast at our hotel then an excursion through San Diego before boarding the noon train that was to take us into Los Angeles. It was a short train ride, and we arrived midafternoon. Once we had checked in at the Roosevelt, we went to the golf course to register and set up a Wednesday practice round for the four of us. Tuesday was set aside for a Los Angeles exploration day.

Our hotel was a Southern California tradition, or so we were told. It was built back in the 1860s just after the Civil War and held many tales of the celebrity visitors that had stayed there over the years. Rumor had it the hotel was haunted by those spirits. Now I don't really believe in ghosts, but allegedly there were several strange sightings of apparitions that had been documented. It certainly had the girls apprehensive, but Sammy and I scoffed at the very idea and promised we would protect them. I do believe that Doreen was grateful that she was not staying in a room by herself; besides, we had become very good roommates.

The old Roosevelt Hotel boasted one of the finest restaurants in all of Los Angeles. It was located in the basement of the hotel, the very same basement dining where the original Academy Award ceremony was held back in 1927. Our rooms were on the fifth floor giving us a spectacular view of the mountains. We each had a spacious suite with a bathroom and a large bedroom with twin beds, and a love seat in a parlor by a fireplace that was in each room. However, this being August, all the fireplaces were inactive. The floors were the original wood from the 1860s, covered by colorful Oriental area rugs. At night one could hear the old floors creak and groan as the temperature turned cooler.

We had settled in for the night, and I was doing some light reading of the local newspaper, waiting for Doreen to emerge from the bathroom. Finally she did, and is now our custom, she came over and gave me a good night kiss before returning to her bed. I turned out the lights, and we both fell asleep until I heard Doreen say, "What was that?" I looked over to her, and in the dim light I could see she was sitting straight up in her bed. Of course, Sammy and I had teased the girls with ghost stories of the hotel, and I suppose that was fresh on her mind.

"What did you hear?"

"I thought I heard someone groaning like they were in pain."

"It was probably just these old floors complaining, I'm sure it's nothing. Try to go back to sleep. We have a big day tomorrow."

"Okay, I'll try. But I am a little spooked."

"It will be alright, I'm here to protect you, don't forget."

I had no sooner laid back down when I heard a noise of some kind, and the next thing I knew, Doreen had jumped into my bed and pulled the covers up over her. "I'm scared. You don't mind if I join you, do you?" I laughed and put my arms around her and pulled her in close. She buried her head on my chest.

"I never mind being this close to you."

"I'll go back to my own bed as soon as I'm convinced we are truly alone in here."

I kissed her and ran my fingers through her hair, and soon we were both sound asleep with no further ghost incident. But she never did go back to her bed, and I found her warmth and the essence of her to be intoxicating.

Our relationship changed that night and only for the better. We met Sammy and Sarah in the lobby the next morning to begin our tour of Los Angeles. Doreen whispered to me as we were walking into the dining room, "Ron, I wouldn't say anything to Sammy or Sarah about last night. Maybe we should just keep that to ourselves at least for now."

"I agree completely. But not that we're hiding anything, it was just a personal experience."

We enjoyed a breakfast of scrambled eggs, bacon, and cottage potatoes, with an abundance of coffee, then ventured into the warm California sun. There were so many famous things we wanted to see, starting with a tour of a movie studio, then a bus tour of the Hollywood stars' homes in the hills surrounding Los Angeles. After that we spent the afternoon at the beach in Santa Monica. We had been told of the Santa Monica Pier that jutted out over the Pacific Ocean. It was referred to as the Pleasure Pier with many attractions and snack food; plus, there was a new carousel that we all wanted to ride. California is truly a magnificent place, and we wanted to enjoy all that we could to the fullest.

After leaving the Pleasure Pier, we walked down to the Venice Beach Boardwalk and took in the myriad of sights that was offered, including several fantastic restaurants and stores. I wanted to get a California souvenir for Mom and something for Robert and Margaret. The girls wanted to shop as well.

So a wonderful day was coming to a close as the evening was upon us. With that, the cool air started coming in off the ocean. We weren't really dressed for the drop in temperature, so we returned to our hotel, had a light dinner there, and called it a night to get plenty of rest for our practice golf game the next morning. It was the beginning of what promised to be a very busy week.

Our Wednesday tee time was at 11:00 a.m., giving us ample time for breakfast and practice before we took the course. As the day wore on, I was astounded at how accomplished at the game of golf that Doreen was becoming. Who knows, maybe she may be a championship level golfer in her own right. Sarah was no slouch as she was playing quite well also.

We finished our round at 3:00 p.m., and Sammy and I went directly to the golfer's meeting, while the girls returned to the hotel to freshen up and prepare for the coming night's activities. All the best golfers were there, including Harry Bonham, John Packard, and Mac Grey. My old friend Jessie Davis finally made an appearance with the same arrogant swagger. It appears he still hasn't learned anything about the polite aspects of the game of golf. All I can say is, Lord, save me from being paired with him again. I was rescued when I discovered that my playing partner at least for the first two days was my old friend from Arizona, the lefty, Howard Ralston.

The purse for this contest was the same as it was in San Diego—$4,000 for first, $3,000 for second, $2,000 for third, with fourth trough tenth each winning $200, with a $200 entry fee. My tee time was set for 9:00 a.m. on Thursday. Doreen and I decided to have an early dinner and listen to some music in a close by jazz club before retiring early in preparation for our Thursday tee time.

The golf course was magnificent and was nestled in the foothills of the San Gabriel Mountains, but it just didn't seem to fit my game. I struggled right from the outset and never seemed to gain traction. So for the first time on this Western tour, it appeared that I was so hopelessly so far behind that I would not be able to finish in the money.

Doreen offered some encouragement Thursday night, but in truth I wasn't really all that upset. Before Los Angeles, this venture had been successful beyond my wildest dreams. Friday didn't appear to be any better as I didn't seem to have my game at all. Sammy pulled me to the side and said, "Look, Ron, you can't win them all. We have done well and have one more tournament before we return to Texas. Maybe you just need some rest." I guess he was right, if you stop and think about it. I had already earned more than enough in winnings to put me well past my stated goal of $3,000 for my college fund. I had paid both Sammy and Mom $1,000 each, which was more than either could earn in almost a year at their jobs back in Dallas. Sammy wasn't complaining and neither was Mom.

Saturday, I teed off in a mood of resignation, and surprisingly I played much better. I suppose being relaxed made for a better game of golf. I decided that these last two rounds would serve to prepare me for our final tournament in California in Monterey Bay. My main focus at the moment was for Doreen's birthday celebration that night as we celebrate her twentieth.

Thinking ahead. I had made reservations at the world-famous Brown Derby and the Cocoanut Grove for Doreen's birthday. So far I had not even told Sammy of my plans, but as we left the golf course and returned to the hotel, I decided it was time to let them in on my secret. "Before we go to our rooms, I want to tell you all that I have a surprise in store for us this evening. I planned this out before we left Texas, especially for Doreen's birthday. Tonight we are dining at the Brown Derby and then dancing at the Cocoanut Grove." Doreen put her arms around my neck and leaned in close, gave me a kiss, and said, "Ron, that's fantastic and so special that you would honor me on my birthday with such a considerate gift. I'm sure we'll have a swell time."

"Sounds grand, Ron, count me and Sarah in."

We returned to our rooms to dress for the evening. We all met in the lobby and Doreen and Sarah as well looked absolutely splendid in their evening attire. We took a taxi to the Brown Derby on Wilshire Boulevard. The restaurant was accurately named as the entrance looked like a "Brown Derby." We walked through the main entrance and were escorted by a tuxedo-clad waiter past walls adorned with caricatures of famous patrons such as Pola Negri, Rudolph Valentino, and others to a high-backed booth. The waiter addressed us as we were seated, "Ladies and gentlemen, welcome to the Brown Derby. I'll be serving you tonight. Would you, fine folks, be interested in hearing a little of the history of this establishment?" I spoke up and said, "Yes, we would be most entertaining. We are all here from Texas for the Los Angeles golf tournament and have heard of your fine restaurant, tell us more."

"Are you a golfer, sir?"

"Yes, I like to think of myself that way."

"Welcome to our fine city, and I hope you do well in your golf career. Now, about the Brown Derby, it was opened just six years ago in 1926 by Herbert Somborn and Bob Cobb, who both were involved in the movie industry. This restaurant immediately became a favorite of movie stars such as Mary Pickford and Cecil B. DeMille, who by the way is a part owner. You just might see somebody famous tonight, for you see this restaurant was designed so that everyone could see everyone else. The tables are set in a semicircular brown leather banquette. All of our waitresses are would-be actresses that wear very short and highly starched skirts hoping to be seen and noticed by a director or producer."

The waiter continued. He had us all enthralled with his tale and the possibility of seeing a famous movie star or director. "You see, unlike many Los Angeles eateries, where service matters more than sustenance, the food here is considered to be excellent. I do so hope you enjoy your evening, now what may I bring you to drink? Just a note, but our coffee is world-famous for its flavor. May I suggest that and water for everyone."

"Sounds perfect, thank you."

As our waiter returned with drinks, I asked, "Are we all ready to order?" Doreen spoke first, "I'll have your famous Cobb salad. I have always wanted to try that." Sarah ordered the pan-seared fish of the day, while Sammy went with charred pork chops with cauliflower, sweet and sour sauce, and hash browns. I chose char-grilled filet of beef with sweet potatoes. The food was quickly at our table, and after dining we all agreed it was as heavenly as advertised. For dessert, Doren and I chose to share a piece of the chocolate mousse cake while Sammy and Sarah shared an espresso cheesecake.

After dinner, Sammy and I enjoyed a cigarette, and we all had another round of their delicious coffee. As we were sitting there enjoying the ambiance, I spotted who I thought to be Carole Lombard entering the restaurant and being ushered to her table.

"Doreen, look over there. Isn't that Carole Lombard?"

Doreen turned to look and said, "Ron, I think you're right, but who is that with her?" I took a second glance. "If I'm not mistaken that appears to be William Powell, her husband."

"Well, we did get to see somebody famous after all, didn't we?"

"Next up, we are going to the Cocoanut Grove in the Ambassador Hotel. Rumor has it that both Loretta Young and Joan Crawford were discovered while dancing there." We carefully made our way across Wilshire Boulevard and into the stately Ambassador Hotel. We walked through an imposing entryway into the Cocoanut Grove ballroom. We were in awe of the grandeur with the Mediterranean styling with tile floors and Italian stone fireplaces with a semitropical courtyard.

We were guided to our table by our hostess. I was curious about the nightclub, so I asked her a question, "Excuse me, miss, but we're from out of town, could you tell us a little about this fine establishment?"

"I would be delighted. Let's see, where should I start. Well, the Cocoanut Grove was opened in 1921 and is decorated in an art deco motif. The club instantly became a mecca for movie stars and star gazers. You'll notice the artificial palm trees. They are left over from the Rudolph Valentino's 1921 movie *The Sheik*. The Academy Award ceremony was held in this very ballroom last year. Several of your Hollywood stars such as Errol Flynn, Jean Harlow, and Clark Gable are frequent guests. They very well may be here sometime tonight, so keep an eye out. You may be rubbing shoulders on the dance floor with the likes of John Wayne or Lucille Ball."

"Thank you, miss, that is very enlightening."

"Oh, and one more thing, our Cocoanut Grove orchestra is excellent, and the singer with the band is Loyce Whiteman. Have a great time tonight."

We didn't see any celebrities, maybe they were there, but we were having such a good time we didn't notice. We danced until the early hours of Sunday morning and returned to our hotel.

This excursion we're on has opened up a new facet of my relationship with Doreen. I find her more dear now than before we left, and I didn't think that was possible. We both readied for bed, but this time she stayed with me and fell asleep with her arms around my neck as I held her especially close tonight.

Sunday morning, I finished my final round, totally out of the money brackets in thirteenth place. We returned to the hotel for one last night in Los Angeles, before boarding our train Monday morning on our way to the Monterey Peninsula and our last tournament in California. The train ride was going to take all day to get to the golf course and resort, but we were all ready for the change.

# 13
## CHAPTER

We arrived at the Monterey Resort at 7:00 p.m. and checked into our hotel. Once we were in our room, we found this to be every bit as delightful as our other accommodations have been along the way. The PGL is nothing if not first-class in the manner in which they treat their members. The hotel was within walking distance of the golf course which was located on a peninsula that jutted out into the Pacific Ocean with fabulous vistas at every turn. What an amazing picturesque course this was going to be. The temperature in Northern California was considerably cooler, particularly for this time of the year with a constant breeze coming in off the ocean.

Tuesday would be a day of orientation and exploration of the region as we adjusted to our new surroundings. Since we had some extra time on our hands and none of us had ever seen San Francisco, we decided to make a day trip there. I asked the clerk about the possible ways to travel and found out that San Francisco was only 112 miles. There was a train that left every morning at 8:00 a.m. and arrived in San Francisco at 10:00 a.m. and returned each day to Monterey at 5:00 p.m. "I can make reservations for you, sir, if you would like. And to help you out on what to see when you are there, I have a selection of brochures that should tell you everything you need to know." Now we were armed and ready to begin our last California experience.

We all reviewed the information and selected several sights to see. Doreen wanted to start with the Palace of Fine Arts located in the Marina District, a San Francisco landmark since it was built in 1916 for the Panama-Pacific International Exposition. From there we went to the Fisherman's Wharf, then the Mission District. Riding in one of the cable cars that San Francisco was world-famous for was essential. The pilot of the car told us the story of the origination of the cable cars. "In the late 1800s, many wealthy San Francisco residents were building homes and living on the top of steep hills. It was almost impossible for horses and carriages to safely negotiate these hills, so the city of San Francisco started to build the cable car lines. By 1889, there were eight different lines running through the city."

We had lunch in Union Square, which was the heart of the city, then it was on to Chinatown which was bordered by Union Square, Nob Hill, and North Beach. Sarah wanted to see the Japanese Tea Garden. The information we had told was that the tea garden opened in 1894 as part of a world's fair and was called the California Midwinter International Exposition. It was indeed a beautiful and peaceful garden that featured an arched drum bridge and pagodas.

Our last stop was the Coit Tower, which according to our brochure was gifted to the city of San Francisco by Lillie Hitchcock Coit, who was a well-known and controversial resident from the late 1800s to the early 1900s. Two draws to the tower are the historic murals on the first level that depicted life in San Francisco and California in the 1920s and 1930s. The second is the view from the top of the tower with a spectacular 360-degree view of the surrounding area. Our day spent, it was time to board our train back to Monterey.

Wednesday morning we were scheduled for our final round of golf in California for the four of us before the start of the tournament on Thursday. We all played well, but my attention was on the next day. I had never managed to win a golf tournament in my brief career, but I was determined to make this one my first victory. The rumor we had heard of a $10,000 first-place prize was just that, a rumor. Actually, $5,000 would be first place money, still the largest purse I had ever competed for, with $4,000 for second place, $3,000 for third, with $500 going to the fourth- through tenth-place finisher. It was a $250 entry fee.

At the players' meeting on Wednesday afternoon, I eagerly waited to find out who my playing partner was going to be for at least Thursday and Friday. I had to ironically laugh when it was announced it would be my buddy, Jessie Davis. Once again he has surfaced into my world. Our tee time was 9:00 a.m. Then I saw Jessie across the crowded room. He hadn't seen me yet, but he was aware that I would be playing with him. I made my way over to him, just to try and shake his hand, the gentlemanly thing to do or so I thought.

"Hello, Jessie, we meet again."

"I'm sorry, do I know you, sir? Just kidding, of course I remember you and what happened the last time we played together. Well, then we were on your home turf, now you are on mine. I assure you we will see different results. You might as well go on home now because I'm going to humiliate you tomorrow to the point that you'll be begging to get off the course and on the train home."

"Jessie, that's awful big talk coming from an amateur like yourself. So why don't we just wait and see what happens tomorrow."

With that Jessie scowled, uttered an obscenity under his breath, and walked off. Some things never change.

As we walked back to the hotel, Doreen posed a question, "Aren't you worried that playing with this obnoxious creep is going to distract you?"

"No, you know what, I really believe he is going to motivate me to play better. I'd like nothing better than to beat old Jessie again."

Our tee time was fast approaching, and as I walked up to the first tee, Jessie was standing there waiting for me.

"Well, Perkins, it looks like to me you have added some weight. I hope you don't think that's going to help you any. Listen, I assume you've never played this course before. Am I right?"

"Yes, Jessie, that's a good assumption."

"Well, Perkins, I have. Many times, but if you're expecting any help from me, you will be sorely disappointed."

"Jessie, I would have been truly astounded if you have ever offered any help to anybody at any time. With that in mind, it will give me great pleasure to wipe you out again, just like I did back in Texas. I want you to keep that in mind."

The first hole was a 325-yard par 4 that had a slight turn to the right around a collection of pine trees and thick underbrush at the 175-yard marker. The conservative play was to hit a brassie off the tee and fade the shot around the turn some 200 yards, leaving a clear approach shot to the green of some 125 yards. An option was to fly the pine trees, thereby shortening the hole considerably. I knew that Jessie was still a powerful man, most assuredly capable of doing just that. But he surprised me and chose his driving iron and followed the fairway perfectly to a position of some 120 yards from the green, in an ideal position. I chose a brassie, and my ball rolled up close to Jessie's, so we were both looking at a safe approach shot of a reasonable distance.

The green was encompassed by sand traps all around, so accuracy was at a premium. I was a bit further out than Jessie, so I went first. I selected a pitching niblick and was able to land within 6 feet of the pin. Jessie followed suit, landed in close proximity of my ball, and we both one putted for a birdie. Jessie made no comment, just smirked and walked to the second tee box.

My confidence soared after a successful start to what promised to be a challenge to my golfing skills. The next hole presented many obstacles. It was a long 480-yard par 5 with a fairway that curved to the right with sand traps that dotted the fairway all the way up to and including the green. There were trees on both sides and thick California fescue grass that was the first cut bordering the fairway. If you pushed your drive too far either way, you were in rough terrain or sand traps, so caution off the tee was essential.

Jessie teed off first and produced an accurate drive of 270 yards.

"Okay, Perkins, let's see you match that."

I smiled at Jessie and stroked a drive of 260 yards coming to a rest in the center of the fairway. "You mean, kind of like that?" I was now only 220 yards out, and I was sure I could reach the green in two. Sammy and I agreed on a brassie, and I was able to lift my shot on a high arc, going right at dead center of the green, rolling to within 10 feet of the flag.

Jessie smiled sarcastically at me, tipped his hat, and went into his swing motion, producing an equally accurate second shot, ending up in position for an eagle putt as well. I knelt down and measured my putt, thinking I saw a slight break to the right just before the hole, and I played it that way. That turned out to be a correct assumption as my ball rolled into the dead center of the hole, giving me a birdie-eagle start for a three under score after just two holes. Remarkably, Jessie missed his putt and had to settle for a birdie. Now I had a one stroke lead over my old nemesis, and I could tell by his demeanor, he wasn't taking it well. I only hoped he had in his mind what happened the last time we squared off.

The third hole was a 355-yard par 4 that turned back toward the Pacific bringing into play unpredictable winds to be considered for the rest of the front nine. But I was prepared for it and knew to play the headwinds coming at us. Feeling confident and against the wishes of Sammy, I chose to tee off with my play club since the fairway was straight, thinking I would leave myself a short chip shot into the green. But I should have listened to Sammy as I hit the ball too high with the wind catching the ball and pushing it too far to the right into a thick layer of pine needles. The wind held my drive to only 200 yards, leaving me with a difficult second shot of some 155 yards.

Jessie gave me a wink as if to say, that's your first mistake, and chose a driving iron. He hit a low, straight drive that left his ball on the right side of the fairway, some 135 yards from the green and in considerable better position than me. From my angle, I would have to try and shape a shot, aiming to the left side of the fairway, bringing the ball back to the right. Hitting off the pine straw was unpredictable at best, for if I over swung and made too solid of a contact, the ball may fly past the green into a sand trap. On the other hand, if I hit more pine straw than ball, the distance would not be enough.

I chose to change my stance, so the ball was forward, trying to hit it low, taking the wind out of play. I chose a spade mashie as my best option. I caught the ball cleanly and hit one of my best shots of the day as I watched the flight of the ball advancing across the green, coming to a rest of some 4 feet from the hole. Even Jessie had to shake his head in disbelief at that one. I putted out and had another birdie, leaving me at four under and safely in the lead. Jessie mishit his second shot and had to settle for a two putt par, leaving him two strokes behind me.

I unexpectedly had started this day out on fire. I took a moment to survey the crowd looking for Doreen. I spotted her almost immediately, tipped my hat to her as our eyes met, and she smiled back at me with a look of pride on her face. She was indeed my inspiration.

I stayed at four under for the rest of the front nine, remaining in the lead by at least two strokes over the rest of the field. Hole 10 was a 390-yard par 4 bordered by the Pacific Ocean on the left. The fairway turned slightly to the left hugging the ocean and a thirty-foot-high drop-off to the Pacific below. If your ball went too far left, then you were solidly out of play. On the right side was a thick stand of sycamore trees and ankle-deep California fescue grass.

So the best shot off the tee would be a slight draw into a stiff breeze coming in off the ocean. I was able to execute a drive of 250 yards that left me on the right side of the fairway, in exceptional position to approach the green still 140 yards away. Jessie's drive exceeded mine by twenty yards. Sammy suggested a mashie niblick, and I agreed as the wind had turned to a left-to-right direction, helping slightly. I hit a high shot into the green, with my ball coming to a rest 20 feet from the hole. Jessie placed his effort some 10 feet from the hole, leaving him in better position to pick up a birdie and a stroke on me. My ball was directly behind Jessie's by 10 feet. He smiled at me and said, "Well, Perkins, I seem to have you in a bind. According to the rules, I don't have to move my ball. You have to go over or around. Let's see how you do." This was a totally legal maneuver on his part, but by now was not considered to be very sporting. But then Jessie had never been accused of being a good sport.

I couldn't really blame him as he was a competitive fellow and was in fact two strokes behind me. I'm sure he saw this as his chance to gain on me. Sammy and I got down on our knees and measured what we thought would be the breaks the ball would take on the way to the hole. We both agreed that if I could begin a path just to the right of Jessie's ball and bring it back to the left on a line that should come close to, if not in the hole, if the speed was right.

When I hit the putt and saw it curve by Jessie's ball just as we wanted, then turn back to the left following the breaks in the green, on a direct line to the hole, I knew it had a chance of going in. The ball was traveling a little faster than we wanted, so when it hit the hole, it did a 360 around the hole and dropped in for a birdie, putting me now at five under for the day. Jessie gathered his composure and made his putt for a birdie, dropping him to now three under par.

I stayed at five under for the rest of the round, and after all golfers had completed the round, I was still the leader, with Jessie at three under, my closest competitor. I realize this was just one day with a lot of golf still to be played, but I felt like I couldn't be beaten. I was on the verge of winning my first tournament, but I knew I had to be careful with my emotions and not get too overconfident.

Doreen joined me as we left the course and walked back over to the resort hotel with Sammy and Sarah along with us. Our accommodations were beyond luxurious with a large suite, featuring picture windows with a view overlooking the Pacific Ocean. Each room had its own fireplace with thick carpeting and couches and easy chairs around the fireplace. The other room contained two twin beds and an adjoining bathroom. The temperature in Northern California, particularly on the peninsula, was considerably cooler than Southern California, dropping into the forties at night, so the fire was a really swell touch.

After freshening up, the four of us decided to explore the city of Carmel-by-the-Sea, really more of a quaint community of two thousand permanent residents founded in 1902 with a famous large artist colony. The hotel manager gave us some tips on sights to see. The downtown was within walking distance of the resort. It presented streets that were lined with art galleries and shops of all description. If you wandered off the main thoroughfare through the side streets, you'll find some lovely hidden courtyards and gardens to explore.

A main attraction of Carmel is the San Carlos Borromeo de Carmelo Mission that was an active Roman Catholic church established in 1770 and famous for its breathtaking beauty. The centerpiece of the mission complex is the basilica church which features a magnificent ceiling, five-foot-thick walls, and a collection of colonial Spanish art.

A can't miss feature of Carmel is the Tor House. It is a stone cottage that sat on a hill just outside of the town. It was the home of the celebrated American poet Robinson Jeffers. He built it for his wife and twin sons. He called it the Tor House, for the craggy knoll it rested on and the view it presented. The history of the house boasted such famous guests as Sinclair Lewis, Charles Lindbergh, Charlie Chaplin, and George Gershwin.

As dinnertime approached, the ranch house restaurant was recommended. The waiter directed us to our table which had a view of the mountains in the distance, such a magnificent setting. Doreen ordered filet mignon with seasonal vegetables and potatoes au gratin. The New York steak with baked potato looked swell to me. Sammy ordered the smoked pork ribs in barbecue sauce with coleslaw and shoestring fried potatoes. Sarah chose salmon ravioli. The meal was topped off with hot coffee and New York cheesecake.

With the sun disappearing over the Pacific Ocean, the temperature started to drop significantly, so we made the decision to return to Doreen and my room for conversation and relaxation in front of a roaring fire. As we sat there enjoying the evening, Sammy said, "Ron, I've never seen you play that well before. It seemed like every chance you took worked out perfectly for you. You were dead-on in every facet of your game. How do you explain that?"

"I don't know for sure, but I've heard of golfers that will have days where every shot is exactly where you want it to be. It just had never happened to me before today. I guess part of it is that this trip has been more successful than I ever imagined, and my confidence is high. Maybe it's also because I have been so focused on beating Jessie that I have pushed everything else out of my mind. Don't forget that having Sarah and Doreen with us has been such a plus, more than you can imagine."

"We have three more rounds, but I believe we are going to win this and walk away with the $5,000 first-place payoff. It all start over tomorrow, and I have to have the attitude that we are all at even par." As it was getting late, Sammy and Sarah excused themselves and returned to their room. Doreen looked at me and said, "Ron, I hope this comes true for you. You deserve to win, and I trust you will." We prepared to turn in for the night, and I couldn't think of any time in my life that I was happier or more at peace.

For the first time in my golfing career, I was in the last group to play, and I fully intended to maintain my lead especially over a bore like Jessie Davis. I met Jessie on the first tee and noticed his attitude had changed from one of irreverence and arrogance to one of solemn dedication to the game. He was finally realizing that I presented more of a challenge than he bargained for.

After the first four holes on the Friday round, I had picked up a birdie to move to six under, and Jessie had only managed pars, so now my lead over him stretched to three strokes. Number 5 was a 175-yard par 3 with the Pacific Ocean on the right with deep sand traps surrounding the green. A stiff breeze was coming across that was affecting tee shots. Sammy handed me a mashie because the wind was blowing from right to left and not helping, plus the fact that the flag was on the back right of the green.

I was able to achieve an almost-perfect tee shot, leaving my ball only 2 feet from the hole. Jessie was just as successful, and we both recorded a birdie, moving me to seven under and Jessie to four under for the tournament. I could see by Jessie's demeanor he was becoming increasingly frustrated by his inability to catch up with me.

The weather so far had been absolutely flawless for playing golf with clear blue skies, temperatures consistently in the high sixties with a light breeze that would only occasionally produce troublesome conditions on the holes that bordered the Pacific. However, the weather forecast for Saturday called for increasingly overcast skies with a distinct possibility of steady rain all day, accompanied by a drop in the temperature in to the forties. Knowing that, I felt like it was imperative to post as many birdies today as possible, for surely they would be hard to come by on Saturday and Sunday.

I was only able to produce one more birdie to move to eight under with Jessie staying close at now five under. The day ended that way, with nobody else in the field challenging us. I felt secure in my first place position, particularly with some ferocious weather approaching. We gathered up the girls and made our way back to the hotel. We decided it was prudent to stay in and have dinner there. The wind was starting to howl as the cold front approached.

We strongly suggested to the girls that if the weather tomorrow was inclement, that they not follow us, but just stay in the hotel. They protested at first, but we insisted, and they finally agreed. Our tee time was at 1:00 p.m., so we had the opportunity to see what the day was going to bring.

Sure enough as Saturday dawned, the temperature had dropped into the high forties, and the wind was kicking up to a steady twenty miles per hour, with a constant steady downpour. Miserable conditions to say the least.

The four of us enjoyed the Saturday brunch the hotel offered and watched the weather conditions deteriorate. The leaderboard remain unchanged from Friday. So as Jessie and I began our day, we were still enjoying a substantial lead over the rest of the field. Sammy and I talked about our approach for not only today, but how to maintain our lead on Sunday.

"Ron, just keep doing what you have been. But maybe not take any chances, just play conservatively unless somebody makes a move on you. With the weather being what it is today, I don't see any possibility of that. Just watch out for Jessie. You and I both know he is certainly capable of pulling off some spectacular shots. I feel like he is going to come at you either today or tomorrow, so just be ready."

"Well, I will, but I am curious about Jessie. I'd like to know more about his background. Ask the other caddies if there is somebody here that is familiar with what he's like off the golf course."

"I'll ask around."

We played the eighteen holes on Saturday without anyone improving their position in these deplorable weather conditions. With the constant rain, the course was becoming soaked, causing for slow play on the greens in particular, something I needed to take into consideration. After we finished for the day, Sammy and I returned to the hotel to our waiting ladies. We were cold and wet and glad to get back to the warmth of our room. I dried off, took a hot bath, changed clothes, and joined Doreen by the fireplace. Not wanting to fight the cold and rain, we stayed in, had dinner, and called it an early night.

Our tee time on Sunday was at 2:00 p.m., so we repeated our routine from Saturday. After brunch, Sammy told me, "I have the information you asked for about Jessie. It took some doing, but according to one of the other caddies, the PGL official, Roy Joiner, knows Jessie quite well and is expecting you to talk to him this morning. I told him you would meet him in the lobby at 11:00 a.m."

"Thanks, Sammy, I'll go look for him now."

I left the restaurant and walked over to the lobby and saw a gentleman sitting there reading a newspaper and smoking a cigar.

"Mr. Joiner? Hello, my name is Ron Perkins."

"Yes, Mr. Perkins, sit down. How can I help you?"

"I have been playing with Jessie Davis here, and I'd like to know more about him. I have never met anyone so brash, arrogant, and downright full of himself. What can you tell me?"

"Okay, I've known the Davis family for quite some time, and what I can tell you is that his father never came home from the Great War, so Jessie never really knew his dad. His mom was a bit of a trollop. After the war, she had to take care of herself and a young son the best way she knew how. She became a heavy drinker, and to support herself, she depended on a parade of men exchanging sexual favors for cash. Eventually she was able to turn her life around some when she managed to land a job as a receptionist at the Ford dealership in San Jose. Jessie's mom was a beautiful woman, so she was never at a loss of attracting men. But between her job and her active social life, she mainly ignored Jessie, leaving him to fend for himself. Jessie as a young boy was unfortunately exposed to a very lonely life as he was never able to find the affection he so desired from his mother."

Roy continued, "Luckily for him, as a young boy, he had an uncle that noticed what was going on and took Jessie under his wing. Now this uncle was an accomplished golfer and started working with Jessie at a very young age teaching him how to play the game of golf. Well, Jessie proved to be a prodigy and starting winning amateur tournament one after another. He turned pro two years ago, still at a very young age. Then last year his mom died, and that's when I noticed a drastic change in Jessie's attitude. So try to understand, that he's really not a bad kid, but still has that little boy inside of him wanting attention."

Armed with that knowledge, I knew now how to approach Jessie and to have some empathy for him and what all he had to overcome to even be here. The weather had improved somewhat for Sunday. It was still cold and breezy, but the rain had subsided as Jessie and I prepared to tee off. But he reverted back to the old Jessie that I had come to expect by saying, "Buckle your seat belt, Perkins. Today, I'm coming after you with everything I have." I just smiled at him and said, "Okay, Jessie, whatever you say." He didn't know quite how to respond to that, so he just walked back over to his caddie to prepare to tee off. The rest of the field after Saturday's round had dropped further back, so now in reality it was a two-man contest.

Jessie and I stayed even through the first three holes. Hole number 4 was a 334-yard par 4. I could tell by the way Jessie and his caddie were communicating that this is where he has decided to make his move. The Pacific Ocean loomed on the right with thick California fescue in the first cut on the left, just in front of a line of sycamore trees. The fairway was straight but narrow. I cautiously selected a brassie to tee off with and drove the ball safely in the fairway at the 200-yard marker, leaving me a simple chip shot of some 134 yards into the green. My assumption was correct as Jessie pulled out his play club in an attempt to go for the green in one shot, relying on a substantial tailwind. Obviously, he felt like it was necessary to be aggressive for the rest of the round in an attempt to take the lead away from me.

He hit a magnificent soaring drive that rode the wind but fell short of the green, coming to a rest still 54 yards out. With my second shot, I was able to land on the green then two putted for a par. Jessie, picked up a stroke as he birdied the hole. We finished the front nine in that position with my precarious two-stroke lead. I knew that if he got hot and I didn't, this championship would slip right through my fingers. I remembered what happened in Tulsa a few years back, so after discussing a strategy with Sammy, we decided to be as aggressive and willing to take chances as much as Jessie was going to do.

We both parred number 10 and walked over to hole 11, which was a 387-yard par 4. This hole was away from the ocean, more inland, eliminating the brisk wind for the most part.

However this hole presented its own set of challenges as the fairway turned at almost a ninety-degree angle back to the right over some very tall pine trees. The turn came at the 200-yard marker, inviting you with the temptation to cut the corner over the pine trees, thus if you were successful, you would drastically shorten the hole. I knew Jessie was capable of pulling off that shot, especially with the wind at our back. I watched as he lined up his shot. He swung down on the ball hard and lifted it up effortlessly over the trees, with the ball landing in the fairway past the turn, now only 130 yards out in an ideal approach position.

Even though I felt like I could match his shot, and in spite of what Sammy and I had discussed, I chose to play it safe trying to protect my two-stroke lead and hit a fade with my brassie that followed the path of the fairway but left me still 190 yards out. For my second shot, Sammy and I agreed that my mashie iron was my best option. I made solid contact with the ball and saw it roll up on the green, but still some 30 feet short of the hole. Jessie executed a precision-approach shot, leaving his ball only 4 feet from the pin, in position for a birdie attempt. I two putted for a par while Jessie dropped in his birdie putt to move now only one stroke behind, with plenty of golf left.

The score remained the same as we came up on hole number 15. Now Jessie was really pressing as the number of holes was beginning to run out. I had not had a birdie all day, and Jessie had managed two. This hole was a straight par 4 of 380 yards that presented a choice of trying to blast a drive over an inlet that cut across the fairway at the 250-yard mark. To clear the hazard, you would have to uncork a 280-yard drive or better to safely land on the other side. If you were able to do that, then it was safe sailing of less than 100 yards into a large wide-open green, devoid of sand traps. It was truly a high-risk, high-reward hole. The wind was not helping, but blowing across the fairway at a right-to-left angle.

Jessie was to tee off first, and there was no question he was going for it. He and I both knew that the last three holes would not present the dilemma that this one does. This was probably his last chance to overtake me. I felt like the championship was starting to get away from me, for I knew that if he was successful, then I would have to follow suit and attempt the same shot. I watched as he tensed up and hit his drive with everything he had. The ball shot off his club, but this time the wind tricked him as just as he made contact with the ball, it gusted right in his face, causing his ball to come up short and drop out of sight into the ocean. I saw his shoulders slump as we both instantly knew that his gamble had not paid off.

That made my decision easy as I hit my brassie short of the inlet coming to a rest 140 yards out. Now I was hitting two while Jessie was hitting three after being assessed his penalty stroke. I was able to pick up my first birdie of the day while Jessie had his first bogey, moving him back to three strokes behind me with three holes left in the match.

The results of hole number 15 seemed to take the wind out of Jessie's sails. He did not challenge me again on the remaining three holes, and I walked away victorious for the first time in my brief professional golf career with a $5,000 first-place prize.

Sammy was delighted with earning another $1,000, and I now had won enough money to not only pay for my college education, but also for Doreen's medical school expense. Our wedding in the spring of 1933 was now all but guaranteed. I watched Jessie walk off, almost in tears as he had his head down, not talking to anyone, not even his caddie, and certainly not to congratulate me. But now knowing about his past and how much this tournament must have meant to him, I felt compelled to at least try to talk to him.

"Jessie, hold up a minute."

"What do you want, Perkins, to rub it in."

"No, man. You gave me all I could handle today. I have to admit to you that I thought you had me there on the back nine. You are a superb golfer with a bright future, and I hope we meet again someday. If you ever need somebody to talk to, well, I'm in the Dallas phone book. That's all."

Jessie looked back at me through red swollen eyes, but the arrogance had totally drained out of him. I thought he looked like a guy in bad need of a friend. "Thanks, Perkins, I'll remember you said that. By the way, the next time we meet, I'm going to beat your brains out." There he was, the old Jessie was back.

As we walked off the final hole, Doreen ran up and threw her arms around my neck, and we were off for a night of celebration, our last night in California. Tomorrow at 6:00 a.m. we were to board our train for the long journey home.

It was way too cold to go out on the town. As the day turned into night, the temperature had dropped into the low forties and the wind was still brisk, so we all went back to our rooms to prepare for our early morning departure. I started a fire, and as Doreen came out of the bathroom ready for bed, she came over and sat next to me by the fireplace and said, "You know, we'll probably never forget this last month. It was kind of like an early honeymoon for us, just delightful in every way possible." I pulled her in close to me, and we kissed. I told her I couldn't agree more and maybe we can come back next year after we are married.

# CHAPTER 14

Monday morning came very early as we were all up and ready by 4:30 a.m. in order to catch our train that was scheduled to leave promptly at 6:00 a.m. for the three-day long trip back to Dallas. Once boarded we caught breakfast in the dining car. We were served just about anything we wanted, and Doreen selected a short stack of pancakes with a side of bacon, coffee, and orange juice. For me, I was in the mood for a mess of scrambled eggs, double order of bacon, sausage, hash browns, coffee, and tomato juice. For some reason, my appetite was way up. I had this indescribable feeling of euphoria. I felt like my future had now fallen neatly into place with a now-successful golf career and the woman of my dreams by my side.

After breakfast we gazed out of the window at the passing countryside as the sun peaked up over the mountains. It had truly been a magical escapade for all involved. We were scheduled to arrive back in Dallas on September 1, giving Doreen only a long weekend before she had to go back to school on the following Monday, Labor Day, as her classes were set to start on Tuesday, September 6.

As we settled into our sleeper berth, Doreen told me of her recent conversation with her mom and dad. "I didn't tell you this, but when I called my parents on my birthday, they told me there was a special surprise waiting for me, but that they couldn't give it to me until the Sunday before I am to leave for school. You don't know anything about what they're planning, do you?"

"No, I can't say that I do. I'm just as mystified as you are. What do you think it is?"

It was safe to say that neither of us had any idea what her dad was planning, but we knew he could be unpredictable, but was always a generous man when it came to his daughter.

The train ride was long but featured some breathtaking scenery along the way. We were all tired and ready to be back home after an exhausting and at the same time, exhilarating trip. I was eager to see Mom to give her this last $1,000. I know that the money we were able to win would make her life a little easier and reduce the number of hours she had to work each week.

Finally, early Thursday morning, we pulled into the Dallas train station. They were all waiting for us, Mom, Robert and Margaret, and Doreen's parents. Sammy's mom and dad were there also; and we all said our goodbyes before going our separate ways, with plans to get together one more time over the weekend before Doreen had to leave for college.

I slipped behind the steering wheel of the Dodge with Mom, and she said, "Tell me all about your journey. It must have been great fun, with all that you were able to see in California. I've never been there, and I've only seen pictures or scenes from a movie, but it looks remarkable."

"Mom, we had a fantastic time, and I have another $1,000 to give you. I finally won a tournament, by the way. I really believe I will do well next season, so much so that maybe you can finally quit your job and let me take care of you for a change."

"That's sweet, Ron. We'll just have to see what happens. On another subject, tell me about Doreen. How did you two get along?"

"Mom, I love her more now than when we left. She was just super, and I can't wait to marry her. She was the perfect partner our entire excursion. We had such fun."

*****

Doreen left the train station with her mom and dad, and as they pulled away, Doreen asked, "Well, Dad, I'm just dying of curiosity. What's this big surprise you have for me?"

"Well, child, I guess you'll just have to be patient and wait until after church on Sunday."

I wanted to give Doreen some time with her parents. We had plans to meet Sunday afternoon and visit our favorite spot at White Rock Lake.

As I was getting ready to leave to pick her up, I heard a car horn. I looked out the window to see who it was, and I was shocked at what I witnessed. It was Doreen sitting behind the wheel of a brand-new car. I ran out of the house to greet her. "What's this?" She smiled at me and said, "This is the surprise my dad had for me, can you believe it? It's mine to take back to school, instead of having to take the train. It's a 1933 Ford Roadster with a rumble seat, and look, it has a radio, heater, and leather seats. It's my favorite color of emerald green with tan interior. Isn't this just the gas? Get in, we'll take my new car to White Rock Lake. I already have a picnic basket in the back."

Doreen was absolutely radiant with her new car. As we sat by the lake, we planned our future and reflected back on how our relationship had grown while we were in California. All too soon, the afternoon was drawing to a close as the sun disappeared over the lake. With one last kiss, we started our drive home. We made plans for me to visit Waco within the next month. I watched as she drove off until she disappeared from view.

Monday was a holiday, but Tuesday meant back to work. I decided to give Mr. Thomas my two-week notice and quit the job at the drugstore, since I really didn't need the extra income anymore. Instead, I wanted to concentrate on my job caddying at the Dallas County Country Club. But a strange thing happened as I reported to work on Tuesday. The club supervisor called me into his office, and I thought he was going to fire me for being gone a month. But no, it was the exact opposite. He offered me the job of club pro, in total charge of the golf course, including lessons for club members. It seems that in my absence, he had fired the existing club pro leaving an opening for me. This meant that in addition to a substantial salary, instead of working for tips, I was now a club member with all the benefits that go with it.

I had swiftly and unexpectedly gone from being a weekend caddie to the man in charge of all golfing operations for the country club. What a turn of events. I couldn't wait to write Doreen and tell her of my even more good news. Maybe now Mom could quit her job completely as I was now capable of supporting the both of us.

The California excursion had benefitted me with $7,500 in winnings, really a small fortune; and now with my new position at the country club, could life get any better? I wrote Doreen of the extraordinary change in my life and expressed how excited I was at the prospect of coming to see her in just a few weeks.

The time flew by, and it was time for my Waco visit to the university and Doreen. My train pulled into the Waco train station, and there she was waiting for me with her usual warm smile. She rushed into my arms and gave me a divine hello kiss.

We walked arm in arm to her new Ford, and she drove us back to campus. Because of the university rules, I was once again staying with her cousin in the boys' dorm. It really didn't matter for Doreen, and I had the whole weekend to be together. Once I was settled in, Doreen picked me up and we took a driving tour of the university and Waco. She showed me sights that I had not been able to see on my last visit to Waco, since that time we didn't have our own personal car at our disposal. This certainly gave us more freedom to do what we wanted.

We parked the car and walked around campus, something that I really enjoyed as I soaked up as much of the university life as I could. Soon we sat down on a bench in the main quadrangle, and I could tell she had something on her mind.

"Ron, can I ask you something? Now don't laugh, but how do you feel about children?"

"Well, I like them fine as long as they belong to somebody else."

"Oh, my goodness, don't you want to have children of your own someday?"

"That was just a joke, of course I want children as long as they are with you. Exactly how many did you have in mind? To tell you the truth, I haven't really given it much thought."

"I'm thinking a boy and a girl, just to balance things out, you see."

"I'm happy with whatever you want to do. I am just so extremely grateful that you are my girl, soon to be my wife."

We sat there for a while longer contemplating our future together and then I had to walk her back to her dorm before curfew.

"Tomorrow, we have tickets to our football game and then a dance tomorrow night. The game starts at 2:00 p.m., and we're playing Arkansas Tech. I don't know if you are aware of it or not, but we have an excellent team this year. We've won our first four games, and I think we're favored to beat Arkansas Tech. Don't worry about lunch, the stadium has the best hot dogs you have ever eaten. You can have your choice of covering your dog with mustard, relish, and onions or chili or all of the above. So bring a healthy appetite. But dress warmly. It's predicted to be a little on the cool side."

"That sounds swell. I can't wait. But I have a question for you. You remember last year you were having trouble with that fellow, what was his name, you know, the one I had to come down here and straighten him out."

"That would be Scott Franklin. No, he's not around anymore, but after your altercation with him, word got out that I was an engaged woman with a boyfriend that knew how to take care of business. So I've had no further incidents."

*****

Doreen picked me up at my dorm. She looked ravishing in a white cashmere sweater with a midcalf blue skirt. She had her hair pulled back and hidden under a black fedora. The university pounded Arkansas Tech as expected 42-16, and Doreen was right, the hot dogs were exceptionally delicious. We had a great afternoon with still the victory dance coming up.

The dance was in the university gym, so all we had to do was walk across campus. Once again Doreen outdid herself, looking lovely in a below-the-knee white dress now with her blonde hair cascading down around her shoulders. We danced past midnight as the girls' curfew was extended for the occasion. Sadly, I knew that tomorrow I was boarding my train back to Dallas, leaving Doreen behind.

I arrived back in Dallas late Sunday afternoon, and Mom was waiting to pick me up. "How was your weekend?"

"Mom, it always ends too soon. We had a terrific time. We went to a football game and a victory dance, and we talked quite a bit about our future together. Our plan is still for me to enroll in the university in January for the spring 1933 semester now that we have the money. Then I suppose you can plan on a January wedding."

"Ron, I am so happy for the two of you. It sounds like you have this all thought-out. Any consideration given to children at some point. I would love to live long enough to see grandchildren."

"Funny you should ask that. We did talk about it and agreed that we do want children, but probably not until she is out of medical school and I have my degree."

As we drove home, I asked Mom, "Are you feeling okay. You look really tired."

"I'm okay, it's just been a long week, but thanks to you and the money you have contributed, I was able to tell my supervisor that I wouldn't be working weekends anymore. You don't know how much that helps me. I can spend more time with you."

Mom was never a physically strong woman at just barely five feet, two inches and slight of build, but emotionally she had always been my inspiration with her determination to provide for the two of us through extremely difficult times since Dad died. Now it was my turn to provide for her.

My new position at the country club is a tremendous boost to my career, giving me added exposure and more practice time. By the time the 1933 golf season begins, I should be primed and ready. I have been quite busy conducting golf lessons, but as the calendar has turned in to October, the weather has started to turn colder, so my instructional opportunities are starting to dwindle down to next to nothing. So I have decided to suspend all golf lessons until the spring of 1933.

We are seeing the first indications of winter as we begin the month of November. It appears this winter is going to be bitterly cold, at least according to the experts. In her letters, Doreen is thoroughly enjoying her new Ford. She likes the fact that she can leave college for home anytime she wants and be here in two hours, without having to consult a train schedule. She is due in on November 23, and we plan to have a large Thanksgiving celebration as the Winthorps are inviting not only Mom and me, but also Robert and Margaret and Sammy and Sarah. Sammy has told me that he and Sarah have an announcement to make and will reveal it at the Thanksgiving dinner.

Mrs. Winthorp set a fine Thanksgiving table with a scrumptious meal of oven baked turkey, cornbread dressing, sweet potatoes, corn casserole, green beans, and fruit salad with hot, homemade rolls. Doreen came in last night, and today is my first chance to see her, but we do have a long holiday weekend ahead of us. Once we were all seated at the table and grace had been given, I turned to Sammy and said, "Okay, now that we're all here, I can't wait to hear your announcement that you've been so secretive about."

Sammy stood up, pushed back his chair, and looked down at Sarah. With his voice cracking and tears starting to well up in his eyes, he said, "I wanted you all to know that we are pregnant. And, Ron, your California trip is responsible. So I wanted to thank you and Doreen for providing us with such a terrific experience."

We all celebrated Sammy and Sarah's good news. This was truly a Thanksgiving to remember.

After Thanksgiving dinner, we adjourned to the parlor for coffee and cigarettes. The radio was playing softly as the conversation continued. Doreen said, "Sarah, that is such good news. We are all so happy for you. Maybe one day Ron and I will have a little one for your baby to grow up with."

"That would be marvelous."

I took Mom home and returned in time to say good night to our friends. Doreen's mom and dad had already retired for the evening, giving me and Doreen some welcome alone time.

"How about we go to a picture show tomorrow night. We haven't done that in a while."

"Sounds swell to me, but do you think the weather will allow us to play some golf at the country club tomorrow. I haven't played since we returned from California."

"It's supposed to be cold, like in the fifties for a high, but sunny and not much wind. So I guess if we dress warmly, it would be okay. Now that I am the club pro, I can for sure get us a tee time."

The next morning I called Robert and Sammy to see if they and their wives would be interested in joining us. Both enthusiastically agreed. My next call was to the club to arrange a tee time. Since it was still Thanksgiving weekend and the weather was at best unpredictable, the morning was wide open for us. I arranged a 10:00 a.m. time, hoping for some kind of a warm-up. Now ordinarily the club frowned on six people playing together, but they allowed it because of the light turnout. Fortunately, the day dawned bathed in sunlight as the temperature rose into the low sixties, a perfectly beautiful day for golf. But by the time we were finishing up, the skies turned cloudy and gray, and a light rain had begun to fall.

We said our goodbyes to our friends, and I drove Doreen home. "I will pick you up at 7:00 p.m. for dinner then there's a new Clark Gable movie out called *No Man of Her Own* that costars Carole Lombard that I hear is very funny."

"That sounds wonderful to me. I'll see you then."

After the movie I took Doreen home with plans to spend Saturday with her. It was too cold to visit White Rock Lake, so the next best option was to take in a matinee. Doreen loved the picture shows, and I couldn't complain as it gave me more time to be with her. The motion picture she chose was *A Farewell to Arms* with Gary Cooper, Helen Hayes, and Adolphe Menjou.

On Sunday morning we went to church together; then it was time for her to pack and start her drive to Waco. I urged her to leave early enough to make sure she made it to Waco before nightfall. We shared one last kiss, then she said, "I love you, and I will see you on Christmas unless you find the time to come down to Waco to see me."

"I love you too, and I sure hope I can do that. I'll have to see how my job goes. I wouldn't think we'd be too awfully busy in December."

As luck would have it, I was not able to make it to Waco. We had to be content with letters and now a once-a-week telephone call, since I had one installed at home during our trip to California. But the month went by quickly, and Christmas was just around the corner.

Doreen was scheduled to leave the University on Friday, December 23, but by that time the weather had turned treacherous when a blue norther had blown in bringing with it a temperature in the twenties accompanied by a steady downpour of sleet and snow that was sticking to the roadway, making the roads slick and erratic and any travel by automobile extremely hazardous.

On that Friday morning, I telephoned Doreen at school, hoping to catch her before she left. I was able to talk to her as she was leaving her dorm. "Listen, I wanted to call you and warn you that the roads are not safe today, at least not up here. Maybe you should rethink driving your car and take the train instead. I checked and there is one leaving Waco at 1:00 p.m. arriving here at three thirty. I would feel more comfortable if you would and I promise to meet you at the Dallas train station just like we used to before you got all fancy with your own car. Please do that just for me."

"Ron, I'll be just fine. I am very cautious, and if I drive I can be there just after lunch. I want to spend as much of Christmas with you and Mom and Dad as I can. I'm too impatient to wait on taking the train. Please don't worry, I love you and I'll see you this afternoon."

And with that we hung up, but I had this feeling of dread that I just could not shake.

I knew that it would take her at least two hours to drive here, maybe more with the weather conditions being what they were. I would be on pins and needles until I was sure she had arrived safely. I had done all I could do to talk her out of driving, it was now up to her. I went to work at the country club to attend to some of my routine duties, and after two hours I put in a call to Mrs. Winthorp.

"Have you heard from Doreen yet? Is she there?"

"Not yet, Ron, but I will let you know the moment she gets here or if I hear anything. Don't worry. I assume you are at work at the country club. I'll call you there as soon as I know something. You know she is a most capable young lady."

I estimated that Doreen should be here before noon or 1:00 p.m. at the latest. As 2:00 p.m. came and went and we still hadn't heard from her, I had this feeling that something was terribly wrong. I hesitated to bother Mrs. Winthorp again as I knew she would call me if she knew anything. So I just sat there in my office and continued to worry and pace the floor. I left around 2:30 p.m. advising Mrs. Winthorp to call me at home.

Finally at 3:00 p.m. my telephone rang, and it was Mrs. Winthorp. I instinctively knew something terrible had happened.

"Ron, this is Susan Winthorp. We're at the county hospital. You need to get here as soon as you can. Doreen has been in a horrific automobile accident. Please hurry."

With that I hung up the telephone, told Mom where I was going, and ran out of the door. I was in such a panic I don't remember at all the drive to the hospital. When I arrived and walked into the lobby, I immediately saw the Winthorps. I could tell by the worried expressions on their face that it couldn't be anything but tragic news.

Through tears and a catch in her voice, Susan updated me on what she knew. "She is in intensive care now undergoing emergency surgery. All I know for now is it happened just north of Waxahachie on Highway 77, and she was brought here by ambulance. A Texas Highway Patrol officer who arrived on the scene shortly after the accident is on his way here to tell us what happened."

Moments later the Texas Highway Patrol officer entered the hospital and walked over to us. "Mr. and Mrs. Winthorp, I'm Officer Jeff Pierce, and I'm here to answer your questions as best I can about your daughter's accident."

"Thank you, Officer, what can you tell us?"

"As best as we can assume, she was traveling north on Highway 77 at approximately sixty miles per hour when it appears she suffered a front tire blowout. That with the icy highway caused her to lose control of her automobile, putting it into a spin, eventually flipping over in a ditch, throwing your daughter out. I am so sorry, do you know how she's doing?"

"No, just that she's in surgery. The doctors haven't told us anything yet. We're waiting to hear."

An hour passed before a doctor came out into the waiting room to give us an update. "Mr. and Mrs. Winthorp, my name is Dr. Paul Wilson, and I wanted to let you know the latest about your daughter's condition. She is under the care of our best operating team, but I must advise you that she has suffered severe internal injuries and head trauma. My team is doing all it can, but it probably would help if you would pray for them and for your daughter. I will keep you informed as her condition changes."

"Thank you, Doctor."

"Would you folks like any coffee? I can have my nurse bring you some."

"No, not yet, but thank you anyway."

I sat closer to Susan and took her hand as we began to pray for Doreen and the surgical team. But I was in a state of disbelief as to how this could be happening. I mean, I just talked to her this morning, and she was fine.

I wanted to let Sammy and Robert know what was going on, so I excused myself and asked the nurse for a telephone. First call went to Robert. "Robert, I wanted to call and tell you that Doreen has been in an automobile accident, and we are at Dallas County Hospital."

"Ron, say no more, Margaret and I will be there as soon as we can."

I called Sammy and Sarah, and they too dropped whatever they were doing to rush to the hospital to offer what support they could.

Once everyone arrived, I attempted to answer all their questions, at least as far as what I knew and what the doctors had told us. They were aghast at the story as it unfolded. Sarah and Margaret began to gently weep out of concern for Doreen and prayed for me and to guide the hands of the surgical team. Sammy and Robert went to the hospital cafeteria for coffee for all, and we settled in for a long night vigil.

I bothered the nurse one more time for the telephone, and she was most courteous and sympathetic to what we were enduring. I wanted to call Mom and tell her that I wouldn't be home tonight. "Mom, she's in surgery, and we have been advised that it's serious. I will keep you posted, but I want you to get some rest and don't worry about me."

"Ron, I'll pray for Doreen and just hope for the best results. You take care of yourself."

This so reminded me of when my dad died and that horrible experience in the summer of 1929. That didn't turn out well. I can only hope for different results with Doreen.

Other than a brief update every two hours, we still didn't know much. I could see the sun starting to appear over the horizon as another day was dawning. Doreen had been in surgery now for over fourteen hours, but finally I could see the chief operating surgeon coming down the hall toward us with a somber expression on his face. He sat down next to Susan and took her hand in his. "Mrs. Winthorp, I regret to tell you that we did everything we could, but we were unable to save your daughter. Her injuries were just too severe, and she had lost too much blood. I am so sorry for your loss."

Susan asked the doctor, "Can we see her?"

"Mrs. Winthorp, her injuries were so catastrophic, I would recommend that you not do that at this time."

With that, the doctor left us to grieve and to try and understand why someone so beautiful and special had been taken from us so suddenly. Susan slumped back in her chair and fainted at the news of what had befallen her lovely daughter.

I was in a daze as I walked outside in the cool early morning, lit up a cigarette, and tried to understand what had just happened. Sammy and Robert joined me, and through my tears I said, "This just can't be true. We are supposed to get married next month and then have children and grow old together. She was my whole life, what am I supposed to do now?"

Sammy tried to console me, but to no avail. He knew I was in no condition to drive myself, so he took charge and saw that I made it home.

Mom was waiting at the door. "What happened, Ron? Is Doreen alright?"

"Mom, she's gone, they couldn't save her. She was just hurt too badly to survive her injuries. I feel so lost."

Now, my tears were starting to flow freely, and I went into uncontrollable sobs. Mom put her arms around me and held me, until I was able to regain some semblance of control.

Sunday, Christmas Day, we held the funeral services as the snow continued to fall. Now I was totally in a state of denial, convinced this wasn't real but must be some kind of nightmare and I was going to wake up any moment. Surely, she can't really be gone, that's not possible. But soon, reality began to sink in, and I returned home with Mom and retreated into my room, desperately wanting to be alone for now and to sort out my thoughts.

## CHAPTER 15

I found over the next few weeks that the only solace I could find was at the bottom of a whiskey bottle. I had managed to find a bootlegger that supplied me with plenty to drink. So I mostly just stayed in my room, drinking rum and whiskey and smoking cigarettes. My boss from the country club came by to offer condolences, and my best friends Sammy and Robert stopped by frequently, but I was inconsolable. Finally, as spring was beginning, I was needed at the country club to resume my duties, but I just couldn't force myself to go back to work. So he had to let me go, but I can't really blame him for that.

Mom tried her best to get me to rejoin society, but I wasn't interested. I felt like I had nothing else to live for, so why try. I stayed totally inactive, barely leaving my room except for an occasional meal, for the rest of 1933. Sammy tried in vain to get me back on the golf tour once the season started, but I would have no part of it. My golf clubs rested in the garage collecting dust. Finally on the first anniversary of Doreen's passing, I visited her grave, just to have a talk with her. "Well, my love, it has been a rough year without you. I don't know what the future holds for me, not much I suppose. I think of you every day." Then the strangest thing happened. A sudden breeze kicked up, and I swear I heard Doreen's voice telling me to get back to the business of living. I know that didn't happen, or did it? Regardless, it made me make the decision to try and put my life back together.

I went home, cleaned up, and shaved off a year-old beard, threw away all the old booze bottles, and emptied whatever I had left down the kitchen drain. Then I got in my Dodge and drove over to the country club to see if I could get my old job back. Of course, that was not possible as long ago they had hired my replacement, but they allowed me to come back and do some part-time caddying. In the lost year of 1933, I was able to live off my 1932 California winnings, and Mom had kept her job, so we were still in good shape as far as financially.

The 1934 golf season was getting ready to start in April, but in my absence, Sammy was forced to move on and give up being a caddie. Fortunately, he had earned enough money working for me to buy out the owner of the filling station where he had once been an employee. He had proven to be so successful that he was able to open up two more locations. He and Sarah had brought a new baby girl into the world and had bought a very nice two-bedroom bungalow in east Dallas for his growing family. Sammy had achieved true happiness with Sarah.

In the first tournament I entered in 1934, I tried the best I could to regain the old form I had in California, but the motivation was just not there. I would catch myself looking into the crowd to see if Doreen was there watching me, but of course she wasn't. I no longer had my old friend Sammy at my side and had to use a club caddie that I didn't know or trust, plus my own instincts were off after such a long time of not playing any golf. I still was not ready for competition.

Mom had been with me throughout the appalling year of 1933 and had been most understanding and supportive. But with the added burden of caring for me and having to continue working at the department store, she was starting to look really worn down. Her health the last few years, particularly since Dad died, had been fragile at best.

The 1934 golf season came and went and was most unremarkable for me, but I felt like by the end I was starting to round into shape. On December 23 I made my annual trek to Doreen's grave site, just to have a chat with her. For some unknown reason, it always made me feel better to try and keep her as part of my life. I decided to work very hard and give the 1935 golf season a go. I was still in need of a reliable caddie, so after talking it over with Sammy, he advised me that an old friend from the past was now available. "You should call Tommy Painter. He is an experienced caddie and his pro just retired, so he might be willing to talk to you."

"Wait, that's the same Tommy Painter that was our old linebacker and took a swing at me in high school."

"The very same."

After a meeting with Tommy, he agreed to come on board and be my caddie for the 1935 season. Now all I had to do was to try and recapture the skill set I had back in 1932. Maybe with Tommy's help and a new attitude, and a new dedication to my work ethic, I might be able to do just that.

The 1935 season started off slowly for us. We were winning enough to barely cover my expenses. My old form of 1932 had not yet returned in spite of the fact that I once again had begun my old weight training regimen, including riding miles every day on my bicycle. Something is going to have to break for me soon. I am beginning to run out of the money I had accumulated on the California trip. That had been my only source of income since the passing of Doreen. And with that my dream of attending the university has faded and become irrelevant, at least for now.

In early April, I noticed a change in Mom's health. She seemed to have lost her appetite. She would prepare large delicious meals for the two of us, then she would hardly eat anything. She seemed more tired than usual, and last night I heard her moaning in pain. Next thing I knew, I could hear her in the kitchen, so I went to investigate.

"Mom, what's wrong?"

"Oh, I'm okay Ron, just a little stomachache. Nothing for you to worry about."

"Of course I worry about you. Maybe I should take you to the doctor tomorrow."

"No, I have to work tomorrow. I'll be okay. Just go on back to bed."

Mom clearly wasn't okay, and as we celebrated her fiftieth birthday on April 28, she was not returning to her old self. We had started using a family doctor by the name of Jonathan Kirby when we moved to Dallas, and as her pain persisted, I was finally able to coerce her into a visit. He conducted some tests, then referred us to a cancer specialist. Of course that diagnosis scared us both. "Listen, Marion, I'm not inferring you have cancer. I just want an expert in the field to take a look at you, that's all." So an appointment was made for the next week with Dr. Gerald Knox.

We went in for testing and waited to hear from him with the results. A few days later he called and wanted us to come back in immediately.

We walked into Doctor Knox's office for our appointment, and as we were seated, he began to tell us our results.

"Marion, Ron, as much as I hate to do this, I feel like I must just come out and tell you straight up what the testing uncovered. Marion, dear, I'm afraid you have pancreatic cancer. I am so sorry."

I asked the doctor, "That sounds really ominous. Is there a treatment for it and exactly what is a pancreas?"

"To answer your first question, unfortunately with the technology of today, there is no known cure or treatment. The pancreas is an organ in your abdomen that lies horizontally behind the lower part of your stomach. Pancreatic cancer begins in the tissue of that organ and can quickly spread to your bowel, liver, or stomach. The purpose of a pancreas is to release enzymes that aid in digestion and creates hormones that help manage your blood sugar."

Mom sat there with tears running down her face and finally said, "Well, Doc, it sounds like a death sentence. Exactly how much time do I have left?"

"Marion, it's hard to say. Probably at best a few months. I have a prescription for you that will help manage the pain, but I'm afraid there's nothing else I can do for you."

We walked out completely devastated at the news. "Mom, you must quit working and let me take care of you."

"Okay, I guess I have no other choice."

We celebrated my twenty-third birthday in June just me and Mom in her bedroom. I spent time caddying at the country club for a few hours a week and the rest of the time tending to Mom and her needs. I was forced to suspend the 1935 season once we knew Mom's diagnosis. I had to tell Tommy that my golf career was over until further notice, and he was most understanding. I did manage to find for him full-time work at the country club for now.

On the night of September 3, I was preparing some soup for Mom when I heard her talking to someone. I knew there was no one else in the house, so I stopped what I was doing and went to check on her.

"Mom, who are you talking to?"

"Your father, he's sitting right there in that rocker, and he tells me that he's here to take me home to heaven."

I looked, and there was on one that I could see anywhere in her room. "Mom, there's no one there."

"Yes, Ron, it's time for me to go. Soon I will be dancing in heaven with your father."

With that, she closed her eyes, breathed a deep sigh, and she was gone. I knelt by her bed and cried until I had nothing left. Now, I was truly alone. We buried Mom close to Doreen, and now I had lost everyone that I loved.

When the 1936 golf season began, I tried my best to put my game back together, but my heart was just not in it. I did not win or place in even one tournament for the full season. Tommy, to his credit, had come back to caddie for me and stayed through the season. I was beginning to think that the magic of the 1932 season was never going to come back. But I made a vow to give my best effort to make 1937 my comeback year. That meant extra work on the driving range and as many rounds of golf as I could play during the off season. I intensified my weight training and rode my bicycle every evening. I now lived in an empty house, so I didn't want to spend any more time there than I had to.

Every year, I receive an invitation from the PGL to join the Western tour and every year I decline. The memories of 1932 still haunt me, but maybe now after five years, I might consider giving it another try. But with no Doreen to be there to cheer me on and no Sammy and Sarah, it's doubtful that I will ever take that tour again.

The first tournament of 1937 was being held at my home course, the Dallas County Country Club. I felt like since I was familiar with the course having played it so many times over the last eight years, that I had a distinct advantage. I was right in my assumption as for the first time in five years, I competed and won first place. Tommy was a main factor in my victory as he proved himself to be a most capable caddie with excellent instincts. I only hoped this would be a harbinger of things to come for this golf season.

We won a couple more tournaments in 1937, enough to keep us going and pay all my expenses with some left over. I made the same arrangement with Tommy that I had with Sammy, and he seemed to be fine with it, especially now that we were starting to win and make some money.

Every year now on December 23, I take the time to go and visit with Doreen. It always seems to comfort me, just to be able to talk with her. I feel like she will always be with me in spirit. Now, I had another date to go and spend some time with Mom.

As we began the 1938 golf season, I had expectations of doing well, probably for the first time since 1932, the last year I was successful. I had changed golf clubs before the beginning of the 1937 season, and by now I had become used to them, and I felt more proficient with my new set. The 1938 season introduced changes in many of the old rules of golf. One was the move away from the Scottish system of nomenclature for the clubs, plus we could now use wooden tees instead of having to pile up dirt. Another important change was removing the rule that if one player's ball was in front of another, he didn't have to mark and remove his ball out of the path of the golfer behind him, forcing him to go around or over the closer ball to the hole. Now all golfers were required by rule to mark and move their ball when on the green.

I most assuredly am still grieving for Mom and Doreen, but I have learned to deal with my emotions and now can function somewhat normally. I am determined to make 1938 my best season ever, and it starts with the first tournament being held at the South Oak Cliff Country Club in South Dallas county, one that I am not familiar with. Many of the old-time golfers are still around such as Harry Bonham, John Packard, and Mac Grey. There are new young bucks to contend with like Tom Harper and Luke Morgan. With the progress of new club technology came the change in the length of the course, as holes were now much longer than they were when I first started back in 1929. It indeed was a new world for me.

Over the years the purse has grown as this inaugural tournament boasts a first-place prize of $5,000, $4,000 for second, and $3,000 for third. Fourth through tenth win $300 and the entry fee is $250. I found out at the players' meeting on Wednesday afternoon that I would be teeing off at 9:00 a.m. with my old friend from years ago, Mac Grey.

The weather for early April in Dallas was spectacular with bright blue skies, full sun, and a light breeze out of the south with temperatures in the high sixties. The first hole was 384-yard par 4 with a dogleg to the left. There were fairway bunkers at the 225-yard marker to avoid, but other than that, there were no further hazards. I was the first to tee off, and I smoked my drive down the center of the fairway, coming to a rest at the 280-yard marker. That left me only 100 yards to the green. Mac was able to follow my lead, and his ball came to a rest just a few feet from my ball. I chose a wedge and aimed directly for the flag that was in the back right corner of the green.

Mac was not as fortunate as he came around on his ball and pushed it too far to the left, leaving him a long putt of nearly 30 feet over an undulating green. I was able to put my ball exactly where I wanted and ended up only 6 feet from the hole. Mac two putted for a par, and I secured my birdie. The second hole was a par 3, and I picked up my second birdie, and Mac birdied the hole as well. I finished the front nine with one bogey, and Mac had all pars as both of us reached the turn at one under for the day.

Occasionally I would find myself looking toward the crowd of people following us, hoping to see Doreen standing there smiling at me wearing her white cotton dress and wide-brim straw hat with her blonde curls peeking out, but to no avail, she's not there. I live a lonely life, still in the house that Mom bought when we first moved to Dallas in 1929. But I have no desire for a social life. I keep myself busy with golf and try not to think about the past.

At the end of the first day, I picked up one more birdie to finish at two under while Mac stayed at one under. I was two strokes out of the lead shared by Luke Morgan and John Packard. Friday was an even par golf day for me. The two leaders improved to five under, leaving me three strokes behind with the weekend to play.

I wasn't that far out of first place, but the weather forecast was for rain and cooler temperatures with wind gusting up to twenty miles per hour. So much more difficult conditions for Saturday. Tommy was prepared with rain gear, and sure enough we watched as the storm rolled in ahead of our 1:30 p.m. tee time, soaking the course and making playing conditions at their worst, but we played on.

We played in these conditions at even golf through a steady downpour until we reached hole number 16. It was a short 253-yard par 4 with a fairway that turned to the left featuring a green that was surrounded with deep bunkers. The wind was at our back, making this a very drivable hole, if you had the nerve and could negotiate a left direction of the fairway leading up to the green. Tommy and I considered our options and concluded that it was time to make a statement and go for it.

I could not have asked for a better result as my ball flew off the face of the club in a high arcing direction following the fairway with enough momentum to make it to the green. We had decided on a three wood instead of the driver mainly because the substantial wind was at our back, thinking that would give me enough force to carry the distance. We saw the fantail of water kick up when the ball finally landed, but from our prospective, we couldn't tell if it made it to the green or not. Mac just shook his head in disbelief and gave me a tip of the cap and said, "I applaud your effort, but I'm not going to try that. I think I'll just play it safe and lay up."

Try to imagine our shock as we walked up on the green and saw that my ball had come to a rest just inches from the hole, giving me a kick-in eagle and now a score of four under par, just one stroke off the lead as Saturday ended. Mac had picked up a birdie to remain at two under.

On Sunday, the weather started to clear, and by the time Mac and I teed off in the second-to-last group, the rain and wind had moved east, leaving temperatures in the fifties but sunny and otherwise mild. After nine holes I was still one stroke behind the two leaders as I had improved to five under. The back nine was going to be the difference.

Hole number 12 was a long and straight 478-yard par 5. Though the fairway was straight, there were several bunkers all along the way and a green that featured hard-to-read breaks. An accurate shot off the tee was essential. I pounded an excellent drive of 280 yards coming to a rest on the right side of the fairway, giving me a perfect angle into the green. Tommy and I agreed on the three wood to encompass the remaining 200 yards to the flag. It turned out to be the right selection as my ball landed safely on the green only 20 feet from the hole. Tommy and I kneeled down to survey which way we thought our putt would break, and it appeared a right-to-left direction was the choice. I was able to make the putt for an eagle, and for the moment I was in the lead by one stroke at seven under.

I managed to protect that fragile one-stroke lead for the rest of the round, winning first place and the $5,000 prize money. Tommy and I celebrated, but it was a hollow victory for me as there was no one else there to help me enjoy this come from behind win.

Whenever I wasn't at work at the country club, I was on the golf course or the practice range honing my skills. That, with the continuation of my physical training with weights and riding my bicycle, began to pay off as I became the top money winner on the tour in both 1938 and 1939, and I was still only twenty-seven. With the 1940 season coming up, I was at the top of my game, but there were storm clouds gathering in Europe and the Far East as both Germany and Japan were becoming more aggressive in their ambitions every day. But according to our government, it was thought that we were not going to be entangled in another foreign war. I continued to play excellent golf through the 1940 and 1941 season. Tommy who had been with me now for several years is probably the best caddie I have ever had.

In late 1940, I bought a brand-new Chevrolet Coupe. It was my first new car in over a decade since that old Dodge. I had made enough money playing golf over the last few years to set me up for life. I started thinking that maybe it was time for me to finally enroll at the university and get that electrical engineering degree that was my goal so many years ago. I knew that as I aged, my golfing skills would start to diminish, so I would need to have a career after my playing days were over.

I finished the 1941 season in first place again in money winnings and tour victories, but now the year is done. Every September 3 since 1936, I visit Mom and put fresh flowers on her grave and sit and talk with her for a while. I miss her every day, unlike my sister, who didn't even show up for her funeral, so we haven't spoken in years. She and her husband had done quite well with real estate investments during the Depression. She always felt superior to me and Mom.

One December morning as I was sitting in my chair reading the morning newspaper and listening to the radio, when a news bulletin broke in, and it was the president of the United States, Franklin D. Roosevelt, with a somber message. His voice made me put down my newspaper and listen closely as he told the nation that Japan had attacked us with airplanes at our military base in Pearl Harbor, Hawaii, trying to wipe out our Pacific fleet. Due to the unprovoked nature of that attack, the president was declaring war on the Empire of Japan. It wasn't long before Germany and Italy declared war on us, so now we were in it for sure. I had a decision to make. I knew that at the age of twenty-nine, I would be much older than the typical recruit, but I felt the need to serve my country.

On December 23, I drove over as I had for the last eight years to visit Doreen and take flowers to her grave. I thought I'll talk it over with her and then figure out what I should do. "Well, my love, I'm here again to see you, and today I have a question. It looks like the United States is headed for war on a large scale. I'm now much older than the usual draftee or enlisted man, but I think I need to join up to help out my country. What do you think I should do?" Of course, there was no answer, but the feeling I suddenly had was that I should indeed follow my instincts and join the Army. "Thank you, I'll do just that, see you next year."

The very next day, on December 24, a Wednesday, I sought out an Army recruiter to enlist. I walked into the recruiting office in downtown Dallas and was greeted by a young Army sergeant. He looked up at me and said, "Yes, how can I help you?"

"Well, sir, my name is Ron Perkins, and I want in the fight."

"Let me ask you this. What are your skills? Where do you think you would be best suited to serve?"

"For the last several years I have been a professional golfer."

"Wait a minute, I thought that name Ron Perkins sounded familiar. I'm from Northern California, and as a young teen, I think I was in the gallery when you won the Monterey Open back several years ago. Was that you?"

"Guilty, that was my first tour victory."

"Mr. Perkins it's a pleasure to meet you. It was your inspiring victory at such a young age that got me interested in playing golf. Thank you. But now back to business, have you thought about joining the USO tour."

"Tell me what is the USO."

"It's the United Services Organization that provides entertainment for our servicemen all over the world. We have Hollywood stars like Jimmy Durante and Lana Turner and musicians like Glenn Miller and the Andrew Sisters, and even some professional football and baseball players. A pro golfer like yourself would be welcome, and it would keep you out of combat."

"Well, you see there's the problem, I want to be in combat, so I think I'll pass on the USO."

"Okay, then what other skills or interests do you have?"

"I've always been fascinated by the power of electricity. We had this old radio years ago, and when it quit working, I took it apart down to the chassis and rebuilt it. It still works to this day. As a matter of fact, back in 1932 I had plans to go to college to pursue an electrical engineering degree. But because of, let's say, extenuating circumstances, I was not able to go. Could be I'll be able to one of these days, maybe after the war."

"How are you with math?"

"I'm not ashamed to say that I am a whiz with math. I really enjoy it. And I've always been mechanically inclined as well."

Next, he seemed to ask a rhetorical question. "You know what I think? I think the Army Air Corp is the place for you. They need personnel proficient with math and electrical systems. After you go through basic training, I'm recommending the Army Air Corp. Since the Japs bombed us, we have had a crush of young men signing up to join in the fight. We have had to open up new induction centers all over the United States, and the one you are to report to is in Fort Worth. Then, it's off to Fort Sill in Lawton, Oklahoma, for your boot camp."

"How long is boot camp, Sarge?"

"It used to be twelve weeks, but because of the urgency we find ourselves in, it has been cut in half and now lasts six weeks."

Since Doreen passed, I have traditionally spent the holiday season with Susan and Theodore Winthorp. They have kind of adopted me, since Doreen was their only child; and since I lost Mom, none of us have any other family to turn to. I wanted to tell them on Christmas that I had enlisted in the Army and would in all likelihood be deployed overseas once I finished my stateside training.

I was ordered to report to the induction center on Monday, January 5, 1942, at 6:00 a.m. sharp. Once I arrived we were ushered into a large room for an orientation of what we would be facing for the next week. Army M.Sgt. John "Jack" Chamberlin called us to attention and told us to take our seat. "Gentlemen, you will be spending the next week with us before you ship out for your basic training at Fort Sill in Lawton, Oklahoma. Our camp consists of the barracks you will be living in, a mess hall, our training center, and the company headquarters. You will be examined and tested to make sure that you are up to the rigors of training and combat. This induction center will allow you as a new soldier to have the chance of getting a taste of Army life. You will be marching, dressing and eating like a soldier."

The sergeant wasn't kidding. After the initial orientation, we were marched over to the barbershop, where we all had our hair shorn off down to only a stubble. Then we were issued several duffel bags worth of equipment and sent through seemingly unending medical exams. Finally, I was able to retire to the barracks where I was assigned a bunk and a footlocker. Included in the gear I had been issued was my uniform and combat boots, dog tags, a mess kit, canteen, belt, and cap.

The next morning we were awakened at 4:30 a.m. by the sergeant flipping on the lights and walking down the center of the barracks hitting a trash can with his baton. Within thirty minutes, we were dressed, up and standing at attention outside of the barracks in the cold morning air. It was a terrifying experience until you got used to it.

After assembly, we were marched over to the mess hall for an extraordinary breakfast—one of eggs, bacon, biscuits, potatoes, and an abundance of coffee. Then it was back out to the training field, where Sergeant Chamberlin addressed us once again, "For the next few days, you will be enduring physical training, classroom time and instruction on how to use an M-1 carbine. This is to prepare you for next week when you report to Fort Sill for your six weeks of basic training."

We spent the next few hours engaged in physical training, then lunch and then a trip to the command post to be issued our M-1. We were trained on how to disassemble, clean, and reassemble our new rifle and how to react to ambushes and booby traps. Once we turned our rifle back in, it was off to the classroom to learn theory of combat skills.

There was always an abundance of paperwork such as in-processing and medical record reviews. The week went by quickly, and the last part of the week was the exit interview. I sat down with a staff sergeant, and he began, "I see here that your recruiter recommended flight mechanical school. Is that still what you want?"

"Yes, Sergeant, I feel like that's what I seem best suited for."

"Well, according to your aptitude tests, that seems to be correct. So your military occupational specialty or MOS will be flight mechanical school at Chanute Field."

"Excuse me, Sarge, but where is Chanute Field?"

"It's in Champaign County, Illinois. Close to the town of Rantoul, about 130 miles south of Chicago. You will be there for 112 days."

The next morning, having completed our week at the induction center, we gathered our gear and boarded the bus at 6:00 a.m. bound for Fort Sill and six weeks of boot camp. So after six weeks there and 112 days at flight mechanic school, the earliest I could be deployed overseas would be around June 15. It took four hours to arrive at Fort Sill, where immediately we were shown to the barracks that would be our home for the next six weeks. It turned out that boot camp was just an intensified and longer version of the induction center. One again, we had our head shaved and were assigned serial numbers. We were organized into platoons where we would sleep, eat, learn together and even did hour upon hours of physical fitness training as a unit. We were trained to follow commands without question. We practiced the same basic skills over and over, marching, loading, unloading, and cleaning our weapon.

Our drill instructor used tough methods to force us to become attentive to every detail and protocol. Even the smallest mistake on our part could result in extra KP or kitchen duty or physical punishment. We trained for hours at the firing range, becoming proficient with our weapon and then there was the obstacle course that we all had to negotiate to graduate from boot camp. It consisted of running through an open field with full pack and rifle avoiding several booby traps along the way. Then scaling a ten-foot-high wall and swing with a rope down the backside over a muddy water-filled pit. Then the last was low crawling under barbed wire for one hundred yards with live machine-gun fire just inches over our head. The six weeks went by quickly, and I managed to graduate at the top of my class. Now it was off to airplane mechanic school in Illinois.

It was a long bus ride from Lawton, Oklahoma, to Chanute Field in Illinois. Once we arrived, we were directed to our barracks and then the mess hall. I didn't realize how hungry I was until the aroma of the wonderful food cooking wafted over me. I got in line and saw that there were multiple choices for dinner. I chose a large, thick rib eye steak with mashed potatoes and corn on the cob, with a green tossed salad. I washed it down with a cup of coffee. After dinner I went to the NCO club for a beer before calling it a night. This was Saturday night, so I had tomorrow to relax and settle in before the class regimen started on Monday morning. I thought about writing a letter but realized I really didn't have anybody to write to. Then it occurred to me to write Susan and Theodore and let them know where I was. After all they were now my adopted family.

# 16
## CHAPTER

Monday morning, we were awakened by the barracks supervising sergeant and hustled down into formation, then over to the mess hall for breakfast. The rest of the day would be spent in a classroom. We filed in and waited for our instructor, Captain Billy Tucker, to begin his lecture. Within moments he arrived. "Gentlemen, today we begin your course of study on how to become an airplane mechanic. As you know there is a war going on, so the time frame for this course has been cut in half. We need to get you in the field as soon as we can. Your individual training here will be under the auspices of the technical training command or the TTC. The term *airplane mechanic* refers to men who maintain airframes, aircraft engines, and accessories integral to the operation of the airplane. These accessories include such equipment as propellers, hydraulic and electrical systems, carburetors, and generators. Your primary responsibility as an enlisted mechanic is to work as a team under a noncommissioned officer called a crew chief. He will be reporting to a nonflying squadron engineering officer. You will be tested several times, and based on your scores, the highest graduates will receive the rank of master sergeant and be designated as a crew chief."

As the weeks rolled by, I learned how to use specialized tools, followed by practical study of airplane structures, operating systems, instruments, engines, and propellers. The part of the course that exposed me to elementary electrical theory and practice as a preliminary to the study of generator and starter systems, auxiliary electrical units, such as lighting circuits and warning systems, electronic turbocharger control system, and ignition system, intrigued me the most.

## THE LOVES OF A LIFETIME

The second part of that class covered electrically operated instruments, including the thermometer and fuel mixture indicators, as well as the artificial horizon and the automatic pilot.

The final weeks covered the airplane's principal structural elements, including wing panels, control surfaces, tail assemblies, fuselage, and landing gear. In the airplane engine curriculum, we studied the principles of internal combustion engines and the construction and operation of air- and liquid-cooled airplane engines. All of this as it applied to the B-24 Liberator. I finished at the top of the class and was promoted to master sergeant and named a crew chief. I was released from Chanute Field on June 19 and given a few days off until Monday, June 29, when I would leave for my assignment in Southern England.

We docked at Liverpool, England, and several hundred of my fellow Americans boarded the trains to our field designation. I was assigned to the 392$^{nd}$ BG squadron in the Eighth Air Force with our base located two miles north of the village of Wendling in Norfolk county. It was now July 1942, and the American forces were flooding into England to support and work with the Royal Air Force (RAF). Col. Glenn Andrews was our commanding officer.

I stepped off the train as we arrived in the quaint village of Wendling. It appears to be a bustling community of around two thousand to three thousand English citizens. I noticed a pub and a hotel and some various shops along the main street. I grabbed my duffel bag and threw it over my shoulder and was told the American camp was some two miles from Wendling. As I prepared for my walk, I heard my name being called. "Sergeant Perkins, over here." I turned and saw a corporal in an Army jeep motioning me over. "Sergeant, the colonel sent me to pick you up. I am Corporal Oliver Bates. Welcome to the war."

It was dusk on a Sunday evening, and as we were taking the short drive, I noticed a young lady on a bicycle headed straight for us. The corporal was too busy talking and taking his eyes of the road until I warned him, "Corporal, watch out, you're headed straight for that bicycle." He quickly jerked the wheel to narrowly avoid hitting the girl, and as she drove by, I heard her comment, "Stupid Yanks, always driving on the wrong side of the road." I saw in that brief moment that she was a stunningly beautiful young woman, probably in her early twenties. She had flaming red hair, and I think deep-blue eyes.

"Corporal, do you know her?"

"Yes, Sarge, her name is Rose Talbot, and she's a native that lives in Wendling but works as a nurse in our hospital. And you may have noticed, she is quite a dish."

Since Doreen passed, I had intentionally taken little interest in becoming involved with anyone; it just hurt too much to lose them. But Rose certainly piqued my interest.

Moment later we arrived at camp. It was a beehive of activity with buildings going up everywhere you looked. The corporal told me that our boys only started arriving here in May and the Army Corp of Engineers immediately went to work erecting barracks for enlisted men, NCOs, and officers' quarters. Plus, a hospital, airplane hangars, and maintenance motor pools along with a large mess hall and administrative offices. He directed me to my quarters, and once I was settled in, I realized it had been a very long day and I was starving. So I took the short walk to the mess hall, and once again I was not disappointed as the Army provides only the best of food. I heartily enjoyed a dinner of fried chicken, mashed potatoes, green beans with a slice of apple pie for dessert.

The corporal had informed me that Colonel Andrews wanted to see me first thing Monday morning. I walked into the colonel's office at 0600 hours.

"Sergeant Perkins, come in, how was your trip?"

"Just fine, sir. Glad to finally be here."

"Well, most of your crew is here and waiting in the B-24 hangar to meet you. Now, I can see from your records that you finished at the top of your class at the airplane mechanic school, and we desperately need you. We're flying missions every day, and quite a few of our airplanes are coming back badly damaged and in need of immediate repair. We're doing sorties into France and some into Germany itself. But that's where we run into trouble. We have fighter escort as far as

France, but there are no long-range fighter planes that can accompany us into Germany. Let me give you some statistics that you may not know about the Liberator. First of all it carries a crew of eleven men. There is a pilot, copilot, navigator, bombardier, radio operator, nose turret, two waist gunners, ball turret, and a tail gunner. They all depend on you and your crew to make sure their aircraft is in top condition and can get them to their target and home safely. I'm going to leave it to you to orient your men on job responsibility and procedure. They are assembled and expecting you. Good luck, Sergeant Perkins. Let me know if I can help you in anyway. Dismissed."

I walked into the hangar to find a B-24 sitting there, and by all I could tell, she was ready for flight. My flight crew of ten men were surrounding her. "Gentlemen, I'm Sgt. Ron Perkins, and I am your new crew chief. I'd like to meet each one of you individually, maybe later on today. But for now, I'd like to make sure that each of us is up to speed on the features of the B-24. First of all, this aircraft is a more modern design than the B-17 with a higher top speed, greater range, higher ceiling, and a heavier bombload. However, that being said, it is more difficult to fly with heavy control forces and poor formation flying characteristics. The positioning of the fuel tanks make her prone to fire, and the high fuselage mounted wings make it more difficult to survive crash landings. The pilot and the flight crew are all aware of this, but it is essential that you know about it also. The B-24 has a spacious, slab-sided fuselage that is built around a central bomb bay with two compartments that can accommodate up to 8,000 pounds of ordnance each."

I stopped and asked if there were any questions so far, and there were none. "Let me continue. The maximum speed of the B-24 is 290 miles per hour, with a 215 mph cruising speed. She is powered by four Pratt & Whitney turbocharged radial engines at 1,200 horsepower each. She has a range of 2,100 miles with a service ceiling of 28,000 feet. The B-24 is armed with ten .50-caliber Browning machine guns in four turrets and two waist positions. This airplane is not heated or pressurized, so all crewmen must wear oxygen masks on high-altitude missions at anything above 10,000 feet. Sometimes the temperature in the cabin can drop to as low as minus fifty degrees Fahrenheit. Any questions? Is this aircraft ready to go?"

"Yes, Sergeant, she has been completely gone through and inspected, gassed up, and ready for the next mission."

I was just about to dismiss my crew and let them get back to work when I heard someone walking up behind me. I turned to see this diminutive figure that probably only stood at maybe five feet, two inches in front of me, but he did have captain's bars on his shoulders. So I saluted and gave him the respect he deserved. "Yes, sir, can I help you? I'm Sgt. Ron Perkins, and I am the crew chief."

"I am Capt. Wally Walton, and this is my aircraft you men seem to have surrounded. I'm here to see if she's ready for her next combat mission."

"Yes, sir, she's all yours."

I instantly liked this little guy; he seemed to me to be supremely confident with a glint in his eyes of possessing a mischievous nature. I knew we would meet again.

I finished the day after pulling maintenance on several aircraft and returned to my quarters. After dinner I wanted to stretch my legs and walk into town and try out that pub I saw when I first came into the village of Wendling. I showered, put on my class A's, and walked into town. The pub was dark and smoky and not as big inside as it looked from the outside, and it was crowded with a mixture of servicemen from the base and local residents. I walked up to the bar, ordered a beer, then turned to take in my surroundings. It was then that I spotted her, sitting at a corner table alone, the same redhead that my corporal tried to run over yesterday. Feeling bold, I approached her. "Excuse me, but I think I owe you an apology." She looked up at me with a quizzical expression and said, "Whatever for. I'm sure I've never seen you before right now."

"Yesterday, you see, my corporal tried to run you over."

"Well, I do remember that, and you should apologize."

"Do you mind if I sit down?"

"Suit yourself, soldier."

I took my seat, but I had a burning question on my mind that I just had to ask. "I'm sorry for asking this, but do you realize that you could be Maureen O'Hara's twin sister. You are every bit as beautiful."

"Maybe you can tell me who Maureen O'Hara is."

"Well, she's a famous American actress."

She started to laugh and said, "I'm just kidding you, I know exactly who she is. And yes, I have heard that comparison before, and I do take it as a compliment. But, soldier, you haven't told me your name. I'm Rose Talbot." She extended her hand to shake mine, and I was momentarily speechless as her mannerisms so reminded me of Doreen.

"I'm sorry, my name is Sgt. Ron Perkins, and I am so pleased to meet you Ms. Talbot, it is miss, I hope."

"Yes, I am unmarried at this time, but, Ron, one never knows what the future holds for us."

I think of Doreen every day, and some nights I dream about her. But it has been a lonely and long ten years since I have had even the remotest of interest in another woman. But Rose intrigues me. We talked for hours that night until we both had to honor our respective curfews. But she did invite me to dinner the next night at her home.

After work, I checked a Jeep out of the motor pool and picked Rose up at the hospital after her shift had ended and drove to her house in Wendling. We pulled up to an unassuming but pleasant cottage, and I had the privilege of meeting Henry and Mary Talbot. After dinner, Rose and I sat in a swing on the front porch. "So, Sergeant, tell me about yourself."

"What would you like to know?"

"Well, for starters, have you ever been married?"

I hesitated, and as I thought back to 1932, I had to fight back tears. Then I decided to reveal a very personal part of my past. "No, I have never been married, but I was engaged with plans to marry. But a month before, she was killed in an automobile accident. That happened on December 23, 1932. I have not been with another woman, well until last night with you."

"Oh, I am so sorry to hear that."

"Then less than three years later, my mom died of pancreatic cancer, so I have been alone for a very long time."

I could see tears starting to well up in her eyes, and suddenly she pulled me in close and gave me the first kiss that I had experienced in a very long time. Rose and I started seeing each other on a regular basis after that night. If I wasn't at work, I was with her. As time went by, I guess we both came to the realization that this was going to be just a wartime fling. The war would eventually end, and I would be going back to Texas, and Rose's home was here in England. In addition to that, I knew that in my mind I was constantly comparing her to Doreen, and in the long run that would not be fair to Rose. So after a few months we both agreed to break off the relationship, with the hope of remaining friends. However, we eventually drifted apart completely, but I will always be grateful to Rose for the time we had together. She was a swell girl that will make some English gentleman a fine wife.

I turned my full attention to the job I was assigned, and in time my ground crew gained the reputation as the most efficient in the Eighth Air Force. Our turnaround repair time on our squadron's B-24s was unsurpassed. Throughout the rest of 1942 and 1943, the war intensified, and the number of dangerous and costly missions into Germany increased.

Since the summer of 1942, the United States Army Air Forces (USAAF) had classified all missions as either strategic or tactical. A strategic mission was an attack beyond the enemy's front line, predominantly production and supply facilities and was by far the most dangerous and risky. A tactical mission supported ground campaigns of which there were none at this time from the English air bases. But from the time I arrived here in July 1942, there have been rumors of plans of an invasion of the European continent.

Now we have been briefed on a large-scale mission planned for the last week of February 1944. Cold and clear weather had been forecast for the operation with the code name Operation Argument that became known as Big Week. On the nights of February 19–20, the RAF bombed Leipzig while the Eighth Air Force put over 1,000

B-17s and B-24s as well as 800 fighters, and the RAF provided 16 squadrons of Mustangs and Spitfires in an attack on 12 German aircraft factories. The B-17s targeted Leipzig for the Allgemeine Transportanlagen-Gesellschaft Junkers Ju 88 production and Erla Maschinenwerk, which manufactured the Bf-109 and Oscherslebel, the plant making Focke-Wulf Fw 190 A fighters. While the B-24s hit the Gothaer Waggonfabrik that produced the Messerschmitt Bf 110 and the Fw 190 Arado plant at Tutow and the Heinkel firm's headquarter at Rostock that produced the He 111. The raids were so successful and caused so much damage that the Germans were forced to move their aircraft manufacturing eastward to safer parts of the Reich.

The next day, over 900 bombers and 700 fighters of the Eighth Air Force destroyed more aircraft factories in the Braunschweig region. Over 60 Luftwaffe fighters were shot down with a loss of 19 American bombers and 5 fighters. On February 24, over 800 bombers hit Schweinfurt and the Baltic coast, losing 11 B-17s. And 230 B-24s hit the Messerschmitt Bf 110 assembly plant at Gotha, losing 24 aircraft. Fortunately, my friend Wally and his crew returned unscathed.

By the summer of 1944, we had been briefed on the planned invasion of Europe on June 6 and all the details and what our part would be. We were to fly over 2,300 sorties over Normandy and Cherbourg with the goal of neutralizing enemy coastal defenses and frontline troops. After D-Day we were assigned attacks on the German oil industry in Germany and Czechoslovakia, but this time we would have the luxury of P-51D and P-38L fighters as an escort.

At the end of 1944, I was advised that a Gen. Thomas Howell had arrived at our camp and was asking to see me. I didn't know if I was in trouble, I didn't see how. I had kept my nose clean the whole time I had been in England, so I was completely taken off guard by what he told me at my first meeting with him. "Sergeant Perkins, please sit down. I would like to offer you a proposition, one that I think you'll find most interesting and challenging. I can't tell you much, for what I am about to reveal to you is highly classified, and you don't have the proper security clearance as of yet. All I can tell you is that you'll be reassigned to something called the Manhattan Project. You will be ordered back stateside to Los Alamos, New Mexico."

"Why are you singling me out? I don't understand."

"You and your ground crew have a sterling reputation and are considered by your peers and commanding officers to be the best and most innovative chief and crew in England. Your country needs your particular skill set back in New Mexico, and you will be promoted to second lieutenant."

"How much time do I have to think this over and give you an answer?"

With that, the general looked at his watch and said, "You have five minutes. Your train for Liverpool leaves in an hour. Besides that, the Jerries are finished, they just don't know it yet. We're on their doorstep to the west, and the Russians are knocking on the door in the east. You're work here is done."

I caught the troop transport bound for New York, and once we arrived, I was ordered to immediately board a train for Albuquerque, New Mexico. Upon arrival, I was informed that I had passed the extensive background check and was cleared for a top secret security clearance. On the way to Los Alamos via staff car, I was able to read some background material on the Manhattan Project. I was astounded at what I read. It seems that we are in the process of developing something called an "atomic bomb." It is based on the discovery of nuclear fission in December 1938 by German chemists Otto Hahn and Fritz Strassmann and its theoretical explanation by Lise Meitner and Otto Frisch that made it possible to create an atomic bomb. It was feared that a German atomic bomb project would develop one first, and that type of weapon would extend the war.

In August 1939, Hungarian physicists Leo Szilard and Eugene Wigner composed the Einstein-Szilard letter, which warned of the development of an extremely powerful bomb of a new type. It urged America to stockpile uranium ore and accelerate the research, thus the beginning of the Manhattan Project. On June 17, 1942, President Roosevelt instructed the Army Corp of Engineers to construct an atomic weapons complex. A weapons lab was set up in Los Alamos,

New Mexico, on August 13, 1942, and Brig. Gen. Leslie R. Groves was installed as commander of the project. On November 25, 1942, Los Alamos was selected as the site for a separate scientific laboratory to design an atomic bomb.

I put down the material and waited to be further briefed by General Groves upon my arrival in Los Alamos. The drive from Albuquerque to Los Alamos only took about an hour, and when I arrived I was dispatched to General Groves's office. As I entered the room, I saw that another gentleman whom I did not know was also in attendance.

"Lieutenant Perkins, at ease. Come in and grab a seat. Let me introduce you to your director of the laboratory you'll be working in. This is nuclear scientist Robert Oppenheimer."

I stood and shook hands with Mr. Oppenheimer and said, "I am so glad to meet you, sir, and honored to be a part of this project, though I'm still not quite sure why I have been selected." General Groves spoke up, "I'll answer that. It's because of your war record of excellence as a crew chief. You came up with some interesting innovations and procedures that made your crew the best in England at their job. You seem to have a unique combination of understanding math and mechanics that make you a prime candidate for this assignment. Welcome aboard."

I was dismissed from the general's office and, with my head spinning, made my way to the officer's quarters. I began working in the laboratory the next morning. We were not allowed to leave the complex or contact any friends or relatives until we had developed the bomb. The months passed quickly as we worked around the clock. It appeared the Japanese were not going to give up even as we defeated them from island to island, moving ever closer to the Japanese mainland. The military command was preparing for an invasion but knew that it would cost at least a million American lives. So our project became supremely important.

We were finally able to detonate an implosion-type nuclear device in New Mexico on July 16, 1945. This led to the development of Little Boy and Fat Man that were used a month later in the bombing of Hiroshima and Nagasaki on Monday, August 6, and Thursday, August 9. It was only after a demonstration of this powerful new weapon that the Japanese finally surrendered, thus preventing a large-scale invasion that would have cost countless American and Japanese lives. The war was essentially over.

The Japanese formal surrender came on Sunday, September 2, 1945, on the USS *Missouri* in Tokyo Bay. On Monday, September 3, I was officially released from my military obligation and sent home. Coincidentally it was the tenth anniversary of Mom's passing. My goal now was to use the money I had earned playing golf and with the help of the GI Bill to finally look at enrolling in the university at Waco, just as Doreen and I had planned all those years ago. I still wanted that degree in electrical engineering.

First thing I wanted to do when I finally got back to Dallas was to find my old friends Sammy and Robert. Sammy now was the father of two precious little girls and had prospered during the war years. He didn't have to serve in the military because he was married with dependents, but he had done extensive volunteer work; and because he was now a wealthy man, he had invested a substantial amount of money in buying war bonds. His service station business had expanded to six locations, and he had plans to franchise more.

Robert and Margaret had brought a son and a daughter into this world, and Robert was still employed by the postal service, but he had risen in his career to the position of postal inspector. During the war, he and Margaret had both volunteered their time at the Dallas VA hospital.

I knew that Tommy had joined the Marines soon after I enlisted, but when I asked about him, Sammy told me that he had been in the Pacific campaign and was killed on Iwo Jima. He had won the Silver Star for bravery above and beyond the call of duty as he had charged a machine gun nest and took out six Japanese soldiers and destroyed their position before they got him. He saved several lives of his fellow Marines in his platoon that day. That sounds just like something Tommy would do. I'm going to miss him.

I still had Mom's house in east Dallas, but I decided to sell it and move to Waco, since I will be spending most of my time there anyway. I let the Winthorps know of my plans and assured them that I fully intended to stay in touch with them, no matter the future.

I went out to dinner with Sammy, Sarah, Robert, and Margaret to advise them of what I had decided my immediate future was going to be. Sammy began with asking me, "What about golf? Are you going back on the tour?"

"You know, I thought about that, but I'm thirty-three years old now, and I'm afraid there are too many hungry young bucks out there just starting their career. So I don't think I would stand much of a chance competing with them. Plus, the game has changed since I've been gone, and the equipment is so much better now than when I last played. I think I would just be lost. No, it's time for me to go in a different direction. I'll still come back to Dallas often, and you all are welcome to come see me in Waco anytime you want to. But I don't enroll until January, so I'll still be here through the holidays."

I went to see Mom and put some flowers on her grave and have a little conversation with her. "Mom, I'm sorry I haven't been to see you the last three years. I was kind of busy with the war, but now I'm back. I wanted to tell you that I am selling your house and moving to Waco to finally start college. Don't worry, I'll be back here every year that I am still alive to see you. I miss you every day."

On December 23, I went to see Doreen, and like I did with Mom, I apologized for having been absent the last three years, but I vowed that I would not let anything more stop me from coming to see her every year. "Doreen, my love, I wanted you to know that I am enrolling at the university in January to finally start on that college degree that we both planned on back in 1932. I know you're thinking it may be a little late since I am so much older now, but this is the first real opportunity I've had to be able to go. I must admit that for years, I didn't think I could stand to walk in your footsteps at the place you loved so much, but I think now it's time. I wanted to tell you that I have remained close to your mom and dad, and that they have treated me as their own child since your passing. Well, it's time for me to go. I love you still, and I will never forget you."

# CHAPTER 17

In January 1946, I did enroll in the university and set up my curriculum for an electrical engineering degree. I wanted to get my bachelor of science and maybe a master's. I no longer have a family or other obligations to speak of, so I can take all the time I need to realize my goal. With my earnings from my golf years still intact plus my Army Air Corps pension and the GI Bill, I am financially set for life. My course load is going to require an abundance of mathematics and basic engineering courses, as well as physics, but this is a curriculum I feel like is right in my wheelhouse.

My decision to sell Mom's house in Dallas was a painful one but turned out to be wise as I was able to find a spacious two-bedroom craftsman within walking distance off campus that perfectly suited my needs. Now I was all set to start my career. With new business opportunities opening up all over the United States, I thought it would be a piece of cake to find an industry that could challenge me and satisfy my ambitions. One area that piqued my interest was a new technology called television. This was a rapidly growing field that was constantly looking for innovation and new ideas.

As I walked across campus that first Monday, following the path that Doreen and I took so many years ago, I could feel her presence. If a breeze picked up, or if the temperature suddenly changed, I knew she was watching over me still.

With my war background and all that I had been involved in the last few years, especially the Manhattan Project, which was now no longer classified, I could refer to that experience on my resume. My future was bright, but I always had this feeling of loneliness.

Except for my brief relationship with Rose in England, I had shied away from any involvement with anyone, not even becoming close and personal with the men that served under me during the war.

But now after fourteen years, maybe it was time to think about opening myself up to other people again. For now my routine was to attend class, take in the library on occasion, and keep my grades up. After my typical day was finished, I would return home and read some, listen to the radio, then call it a night. I went through the spring and fall semester in 1946, pausing only long enough to return to Dallas for Thanksgiving dinner with the Winthorps, a tradition we had maintained all these years. It also gave me the opportunity to make my annual visit to Mom.

I would return to Dallas for Christmas staying with the Winthorps and visiting Sam and Sarah and spending some time with Robert and Margaret and their burgeoning families. Of course, I would take flowers and visit Doreen on December 23.

"I wanted to let you know that I am doing very well in my college studies, and I desperately yearn for you to be there with me, just like we planned. I miss you as much now as I always have. I guess that feeling will never go away. I love you, and I'll see you again next year."

I'm now starting the spring 1947 semester, my second year at the university. The courses will now be more intense and difficult, requiring more study time. I have no other interests, so that should not be a problem. I keep mostly to myself, but I have made a few casual friends along the way. It's hard for me to identify with these kids since they are all so much younger and less experienced in life than I am. One of the places I like to go to study is in a cubby hole of a snack bar in the student union building. During the day, it is mostly deserted and quiet, and I can concentrate without interruption. I was there one day in the late spring, minding my own business and totally engrossed in my studies, when all of a sudden there was a crashing sound of falling textbooks. I looked up to see this somewhat bewildered girl drop all her notes and books on the ground in front of me.

Being a gentleman, I closed my textbook and rushed over to help this poor girl retrieve her belongings that were now scattered all over the snack bar floor. It didn't hurt that she was a quite lovely young lady. "May I help you, miss? You seem to be in some distress." She smiled at me a most fetching smile that seemed to light up the room and said, "Thank you, I obviously need help. I guess I overloaded myself." We collected her belongings, and she said further, "I so appreciate your kindness, let me buy you a cup of coffee. It's the least I can do." This girl intrigued me like no other had in such a long time. Don't get me wrong. Over the years I had passed on many opportunities as I always measured them against Doreen, and they all failed. That includes Rose, my English friend, who came closer than anyone else at capturing my affection. But there was something different about this young lady, and I wanted to know more about her.

"I would love to have a cup of coffee with you. My name is Ron Perkins, and you are?"

"Hi, I'm Kathleen Winston. I am a graduate student here, studying for my master's degree in nursing. How about you, are you a graduate student also?"

I laughed and said, "No, I'm just old. I waited until after the war to start my college career. Perhaps, I'm a little late, but I am now a sophomore pursuing a degree in electrical engineering."

Kathleen was a vivacious girl with shoulder-length strawberry-blonde hair, and she stood about five feet, four inches tall. She was slim and athletic with soft brown eyes and as beautiful a girl as I had noticed in years. We sat there and talked for over an hour. Her personality bubbled over with enthusiasm and optimism, and she reminded me in so many ways of Doreen. I think Doreen would have instantly like her. I assumed that I was several years older than her, but it didn't seem to matter.

"My it's getting late. I was so enjoying talking with you that I lost all track of time. Do you think we could meet again soon?"

I was so enthralled with her, for the first time in it seemed like so long, that I was slow to respond, "How about dinner tomorrow night? Would that be too presumptuous of me?"

"No, not at all, I think that would be fun. I live in a boarding house on Eight Street, do you know of it?"

"No, but I'll find it. Is seven okay with you?"

"Sounds perfect, I'll see you then."

I had not had this feeling about another person in so long that I almost forgot how to act. She had ignited a passion in me after just a few hours that I thought had died with Doreen. I wanted to tell her of my past so we would have a clear understanding of each other right from the beginning if this relationship was going to go anywhere.

I wanted to take her to this great little homestyle restaurant where you could get any kind of food that you desired from a Mexican cuisine to steaks and everything in between. When I picked her up, she answered the door wearing a stunning dark blue dress with a white wide-brim hat with her blonde hair framing her face and featuring her beautiful expressive brown eyes.

Once we were seated at the restaurant, I asked, "So tell me more about yourself and your family. You didn't tell me last night where you were from."

"I'm from a little town in far West Texas called Hale Center, and no you would have never heard of it. It's just a small farming community close to Plainview, Texas. My parents live there with my younger brother, and I have an older sister that goes to the college in Canyon."

"Why did you choose to go here, it's so far from your home. Not that I'm complaining."

"Mainly because of the quality of the nursing school. It's the best in the state. And how about you, any brothers or sisters?"

"I have an older sister, but we don't really get along. I haven't seen her in years. My mom and dad are both gone, so I really don't have any family left. One thing you don't know about me is that back in the 1930s I was a professional golfer, and I did quite well on the tour."

"Ron, that's fascinating. Do you still play professionally?"

"No, I gave it up because of my age, and I wanted to pursue a college degree. I just play for fun occasionally now. Do you play?"

"Oh, no, but I would love to learn to if you were of a mind to teach me."

Kathleen was becoming more and more attractive as the evening wore on.

"I do want to tell you something personal about my past that I feel like you need to know."

She had this worried look on her face and said, "My goodness, whatever could it be?"

"Back in 1932, I was engaged to be married to a young lady by the name of Doreen Winthorp. But she was tragically killed in an automobile accident a month before we were to be married. The last time I had even the remotest resemblance to a serious relationship was during the war in 1942 in England with a girl by the name of Rose. Even then, it was a brief friendship that only lasted a few weeks. The reason I'm telling you all this is to be perfectly honest with you that even after fourteen years, I'm not sure that I am totally over Doreen. It's possible that I never will totally be able to forget her. But I do want to see you again, if you are willing."

"Ron, I am sorry to hear of your loss. But like you said it was fourteen years ago. Maybe it's time now for you to move on, and if I can help with that, I certainly want to."

"I want you to know that I do want to see you again as soon as you will allow it. And yes, you are most certainly right, it is time for me to start moving forward."

We stayed at the restaurant for another hour and then sat in my car for a while longer talking about every subject you could think of. Then as the hour was getting late, I walked her to her door; and as I extended my hand to shake hers, she squeezed my hand and pulled me in close and gave me my first kiss in many years. It was sensual and made me feel weak in my knees.

My new interest in Kathleen did give me mixed feelings. I was torn between my loyalty to Doreen and my desire for new companionship with this exciting new person that has suddenly entered my life. After that first dinner, my relationship with Kathleen grew to the point that we were seeing each other on almost a daily basis as my affection for her grew with each time that we were together. I just couldn't explain my nagging feeling of guilt.

In early 1947 I decided to buy a new car. My life was going well, and my old 1940 Chevrolet was on its last legs. So I chose one beautiful spring day to go automobile shopping. The one that had caught my eye was a snazzy Mercury convertible that I had seen advertised on billboards and in the newspaper. So I drove my old Chevrolet coupe into the dealership. Sitting there on the showroom floor was exactly what I was looking for. It was a Canary yellow convertible with tan leather interior. She was a V8 with 100 horsepower and a three-speed manual transmission. This Mercury was fully loaded with a radio and heater, fog lamps, and wide whitewall tires. She was truly poetry in motion. I had never seen such a magnificent automobile before.

They offered me $200 for my Chevrolet, dropping the price of the Mercury to just a shade over $2,000. I paid for the Mercury with a bank draft and drove her home. First thing I wanted to do was surprise Kathleen with my proud new purchase. I called her up on the boarding house common telephone and asked for her. "May I speak to Kathleen Winston, please."

"Just a moment, I'll tell her she has a telephone call."

I only had to wait for a few seconds until I heard her sweet voice on the other end of the line. "Hello, who's calling?"

"Hi, it's me. I have a surprise for you. Can I drop by?"

"Oh, I like surprises. Sure, come on over. I'm here for the rest of the day, I've finished all of my classes."

I drove over to Kathleen's boarding house, and she was sitting on the swing on the front porch waiting for me. Of course, she didn't recognize the car, so I came to a stop, revved the engine to get her attention. "Hey, missy, want to go for a ride?" Kathleen looked up and smiled, then ran down the front steps to greet me. "Oh, this must be your surprise. What a sensational automobile. Can we go for a ride?"

"Absolutely, hop in."

"Wait, let me go get a scarf, then I'll be ready."

Kathleen jumped in and slid over next to me, and we were off on a beautiful sunny spring day for a drive around the park. The low rumble of the dual exhaust was a symphonic accompaniment to the music of Francis Craig singing "Near You" on the radio. We stopped by the carhop drive-in for a Coke and then back to her house with plans to take in a movie later.

"Have you decided what you want to see?"

"There's a new comedy that just came out called *The Ghost and Mrs. Muir* that I have just been dying to see. Would that be okay with you?"

"Sure, anything you want to see is A-okay with me. What's it about?"

"It's about this young widow that moves to the seashore with her daughter to an old cottage. On her first night there she is awakened when she sees an apparition of the former owner, an old sea captain. Then the story evolves from there. I don't want to give away any more than that."

"Sounds great, I'll pick you up at seven."

*****

The movie was superb, and on the way home, Kathleen asked me a question, "Ron, we are almost at the end of the semester. I was wondering what your plans for the summer are."

"Well, I have already signed up for the first six-week summer school session. I want to graduate either ahead of schedule or at least on time. Why do you ask? What are you doing for the summer?"

"I'm going home to west Texas, and the reason I asked was I hoped you would come out to my home and meet my family and spend some time with me."

"I'm committed to the first summer school semester, but not to the second. I could come out there somewhere in mid-July if that would be acceptable."

"I would love that."

We were down to the last two weeks of May and the spring 1947 semester. Kathleen and I spent quite a bit of time at my off-campus house, but she had never spent the night. I had not really pushed the issue of intimacy, not wanting to run her off; but in all honesty, it was something I desperately wanted. Then the last Friday night before the end of the semester, I had taken Kathleen out to dinner and then over to my house to relax and sit on the couch and listen to the radio. The song "Peg o' My Heart" by the Harmonicats came on, and Kathleen asked me a question, "Ron, can I ask you something?"

"Sure, fire away."

"How do you like your eggs in the morning."

At first I didn't grasp what she was trying to tell me, but I could tell by the wry smile on her face that she was subtlety trying to communicate with me. When I finally woke up, I pulled her close to me, and we embraced and shared a long and passionate kiss. Our relationship changed for the better that night. The next morning I got up and went into the kitchen to make coffee, and when I returned she was awake. I sat on the side of the bed and had a question of my own. "Kathleen, how long have we been seeing each other?"

"I would say around three months."

"Do you think that's long enough for you to be comfortable with me telling you that I love you?"

"To tell you the truth, I didn't know why you waited that long. For I certainly feel that way about you. I love you too, Ron."

We spent a glorious weekend together, and on Monday, I regretfully put her on a train bound for Amarillo. I knew it was going to be a long six weeks before I would see her again, so I immersed myself in my work, eagerly anticipating the day that I would board that same train for Amarillo on July 14.

That day finally has arrived, and I am so eager to see Kathleen, I can barely contain myself. The train ride seemed to take forever, but finally we pulled into the Amarillo station. I disembarked, and there she was waiting for me on the platform. We rushed to each other, kissed, and she said, "I am so excited to see you. Six weeks of separation is too long. Promise me it will never happen again."

"You have my word. I couldn't wait to get here to be with you. I'm eager to meet your parents."

We took the short drive from Amarillo to Hale Center and to Kathleen's home. It was a large and handsome ranch-style house. We parked her car and walked up to the front door, where her mom and dad were waiting to greet us. "Hello, Mr. and Mrs. Winston, it's such a pleasure to meet you."

"Ron, I'm Hubert and this is my wife Sally, and we have heard so much about you. It seems like we already know you. You have really captivated my daughter's heart. Welcome to our home."

After introductions were concluded, Kathleen showed me to the guest room. "You'll get to meet my whole family this week. I didn't expect my sister, Mary, to be home from school this summer. But she has graduated and decided to stay here until this fall when she is off to New York. She graduated from college with a bachelor's degree in both finance and business and is off to go to work on Wall Street for a brokerage firm. She's very excited about that. My brother Paul is in high school and will graduate next year and for some reason wants to go into the Army. There you have it, that's my family. You'll be able to meet them all at dinner tonight."

Their home was a large five-bedroom house with three bedrooms in one wing and the master and guest bedroom in the other, with a full bathroom located at each end of the house and a half bath in the center with the kitchen and living areas also located in the center of the house. It was a beautiful and comfortable home, not elaborate or pretentious at all.

An hour later, I could smell the aroma of a wonderful meal being prepared by Kathleen's mom. She had told me prior to my arrival what a fantastic cook her mom was.

As we were waiting to enjoy dinner, I was able to meet Paul and Mary, both just as charming as Kathleen. Obviously, they had been brought up by kind and courteous parents. Once we were seated and grace had been given, Mr. Winston asked me a question, "Tell me a little about yourself, Ron."

"Well, sir, before the war, I was a touring golf professional. Then in the war, I was stationed in England at the rank of master sergeant as a crew chief on a B-24 bomber ground crew. Then in the last days of the war I was promoted to second lieutenant and served in the Manhattan Project in Los Alamos, New Mexico. When I was released from active duty, I decided to enroll at the university in quest of an electrical engineering degree, and that's where I met your lovely daughter."

I became so engrossed in telling my story that I failed to notice that all had ceased talking and were listening to me tell my story. Finally, Mr. Winston said, "My goodness, what a story. It literally took my breath away, listening to all that you have accomplished in such a short amount of time. Most impressive, Mr. Perkins, most impressive." Paul spoke next, "Say, Ron, do you think you could help me improve my golf game? The reason I ask that is I play football for my high school, and I am on the golf team, but my game could certainly stand some improvement. I seem to have a major problem with my short game."

"Sure, Paul, I'd be more than happy to help and give you some tips on what I've learned through the years."

After dinner we retired to the den for coffee and conversation as Kathleen sat next to me on the couch. Paul excused himself and went to his room. It was getting late in the evening and it had been a long day, so we all retired for the evening. The next morning I dressed for breakfast; and as I came out of my room, I simply followed the aroma of brewing coffee. I walked into the kitchen and quickly saw that I was the last one up as they were all waiting on me.

Paul was the first to see me, and with an excited voice, he said, "Hello, Mr. Perkins, welcome. I have to tell you that I looked you up in a sports almanac I have and found that you were not just a run-of-the-mill touring pro, but in the late 1930s you were the champion of the PGL for like three years running. I bet you can help me with my game. When did you start playing golf for the first time?"

"Paul, how old are you?"

"I'm seventeen, sir, why do you ask?"

"Because that's exactly the age I was in 1929 when I was first introduced to the game of golf by my best friend Robert Hays. I was able to catch on quickly, but I didn't win my first tournament until three years later in 1932. So what I'm telling you is that if you want to excel at golf, it takes dedication and patience. I would be delighted to give you some instruction if you want."

About that time Kathleen joined in, "What about me? I want to learn too." I had to laugh and say, "Well, I didn't bring my clubs, but if you have a set and a practice range close by, we could go anytime you want and spend a few hours."

"I do have a complete set of Spaldings, and we only have a driving range in Hale Center, but we can play a round of golf in either Amarillo that is only eighty-three miles north of here on Highway 87, or we can go into Plainview that is just seven miles. There are plenty of courses around."

"Okay, young man, why don't we go to your practice range this afternoon and then maybe later in the week, we can actually play a game of golf. I can play out of your bag, if that's okay with you."

The boy turned out to have talent and a promising future in golf. I felt like if I worked with him enough, he could be good enough to get a golf scholarship. By the way Kathleen, as I already knew, was a very athletic girl, and she too took to the game with ease and an unexpected level of skills. My planned one-week stay in West Texas turned out to be three weeks, before I returned to the university to ready myself for the fall 1947 semester.

I preceded Kathleen back on campus by a couple of weeks to prepare for the fall 1947 semester. We continued to accelerate our relationship to the point that we were for all practical purposes inseparable. But I still had this nagging feeling of guilt in the back of my mind, and with the holiday season coming up, I felt the need to try and clear my conscience. Kathleen had made plans to spend the semester break and the holidays in Hale Center, and of course I was invited, but I declined and decided to stay for holidays in Dallas with Susan and Theodore and spend some time with my old friends. Without much explanation, Kathleen understood and reluctantly agreed.

I can't explain why I had this overwhelming feeling of guilt, like I was cheating on Doreen, but I wanted to discuss it with Susan and Theodore and inform them of this new person that has come into my life. On the day before Thanksgiving, the Winthorps met me at the train station and insisted I stay with them for the holidays. I was eager to unburden my heart to them.

After dinner, as we were sitting in the parlor, I thought I would approach the subject. "I have something to talk to you two about, and I don't quite know how to begin, so I'll just jump right in. I found somebody that I've been seeing since last spring. Her name is Kathleen Winston, and someday I would like for you to meet her. I do feel somewhat guilty about this new relationship, but it has been a long time since we lost Doreen. I guess I want your opinion and maybe your blessing."

"Ron, we both felt like for a long time now that you needed to finally move on with your life and find somebody else to love the same way you loved our Doreen. As you said, she has been gone for a while now, and I assure you she would want you to find a girl to make you happy, just as we do. We want you to have a fulfilled life. You know we think of you as our son. We would really like to meet your young lady. Maybe you can bring her up here the next time you come to visit us."

I was somewhat surprised and relieved at their reaction, but I wanted to go and talk to Mom and Doreen about it too. So I decided to break with my usual routine and visit them both this holiday. I knelt first by Mom's grave and placed the flowers I brought and started telling her about my new friend. "Mom, I wanted you to know that after all these years, I have finally been seeing someone on a serious and regular basis for the first time since Doreen passed. I wish you were here to meet her. She's a lovely girl named Kathleen Winston, and I know you would love her as much as I do. Anyway, I love you and miss you every day."

The next step was going to be the hardest in my mind as I sat down on the ground, placed the flowers, and began to unburden my heart. "I know I'm here a little earlier than usual, and I will come back on December 23 to see you again, but I have something I need to tell you. It's been fifteen years since you left us, and I now have somebody new in my life. I want you to know that I will always love you, and I will never forget you, but it's time for me to move on with my life. I hope you understand. I talked to your mom and dad, and they approve, and I believe if you could meet her, you would love her as much as I do. So I will be back in December, and this will never change as long as I draw breath. I will come see you every year."

I returned to Dallas alone for Christmas, feeling like Kathleen wasn't ready to meet Susan and Theodore, but she was most sympathetic and understanding of the emotions I still felt for a long-ago lost love. I think she appreciated my dedication and loyalty. With the holiday season over, we were ready to start the spring 1948 semester. Kathleen was scheduled to finish her master's studies by the spring of 1949, so I decided to increase my course load to match her and graduate in three years as well.

Paul had absorbed what little I could instruct him on and did drastically improve his golf game to the point that he was offered a golf scholarship to West Tech in Amarillo. Then one night in late spring, Paul called me, "Ron, this is Paul. I am graduating in two weeks, and I was wondering if you could be there. Kathleen has already told me she would. It would mean a lot to me."

"Sure, I'll come out with your sister, I wouldn't miss it. Thank you for inviting me."

"One other thing. I have entered in an amateur tournament in Amarillo in June, and I wanted to ask if you would consider being my caddie."

"Paul, I'm flattered. A good caddie carries a lot of responsibility as you probably know. Are you sure you want an old warhorse like me on your bag?"

"Yes, sir, I would be honored."

"Well, Paul, I will agree but only on a temporary basis. Eventually you will need to find one of your peers that you trust and feel like you can rely on to be your caddie on a permanent basis. I had the luxury of having a great caddie on my bag when I was coming up."

In all honesty, I was thrilled to once again be on the course in competition in any capacity. It would give me the opportunity to relive vicariously my youth through Paul. I hadn't competed since before the war.

I watched this young man improve and blossom into one of the best golfers on the amateur circuit. "Paul, I truly believe after you graduate from college, you will easily qualify for the PGL tour. I will be there to cheer you on as much as I can."

Kathleen and I continued on a path of making our relationship permanent, and in the spring of 1949, as we were both set to graduate, I made a decision. "Kathleen, I need to ask you something." As I went down on one knee in front of her and held her hand, I felt her tremble as she put her other hand over her mouth as tears started to flow; she knew exactly what I was about to do. "I love you, and I have waited for this day for two years. Will you marry me?" With that I produced an engagement ring from my pocket for her approval. She sank down on her knees and wrapped her arms around my neck, and through tears and kisses, she said, "I absolutely will marry you, but I have only one question. What took you so long?"

We set the date for November 4, 1949. I asked Robert as my oldest friend to be my best man. We decided to have the ceremony at the church in Waco we had been attending since my freshman days. I arranged for travel by train for Kathleen's family and for my friends from Dallas. I invited Susan and Theodore, but because of some health problems that Theodore was going through, they unfortunately had to decline. "I am so sorry to hear that. I was really counting on you being there. But I understand. Would it be possible for Kathleen and I to come see you for the Thanksgiving holiday? I really want you to meet her."

"Ron, we would love to see you then, but only if you and your lovely bride agree to stay with us."

"You have a deal, we'll see you then."

Our wedding was a day of glorious celebration for two people who are fatally and completely in love. The ceremony was performed with friends and family in attendance. At the reception, Robert pulled me aside and said, "Ron, I am so happy for you. I know you have needed someone special in your life for an awfully long time. We all loved Doreen, and none of us will ever forget her, but you are way past due to find a new love in your life. Congratulations, man."

We hurried to the train station to catch the Sunset Express train bound for Palm Springs, California, for a two-week honeymoon. We had booked a luxury suite, and the accommodations were first-class all the way. It was late Saturday night as we got underway, so it was an early dinner and then back to our suite to enjoy our honeymoon night.

The next morning, we slept in late, then made our way to the dining car for a scrumptious breakfast. The extraordinary feature of train travel is the excellence of their food. We dined on eggs, toast, hash brown potatoes, bacon, sausage, coffee, and orange juice. We ate like this was going to be our last meal. I suppose we worked up an appetite. "Let me be the first to wish you a happy birthday. Now that you have your anniversary on November 4 to go with your $32^{nd}$ birthday on November 5, it will be easy to remember. I have reserved a room for us at the Hotel Del Tahquitz resort in Palm Springs for our two-week stay. I was told that the Hollywood movie stars prefer the Hotel Del Tahquitz. Maybe we'll see somebody famous. I wanted to let you know that I have ordered your birthday gift to be delivered to our room there so we can enjoy it while we are in California. I do hope you like it."

"You must give me a hint, I have no idea what it could be."

"No, that would just ruin the surprise. You'll just have to wait."

"Can you at least tell me what we'll be doing during our stay there."

"To begin with, I have booked us on a bus tour of the movie star homes. I understand quite a few of them have second homes in Palm Springs."

"That'll be fun, but what else?"

"Well, there's hiking, sightseeing, casinos, horseback riding, and on and on. Believe me, we will be totally entertained."

Soon enough we arrived at the Palm Springs train station in beautiful, lush downtown. But I must say as we looked out of the windows of the train as we passed through a desolate scene of nothing but sand and mesquite bushes, I was beginning to worry that I had made a mistake. But I needn't have been concerned, for Palm

Springs is truly an oasis. The temperature as we stepped off the train had to be in the high seventies or low eighties with an abundance of sunshine. When we left Texas, it was overcast and in the forties. So this was a welcome change.

We took a taxi to the Hotel Del Tahquitz which was an impressive structure in early Spanish Mission motif. We were guided to our luxurious room which had a panoramic view of the mountains that surrounded Palm Springs. In the corner was the surprise birthday gift I had arranged for Kathleen. At first she didn't see it, but then as she surveyed our suite, she said, "Oh my goodness is that my birthday gift?"

"Yes, I hope you like it. Since I still have my PGL card and a relationship with Spalding golf clubs, and I still have some influence in the golfing community, I ordered a set that was custom-made to fit your height. And I had them make me a new set as well. Tomorrow we have a tee time at the resort golf course so you can immediately try them out. I hope you like them."

"I love them, I've never had my own set. I will cherish them always."

We arrived for our tee time the next morning. Using new clubs for both of us required some adjustments, but by the back nine we were performing well. I hadn't played much golf since coming back from the war, so I was understandably rusty. Kathleen, on the other hand, once she acclimated to her new set of golf clubs was striking the golf ball with accuracy and consistency. She was indeed a natural golfer.

During our two-week stay, we dined at the finest restaurants and ventured out to the Dunes casino for some blackjack and to take in one of their fabulous floor shows in the casino nightclub. We visited the Chi Chi nightclub and the Cove club. The first week we were there we took the fascinating tour of the movie star homes including Bob Hope's and Lana Turner as well as Alan Ladd. But by the end of the two weeks we were approaching exhaustion trying to take in all there was to do and see in Palm Springs, so when our train pulled out, we were more than ready to return home and start our new married life together.

# 18
## CHAPTER

We arrived back in Waco on November 18, less than a week from Thanksgiving. Kathleen and I agreed, and I had already notified Susan and Theodore of our intention to spend Thanksgiving with them. So we left Waco on Wednesday, November 23, bound for Dallas. I decided to drive the Mercury instead of taking the train to give us a bit more flexibility in our schedule while we were in Dallas. I had so much I wanted to show her. "As you already know, I visit my mom and Doreen's grave every year during the holidays. I hope that is okay with you if I continue to do so. I won't make you go with me if you don't want to."

"Ron, I know how important that is to you, and of course I'll go with you."

Kathleen and I visited Mom and Doreen's final resting place on December 23. Then we spent the Christmas holiday in Hale Center with Kathleen's family returning to Waco to celebrate our first New Year's Eve as a married couple. We welcomed in 1950 with unbounded optimism about our future.

In January I applied for and was hired by the new television station in Waco as, of all things, a camera operator at the astounding annual salary of $4,000 a year. I had to smile at being told what my salary would be as I remembered back to my days as a golf pro where I would make more than that on a good weekend of playing in a tournament. That being said, that wasn't my objective. I wanted into the television industry any way I could get there. At least now I had my foot in the door.

Kathleen was hired by the Waco General Hospital as an entry-level nurse. Now, we were both gainfully employed and living in my small house just off campus. I would have been happy in that situation for the rest of my life, but I knew that life has a way of throwing you a curveball. In the early spring, Kathleen started complaining of being tired more so than usual. We tried to explain it a way as a symptom of her working too many hours at the hospital. But then the headaches started followed by early-morning nausea. I finally convinced her to visit her doctor.

As we sat there waiting for the doctor to return and dreading to hear what he might say, he finally walked back in, strangely enough with a slight smile.

"Well, Doc, what's wrong with her? Why is she feeling ill all the time?"

He smiled one again, sat across from us, and said, "Mrs. Perkins, the only thing wrong with you is that you are pregnant. Congratulations." This was something we never expected as we both felt like we were both too old to have children with me almost thirty-eight and Kathleen at nearly thirty-three, but I guess miracles do happen.

We walked out of his office jubilant at the news. We were going to have a welcome new addition to our family. By the fall season, Kathleen had to take leave of her job as she was now six months pregnant, with a January 1951 birth planned. Money was no problem as I still had my Army pension and my savings from the golf tour to more than make up for losing Kathleen's salary. Like I said, life does throw you a curveball every now and then, but this was a welcome change.

With the television industry in its infancy, this new little station in Waco was not only understaffed, but had very few people employed that understood any of the principles of electronics to be able to fully execute their function. Particularly our station manager, that had been a reporter for the Houston newspaper who was in this job way over his ability and I think was hired out of desperation.

I finally went to the ownership of the station and pleaded my case to replace him as manager. I pointed out my qualifications.

Finally a month later they called me in for a meeting and announced they had fired him and were appointing me to take his place. What helped my case more than anything else was the fact that this station was becoming the joke of the industry. They could barely get any programming on the air at all until I took over. I added some new and necessary procedures and changed the way the programming was carried out. Before long, we had gained respect and the reputation as a quality business once again.

On January 10, 1951, Kathleen gave birth to a healthy beautiful baby girl that we named Martha Marion Perkins. The Martha was in honor of Kathleen's grandmother, and of course the name Marion was for my mom. It always amazes me how quick life can change without warning. In February, a network executive came into our station unexpectedly and asked for a meeting with me.

"Mr. Perkins, my name is Chester Thomas, and I am the vice president of the National Network, and I have come here today to talk to you in person. We have taken notice of how you have turned this television station around in less than a year, and we would like to explore your feelings on coming to work for the network. We want to make you our chief of research and development. It would require moving to Los Angeles, California, but you would receive an annual salary bump up to $20,000. We would pay off your existing home and all you and your family's travel expenses. Does that sound like something you might be interested in?"

"I am overwhelmed by your more-than-generous offer, and yes I am most certainly interested. But can I have the day to discuss it with my wife and get back to you tomorrow?"

"Yes, but be advised, I am leaving on the train in two days, and this offer goes away if you haven't accepted by then."

"No problem, I will talk to you tomorrow."

I called Kathleen at home, "Hi, are you and Martha doing okay today?"

"We are just fine, what's up?"

"I have some exciting news, and I am coming home right now to discuss it with you." I walked into the house, and Kathleen had put Martha down for a nap. "I just had this most interesting conversation with a gentleman by the name of Chester Thomas who is the vice president of the National Television Network. He has offered me a position with the network as head of the research and development department with an annual salary of $20,000. But it would require that we move to Los Angeles, California. What do you think?"

"First of all, let me catch my breath. Now, that is certainly great news. Is that something you want?"

"Yes, of course, but only if you are okay with it."

"I've wanted to go back to California since our honeymoon in Palm Springs. Do you think I could find work out there?"

"I'm sure of it. They're bound to have hospitals in California too."

"I suppose they have golf courses, don't you think?"

"I know they do, remember I played there back in 1932."

"Then why aren't we packing?"

I went to Mr. Thomas's hotel and met with him to accept his offer. "My wife and I are enthusiastically accepting your most generous offer. When do you want me to report for duty?"

"Mr. Perkins, I already have the wheels in motion. We will expect you within the month, if that's acceptable to you."

"I'll see you then, sir. And thank you."

I wanted to make one last trip to Dallas to tell the Winthorps and introduce them to our baby girl before we left for California and to also swing by and tell my friends Sam and Robert. Susan and Theodore were delighted to meet Martha, and I invited them out to California, but I knew that Theodore's health was rapidly failing, so that wasn't going to happen.

*****

We settled into our new home in the Hollywood Hills, close to the studio, and for the next two years our life was perfect. We continued every December to return to Dallas to visit Susan and Theodore and my old friends and of course to keep my tradition of dropping by Mom and Doreen's grave site. Then in early 1953, Susan called me with the bad news that Theodore had passed away, leaving her alone. I immediately insisted that she let us move her out to Los Angeles so I could see to her for the rest of her days. She had after all taken care of me after Mom passed.

Kathleen and I joined the country club in Hollywood and played together almost every weekend. She was hired as a nurse supervisor at a hospital close to us. As the years passed, we watched our little girl to grow into a beautiful child, just like her mom. I was living the life I had always dreamed of.

The End

# Golf Club breakdown comparison

| | |
|---|---|
| Play Club | Driver |
| Brassie | 3–wood |
| Spoon | 5–wood |
| Baffy | 7–wood |
| Driving Iron | 1–iron |
| Mid Iron | 2–iron |
| Mid-Mashie | 3–iron |
| Mashie-Iron | 4–iron |
| Mashie | 5–iron |
| Spade-mashie | 6–iron |
| Mashie-Niblick | 7–iron |
| Pitching-Niblick | 8–iron |
| Niblick | 9–iron |
| Jigger | Pitching or chipping |

# About the Author

James B. Styles is a native Texan, born in Fort Worth, and he grew up and attended high school in Beaumont. James has a BA degree from Baylor University in journalism. Writing has always been an interest of his, which led to a column for his high school newspaper, then composing technical manuals at his first job out of college in the aerospace industry, to now writing novels. James was self-employed for the last seventeen years until he sold his business in 2015 and spent many years prior to that in the automotive industry. James currently lives with his wife, Ann, and he has a daughter and a stepdaughter. His family attends a local church regularly, and he has an interest in classic cars and playing golf. James also published his first book with Covenant Books, *Through the Glass Darkly*, in 2020.

CPSIA information can be obtained
at www.ICGtesting.com
Printed in the USA
FSHW010946080421
80224FS

9 781636 305684